For Mom, Dad, Ezra, Jake, and Jonah.

There is no better life than the one
I share with all of you.

A FAE IN FINANCE

HOW TO DO BUSINESS IN FAERIE: BOOK ONE

JULIET BROOKS

orbitbooks.net
orbitworks.net

Copyright © 2025 by Juliet Brooks

Cover design by Alexia E. Pereira
Cover illustration by Chloe Quinn
Cover copyright © 2025 by Hachette Book Group, Inc.
Author photograph by Grant Germano

Orbit
Hachette Book Group
1290 Avenue of the Americas
New York, NY 10104
orbitbooks.net
orbitworks.net

First Edition: October 2025

Orbit is an imprint of Hachette Book Group.
The Orbit name and logo are registered trademarks of Little, Brown Book Group Limited.

Library of Congress Cataloging-in-Publication Data
Names: Brooks, Juliet author
Title: A fae in finance / Juliet Brooks.
Description: First edition. | New York : Orbit, 2025.
Identifiers: LCCN 2025013545 | ISBN 9780316587686 trade paperback | ISBN 9780316587662 ebook
Subjects: LCSH: Fairies—Fiction | Women in finance—Fiction | LCGFT: Fantasy fiction | Humorous fiction | Novels
Classification: LCC PS3602.R644276 F34 2025 | DDC 813/.6—dc23/ eng/20250602
LC record available at https://lccn.loc.gov/2025013545

ISBNs: 9780316587662 (ebook), 9780316587686 (print on demand)

Chapter 1
In Which I Compose a Presentation

My manager's email was titled *YOU ARE LEADING THE CLIENT CALL.*

1. *Do not commit to, agree to, or provide a deadline*
2. *When he tells you he needs the deliverable tonight, hum noncommittally*
3. *Do not say any sentence including the words "you will have it by"*
4. *I mean it, Miri: DO NOT MAKE ANY COMMIT-MENTS WHATSOEVER*

I will be listening in but will not speak.

Jeff

I stared at the email for a moment, twisting the thin gold

band on my index finger. Doctor Kitten, the black and white cat on my lap, also stared at the email for a moment.

I giggled. Doctor Kitten glared up at me, disturbed by the movement. "Sorry, it's just kind of funny," I said, scratching his head.

Obviously I wouldn't agree to anything the client asked— obviously I wouldn't bind myself in promises or pearls for the Princeling. But there was something mundane and hilarious about this note, delivered via Microsoft Outlook and not scrawled in black ink on the soft underside of a torn bit of bark.

I tapped my fingers lightly on the keys, unsure whether Jeff wanted me to confirm receipt. He might just find the extra email irritating.

Finally, I sent a quick *Understood; thank you.*

When I shifted in my chair, my thighs stuck to the faux leather. The tiny window air conditioner was more enthusiastic than efficient, and I was already sticky from the summer heat. I had two screens glowing an unnatural blue in front of me: my silver work laptop and my larger second monitor. The artificial light hurt my eyes.

Doctor Kitten remained stubbornly nestled on my knees, despite my attempts to remove him. In the background, my "Pop Punk Hits of the 2000s" radio station started its third Good Charlotte song, putting me in exactly the wrong mindset for a client meeting.

The computer pinged—the soft insistent *blip* of a Microsoft Teams meeting—and the pop-up on the lower right-hand side of my screen invited me to *Join Meeting*. Of course the Princeling had started it early.

"Robot Overlord, please stop the music," I said, and the speaker turned off.

I joined the meeting, my left hand curled around a glass of what used to be iced tea.

The Princeling greeted me the moment the meeting loaded. "Hello, fair one," he said, his voice distant and tinny.

"My lord," I replied, scanning the attendees for Jeff. The Princeling's unfairly attractive retinue had all joined, sharp faces against the artificially blurred backgrounds of the video software. No sign of Jeff, who seemed to feel that while timeliness may be a virtue, he'd never agreed to be virtuous.

"Share the agenda," the Princeling instructed. I couldn't tell if he was frustrated by my slowness, if he expected me to have it up and shared already. Perhaps I should have.

I shared my screen, the agenda now visible to everyone.

"Not much today," I said, and my voice cracked. I wasn't really new to this job anymore, but still in the liminal space where I didn't know whether to start without my manager. Jeff wouldn't talk, but he'd said he wanted to observe. "We should be done soon." I shifted in my chair, which tilted backward unbidden.

The Princeling smirked, raising an eyebrow. "I knew I sensed prophecy in you," he said.

I blanched. *Did I just promise something?*

"Not a prophecy," I replied, frozen in place. "Just a guess." My phone buzzed from the far side of my desk, beyond the lukewarm tea.

"She has prophecy, though," the Gray Knight said, coming off mute. A loud shriek came through her mic, then cut off abruptly. "Look at her fractured eyes."

Fractured eyes? I'll fracture your face, I thought, because I'd spent half the night rereading the death-by-magic-flower adventures of *The Jasmine Throne* and the rest of the night formatting PowerPoint footers. Both of those activities made me feel murderous.

"'Tis true," said another—the Red Knight. The Red and Blue Knights should have been indistinguishable, with equally shiny spills of untamed chestnut hair, penetrating eyes the frozen brown of soil packed down under an ice melt, and shoulders broad enough to splinter a front door. Fortunately, the knights always wore their colors. "Observe the tilt in the zygomatic bone," the Red Knight added, gesturing with his pointy, dimpled chin.

"Anyway," I said, before they could begin discussing my cheekbones in earnest. "Today we just want to talk about the seller's presentation, to make sure it lines up with your expectations." I stopped again. My phone buzzed several more times, lit up by a flurry of messages in my Games Games Games group chat. I flipped the screen face down and tried to stay focused.

"Yes," the Princeling said. "The seller's presentation. Do you truly think mortals will buy our acorn cups and cobweb curtains?"

"Um," I said, wishing my manager would join already. "Jeff says people will buy anything if you have a celebrity endorsement."

Jeff believed that many things could be simplified by the mention of a "celebrity endorsement" but hadn't yet explained how to obtain one.

None of the faeries appeared reassured by this statement. "And I think that people will want to buy faerie-made products either way," I added.

The Red Knight unmuted himself and heaved a dramatic sigh. "Would that this debasement were not required."

The Blue Knight remained muted but rolled his eyes with gusto.

"Look," I said. "I think it's a really good thing we're doing. An important thing. It'll help people know you—know faeries. Help humans and faeries…be friends. You know, like, uh, globalization." I winced, experiencing the unique brand of agony that only comes after one has opened one's own mouth.

"*Globalization*," the Princeling repeated, his face wrinkled in either immense pain or disgust. "I know this not. Let us continue. I have many councils scheduled today, sorceress."

"Right." I glanced at the attendee list. Still no Jeff. "Not a sorceress. But let's get started. We've got a valuation range for the company."

I glanced up—with the Princeling, I was never sure how much to explain. "We think that we have an exciting story for investors, because of the, uh, supernatural element."

Jeff always said "supernatural element." Jeff said that if a celebrity wouldn't endorse a product, you could just write *supernatural element* on your materials to achieve a similar effect.

"You have mentioned," the Princeling noted dryly. "Is there no progress, then?"

"No, there's a lot of progress! Did you get the new pages we sent?" I leaned forward, smushing Doctor Kitten a bit in my lap. He still wouldn't move.

The Princeling sighed. "Yes. They were not to our taste."

This was why Jeff was late, really. He'd taken a strong dislike to our client, in part over differences in creative vision. And to be fair, I also found the Princeling's vision . . . *creative*, for lack of a better word.

"Okay, that's fine," I said. "Can you let me know what worked and what didn't?"

"What worked?" the Princeling repeated. A tiny crease had come between his peaked brows, and I remembered that faeries are quite literal.

"Uh, what you liked about it," I amended.

"Oh," he said, almost brightly. "Nothing. I liked nothing."

Faeries cannot lie. I fought the urge to cringe.

"Okay, cool," I said instead. "That's, um, a good start." It was not really.

"I do not believe it is an auspicious start," the Gray Knight said, coming off mute again. Her filter had slipped; she was leaning against a tree, silvery bark and silvery eyes and the cheekbones of a movie star. I flushed at the dismissal in her tone and tried to focus. She held her camera at an odd angle, tilted down toward the part in her hair, which should've been unflattering but just made her look sharper, mesmerizing like the thin blade of a knife.

"I have heard humans say that," the Princeling told her. "It means naught."

"Right," I said.

"This means correct," he added.

"Right," I said again. I felt that I had perhaps lost the plot a bit. "Um, so, Jeff says that buyers will be used to seeing a presentation like the one we shared with you," I told them. "So maybe we can think about keeping some of the elements of that presentation—"

"Miri, Jeff here," Jeff interrupted, brusque. "It's all good, let's do what the Princeling asks." He hadn't turned on his camera. I pushed the annoyance off my face. He'd said he wouldn't speak.

"Okay, well, um, my lord," I said, voice rough. I reached with shaking hands to pet Doctor Kitten, who sensed my stress and took this opportunity to jump from my lap. "What would make this presentation more agreeable to you?"

"If it were expulsed from the world," the Princeling said, "and expunged from the books of heaven and hell."

We stared at each other through the cameras, his long face earnest and his green eyes somber.

I cleared my throat. "So, ah, if I can't do that, what would work?"

Silence.

"More green," the Princeling said, after a long, considering pause.

"And more leaves," the Gray Knight chimed in helpfully.

The Crone, the Red Knight, and the Blue Knight—the others in the retinue—did not speak but nodded in their respective frames.

"Miri can add more leaves," Jeff said, which seemed unfair to me because our graphic design and software budget was approximately seven dollars and a pack of washable markers.

No one was giving me funds for a glue stick, let alone for digital art packs.

"Yeah, totally," I said aloud.

"We shall see," the Princeling said. "When will you provide us with this new document?"

"Soon," I said.

"Will you provide a span of moon or sun?" the Princeling requested. *Do not agree to a deadline.*

I waited for Jeff to speak.

He didn't.

My air conditioner huffed indignantly.

"Perhaps within the arc of this day," the Princeling prompted.

"Uh, we'll do our best to get it done soon," I said. *Do not commit to a deadline.*

"Very well," he said, and in one moment his entire retinue had signed off.

"Jeff?" I asked, hoping to talk about the art packs. Silence.

With a sigh, I exited the meeting.

I really had to pee, but the second I stood up, Jeff pinged me on Teams. I answered right away.

"You need something," he said accusatorily as soon as the call connected.

I debated saying *You called me*, but that wouldn't be productive.

"How do I add more leaves to the presentation? Do we have access to leaf art somewhere?"

"How the absolute fucknuts am I supposed to know?" he snapped.

"Uh." I didn't have my camera on, so Jeff couldn't see how my eyes were wide with exhaustion and stress. "I don't know. You agreed to it, so I thought you might have an idea."

"No, I just don't want to deal with their moronic bullshit anymore, Miri. They're the *stupidest* people I've ever dealt with, and that's saying something."

"I don't think they're stupid," I said, hunching my shoulders and staring at the computer screen. *The Princeling doesn't need a human girl who can't throw a punch to defend him* went the voice in my head.

Jeff huffed. "Okay, *Glinda the Good Witch*." The impassive circle bearing his initials stared back at me.

I flinched at the attempted insult but didn't reply.

The voice in my head, which is of the dual opinions that violence solves everything and that I am bad at violence, growled. But the voice in my head had also never felt so defensive of a client, supernatural or otherwise. Ugh—truthfully, I'd never even *thought* about anyone so much outside of work before. I tried to tell myself something magical was at play, that I was falling under some faerie spell—

Exactly the type of prejudiced bullshit I'd have called anyone else out for.

"Don't we just need to teach them what's normal for the industry?" I ventured, after some tense mutual silence.

Jeff snorted. "No. Just do what they want. It's fine. Everyone who sees the presentation will know it's because the client is a faerie, and faeries are crazy."

This sounded like a logical fallacy. It also sounded like something he wouldn't say in the office, where our few faerie and werewolf colleagues could hear him. The vampires would remain blissfully ignorant via the simple expedient of not coming into the office until after dark.

"Okay, but the leaves?" I prompted.

"Just google some free leaf graphics, I guess." He sounded distracted. No doubt he was, already reading a different email.

"Okay," I said. "Do you want to see it before I send it?"

"No, I don't care. The whole thing is stupid."

I rubbed my eyes. "Okay," I said again. I felt a lump in my throat, frustration burning hot behind my eyes.

He hung up without another word.

I glanced around my living room, feeling itchy and stagnant. I desperately needed a walk but was afraid to leave the apartment, worried that as soon as I got out the door someone would call me about work.

Sighing, I opened the PowerPoint document titled *Faerie Trade Goods* and stared at the front page again. The entire presentation touted the sedate colors of our bank, a sea of blues in RGB (0, 0, 255) and (0, 180, 255) and (70, 20, 230).

I thought about the best way to change the presentation. I could mock up a few slides and send them to the client, but if Jeff saw that email he'd be annoyed that I didn't ask him to review, even though he'd just told me not to. I could try to find a style guide for our company (the style guide does not exist; this was just stalling). I could stuff my face with tofu noodles and then deal with another irritated lecture from Jeff when I didn't get this done as quickly as he wanted.

With another sigh, I opened the Noun Project on my computer and searched *leaf.* A bunch of black and white icons appeared. I glanced longingly at the sliver of afternoon sunlight bravely reflecting off the windows across the street while the results of my search loaded. Cartoon maple, clover, and ginkgo leaves filled my screen. I probably should've asked for slightly more guidance from the Princeling.

Doctor Kitten mewled and hopped back into my lap. He looked as annoyed as I felt, which was kind of unfair, because he didn't have to make any PowerPoints and *his* ability to sell this stupid company likely wouldn't impact faerie-human relations for the foreseeable future.

Oh, and I still had to pee, but I couldn't get up because Doctor Kitten had settled in for a long scratching session, and also if I got up I would possibly be pinged on Teams.

I looped my arms awkwardly over Doctor Kitten, who was smugly coating my shirt in white cat hair, and started to type.

———————————•———————————

I shouldn't have gone out with Thea and Jordan. I should have stayed in my musty apartment and worked. But Thea had texted me just as I felt the phantom oozing trickles of my own brain fluid down my neck, so I'd shut my laptop and agreed to meet them at the convenient restaurant beneath my apartment.

Thea, my first absolute best friend in the whole wide world, stood waiting in the entrance, wearing her summer uniform of jean shorts and a tank top. When she saw me, she strode across the almost steaming pavement and swept me into a hug. "Hey," she whispered, squeezing me until I lifted onto my toes. I hugged her back; even just seeing her face improved my mood.

I felt someone barrel into me from behind and realized the arms of my other best friend, Jordan, had come around both of us. I sighed and sagged between them, a boneless noodle being supported by her two besties.

"Let's eat, I'm starving," Jordan said fervently into the back of my skull.

"Same," Thea agreed. "I had meetings all day and had to skip lunch!"

Jordan let go of us, and then Thea and I parted. "You could've eaten if you'd texted the group chat less," Jordan said, leading us into the restaurant. "No one cares about your character's lists of attacks; this one shot is about a game show."

I snorted.

"Jordan, I'm spending my entire Saturday playing Dungeons and Dragons with you," Thea said. "And I don't even *like* Dungeons and Dragons. So you will appreciate the effort I put into my character, even if all we do is role-play *Jeopardy!* as orcs."

The host, who'd heard the end of this little tirade, hid a smirk behind one hand.

"You're coming Saturday, right, Miri?" Jordan asked as Thea requested a table for three.

The host led us through the dimly lit low room to a booth at the back, where the worn vinyl seats and exposed brick wall waited in muted reds. I sagged into the booth and leaned a shoulder against the wall for support.

"I...don't know," I said, while the other two slid in across from me. I tensed up at the twinned expression on their faces: This was an intervention. I was about to be intervened. Again.

"You need to take care of yourself," Thea said. I tried to hide how piercing I found both her remark and her speckled hazel eyes by staring at the menu, where absolutely none of the words resolved themselves into anything recognizable. Since this was a burger joint, that was probably a function of my currently limited brain power and not a language barrier.

"I *am* taking care of myself," I muttered, toying with my ring.

"Miri, this is worse than your old government job," Thea said. She reached across the table to hold my hands, stilling the frantic motion of my fingers. I stared at her clean, short nails and held my breath. "At least there, you were making some kind of positive difference for supernatural people."

"Integrating supernatural folks into business is the best and fastest way to reduce prejudice," I said, mulish. "And at least I can afford my apartment now," I added, since one of their (fair) gripes with my last job had been the low pay.

I got the impression of a waiter from off to the left; a disembodied voice asked what we wanted. "Grilled cheese and tomato soup," I guessed, and that must have been on the menu because no one said anything. My friends ordered, but I couldn't really hear them over the buzzing irritation in my own ears.

"Miri," Thea exhaled. "Financial services don't make a positive impact." She squeezed my hands for emphasis.

"In fact," Jordan added, in the voice that meant he was being clever, "the biggest measurable impact of financial services is that you've missed every important life event and several fantastic romantasy books since you joined that company."

My phone buzzed in my pocket. I glanced at my friends, whose twinned expressions had turned simultaneously disapproving.

"It's work," I said. Thea let go of my hands and propped her chin on her fist. Jordan made a face.

I yanked my phone out of my pocket. It was an email from Jeff, which had the subject line *WHY AREN'T YOU ONLINE?* and absolutely no other text in the body.

Wordless, I turned the phone for them to see.

"What a dick," Jordan exploded.

"Has he never heard of dinner?" Thea asked with righteous indignation.

"I'll get dinner to go," I said, pushing down the guilt as I slid out of the bench seat and toward the front of the restaurant. "And pay separately."

Before either of them could voice displeasure, I stalked away.

———————————— • ————————————

I finished my draft of the deck around two a.m. I stared at the cover page on my computer for several minutes, now adorned with green, leafy borders that had taken forever to format. But I was finally satisfied that this would please the Princeling.

I stayed seated at my desk, eyes scrunched shut, and wondered whether I should send it to Jeff or straight to the Princeling. Jeff had said he didn't want to see it, but we'd played this game before—if I didn't send it to him, he'd likely ream me out in the morning. I pulled up a blank email and wrote:

Hi Jeff, please see attached the draft for the client. Please let me know if you want to take a turn or if I should send it over.

I attached the draft, confident that it was flawless and also that Jeff would find or fabricate some mistake. There was nothing more to do, so I stumbled into the bathroom to brush my teeth and wash up. I was too tired to shower, and when I got into the bedroom I flopped onto the bed, butt-up on the mattress. I didn't even have the energy to lie flat.

Doctor Kitten hopped up next to me and mewled, annoyed.

With a groan, I rolled onto my back, my eyes still shut. Glowing green leaves danced behind my eyelids. The conversation with my friends floated up from my subconscious to join the terrible, stupid party in my brain.

My team was the Supernaturals and Preternaturals Banking and Brokerage Group Business Development chapter of Tartarus, the fourteenth-largest financial services firm in the world. I'd joined four months earlier to help companies with nonhuman founders and inclusive business plans raise money. On nights like this one, it was hard to see the connection between my work and the world I wanted to build. But business was fast, and government was slow, and I'd hoped—well, at two thirty a.m., it didn't matter what I'd hoped. It mattered that I got four hours of sleep.

Doctor Kitten stepped onto my stomach, making biscuits with his front paws. It hurt. I sighed and put my hand out, feeling in the darkness for his head. I scratched behind his ear until he settled on my chest. We both fell asleep on top of the covers.

My dreams were restless, full of the Princeling, broad and cold. He sat at the foot of my bed and watched me, his green eyes glowing in the dark, just like those damn leaves. When I kicked out, he put a hand on my ankle, holding me in place. "Human girl," he said. "You do not yet know what you will give me."

I woke up exhausted, having slept through four separate alarms.

Chapter 2
In Which I Receive Career Mentorship

It was an in-office day. I arrived at eight thirty in the morning and set up at my desk, plugging my laptop into the docking station, logging into the system, then kicking off my sneakers and sliding my feet into the heels I kept under the desk. The shoes pinched my toes even more than usual this morning.

My computer pinged and my pulse spiked. I jabbed at the mute button. Luckily, it was only a daily industry update, something I could easily delete. I didn't even skim the headlines on those emails anymore. I knew what they would be: snippets about Elf off the Shelf, the elvish home goods company that had hurled the supernatural into public consciousness four years ago; the capital raise for the fitness company founded by six vampires ranging in age from four hundred to nine hundred years old—all of whom swore by "this one simple routine to stay fit"; and some other new entrant, a company started by an entrepreneurial immortal with wings, claws, or fangs.

Soon my colleagues would come in, and I would be surrounded by men in matching white button-down shirts who made me feel completely alone.

On cue, Corey rounded the corner and plopped into the cubicle next to mine.

"How was your evening?" I asked him, though I already knew what he would say—

"Terrible," he said, "I worked until two a.m."

I didn't know what he spent all this time working on. He didn't have a deal going. Or any clients. Or a manager. He spent all of this time on his computer doing…PowerPoints? Research? One time, I saw him rendering a video game background in MS Paint.

"Bummer," I said.

He shrugged.

I sighed, still trying to engage him in conversation for some reason. "You hear we might be going to Faerie soon?" I asked. *We* meant me and Jeff.

"Yeah, travel sucks," he said.

This didn't feel like the appropriate response to being told your colleague was one of the first humans invited to Faerie in centuries.

Or at least one of the first humans *publicly* invited.

Jeff rounded the corner, wearing a full pinstripe suit and matching blue tie that made his skin look positively pink. He was always clean-shaven and had reached the age where men's chins start to sag into their neck, no matter how slender they are.

He grunted toward us and strode past into his office.

This was a good greeting, for Jeff.

I turned back to my computer and alt-tabbed over to an Excel spreadsheet, shushing my roiling stomach. Maybe it would be a calm day after all.

"Miri, get in here!" Jeff barked from his office at the end of our row of cubicles. "When you have a minute," he added, perhaps for the benefit of a colleague walking by.

When you have a minute meant *now*. I pushed away from my desk and stood, my knees cracking. So much for calm in the office.

The thirty steps to his office were muffled by the gray carpet and punctuated by sharp pains in my big and pinky toes. I leaned against the doorframe.

"Jeff," I said, because he'd already turned back to his computer.

"Miri," he said. "What do you need?"

I blinked, unsure what to say. He'd just called me over like, fifteen seconds ago. "Uh, did you—uh..." I stopped, stumbling over my words. Jeff's window looked over New York City, out west to the Hudson and Jersey City. Up into the endless sky.

"Oh, yeah," he said. "We're going to dinner tonight in that shithole. Dinner's outside, can you believe it?"

"We're going to Faerie *tonight*," I said in disbelief.

"Yes, the Duke said tonight."

"Princeling." The title of Princeling didn't exactly mean a *prince* or a *king*, wasn't a name like *Rowan* or *Oberon*, and wasn't a descriptor like *Fairy Godmother*.

The Princeling just *was*. And most of all, what he *was* was in charge of everything Faerie. The very few public statements we'd gotten about the Fae bore his signature, and the faeries who'd come out of the woodwork to join the mortal realm all claimed loyalty to him. As far as I could tell, he was their ultimate authority.

"Yeah, Princeling. I know." Jeff stuck his pinky in his ear and started scratching.

I shifted my weight away from the doorframe. "Are we bringing our own food?"

Jeff finally looked at me, his eyes narrowed. The purple bags under his left eye were bigger than the bags under his right. "Why would we do that?"

I rubbed my thumb against the gold band on my index finger, queasy. "Um. Doesn't faerie food trap you in Faerie?"

Jeff snorted. "Food can't trap you somewhere, Miri," he said, his tone cool. He leaned back in his chair. "That's the dumbest thing I've ever heard."

I swallowed. "Jeff, I—"

"Where did you even hear that? Seriously." He chuckled, shifting in his seat. He'd taken off the suit jacket and I saw the perspiration stains under his arms.

"It's the only legend they've confirmed, actually," I said. "There's a New York City Department of Public Health advertisement campaign about it in the subways."

Had he not seen *Just Say No*, the campaign they'd enacted when faerie fruit sellers started popping up on street corners? Had he not noticed their slitted pupils and their berries that gleamed golden like little spheres of sunshine?

"I don't take the subway," Jeff said, matter-of-factly. Of course he didn't.

"I'll grab us takeout," I said.

"You'll embarrass our hosts if you do that!" he snapped.

I gulped.

"Don't bring any food, Miri," he said. "We need this dinner to go well."

Jeff stared at me, blue eyes cold like the wind between the buildings in the winter.

"O-okay," I said, my stomach tight. I just…wouldn't eat anything. And if Jeff wanted to get himself stuck in Faerie, there wasn't anything I could do about it.

I shoved down a wave of nausea and left his office.

———————————— • ————————————

At lunchtime I took the elevator downstairs and stood in the courtyard of our building, staring at my phone.

My mom had called me three times that morning. I'd let the calls go to voicemail, keenly aware that her friend Mrs. Phillips's nephew had just tragically broken up with his fiancée and moved to New York City and this meant that I was about to be conscripted into a blind date.

With a sigh, I called her back. The phone rang once before she picked up. "Good afternoon!" she said, sounding delighted. She always sounded delighted to hear from me.

"Hi, Mom," I said, ready to derail. "I'm going to my first client dinner tonight."

"Oh, sweetheart!" she squealed. "Are you excited? What

are you going to wear?"

I groaned.

"The black suit," she said firmly. "And don't forget makeup."

I pictured my mom sitting at the kitchen table and playing solitaire on an iPad.

"Do you have shoes?"

"Yes, I have shoes," I said, scowling into the middle distance. Two young men in suits scurried past me.

"The black pumps?"

"Mom, I think Faerie is on a hill, or under a hill, or something. I'll wear my sneakers."

I paused, expecting her to argue.

"I had a dream about this," my mom said suddenly.

"Witch," I said, grinning. We'd joked that my mother was a witch for years, even before anyone knew the paranormal existed.

"Miri . . . be careful," she said.

I blinked. My mother wasn't usually this circumspect in her warnings.

"Mom, I'm always careful." I started toward the little marketplace in the northeastern corner of our building. "I'm going to grab lunch."

"Miriam"—usually my full name was a bad sign—"it wasn't a good dream."

I twisted my gold ring from my index finger onto my thumb. "Did I die?"

My mother hadn't predicted anyone's death, exactly. But still. Sometimes she dreamed about a person dying, and then they died, not in the way she'd dreamed of, and while I wouldn't call that a *prediction*, I also wouldn't call it *optimal*.

"You were in a cage," she said, "too small to stand in, and the bars were woven branches and ivy, and you were so thin."

"That probably made you happy," I said, trying to sound glib. "Me being thin." I walked into the marketplace and looked around at the food options. Bao buns, tacos, three different sandwich shops, a blood shake pop-up bar with evening hours, and a vegan grain bowl place.

My mom was silent.

"Mom?"

"I love you no matter what size you are, honey," she said.

I stopped at the vegan grain bowl shop. "Mom, I know," I said. "I'm sorry, that was a bad joke."

"Please be careful, Miri. I don't want to lose you."

I swallowed around the lump in my throat. I wanted to ask follow-up questions, or reassure her, or tell her she needed to go into business as a fortune teller because she was really freaking me out.

But I was in a crowded, public place. "Sorry, I gotta go, Mom. Love you."

"Wait!" she exclaimed. "Did you know Mrs. Phillips's nephew Ra—"

I hung up.

When I got to the front of the line, the cashier smiled at me. We'd become buddies these past weeks, by which I mean the cashier smiled at me and I narrated a budding friendship on top of it.

He slid my rice and lentil bowl across the plywood counter and I tapped my credit card. "Thanks," I said, staring down at the unappealing brown patties covered in thick, tasteless mango chutney. The vegan grain bowl shop rarely had a line, for reasons beyond mortal comprehension.

I started for the door, clutching my sad lunch in one hand and my phone in the other. My music had started as soon as I hung up, and an indie lesbian steal-your-girl anthem drowned out the chatter in the hall. A gaggle of men in suits parted around me. One of them bumped my right hand, almost upending my bowl.

The frustration boiled within me as I beelined for the door. My fingers drummed on the back of my phone case. My steps were longer, faster, staccato on the polished concrete.

I just needed to breathe. In through my nose. Out through my mouth. Deep breaths over and over until I made it into our building's lobby and then to our elevator bank.

Just as I walked into an opening elevator, someone else walked in next to me. I didn't see him, but I felt his arm brush my shoulder as he passed me, hurrying to lean against the back wall, the mirror reflecting the knot of black curls at the base of his neck.

"Sahir," I said, and inclined my head. I paused my music but left my headphones in.

"Miriam," he replied, with a slow blink back at me.

"Hold the elevator!" someone called out. I stepped forward and stuck my arm out, entering a battle of dominance with the closing door. The door submitted, reopening.

The man who'd shouted came into view, eyes flicking from me to Sahir. His nose wrinkled. "It's okay, I'll wait," he said.

I withdrew my arm, following his gaze. His gaze led to Sahir, whose pointed ears and sharp features marked him

Fae. Sahir's eyebrows contracted as he realized what had happened.

The elevator doors slid shut. I leaned against the wall next to Sahir, staring at the curve of his crooked nose. His visage never ceased to fascinate me, though I knew it left many in the office unnerved.

He'd pursed his lips; his eyes were fixed on the stainless steel doors.

"How are you?" I asked, suddenly desperate to distract him.

"Weary as a winter lamb," he said, without looking at me.

"That sounds, um, bad," I said.

"We live to feel," he replied, "and cannot feel joy without pain."

"Which is why you went into banking," I countered.

Sahir's lip quirked, though his head didn't turn. "Sharp tongue for a soft woman," he said.

"I've got rock-hard biceps," I replied, flexing. He couldn't see them through my jacket, of course, but he finally smiled at me—the expression rounded his craggy cheeks, softened the bitterbark brown of his eyes into something more like molten chocolate.

"Apologies, Miriam," he said, and chuckled. "Soft you are not."

I smiled back. "We're going to dinner with the Princeling tonight," I said.

The elevator came to a stop and the doors opened on our floor. Sahir gestured for me to precede him into the stark white hallway.

"My liege may lay bounties before you," Sahir said, pulling

out his wallet. The wallet looked like two dried autumn leaves sewn together, but before I could examine it, he drew his key card from a fold and slid the wallet back into his pants.

"I'm sure he will be generous," I replied.

"My liege will offer gifts and curses." Sahir tapped on the card reader and then opened the door for me. I tried not to stare at his broad back, the ripple of his shoulders beneath the taut fabric of his black suit jacket. Until I'd met Sahir, I'd always been able to compartmentalize *attractiveness* and *coworkers*: They existed in different and unconnected circles. Sahir had unfortunately turned those circles into a Venn diagram.

"Everyone offers gifts and curses." I flipped my hair and traipsed past him. "No point worrying which is which until the time comes." Every time I spoke with Sahir, the part of me that thought I was a sassy sword-wielding protagonist in a fantasy novel took over.

"Good day, Miriam," Sahir said, turning right. I turned left past the giant painting of our founder, then three rows of cubicles, and finally slid into my rolling chair.

My team was in the office now, in the three cubicles around mine.

"What's for lunch, Miri?" my colleague Levi asked, glancing over at my desk. I stared at the wide laminated surface, my pink reusable water bottle in one corner and my coffee thermos in the other.

"Grain bowl," I muttered, sliding my key card into my computer.

"You gotta eat more protein, princess," he said, helpfully. "That's how you get gains."

Levi believed in one macronutrient: protein.

"No pain, no gain," I said, to say something.

He laughed. I looked over at him; his gelled brown hair had been slicked back into four distinct ridges, presumably where he'd run his hand through it. He was in his shirtsleeves, leaning back in his chair.

"Don't report me to HR for calling you *princess*," he added, his voice slightly too high to convince me he was joking.

I shrank down in my chair a bit. "I wouldn't," I said.

The silence settled, thick and viscous like a bathtub full of Jell-O.

I glanced around our group.

"Jeff and I are going to Faerie," I told Levi, trying not to sound nervous. I told Levi so I wouldn't text Jordan and Thea, who would absolutely blow up my phone, and probably show up at my workplace in the hopes of tagging along.

"Yeah, so, the thing about client dinners is, you cannot get too drunk," Levi said, which was the only wrong response. On my other side, I could feel Corey perking up.

"There go my plans," I muttered, clenching my thumb under my other fingers. I should've just texted my friends, because as unhelpful and culturally insensitive as an entourage of twenty-somethings in cosplay would've been, I knew it would be better than whatever wisdom Levi was about to impart.

Levi nodded earnestly. "I know you will want to drink. I know you think you can outdrink them. But don't. One time I double-fisted Jameson and ended up under a table narfing in a client's bong and jangle, if you catch my drift." I stared at him; it wasn't that I didn't believe him, but I honestly couldn't believe he was saying it out loud. On my left, Corey snorted.

"It wasn't the client who told us he would fuck all our mothers," Levi clarified, because this was obviously something that needed clarifying. "You remember that story, right? Anyway he wasn't happy when I upchucked on his Chucks."

I blinked at Levi. The others had turned around to listen to him, as they always did when anyone talked about the "good old days" of banking. Now whenever anyone wrote *fuck* in an email we got a compliance notice, and Jeff had to give us a lecture, which I personally found hard to internalize when every third word out of Jeff's mouth was *fuck*.

But in the good old days, which were somewhere between five and thirty years ago, you could spank a secretary or call an analyst "a smeared crust of dogshit on the underside of an old boot" and that was a fine thing to do.

I opened my bowl and stuck a fork into it, the gloopy mass immediately sticking to the utensil.

"But did you guys close the deal?" Corey asked, his face brighter than usual. Corey had once said "investment banking is sexy" in a meeting and meant it. Since Corey didn't appear attracted to any of our colleagues and had never referenced a romantic partner of any kind, I wasn't sure where he got that from.

"Oh yeah. One-point-three million fee," Levi crowed.

"Nice," Matt chimed in from the other side of the aisle.

I ate a bite of chewy brown goop, staring at a report on my computer and trying to erase that conversation from my head. In our operational model, the logistics of scaling one gnome under a tree into a faerie factory flattened into revenue and expense lines.

"Levi," I said, "do you think you'll have a chance to help me with this model soon?"

"Sure," he said, not looking at me. "What's the issue?"

"Well, they don't really have a business plan to scale, so I don't think the numbers make sense."

"Miri," Levi said, in the tone he reserved for me. "We don't worry about the assumptions, remember?" He separated each word, like he wanted to make sure I could digest them. "It's not *our* problem if they can do it or not. It's the investor's problem."

This wasn't true, and as I had recently taken my licensing exams, I probably could have pointed Levi to the relevant regulation stating otherwise. But it absolutely wasn't worth arguing with him.

"Sorry, I forgot," I said, staring at the computer. I hit F2 and started auditing the model, because we had to get it out to the client before we went to dinner.

Not that Levi or Jeff cared what I did regarding our client. Levi didn't really engage with them, and Jeff hated them passionately.

I took another bite of grain mass and squeezed my eyes shut. It was going to be a long day.

———————————— • ————————————

At seven thirty p.m., Jeff came out of his office to talk to me. No one had given me details about when we'd be going to

Faerie, or how we would get there, but I'd learned not to ask questions.

"Hey, Miri," he said, standing over my chair. I spun the chair to look up at him and immediately regretted it. He was slightly too close for me to stand up, his knees almost touching mine.

"Hi, Jeff," I said, staring into his nostrils. He glowered down at me, like a stilt walker at a Ren faire who'd just tripped over a stroller.

"Let's get in the car."

I glanced at my own shoes and almost bumped my head into his stomach. "I wanted to wear sneakers," I said, unsure if I was asking for permission or stating a plan.

"Wear sneakers, I don't care," he said, leaning an elbow on the divider at the edge of my desk. I watched it tilt precariously. "They're magical creatures, Miri, they don't know about fashion."

I didn't know about fashion either.

"Okay." I spun back around—Jeff still standing behind my chair—and slid my shoes off. I waited for him to move, but he didn't, so I had to toe around under the desk for my sneakers without sliding back into him. After a few seconds, I found them and hitched myself into a backbend to get into the shoes without moving the chair.

"Let's go, Miri," Jeff said.

Assuming he'd moved, I twisted out of the seat and bumped into him. Jeff grabbed my arm to steady me. "Jesus, balance much?"

I frowned up at him. He let go and led the way out into the

elevator bank, talking. I grabbed my computer, shoved it in my backpack, slung the pack over my shoulder, and followed him.

By the time I caught up, I'd clearly missed a few sentences.

"But anyway, the thing about clients is they're always right, but they're never right. You shouldn't ever seriously listen to a client, but you should always agree with them." He jabbed his finger on the down button, so hard his nail went white.

"Oh, interesting," I said, following Jeff into the elevator. He stood in the middle of the car, facing the back wall, so I inched left around him and leaned against a side wall.

"The client will have a lot of opinions, but you don't need to pay attention to them. But if they ask why you didn't do something, you just say you'll circle back to them on that. Then you can forget about it. That's what I do," Jeff said, in a distressing stream of consciousness. I wondered if the elevator would move. I wondered if Jeff intended to lean against a wall at some point. "Also, it sounds like they're sending a car for us," Jeff added, when I only nodded in response.

"Faeries don't drive," I said, staring at the television screen blinking stock market updates in the right-hand panel. The elevator began its descent.

"Clearly they do, Miri, and don't contradict me tonight. It looks bad." He straightened his tie. I glanced down and saw he was still wearing his nice shoes. I wondered if Jeff *did* care what the Fae thought of him.

Faeries can't *drive*, I thought. *They're not allowed to in New York.* New York State wouldn't let faeries on anything faster than a moped, ostensibly because of concerns that the pure metals in vehicles would weaken them, leading to drowsiness while driving.

The Princeling had never commented on this regulation one way or another.

"Okay, sorry," I said aloud as the elevator door mercifully opened.

Jeff strode toward the southern turnstile and out into our opulent marble lobby, which had been designed by a man who was apparently trapped in the Parthenon for thirty years and was also apparently twelve feet tall. The security guard leaned against a fluted column, glaring inward at the vast misery of his own psyche. I waved at him, but he didn't see me.

When we reached the glass revolving doors, Jeff shoved forward forcefully. I scurried into the next slot.

It was late enough that the sun had phoned it in and hung in the sky unenthusiastically, pierced by spires. But the city shone bright and angry around us, pulsing with life. Across the street I saw a gaggle of middle schoolers, wearing sweatpants and flinging their skateboards around, shrieking like banshees. Behind them, three banshees sat sedately conversing at the wine bar we sometimes went to after work, nursing long-stemmed glasses of red.

A giant delivery truck rumbled to a stop in front of them, *Tornado & Sons Tender Tenderloins* emblazoned in green on the side.

"Tornado tenderloins are tough," Jeff told me. "Werewolf owners. They probably chew the cows to death. And their logo isn't centered on the truck. Bad design, I don't know how they sell anything."

Before I could respond, a gaggle of cargo-shorts-clad tourists who'd clearly bought Yankees caps as camouflage started gasping and pointing. A few New Yorkers leaving work in their somber black suits also cast surreptitious glances away from their phones and toward the commotion.

Following their focus, I saw a faerie knight turn onto our street, astride the biggest horse I'd ever seen (though in fairness, the only other living horses I'd seen were the carriage-pulling ones in Central Park).

The knight was resplendent in perfectly tailored monochrome, silvery garb that glittered in the halogen streetlights. Her sparkling silver hair cast sharp shadows across her even sharper cheekbones. Her somber silver eyes glinted in the dying summer sunlight, so bright even down the street that they made the orange cast of early evening seem dim. She radiated confidence, like she was the protector of any land she set foot on, not just her own home in Faerie.

The Gray Knight, in the flesh.

She led two other horses, each half as wide as a car, and stopped in front of us. When the Gray Knight slid off her horse—a gorgeous dappled gray, twice as tall as Jeff—she turned to me first and inclined her head.

"My lady," she said, her hand outstretched. I went to shake it, but she brought my hand to her lips and kissed my knuckles, staring up at me through the thick fringe of her lashes. "May our first real meeting be a boon and a blessing."

"I am honored to meet you in person, fair one," I replied. *Fair one* just felt like the move, I don't know. But it seemed to please her, because she smiled against my fingers and pulled away.

I glanced at Jeff, who had shifted so his own hand dangled in front of him, limp and ready for a kiss.

She straightened. "Jeff," she said, staring at him. He dropped his hand back to his side.

"Gray," he said.

The Gray Knight gestured toward the horses. "I bring you transport for our evening's revel," she said. She led me to the nearer horse, a brown animal with an almost golden mane. "Let me help you mount," she said, holding her hand out to me.

Jeff chortled behind us.

"Thank you," I said, reaching for her. She ignored my proffered hand. In a fluid motion, she slid both hands around my waist, thumbs under my backpack, and before I could gasp, she'd lifted me onto the horse.

I was startled: That lift would've been a challenge for almost any human, and she'd done it with neither fanfare nor difficulty. A not unpleasant shiver ran up my spine. I shook my head and tried to ground myself, splaying my hands on the horse's neck.

Though I could have sworn the horse's back was bare when I stood on the ground, I sat in a saddle with a round knob protruding from the front.

"What's their name?" I asked, shifting forward on the horse's back and patting the thick neck.

She looked up at me, her gray eyes swirling with stars. "A name is a powerful thing," she said. "But you may call her Sparkles."

"Sparkles?" I repeated.

The Gray Knight had already moved toward Jeff, who seemed determined not to accept her help. He kept trying to climb the other horse, his hands grabbing awkwardly at its back and side. He'd hitched one foot against the horse's leg, and I was shocked that he hadn't been trampled to death.

She examined him for a moment, her head cocked predatorily, and then put both of her hands on his side and shoved him up, like a barrel over a waterfall. And then she went back to her own silvery-gray horse—were they *matching*?—and she *leapt*. She was like a lion in a nature documentary, or like Doctor Kitten trying to get on a counter. She tensed, and I could almost imagine a tail twitching as she found equilibrium—

No. I wasn't imagining it; she had a tail, a thin silver one, like a birch branch against the sky. I gaped at it, hypnotized—they didn't all have tails...did they? The Princeling had wings. How did I not know that faeries could have tails?

Our horses moved of their own accord, into a single-file line going down 44th Street. Jeff had righted himself, though he rode before me like a man who had never straddled anything in his entire life. In front of him, the Gray Knight sat comfortably astride her horse, her shoulders back and her head twisting from side to side as she took in her surroundings. Whenever she looked at me, I felt my back straighten, my shoulders pull away from my ears. Our eyes met and I flushed, flustered by the force of her full inhuman attention. I looked away.

"Sparkles, do you obey traffic laws?" I asked the horse, patting her shoulder. She didn't say anything, but her ears tilted back.

At least I didn't have to make small talk with Jeff as the horses turned north on Sixth Avenue.

Tourists stared in awe as we rode down the street, and a kid on the sidewalk did a double take when he saw us, but for the most part, the native New Yorkers had seen weirder. I worried about Doctor Kitten for a moment—he didn't like to be alone for too long—but I'd be home later tonight, and he'd get to ignore me to his heart's content.

We entered the upper fifties, and I wondered if we were headed for Central Park. No one had confirmed it, but people said there was an entrance to Faerie somewhere inside.

Sure enough, the horses crossed 59th Street, going north up Center Drive. The sickle moon, weirdly visible hours before sunset, disappeared behind a cloud and was suddenly gone. The moment we passed between the low stone walls, the air around us quieted, like the squirrels and pigeons were preparing for a performance. The world darkened, the trees thicker and the sky more velvet than gray. I could hear Jeff wheezing ahead of me.

The trees grew harder to avoid on horseback. A branch softly brushed my face, and then another, and I closed my eyes to avoid getting poked.

I felt Sparkles turn, stepping off the path. A rush of air brought wafts of heather and mown grass; everything felt subtly different and simultaneously unchanged, like we were a toy race car jumping from one track to another.

I opened my eyes, and gasped. It *was* still the park…but it wasn't. The colors had brightened so I could see—not like daylight, but like a movie set, with muted light throughout the open area in front of us. There was a wide plain laid out at Sparkles's feet; it ended abruptly at a wall of trees on the horizon. I could see each trunk, the moss growing up from rich dark earth, the shifting shadows made by rustling leaves.

And there was no moon. Stars spun overhead in silver whorls; filaments of liquid mercury spilled across the black velvet sky.

I felt the breath catch in my chest. *Faerie.* The wide, hard-packed patch of dirt before me was *Faerie.*

We'd come out—in?—a few yards from a long wooden table, set with plates and bowls that shone dimly. Off to my right, a path led toward the uniform mass of a hill.

Arrayed before us stood the Princeling and the remainder of his retinue: the Blue Knight, the Red Knight, the Crone, and Sahir, whose place in the Court I still wasn't sure about—though I was glad to see him here.

"We could've carpooled," I said to him, forcing a grin to hide my awe. He came toward me and held out his hands.

"I doubt you would have been delighted by my steed," he said as I fell, ungainly, into his arms. He caught me with ease. Sahir slid me down his body, gently, until my feet touched the earth. I tried not to feel how warm his palms were against my spine.

Determined not to be creepy, I pushed away and turned to the horse.

"Thanks, Sparkles," I said, and patted her on the shoulder as high as I could reach. She tossed her head and stalked off into a wide meadow, radiating the self-satisfaction of a quadruped who'd vastly exceeded expectations.

Jeff sat on his horse, frowning at the Princeling, who had come to stand by his side. The Princeling was *much* taller than I'd expected, towering over everyone present, but otherwise looked exactly the same as he did on the video calls: the slightly sharper features inherent to most Fae, with a nose like a weapon and shoulders that made me think about the month in college I'd spent binge-reading romantasy and pining over brooding magical dudes. He was basically straight from the pages: broad, with a wide chest and a triangular torso that hinted at hours spent in physical combat but were probably just physiological. His green eyes sparkled like faceted peridots as he took me in.

And there were his wings—smaller than I'd expected, from what I'd seen over his shoulder on camera. They were composed of soft-looking feathers in an array of greens and golds, though they were almost translucent; I could imagine them catching the light so beautifully when outstretched.

Without looking away from me, he held his arms out to Jeff, offering assistance on the dismount.

When Jeff glanced over and saw that I was already on the ground, his face flushed and he shook his head, instead flinging himself off his horse into space. He landed on the Princeling with a loud "Oof!"; the Princeling buckled but didn't fall. There was no gentle release, though, and the Princeling let Jeff stumble away.

Jeff straightened up and nodded at me, a jerky motion that meant *get over here*. I went to stand next to him and inclined my head to the Princeling. "My liege," I said.

Obviously, the Princeling was not literally my liege. But

what do you call a liege who isn't yours? *Mister Liege? Their Liege? Hello, Someone Else's Liege.*

Jeff grunted, which meant *I should be talking.*

"Lady of the True Dreams," the Princeling said to me. That was at least better than "sorceress." His green eyes were almost dappled, like sitting below a tree in midsummer.

He turned to Jeff. "Jeff."

"Well, I'm starving," Jeff said, and chuckled. "Should we eat and talk?"

My stomach tightened. Was he just…not going to listen to me at all? I stared at the Princeling, who looked back like he could read my mind.

"Yes," he said, with a smile that made his lips thin and white, "we should eat and talk."

Chapter 3
In Which We Meet the Obligatory Climate Protester

The Princeling led us to the table. Small three-legged stools clustered around the two long sides. At the head of the table stood a silver throne. He stopped beside it.

"Sit by me," he said to Jeff. I looked at Jeff, not sure whether to follow, but someone grabbed my arm.

"You'll sit with us," Sahir said, his breath tickling my ear. I stiffened, but he pulled me toward the other end of the table, next to the Gray Knight. When I looked up, a crowd of people I'd never seen before had filled the empty chairs.

"It is an honor to dine at the Princeling's table," the Gray Knight said in my other ear, almost in warning. "Many supplicants will take a seat, if there are spaces." She put a hand on my shoulder and guided me onto a stool. Then she slid my backpack from my shoulders before I could protest.

I had to crane my neck to look past Sahir at the Princeling and Jeff. Jeff was already holding a wineglass in one hand and spearing a potato with the other. I felt the bile rising in my throat and tried to say something, but the words caught. If he got stuck here, he'd blame me, but I couldn't insult our hosts by calling out to him. I tried to signal to Jeff to put the fork down, but he didn't notice at all.

"The Princeling has provided mortal fare," the Gray Knight said, clearly following my panicked gaze to Jeff's potato-filled plate. "Those potatoes are from a place called Idaho."

When I looked back at my own plate it was full—of something that looked suspiciously like the grain bowl I had had at lunch. A gloop of saffron-colored mango chutney dripped off one of the lentil patties.

I frowned at the Gray Knight. "So the food is…" I didn't want to say *safe*. "For human consumption?"

"You are a human," she replied slowly, inclining her head. She sounded a bit insulted. "And the food is for your consumption." Her hair fell forward over her face, a glittering silver curtain separating us. I winced.

"Your caution does you credit, Miri," Sahir said, putting his hand over mine. His touch burned, and I noticed the cold bite in the air for the first time. I shivered.

He slid his hand up to my shoulder, clear eyes and a single dark curl waving its way down his broad brown cheekbone. He smiled warmly at me.

The Gray Knight ran her hand up my arm to my other shoulder and squeezed reassuringly. "Eat," she said, tilting her chin toward my plate.

Involuntarily, I glanced at Jeff. He caught my eye and waved his fork, flinging some sauce onto the table. The Princeling, grimacing, flicked his index finger and the sauce disappeared in a spray of green sparks.

I looked back at the Gray Knight, torn between concern and the ingrained desire to be a polite and unproblematic guest. "Is this from that grain bowl place below our building?"

She frowned. "I do not know what that means," she said.

"Miri, it's delicious," Jeff shouted, ten decibels louder than anyone else. The entire table fell into an uneasy silence.

The Princeling raised a hand toward me, palm up. "The maiden is discomfited because she fears our food," he said. "She is wise and just in her concern, but she will not be harmed."

He'd just turned the table into a stage for our conversation, and the faeries between us were an audience. I looked down, anxious. If I continued not to eat, I'd seem surly and ungrateful, and Jeff would be upset with me.

Instead, I nodded toward the Princeling and Jeff and picked up my fork.

The Princeling nodded back, and the conversations resumed around the table.

"I still don't know your name," I told the Gray Knight, staring at my plate. I could feel her and Sahir both looking at me and wished I had worn concealer to the office. I had at least ten red spots on my right cheek. When I leaned forward to get closer to the plate, my waistband strained against my stomach.

"As I said," she said, soft and stern. "A name is a thing of power. I shall not share mine lightly."

I cringed. "Sorry." I stuck the fork into the lentil patty, scooping up some chutney and a bit of rice, too.

I stared at the gooey forkful of food. The forkful of food stared gooily back.

What did the Princeling mean, *she will not be harmed*? Was there any hidden meaning in there? And the Gray Knight had said it was for human consumption. But what did *that* mean?

I snuck a glance upward. Jeff was staring intently at me, fork clenched in his fist. I didn't need telepathy to know he was thinking *Eat it or you're fired.*

Jeff had already demolished his plate of food, and nothing had happened.

I took a bite.

Nothing continued to happen, except that this batch of lentil patties was actually flavorful; the rice had some sort of lovely aromatic in it that filled my nose as I ate, and the chutney on top was sweet and slightly spicy, with bits of juicy mango hitting my back teeth as I savored the bite. The flavors warmed me in a way I hadn't expected; my limbs were tingly, my stomach sated in a way food court fare doesn't usually accomplish. I had no idea how they'd managed to get this to taste this good; maybe Sahir had charmed the cashier in a way I couldn't and actually gotten the delicious stuff they advertised. I'd ask him to order my lunch the next day so I could copy what he did in the future.

"Miriam means no ill," Sahir said around me, continuing a train of thought I'd almost forgotten. "The humans find titles discomfiting, Gray Knight."

"Her comfort is not my prerogative."

I swallowed another bite and turned to the Gray Knight again. "My apologies, lady," I said, straightening my spine, "for any unintended offense. I am not owed your name."

She tilted her head in acknowledgment, but before she could speak, a commotion broke out from the other end of the table. It sounded like something shattering. I looked up and saw that someone had thrown an acorn onto the table. It had broken the Princeling's glass.

"Do not do this, Princeling," a woman said. Her voice carried, and she stood a little away from the table—she wanted everyone to see and hear her.

"Who begs a boon of me?" the Princeling asked. He had propped his head up on one hand, the other hand dangling a silver fork. He sprawled in the silver chair, long and lavish, and stared at her. I nearly bumped Sahir's shoulder trying to see her.

She was just as regal as the Princeling, with blazing blue eyes and hair like river reeds, sticking up on her head like a crown.

"It is the obligatory climate protester," Sahir murmured, so quietly I might have imagined it. He hadn't turned to look at her, and his nose brushed my cheek.

"I speak for the rivers," she said, "and for the trees."

I am the Lorax ran through my mind, in a very unfortunate loop.

"Name yourself, nymph." The Princeling wasn't even looking at her now; he had his eyes on his fork and spun it on the tabletop on a single tine. A few of our tablemates had resumed eating.

"If he does not know her, she is not of his Court." Sahir's

black hair lay in a loop on my collarbone, curling under the lapel of my suit jacket.

"There are other Courts?" I whispered.

The protester continued: "I am the voice of all concerned. I am an emissary of the Queen."

Around the table, everyone lapsed into preternatural stillness. The Gray Knight, on my right, had one hand at her waist, where a slender handgun was slung on a belt she hadn't had earlier.

"Oh, so there's a Queen now?" Jeff asked, with a level of snark I had never achieved in my life. I swear I felt my ribs clutch convulsively at my heart.

"Our guest speaks," the Princeling said, straightening. His mouth tightened. I clenched my hands and tensed my thighs, ready to spring onto the table and protect Jeff if needed.

The Gray Knight caught my eye and raised an eyebrow. I could almost hear her thoughts: *You're going to jump in front of* him? I shrugged, as if to say *He's my boss.* She raised the other eyebrow, perhaps indicating *Your paltry power structures mean nothing to me, mortal.*

I redirected my attention to Jeff.

"What's the issue?" Jeff asked. "I can mediate. That's part of our contract, you know." Absolute silence. He chuckled with the panache of a donkey playing piano. "That's why you pay me the big bucks."

There was a murmur of unease. Across from me two faeries in diaphanous dresses with gray skin and black eyes slid off their stools and into the darkness. The Princeling looked around the table.

"Please continue," he said, and gestured at Jeff.

Jeff frowned at the protester. "What's the problem?"

The faerie woman stared at the Princeling. "Am I to fling myself before a mortal, a creature my Queen would kill on sight?"

"It would amuse me," he replied, "if you did."

She tossed her head, the crown-of-cattails hair bobbing. "This proposal to build a company is the end of our way of life," she said, still staring at the Princeling.

"If she says it, does that mean it's true?" I whispered to Sahir, my lips brushing the thin ridge of his ear.

"She believes it so," he replied. I shivered.

"Your factory will poison our rivers, and human greed will poison our lands."

"She has no prophecy," the Gray Knight whispered, helpfully, into my other ear. "Look at the eyes." I did. Blue and bright against the night sky, gleaming with reflected starlight. Nothing about her eyes screamed *I have no prophecy* to me.

"And, Princeling, your fondness for humans has not gone unnoticed by my Queen. Desist," she finished, "or the Queen will consider your lands forfeit. She will raze your factory and rule your Court."

That sounded *very bad*.

"This is ridiculous," Jeff said. "We're bringing you progress. And your lands are just the inside of Central Park, which isn't yours."

I slouched down. Maybe no one would notice I was a human.

The nymph turned to the Princeling, as if to say *Well?* He looked around the table again, at his people. No one looked pleased.

I wasn't an expert in faerie politics, but this altercation appeared not to have gone his way.

"Jeff, your presence at this meal has illuminated for me many things. I excuse you."

The nymph, message delivered, turned and sauntered back into the darkness.

Next to me the Gray Knight stood. I stood as well.

"Not you, Miriam Geld."

"I—what?" I put my hands on the table. Glanced at Sahir, who was staring at the Princeling. "I thank you for your hospitality, my lord, but I must leave with Jeff."

Two horses appeared over a ridge, their hooves clacking on the stone embedded in the hill. Neither was Sparkles.

The Princeling shrugged, still slouched across the arm of his chair, his wings dangling beneath him. "You partook of our food and will remain in our lands."

"Sorry?" I asked, my hands convulsing on the wood. I could feel twelve sets of eyes on me, strange alien eyes. My heart began to thump rapidly.

"You consumed faerie food, Lady of the True Dreams. *You are ours.*"

My body locked up, and I took stock of myself: no new sensations, nothing out of the ordinary beyond a panicked emptiness growing in my stomach.

"No I didn't! I had a grain bowl, for fuck's sake," I said. This was perhaps not my proudest moment. I looked at Jeff, my eyes watering. "Jeff, tell him—"

I couldn't believe I'd eaten the food—I'd *known better.* There was a *subway educational campaign.*

"Look," Jeff said, turning to the Princeling, "you can't take her, she's the only junior on our deal team."

The Princeling raised an eyebrow. "You will fulfill the terms of our bargain, Jeff. You will complete our transaction." He didn't move otherwise. A small part of my brain felt immense envy at the menacing way he lounged.

Jeff held his hands up in a placating gesture. "Yes, but it would be easier with Miri."

This was his argument?

"She is ours."

Faeries couldn't lie.

I stared around the table and saw a dozen strange faces grinning back at me. So this was the play, then. This was the power move, and I was the pawn.

"Jeff, please," I said, and my voice cracked.

"Miri didn't eat your food," Jeff said, staring at the Princeling. "She had a, what was it, a grain bowl. You didn't eat anything else, right, Miri?" He sounded bored and annoyed.

"What? No, of course not."

Jeff shrugged. "I don't know. You like snacks. You eat a lot of those—what are they called? The corn chips."

I gaped at him.

"Tortillas?" one of the faeries at the table asked, a man with wings so white they glowed against the night sky. Everyone turned to stare at him, and he shrank in on himself. "They're called tortilla chips," he said, doubling down even as his chin dipped. "Do you like go-hawk-a-molo?" he continued, directing this question at me.

The emotion I felt at this moment has no name.

"Do you mean *guacamole*?" the guy next to him asked. The guy next to him had a ridge of horns on the sides of his face, like a triceratops.

"I know not. It is made with avocado." Perhaps feeling that his audience required more context, he added: "My uncle who works at the Bronx Zoo showed it to me. You mash it up with a lemon and some pepper flakes."

Even the night had gone silent.

"Everyone likes guacamole," the guy next to him said.

I had the strangest sensation, like my entire body was ossi-fying where I stood. I could do nothing but stare.

"She partook of our food," the Princeling said, implacable as the tide. "My people sowed the seeds and harvested the grain."

Jeff threw his hands up. "So what? You know she didn't mean to!"

"I did not make this rule," the Princeling replied. "It is an old magic. If she tries to leave, it will not end well for her."

For the first time, Jeff looked around the table and saw the sharp faces of the inhuman strangers he'd eaten with. "Well, what do you want from her?"

The Princeling pointedly ignored this question. My heart beat wildly.

Through the roaring in my ears, I managed to form a coherent thought: *What* does *he want from me?*

"It is what the old magic requires. The lady stays," the Princeling said, serene.

Jeff frowned at me, taking me in.

"You have Wi-Fi here, right?" he said to the Princeling.

My jaw snapped shut.

"Of course," the Princeling said, in a tone that conveyed *How did you think we had been communicating with you?*

"Miri, I'll see you on the call tomorrow," Jeff said. He turned to the Princeling. "She needs to be on the call, okay?"

"She will continue to work on our deal, and I shall not harm her," the Princeling said, which was:

A. horrifying,

B. more than Jeff had asked for, and

C. too specific for my liking.

The Princeling looked at Sahir. "There is a room for her in the Court, in the central corridor. You will find her name upon the door."

"But I can't stay! I don't belong here! And…and I have a cat," I said, crying in earnest now.

Everyone ignored me. The Gray Knight had approached Jeff and held a hand out to him. He took it without looking at me again, and she hoisted him onto his horse.

Sahir grabbed my arm and pulled me away from the table. I tried to fight free, but his hand was iron around my biceps.

"What did you do?" I sobbed. There was already snot running along my upper lip. I could feel it cooling in the night air.

"Don't speak," he said. "And stop crying, now."

Whether it was magic, or just shock, I did.

"What did you do?" I repeated, stumbling over my feet as he dragged me away. His face was frozen in something between terror and determination.

"I have done many things, Miriam," he said, walking faster. I twisted my shoulder but he didn't loosen his hand. "Chin up, eyes forward," he added.

"Where are you taking me?" I scrabbled against his fingers with my free hand. He grabbed it and held it in front of us. We probably looked like the worst dance partners in a tango competition.

"The Court. Stop talking."

I tried to open my mouth, but this time he'd clearly bound me with a spell.

I jerked against his hand but couldn't pull loose. So I looked around as he half led, half carried me along a narrow stony path. I didn't recognize the topography of Central Park; we should have been heading directly into the reservoir, but instead we were walking toward a hill, probably no taller than one of the brownstones bordering the park, and dotted with gaping holes. Sahir went straight toward the largest hole, a wide arch set into the middle of the hill. The arch was made of unsupported dirt, and clumps of grass clung to the sides.

We passed through into a long brown tunnel, dotted with rough-hewn wooden doors. I tried to speak again and managed a low croak. I felt the words building between my lips, like a carbonated drink.

He glanced at me, an expression like surprise flitting across his face. He wrinkled his long hooked nose. "That is a powerful spell. You have some gift, at least," he said, sounding irritated. Then he looked away, his gaze flicking from door to door.

Without warning, he flung open a door on his left and spun me into a large, low room. The room was lit by glowing orbs that seemed to dance along the ceiling. There was a wide bed against the left wall and a desk beneath the window.

Sahir shut the door while I looked around. Along the far

wall stood a stone basin, a cascading waterfall, and what (thank god) looked like a fully functioning porcelain toilet.

"What is this?" I rasped, my voice suddenly mine again.

"This is your room." Sahir leaned against the shut door and crossed his arms over his chest. I stared at his implacable face. He'd left his hair loose, and it tumbled around his ears and cheeks, dangling at shoulder height.

He stared back at me.

"Why do I have a room here, Sahir?" I tried to modulate my voice, but I could hear it rising. "How long have you planned this?"

"You have a room here because you are a guest. I had no hand in the planning."

"Guest? *Guest?* I'm a prisoner!" I snapped, and put my face in my hands.

There were several moments of silence. I wondered if he'd left.

He sighed, like he'd been holding his breath for as long as he could. "You are not a prisoner, Miriam." Which meant he didn't think I was, at least. "And I am sure the Princeling has made you his guest for a reason." Which meant he didn't know anything.

"That's the dumbest thing I've ever heard."

When I looked up, he was rubbing the bridge of his nose. "It is probably not the dumbest thing you have ever heard, and if you were unable to lie, as I am, perhaps you would speak less."

Rude.

"Sahir, what is going on? I'm very tired and I need to feed

my cat, and I don't know what the Gray Knight did with my computer."

As soon as I said that I patted my pocket, frantic, and found my phone still there. "Do you get cell service here?"

He growled. "Humans," he said.

"*Humans?* You guys kidnapped me, Sahir! I would get off my high horse if I were you!" I shoved the panic down and yanked my phone out, staring at the screen. One text from my mom, two from Thea, and sixteen messages in Games Games Games, the group chat.

Would I never play a board game with my friends again? I dropped the phone to the bed and then sat down, heavily.

"*I* did not kidnap you."

"Please take me home," I said.

"You are home."

At that, I screamed at him wordlessly and chucked the nearest object—a small throw pillow covered in a sandy knit pattern—at his head.

He ducked and groped for the doorknob. I hurled myself upright, off-balance and hurtling toward him with my hands outstretched in claws.

Sahir slipped out the door and slammed it shut behind him.

I didn't stop and flung myself at it. The door didn't open, but it *did* knock the wind out of me as I slammed into it.

"Sahir!" I screamed, banging my fists against the wood. Silence.

I slid to the floor and crawled back toward the bed, sobbing so hard that each ragged breath sent me lurching to the side. When I got there, I pulled the blankets down onto the floor with me, and lay on my side, my face buried in the crook of my arm. The waterfall shower—was it just always running?—poured in a soothing cascade. I drowned it out with my heaving sobs.

I cried until I couldn't breathe, until my throat and eyes and cheeks all hurt.

The tears wouldn't stop. I reached for my phone, which had fallen to the floor beside me, but no one I called would be able to help me.

And beneath all of it the rage was building—I had *trusted them* and I shouldn't have.

I had trusted Jeff, and Jeff hadn't protected me.

Chapter 4
In Which I Explain My Cat's Name

I woke up from dreams of a stony riverbank and a bizarrely attractive picnic basket, lavishly appointed with a gingham blanket and gloriously curvaceous woven wicker sides.

My feelings about the picnic basket were so vivid and distressing that it took me a minute to remember where I was. I lay on the floor with a pounding head and dry face. I ground the heels of my palms into my eyes but the pounding didn't stop. I covered my ears, scowling.

The pounding continued.

This, I realized, was because someone was knocking on the door.

With a groan, I heaved myself upright. I had to pee terribly. "Hello?" I called, my voice hoarse.

"Wake up, Miriam. You should eat before your morning call."

"I'm awake." I stalked across the wood floor—still in my sneakers—and yanked the door open. Sahir stood outside, dressed in a gray suit with silver threads. His black hair was pulled back into a small bun at the nape of his neck. In one hand he held a large cat carrier, and on the floor next to him was a suitcase that looked a lot like mine.

His hands were both covered in red scratches, and there was a long thin line down his throat like a claw mark.

I frowned at him, then at the cat carrier.

"What is this?"

"You seemed distraught about the cat, so I found your address in the employee records and brought it here." His lip curled. "Your cat is very irritated."

"Maybe because you're very irritating," I snapped, and dove for the carrier. I lifted it up, arms shaking. Doctor Kitten was indeed inside, staring at me with the disdain he usually reserved for my neighbor's dog.

"You are welcome," Sahir said, his lip curling as he glared with an identical expression of disdain at the back of the carrier. "Now leave the cat here, and change into something clean. We will go to breakfast."

"He needs food, too." I went back to the bed, nearly tripping over the nest of sheets on the floor, and opened the carrier to let Doctor Kitten out. He just sat there, staring up at me, breathing hard. I put a hand on his back, feeling the warmth of his fur, shushing him in what I hoped was a calming way.

Sahir inclined his head. "Of course he needs food."

"And litter." I glared at Sahir.

Sahir's dark eyebrows had drawn together over his brown

eyes, and he looked like a glowering portrait in a very old house. "Miriam, I brought your cat everything he needs." He waved his left hand, a languid, too-long gesture, and something shot past me. When I turned around, Doctor Kitten's food and water bowls sat next to the desk. His litter box was in the corner next to the toilet.

"Now change so we can depart, please," Sahir said, closing the door.

I started to turn back to the door but stopped halfway, because my suitcase had appeared on the bed next to Doctor Kitten's carrier, unzipped. I snatched up the shirt on top, not caring what it looked like, and scuttled over to the toilet to pee.

Doctor Kitten followed me and rubbed his head against my calves.

He sat on my foot while I washed my hands and splashed my face with water, and mewled when I slid out from under him.

After I put the new shirt on, I picked him up and nuzzled his face. He licked my chin and wiggled until I put him down on the bed.

Then I picked him up again and took him to the door.

"Ready," I said, hefting Doctor Kitten in one arm and opening the door with the other hand. Sahir frowned at me.

"You are not bringing the cat, are you?"

"I am bringing the cat." I set my jaw and glared at him.

He sighed in a way that indicated decades of suffering.

"I'm sorry you're inconvenienced by my kidnapping, Sahir," I said. "Please feel free to release me at any time."

"You do not seem to understand." He stalked down the

hall, farther into the hill. I glanced in the direction of the exit but couldn't see any light.

"You said that last night." I shifted Doctor Kitten so I was cradling him like a baby. He stuck his white front paws in the air, toe beans on display, and lolled his head over my forearm.

"It was true last night as well."

"Then *explain*," I snapped.

Sahir's jaw set, and he spoke through clenched teeth. "Perhaps humans cannot understand. Faeries are *just* and *fair*. If the Princeling committed a wrong against you, he will make it right. And if he detained you from your chosen path, he did so for a reason."

I *tsk*ed a hopefully dubious *tsk* but had nothing to say. Sahir was just a guy on the other end of a customer service line: fundamentally powerless, shoved into my path so I could abuse him verbally and encounter the manager completely exhausted.

He glanced down at me, brow furrowed. "You did not call the police last night."

I jerked to a stop. "What on earth would the police do against faeries?" I imagined a bevy of police officers pouring into Central Park and then maundering about on their Segways, looking for a glimmer of light, a tear in the fabric of human reality.

"You have not told anyone." It wasn't a question.

"Creepy that you know that, but no, I haven't, because I'm hoping you'll all come to your senses and let me go."

"I know you. Will you tell any humans?" He sounded curious but not concerned.

I wanted very desperately to ask questions, like *Can we reprioritize for a moment?* or *Do you feel that your unfailing trust in your leader is truly warranted?* But I needed Sahir on my side if I was to get out of here. So instead, I said, "Jeff knows."

He shrugged. "Your colleagues may know," he said, trailing a hand along the wall. "But they are unlikely to care."

Ouch.

Specks of dirt dusted down in his wake.

Sahir turned right at a break in the corridor and led me along an identical brown hallway, lit at intervals by chittering will-o'-the-wisps. They swooped and dipped down from the ceiling like hawks riding imperceptible air currents, tiny bodies subsumed by their own luminescence. I squinted but couldn't discern their shapes.

Instead of continuing to batter my own self-esteem, I suavely changed the subject.

"Don't they get bored?" I asked, nodding at one.

He looked at me. "Who?"

"The, uh, lights."

Frowning, he stopped in front of a large wooden door. "This is our communal dining hall. Do not embarrass yourself."

"I don't want to eat faerie food," I protested.

"It is a little late for that." He pushed and the door swung inward. "And I do not know if the will-o'-the-wisps get bored, Miriam. Do pigeons get bored? I suppose you will have to ask them."

Inside, the communal dining hall looked depressingly like a high school cafeteria, a large room full of long tables. Along the far wall, three faeries stood behind a counter, serving scoops of food to a line of people with wide wooden trays. Behind the counter I could see windows into a kitchen area.

There were rows of tables like the one we'd sat at the night before, long wooden rectangles crowded with stools. A series of small holes in the ceiling let in light, and more tiny faeries flitted through the air above the tables, bringing flashes of illumination with them.

I didn't see the Princeling or any of his retinue.

"We will eat here, and then I will bring you to your room before I leave," Sahir said.

"If you're going into the office, why can't I?"

Doctor Kitten had started getting restless so I hefted him over my shoulder, his front paws on my back and his back paws on my stomach.

"You must not leave Faerie," the Gray Knight said, appearing out of nowhere to glower like a very hot and foreboding bodyguard next to me. Sahir walked toward the food line. I felt the eyes of everyone in the room on us as the Gray Knight and I followed him.

But Thea and I had spent a summer teaching ourselves Elvish so we could read the inscription on the One Ring in its original language. Jordan had once created a monthslong campaign whose mechanics hinged on the precise wording of a mysterious letter. I was primed for verbal loopholes, is the point.

"Must not or cannot?" I asked the Gray Knight.

Sahir grabbed a tray for himself, looked at me with the cat over my arm, and then grabbed a tray for me, too.

The Gray Knight said nothing, the haughty tilt of her chin almost but not quite hiding the way she clenched her jaw.

"*Must* not or *cannot*?" I repeated, glaring at her.

"Must not *and* cannot," she snapped. "The food you consumed has altered your body, and the attempt would disintegrate you into a fine mist of blood and bone shards."

I recoiled, thinking about how the grain bowl had warmed me, how my arms and legs had tingled. It clearly wasn't from the spices. It was magic.

I clutched Doctor Kitten tighter. I'd been such an idiot.

She pointed to Sahir, who was putting a bowl onto my tray. "You might enjoy the porridge, Miriam. It is made with wilderberries." Then she stepped ahead of us in line, skipping the porridge entirely.

"Sahir," I pleaded, hoping he'd intervene, but he kept his back to me. We went along the line together.

The first faerie serving breakfast scowled at me. I stared back, the word *cannot* pounding along my veins with every frantic beat of my heart.

The second pretended not to see me. The third—who looked like a Dallas Cowboy with a day of stubble, big arms, and the faded blue eyes of a person who spends all his time in the sun—nodded in greeting.

I blinked.

Sahir led me back across the wide room to the table closest to the door, where the Gray Knight had already made herself comfortable. Her silver hair lay in a thin sheet down her back, and her silver tail flicked in time to some music only she could hear.

"My lady," he said, hooking a stool with one foot and straddling it. He put both of our trays down with the expected inhuman grace and then glanced at me.

I put Doctor Kitten on the table. "Please sit," I said. Doctor Kitten stared at me for a second and then sat.

"She brought her familiar to breakfast?" the Gray Knight asked Sahir. She had the loveliest cheekbones, high and broad against her narrow chin. "Did you not advise against this?"

"Miriam is unwilling to hear advice at the moment," Sahir said, his fist clenching on the tabletop. The smooth line of his suit rippled over his forearm. I wondered if faeries had similar circulatory systems to us, if the vein in his forearm would pop when he flexed.

With a violent internal shake, I refocused my attention on the Gray Knight and my literal imprisonment.

"If I eat this food, will I get…more stuck in Faerie?" I tilted my head, took in the slope of slender neck into delicate trapezius.

Seemingly determined not to engage, Sahir picked up his spoon and started shoveling porridge into his mouth.

"More stuck?" The Gray Knight glanced at him. My eyes caught for a moment on her free hand, laid out on the table, slender fingers close enough that I could have reached out and brushed my fingertips along her nails. I looked away, feeling a hot flush creep up my cheeks. "You will become no more or less *stuck*, as you put it, no matter what you do, my lady."

With his left hand, Sahir snatched up a slice of bread with jam and took a huge bite. He had a smear of blue on his full upper lip. I fought the urge to wipe it away.

"How do you come up with these nicknames?" I stared at

my plate. There was a bowl of porridge with golden berries on top, two pieces of toast spread with blue jam, and a glass of almost-orange juice.

"What is a Nick-name?" The Gray Knight rolled her shoulders back, like she was preparing for a fight. "Is it like a true name?"

"What you call me." I put a hand on Doctor Kitten to stop him from squirming. "Lady of the True Dreams or whatever."

"A title?" The Gray Knight finished her last bite of toast and pushed her plate toward the center of the table. Doctor Kitten stretched out to lick her plate clean. I snatched him back before he could make contact; I had no idea if cats could get stuck in Faerie, but I wasn't planning on finding out.

"This is unhygienic," she added, eyeing him dolefully. He'd borne my intervention with bad grace and now stretched out on his side across the table.

"We're in a giant dirt building," I muttered. "And Doctor Kitten is clean."

"The cat is not a doctor, I do not think," Sahir said. "A name that is a lie."

"Well, he's got his PhD," I started, "only I'm his supervisor and I'll never put him up for tenure. You could call him Adjunct Professor Kitten if that's better."

Both of them stared at me, eyes silver and brown.

"Is this a—" the Gray Knight started, and stopped. She put her chin on her hand and stared at me, like I was some sort of specimen. "Is this a riddle?"

"It's a commentary on the state of academia," I said, twirling my ring around my finger.

Sahir dropped his spoon onto his tray with a clatter and

turned his entire torso to glare at me. "You have given your cat a name that is a commentary?"

"Well, aren't all of your names commentary?" I stuck my spoon into the porridge-type thing.

"Our names are *truth*," he growled. "Names are truth. Your cat's name is a lie."

He was, I felt, unjustified in his irritation.

"What's the endgame with keeping me here?" I spooned porridge into my mouth. My eyes rolled back in my head. The berries were sweet and juicy, with enough of a bite to balance the smooth creaminess of the oats. I took another bite—blissful. It was so hard to stay annoyed when this was probably the best breakfast I'd ever eaten in my life.

"What is a game at the end?" The Gray Knight looked nonplussed.

"You know, what will my being here accomplish?"

"Do not ask questions we will not answer," the Gray Knight said, already sounding tired.

I looked to Sahir, who had scarfed down his entire breakfast. He still wouldn't make eye contact with me. "I am going to work," he announced. "The Gray Knight will take you to your room before your morning meeting." He'd clearly decided to foist me off as soon as possible.

"It's at nine a.m.," I said automatically.

Sahir stalked out of the dining hall, shoulders tense as he slammed the door open. It swung quietly shut behind him.

"Oh, so it's on double-sided hinges," I said.

The Gray Knight frowned at me. "You are quite calm," she said. "I anticipated more…shrieking."

"My dad says I'm good in a crisis," I said. "But I'm shrieking on the inside, I promise." I sounded cheerful to my own ears. "Anyway, why can I call him *Sahir* but I have to call you the Gray Knight?"

"I am in the Princeling's retinue," she said. "And as Sahir said, names are truths. I am the Princeling's Gray Knight."

She stood up and nodded at me, indicating that breakfast was over. I hooked Doctor Kitten around the middle and followed her into the hallway.

"So do you change colors? Could you be his Blue Knight if he wanted?"

Unwilling to divulge the great secrets of her Court, the Gray Knight remained silent. I trailed behind her, shifting Doctor Kitten in my arms so that his slowly extending claws caught on my shirt and not the tender flesh of my upper arm.

Though so far, all of the hallways I'd been down looked the same, I felt fairly sure that the Gray Knight was leading me along a different path than the one I'd walked to get to the cafeteria. I cleverly deduced this when she said, "We have time before your meeting; the Princeling will speak with you now."

Good. I didn't care that I wasn't really presentable or that Doctor Kitten was still wiggling in my arms trying to get free.

It was time to get answers.

We finally stopped in front of a door inlaid with tiny blue and gray and green gems that glittered in the variegated light provided by the luminescent wisps darting overhead. Taken together, the gems gave the impression of a sheer cliff face, pockmarked by moss. The unsteady colors and brightness lent the blue gems life, and they flowed from the top left corner of the door down to the bottom right like sun-drenched droplets down a torrential waterfall. Or *was* it the lights—was there some magic animating the mosaic?

Before I could decide, the Gray Knight swung the door open and strode inside. I stopped on the threshold. The room was smaller than I'd expected, with a throne on a dais across from the doorway, and several chairs along either wall. Otherwise, the room was empty—no garish decor on rustic shelves or grand portraits of the Princeling on the walls. The Princeling sat on the throne. He was resplendent in a matching shirt and trousers embroidered with shining silver threads, legs splayed in a way that looked almost vulgar, his expression one of boredom. The Gray Knight stationed herself at his side, her eyes trained straight ahead.

"It is time to explain to you some measure of my plans," he said, instead of *Good morning*.

"Please do." I strode into the center of the room and planted my feet, trying for a power pose. When I first went into finance, I'd watched this video on YouTube about how to stand in front of director-level executives to command respect. Now seemed like as good a time as any to try to bring that sort of confidence into a room. Doctor Kitten mewled, so I shifted him onto my shoulder.

The Princeling inclined his head. "You are here in part as a response to the unrest among my people about our new company."

I raised an eyebrow. It had been clear from the dinner that not every one of the Princeling's constituents supported his working with humanity, but I wasn't eager to be a response to any unrest.

He cleared his throat, glanced at the Gray Knight. She didn't move: She continued to stare at nothing.

"The Queen is plotting an incursion upon my territory," the Princeling said. "What do you know of Faerie politics?"

"I didn't know there was a Queen," I admitted, shifting Doctor Kitten's weight in my arms. "So probably not much. I thought you were in charge of the whole realm."

At this, the Gray Knight shot him a look. It was hard to interpret, dark and a little frustrated; did she not want him to share this information with me?

But he continued as though he hadn't noticed. "There are several rulers in Faerie," he said. "And our people bind themselves to us only so long as they *feel* loyalty. We protect them, and they support us."

"Okay," I said, watching the restless flutter of his iridescent wings. They beat against his chair, trapped between his shoulders and the heavy silver throne.

"My nearest neighbor is the Queen, who rules a cold, cruel Court. She is a monster, with shark teeth and a shark's heart. If she wins the loyalty of my people, she will not stop: Her incursion will continue through Faerie, and maybe into New York, where they will hunt humans for sport."

Throughout this little monologue, his wings beat faster and faster, until he'd kicked up a little maelstrom in the room: My hair whipped around my head, and Doctor Kitten burrowed into my arms.

"Hm," I said, hoping I sounded thoughtful and not unbelievably freaked out.

His wings stopped moving.

"I don't know how I can be particularly helpful there," I admitted. "I don't have any military experience. Have you considered requisitioning a general?"

Clearly already done with my bullshit, the Princeling plowed on.

"We need an example of a human, akin to the ones we might encounter outside, so that my people can become used to you and see that your kind is no threat to ours."

I ground my teeth. "I'm not going to be a very useful show pony," I bit out.

The Princeling leaned forward, shoulders tense, like a lion deciding whether to pounce. Belatedly, I realized I now lived in this guy's realm. Possibly forever. I took a deep breath.

"If you'd just told me what game you were playing, we could have worked together," I said. "There was no reason to trap me here." *Away from my family,* I couldn't say. Couldn't remind him they existed, lest he bring them to me.

He tapped his fingers on his chin. "This *game,* Lady of the True Dreams, is older than your life, and has consequences far broader than your existence. Let us be honest with each other."

I stared up at him, frustrated with myself more than anyone else in the room. I'd trusted the faeries, because they were pleasant to be around and, though I was loath to admit it, pleasant to look at. And...because I truly wanted to believe they were trustworthy. Faeries were supposed to be *better* than humans—or at least worse in more interesting ways—not play the same stupid games as us.

"Honestly? I want to go home."

Doctor Kitten must have smelled my brains steaming with

rage, and stuck his nose in my ear to investigate. I pulled him away, never taking my eyes off the Princeling.

The Princeling sat up, impassive. "This is home for you now, my lady. As your lord, I will give you a task in our lands. You will teach my people about your people, and in this way prepare them to enter the mortal realm safely." He paused, considering. "More safely than the vampires did, at least."

I opened my mouth.

Blinked at him.

Closed my mouth.

"Are you—are you serious, right now?"

The Princeling looked surprised. "Yes."

"You want me to teach a *human class*?"

"I would not call it a class," he said. "Perhaps a lecture, or a practicum." He tapped his fingers on his knee, staring over my left shoulder. He looked a little uncomfortable. *Good.*

I didn't speak until he made eye contact again.

"You kidnapped me . . . to teach a class. That's your solution to this Queen problem. You're going to run an educational campaign against her *military incursion* and hope the power of *knowledge* saves your Court."

We stared at each other.

He didn't blink.

I didn't blink.

The Gray Knight cracked her neck, her face passive.

"Does Sahir know why you took me?" I demanded.

He shook his head. "Sahir is not my knight. He knew only that he should sit with you during our first meal and make sure you felt safe."

Well then.

"He's your spy, though," I tried.

The Princeling waved a contemptuous hand. "I do not need Sahir to spy for me." But his eyes flicked to the Gray Knight.

"And her?"

"My Gray Knight knew, of course," he said.

I stepped away. "I want to go back to my room, please," I said.

For a moment, I thought he would protest: He raised his eyebrows, as if preparing for us to duke it out by staring wordlessly at each other with progressively more incredulous expressions. But then his brow furrowed and he ducked his chin.

"I have other stratagems as well," he said, almost defensively. "You cannot expect me to share all of my plans with a single mortal girl."

I gnawed my lip. "Sure," I said.

"Is there anything you want to discuss before you leave, lady?"

I didn't know how to bring up my family and friends without getting them dragged here as well, just like my cat.

"I'm uncomfortable being here without anyone from the outsi—*my* world knowing where I am. Though I'm unsure if it would be wise for me to disclose my location," I said, cautiously. "It might cause negative feelings in the human realm…a kidnapping might lead to stronger regulations on faeries, which neither of us wants."

The Princeling stood up and stepped off the dais, the

movements so fast I couldn't track them. He was before me in a blink, a hand on my chin.

I tried to twist away, but he pulled my chin upward and looked into my eyes.

In the fantasy books I'd read, this was usually a very sensual moment. Perhaps I should have wondered if he would kiss me. But that wasn't the vibe. His fingers pushed my cheeks toward my lips harshly, and though it hurt, I did my best to keep his gaze and not let him know that I was scared out of my mind.

"Interesting," he said, searching my eyes.

"I-interesting?" I asked, in a squished sort of voice.

My neck started to ache. Doctor Kitten, who'd borne all of this with remarkable calm, twisted his head and bit the Princeling on the wrist.

"Demon creature!" he shouted, jumping backward.

"He's not a demon," I said proudly, cradling Doctor Kitten's head. "He was just annoyed because you were in our personal space."

"Space cannot belong to a person," the Gray Knight stated. She'd been so quiet I'd forgotten her presence. But if I didn't know better, I would have thought she was fighting a smile.

"Perhaps one day I will ask for your opinion on these matters," the Princeling said. "But for now, allow me to worry about...*feelings* in the human realm." He ran the pad of a finger over his wrist, the red scratches disappearing beneath green vines of light. "And please consider my request. Your cooperation is desired."

He turned away from me, presumably to go back to staring at the ceiling.

Without anything more to say, I backed out of the room, my left hand over Doctor Kitten's head, just in case.

And then I stood in the hallway and waited until the Gray Knight deigned to join me.

She came out quietly, after enough time that I was fuming.

Ignoring my glare, she led me back the way we'd come, right and then left. I tried to count the doors between mine and the turn but couldn't keep track.

"How many people live here?"

She stopped in front of a door. I looked at it and saw that it had my name burned into the wood: *Miriam Geld*. It was a punch in the gut, a brutal reminder that threatened to shatter me.

"You will understand, Miriam, why I do not answer that question." She didn't even look at me as she spoke.

"I won't understand, actually," I snapped. "I haven't understood *anything* you've done. What am I going to do with the information?"

But she'd already started down the hallway.

Chapter 5
In Which I Call My Mother

When I got into the bedroom and put Doctor Kitten down, I realized I had no idea how to log onto the internet. The desk had three monitors now, and my computer had already been hooked up to them. My key card sat on the desk next to the external laptop and mouse they'd left me.

And there, next to the computer, my cell phone sat on a wireless charger. I didn't remember what I'd done with it last night.

But they'd *left my phone for me*. That told me, more than anything else, the truth of my captivity: They weren't worried who I told about my imprisonment.

They *should* have been worried; I wasn't sure if the Princeling realized what he had done, what he was risking in taking me this way. If I revealed that I wasn't here voluntarily, human-faerie relations—already tenuous at best—would sour rapidly.

Frustratingly, it seemed like I cared more than he did about how faerie integration went. I'd taken this job in the first place because I believed business success was one of the fastest ways to integrate supernaturals into human society.

Obviously, I hadn't been listening when Jordan tried to explain that investment banking probably wouldn't build the bridges I thought it would. I missed his oversized fashion glasses and his always-right attitude so much right now. I missed Thea, too, her natural way of understanding others, and her warm hugs that were just the best.

Would I ever get another hug from my best friends?

I walked over to the desk and tapped on my phone screen. It lit up. Eight forty-five a.m., six text messages from Thea, forty-five messages in the Games Games Games chat, and a missed call from my mom. My throat tightened. What could I even tell her?

I stared out the window. In the daylight, I could see more clearly. Despite my impression that the corridor was flat last night, I was high up in the hillside, towering over an unfamiliar landscape. As in Central Park, there were gray uncovered rocks and winding dirt pathways among wide green swaths of meadow, but unlike the human side, the foreboding edge of a dense forest bounded one horizon. My eyes felt weird—I almost thought I could see individual blades of emerald grass swaying in a breeze, like the window was magnifying what I wanted to explore. I tried to reach through the window and slapped my hand into an invisible barrier.

Magic. I was touching magic.

Something in my stomach fluttered. I shouldn't be pleased

about anything, of course. But—I imagined a conversation with myself at eight years old.

Eight-year-old me would be sitting at our kitchen table, in one of our wooden chairs with the rounded backs, her bare feet kicking at a table leg.

Miri, I would say, trying to sound calm and soothing. *You got stuck in Faerie.*

EEEEEEEEK, younger me would reply. *THIS IS THE BEST NEWS EVER.*

I would put my hand to my head at this point. *No, Miri, this is* bad *news. They kidnapped your cat, too.*

Younger me would probably be vibrating at a frequency strong enough to break her own chair. *You mean I'm in a magic realm, and I get to keep my cat?*

I'd search for something to upset her. *Miri, Mom and Dad aren't here.*

A pause. *Well, we can go visit! And did a faerie prince fall in love with us yet? Are we really pretty?*

The Princeling—I would stop. Green eyes, tunic open at his throat to show the smooth column of his neck. *Is cruel.*

But she was a child, with a little-girl smile, one tooth missing, too many freckles. *You'll make him nice!*

In my head, I sighed. *Miri, it's time for me to explain the harmful trope of fixing a broken man.*

And then I stopped. What the hell was I doing?

I wrenched myself out of that little fantasy and shook my head, scrunching my eyes shut. My hand was still on the not-window. I looked for the sun but couldn't see it in the sky.

Nothing for it but to dial into our team meeting, so I booted up my computer.

Maybe it was the magic, but the computer turned on faster than usual, and I had set up the meeting screen before nine a.m.

The Wi-Fi—named FairFolk 'Fi—had no password. I sat in the virtual waiting room and shot a quick text to my mom. *Call you when I can.*

Corey let me into the meeting. I stared at his initials. He came off mute.

"Hey, Miri, you aren't in today?" He sounded so normal.

"What?" I gasped. "Jeff didn't tell you?" But I was still muted.

Should I tell him? Did Jeff want me to keep it quiet?

Fuck that. I tapped the spacebar and came off mute.

"I got trapped in Faerie, Corey," I said. "Jeff really didn't tell you?"

"What?" His shock sounded genuine. "How is that even poss— Miri, *did you eat their food*?"

"I—"

"Miri, there's a *subway campaign about this*," he said. "Don't you even look up when you're on the train?"

I could feel my eyes watering again, but I didn't want to cry on a work call.

"Yes, thank you," I snapped. "I told Jeff that yesterday. They tricked me. I thought it was a bowl from Grain Up."

"That place is terrible," he muttered. "I could've told you it would ruin your life."

Matt and Levi both dialed in at the same time. "Morning," Levi said. Matt didn't say anything.

We all sat in silence for a few minutes, waiting for Jeff.

His name popped up, and he said, "Jeff here."

No one said anything.

"Can you all hear me?" he asked, at the same time that Levi started to say, "Hi, Jeff."

Both of them fell quiet.

"Corey, you have the agenda?" Levi said after a second. Doctor Kitten jumped onto the desk next to me and tried to write a sentence on my keyboard.

"Is Miri on?" Jeff asked, like he couldn't see my name. I lifted Doctor Kitten off the desk and put him on the floor.

"I'm here, Jeff," I said.

"Miri will be working remotely for a bit."

I muted myself in order to say a series of very rude words. Doctor Kitten hopped onto the desk again, looking at me with what I thought was sympathy.

I unmuted myself.

"I'm stuck in Faerie," I said. "Jeff, I'm stuck in Faerie. I am not working remotely because I want to. I am *trapped*. In *Faerie*." Doctor Kitten climbed onto the windowsill and I grabbed for him, unsure if the magic barrier would work for him, too. I caught him under the arms and hauled him back.

"Yes, well, I didn't know if you wanted me to share details of your personal life."

I went on mute again and devised a new set of creative sentiments, involving Jeff, a waffle maker, and various bodily excretions.

I unmuted myself.

"This isn't my personal life, Jeff. I got stuck in Faerie on a work trip."

No one said anything.

I took one of Doctor Kitten's paws and tried to put it out the window. It came up against the magic barrier, so I put him down on the desk again. He probably wouldn't fall out the window.

"Miri, we don't have a ton of time, I have a hard stop at nine thirty," Jeff said. "And the rest of you, since this is a work issue, I expect it to remain in the office. Don't share with CBS, okay? I don't want us on the news. Now, Corey, do we have any new pitch meetings coming up?"

"You absolute towel rack made of dog shit," I muttered.

I had not muted myself.

"Excuse me?" Jeff said.

"Sorry, talking to my cat."

Doctor Kitten hopped back onto the windowsill and leaned against the magic barrier, staring at me.

"That poor cat," Matt said.

"We don't have any pitches coming up, Jeff," Corey said.

"We have the dairy company with the new yogurt for werewolves," Matt chimed in.

I cringed.

"That's supernatural," Matt added, when no one spoke.

"Matt, there's a reason they are spinning off the 'dog food for your human' brand three months after they launched it," Jeff said, displaying sense and making me hate him more.

"Fine, then we don't have any new pitches," Matt said, petulant. I pictured him crossing his arms at his desk. Were all of them at their desks except me?

"Okay, does everyone know what they're working on?" Jeff asked.

No one answered.

"I'll take that as a yes, and let's end early so I can have a few minutes back."

"Wait, Jeff—" I said, but they'd all already hung up.

Was I just supposed to, like, do work?

On cue, an email came in from Jeff.

Hi Miri,

Please take some time today to think through our strategy for the presentation. Remember it is due to the client at the same time as the final iteration of the model. When I reviewed it last night, I saw several mistakes and formatting errors.

Jeff.

Gritting my teeth, I opened our shared file drive and found the latest version of the presentation. I double-clicked on it, sighed, and stared at the outline of my black and white cat against the impossibly blue sky.

———————————•———————————

When the clock on my computer showed one thirty p.m., I stood up.

It was time.

I picked up my phone, the miserable pit in my stomach gaping. I was the most afraid I'd been all week. Standing, knees locked, I pulled up her contact and hesitated.

No.

I considered the room and sat back down in the chair, phone in my hand.

No.

The bed? I sat gingerly on the side without my suitcase, and then pulled my knees up to my chest.

No.

The floor, maybe. I slid down onto the floor and stretched my legs out in front of me.

I didn't *have* to tell her. I could just call her and lie.

Except I couldn't. I *wanted* to. But I couldn't.

For a moment, I considered telling Thea or Jordan or my dad first. But there was no putting this off.

I had to call my mother.

Before I could talk myself out of it, I tapped the call button. The ringing started with surprising alacrity for cell service in a pocket realm, and I made a mental note to ask the Gray Knight about their service provider.

"Miri?" my mom asked, her voice cheerful through the phone. "How are you?"

"Mom, I'm trapped in Faerie and I can't get out or I'll explode into blood mist and bone shards," I said in one breath. "But you don't need to worry because I have Doctor Kitten and I'm fine."

"Oh?" my mother asked, in a tone so far beyond hysterical that it veered back into calm. The calm then shattered with violence.

The light emitted from the sun takes eight seconds to travel the ninety-three million miles from thither to hither.

The sound my mother made next took approximately thrice that time to die down.

"Mom, it's okay," I kept saying, staring at the patch of brown wall underneath the window. I felt better now that I'd told her. The first half of the hard part was over.

"Who's keeping you there?" she asked, in a voice octaves above human comprehension.

"The Princeling. He's...in charge."

"I'm going to march over there right now and give that man a piece of my mind!" my mother said, initiating the second half of the hard part.

"Mom, it's fine. I'm talking to him."

"Put him on the phone! I have something to say!"

I took my ring off and twirled it between my fingers, staring at the glints of light refracting off its surface. "Mom, it's fine. Please."

"He can't *keep you*," she snapped. And then—"How did this even happen?"

Oh lord. Oh heavens and earth. Oh sweet parboiled mayonnaise-smothered corn.

"Um...They tricked me."

I scrunched my eyes shut against her next tirade. Unfortunately, sound doesn't enter your brain through the eyeballs.

Eventually, she ended on her fourth "Make him let you go!"

With a sigh, I slid all the way onto the floor, staring up at the faerie flittering by the ceiling.

"Even if he could let me go, which he can't, faeries don't work like that, Mom."

"Our next-door neighbor Mrs. Jackson is a vampire, and *she* would let you go."

The ceiling had lovely striations in it, veins of gray and brown rock and mineral.

"Okay, I'm not sure why you think Mrs. Jackson would kidnap me in the first place, but I *meant*—"

"Miriam!" she scolded. "Is now really the time to be sassy?" Which, fair enough.

"Look, Mom, all I mean is that faeries have a strong sense of fairness. If the Princeling were in my debt, then maybe it would be different."

"Then put him in your debt," she said. She sounded gentler now that we'd moved on to the advisory portion of our call.

"How am I going to put a faerie prince in my debt?" I groaned, closing my eyes. Doctor Kitten mewled, so I opened my eyes again.

"You could…save his life from an assassination attempt?" she suggested, sounding hopeful.

I remembered the Princeling earlier that morning, moving so quickly I couldn't track him with my eye.

"That's definitely an option," I said brightly.

"Do you have better ideas?" she snapped. I squeezed my eyes shut.

"He wants me to teach a class about humans," I said. "Maybe he'll bargain?"

I didn't feel particularly hopeful about the idea, but my mom latched onto it with the vigor of a leech leaping from a beaver dam onto a human ankle.

"Yes, bargain with that!" she said. "He wanted it enough to kidnap you, right? It must be important to him."

Doctor Kitten and I stared at each other.

"I guess so," I said, still so baffled I couldn't feel angry.

"Then bargain with that," she said, in the voice she used when she considered a matter settled.

"That's a good point, Mom, I'll do that now."

"Are you just saying you'll do that now, and then you're going to put it off?" she asked.

"While that is certainly my modus operandi, no, Mom, I am not just saying that."

I could hear her chewing on a pen cap over the phone. "Do you want me to come get you?"

The thought of my mother storming Faerie with nothing but a pocket full of used tissues and her force of will gave me major anxiety. "Not yet, Mom. But I'll let you know. I love you."

I hung up before she could say anything else and levered myself upright.

"I'm gonna get lunch, Doctor Kitten," I said. "Do you want to come?" I walked toward the door, but he stayed on the windowsill, staring out at two strange-looking gold birds who'd come to roost on the other side of the magic barrier.

"Okay, traitor." I opened the door and turned left. Then I paused.

Maybe lunch could wait…maybe I should be exploring the mountain to find secrets or a way out instead.

Sure, if I wanted to get eaten by a dragon or locked in a cave or turned into a flower or some nonsense.

I started down the corridor, forcing myself to observe more. I counted the wooden doors on my left, at least, to get a sense of where I was so I could find my way back.

One. Two. Three.

One of the will-o'-the-wisps darted away from the wall and floated next to my cheek. I glanced over. He was a tiny humanoid creature but had six limbs, the two extra protrusions coming from his midtorso like a fly's. He had a fly's eyes, too, multifaceted and refracting extra light. I couldn't tell where the glow came from—maybe it was all over his skin. He also wore something that looked like a diaper made from an acorn.

"Hi," I said. He cocked his tiny head. If he recognized human speech, he didn't give any indication.

I came to the break in the corridor and realized I had stopped counting doors. With a sigh, I turned right, determined to pay better attention this time. The will-o'-the-wisp followed along, brightening as we got closer to the dining hall.

When I pushed the door, warm and rough beneath my fingers, my new friend flew inside without a backward glance, giving off spurts of bright light like Morse code.

I followed slowly, staring around the room. It was fuller than it had been in the morning, and again everyone turned to look at me. Gulping and trying to make myself look small, I hurried over to the buffet line and grabbed a tray.

The same three people stood serving food. This time, I tried to keep my gaze down at the food as I passed, though it was still hard not to glance at them.

The first faerie didn't put anything on my tray and scowled again when I stopped. She had slitted pupils and vivid green scales on her cheeks. She appeared to be serving bowls of a thick brown soup. I could see something like peas and potatoes floating in the pot, which resembled the sort of witches' cauldron a high school production of *Macbeth* would splurge on.

The second faerie, when I approached, stared down at his platter of sandwiches—sandwiches?—but pushed one toward me. I picked it up and put it on the tray.

The third had blue eyes shattered through with gray lines like shards of broken glass. He met my gaze. He put a bowl of leafy vegetables in blues and greens onto my tray. And he smiled. He smiled like a gift, with a wall of blinding white teeth against his pink lips. Shocked, I felt my mouth turn up in response.

"Lady," he said, with a gracious half bow.

"Thanks," I croaked. I felt his eyes follow me back to the same table where I had sat that morning. It made the other eyes feel lighter.

As I sank onto the stool, I felt a rush of wind, and suddenly the Princeling sat across from me, the Gray Knight on his left and the Crone standing behind him. He'd changed into less formal clothes than he'd worn earlier—a plain green shirt, darker than his eyes, and soft trousers. "Lady of the True Dreams," he said with a kind smile. I wondered if it was genuine.

"Princeling." I inclined my head but couldn't keep the irritation off my face. He saw it and his mouth twisted.

"How do you find your accommodations?" he inquired, politely. I wondered what would happen if I punched him in the face.

On his left, the Gray Knight cracked her knuckles like she could hear my thoughts. She was wearing a pewter gray blouse, and it made her hair shine against her shoulders like a river in moonlight. I mean, to be honest, she was just very pretty.

"Does my hospitality lack?" the Princeling prompted. I flushed and turned my face away from the Gray Knight.

"I—" I stopped. Would he pull our contract if I was rude?

Did I care at this point?

I imagined trying to interview for a new job while in Faerie.

Hi, it's Miri here, thanks for taking the time to chat. Sorry about the weird lighting, my night-light is alive and he's really acting up. Anyway, I am so excited about your human job in the human world, where I totally live and pay for food and housing—

"The room is lovely, my lord," I tried again. His eyes were intent on my face. "But would I not serve you better from my office?" I clenched my hands together in my lap. I felt so cold I was shaking. "I cannot work as well with my team from your realm."

"You serve me best where I have placed you," the Princeling replied. He sat back and put one hand on his knee.

"And how do I serve you here?"

"With a smile, I hope." He still didn't look away. I tried to meet his gaze, but I couldn't. Had he just told me to *smile*? I would rip his *face* off—

"My liege—" I started, but he cut me off.

"Was Jeff fair to you this morning?"

Startled, I jerked my hand up to my face, sending my tray of untouched food flying. The salad bowl clattered across the table and landed on his chest.

Neither he nor the Gray Knight moved. The Crone sat down on his right and stared at me, too.

"Oh—fuck—I mean, oh—shoot—I am so sorry—" I scrambled out of my seat and started around the table toward him, but he waved a hand and the food disappeared, tray and all. There were no stains on his green shirt.

"Think of it no more." It might have been a command. "But answer me, if it please you." He waved an imperious hand, and I slumped down onto the stool.

It does not please me, I thought. "Jeff was…Jeff." Frustration buzzed inside me. I didn't owe Jeff anything—but I wouldn't criticize him and risk the success of the faeries' company.

Still the Princeling's eyes never left me. I felt them, even though I stared down at the table. I tried to trace a vein in the wood with my finger and lost track of it.

"I know what you said to Sahir," the Princeling said.

"What I said to Sahir?" I repeated. He glanced at the Gray Knight and jerked his chin. She stood up and went toward the food line. "I'm sorry, my lord, I don't know what I said to Sahir."

The Crone rolled her eyes—the action looked strange in her wrinkled face. Today she wore a blue cloak, the hood over her brow. Her eyes, glittering black, stared out from the folds of the fabric. I wondered if cloaks were comfortable.

To my surprise, she spoke. "Everyone offers gifts and curses," she said, in a terrifying mimicry of my voice. I clapped my hand to my own mouth, shocked to find it shut. The Crone mimed something, her left hand coming up to her neck and then flicking backward, nails brushing her hood.

Did she just pretend to flip her hair? "No point worrying which is which until the time comes."

"Did Sahir relay this to you?" I asked aloud.

Another eye roll from the Crone.

"I am a Prince of Faerie, lady," the Princeling said, his voice soft. "My methods are my own, and my knowledge mine until I share it. Ask no more impertinent questions."

So he'd just confirmed they were watching me, and I should assume they heard everything I said.

I wanted to hunch my shoulders and give up, but the thought of my mom stalking into Faerie to demand retribution spurred me on. "I have considered your...offer, my lord," I said, choosing my words carefully.

"Indeed," he said. He sounded casual, but he flicked his wrist and a bramble of green sparks burst into being around our table, shielding us from the others in the room. No one screamed at the sight of magical bushes exploding into existence, so it must have been fairly normal for the Court.

"I will teach your people of my people, in exchange for your assistance in freeing me from this realm." My eyes burned. I stared at the green magic behind him, willing the tears not to fall.

"You know that you cannot leave," he said, his words as slow as mine. I inhaled. Exhaled. "Or, rather," he corrected, "you cannot leave and live."

Finally, I found the courage to meet his gaze. "My lord, within the bounds of faerie magic there must exist some spell to aid me. I ask only your resources in looking for an answer."

We looked at each other. "Oh, and a vow not to stop me if

I do find a way home," I added. "I seek no promise from you regarding the outcome."

We sat. No one spoke. The Gray Knight forced her way through the magic green brambles, carrying a tray of food, which she dropped on the table. She had a few green leaves dissipating in her hair, and a tiny green bur on one shoulder. She looked irritated.

"Eat," she said, rejoining the Princeling and the Crone across from me.

For a moment I wasn't sure if she spoke to me or to the Princeling, but he pushed the tray toward me.

"Is this new life in Faerie a gift or a curse, lady?" the Princeling asked.

I frowned. The obvious answer—*A curse, you insufferable man*—was also obviously wrong. "It depends on your perspective," I said. "And perhaps it depends if you agree to my bargain." I sounded cool, calm, collected. Suave, even.

Internally, I was shitting myself. But I was more afraid of telling my mom that I was never coming home than I was of the Princeling.

"Eat," the Gray Knight interrupted, pointing at the tray.

I picked up half of the sandwich and stared at it. Some sort of spread that looked creamy and purple had been slathered thick through the middle, and sprouts with crisp white roots stuck out from the sides. I tried to take a bite but couldn't; my throat had started to close, the way it always did before I cried.

The Princeling sighed. "It is an intriguing proposition," he said. "And I do not lose much. Nor do I gain much. Your presence here will provide my people with some knowledge of humans, with or without your active instruction. Perhaps that will be sufficient."

"My lord, I will serve Faerie better in the human realm," I said, dropping the sandwich and pushing the tray aside. I'd lost the battle with my tears; I could feel them leaking down the side of my nose. I leaned across the table toward him. "I can advocate for you better in New York. I can help you integrate into human society. If we get enough investors for your company, people won't care what species you are."

His eyes flashed. "You presume much, lady, about what will help my people."

I shrank back, mortified and horrified. "I didn't mean—" I started, but he cut me off.

"It is interesting. I do wonder…" He glanced at the Crone, who nodded minutely.

"Then here is our bargain," he said, splaying his hands out on the table. "You will teach my people of humans, whenever they ask and whatever they ask, for thirty years. For that period, you will also retain your job—this should be manageable for you. And if you can complete both of these tasks to my satisfaction, then all of my resources will be laid at your feet."

Thirty years????? I didn't want to be starting an escape post-menopause. And what resources was he talking about anyway?

"*One* year," I said. "Not thirty."

"One year, thirty years," he sighed, waving a hand in exasperation. "I forget myself. Your lives are short."

He glanced at the Crone again. Though her face appeared not to change, he turned back to me with a frown. "Ten years," he said, "or do not take the bargain."

He held a hand out to me across the table; it was completely smooth. No tendons, no veins. Just a covering of unblemished skin like the stem of some creeping ivy.

Before I could think, I took it and jerked back at the shock I felt in my palm.

"The bargain is sealed," he said, a tiny smile creeping onto his face.

I glanced down at my palm—a long white scar appeared, like a single blade of grass. As I watched, it faded back into my skin, dissolved into my blood. Then it was gone.

The Princeling did something with his fingers, and the green brambles dropped.

I expected him to leave in a dramatic and exceptional manner, the Crone and the Gray Knight flanking him. But instead, he leaned back, settling onto his stool.

"Thank you. I don't want to be here forever," I said, feeling vaguely embarrassed, like I was turning down a second date. "It's not personal."

The Princeling nodded. "Change is no easier for us who live beneath the hill."

"Are we *beneath* a hill?"

The Princeling's shoulders loosened. "We are . . . sideways. Above. Inverted. And beneath, yes."

How did faerie truths apply to such nonsense? I looked at the Crone, as though she would provide some insight.

"Look," I started, and stopped. "Sorry, I mean, my lord, please, look."

"Why do you speak this way?" the Gray Knight interrupted.

"What?"

She'd leaned forward, forearm on the table, her body tense. Her hair fell forward around her cheeks in sleek curtains. "You speak and stop and speak. You apologize when there is no wrong."

"Well…I'm a woman in the workplace." I frowned at her.

"This is…poor reasoning."

"I—" It was poor reasoning, yes. "I cannot defend the logic, fair one."

"You evade as surely as one of my own subjects," the Princeling said. "And I have ignored my subjects for long enough." He made to push back from the table.

I felt like the deflated remnants of a Halloween pumpkin watching Thanksgiving guests walk into a house. And he'd given me no *practical* information—how would this teaching thing even work? Would I get a classroom? Were we putting flyers up?

Was I getting paid?

"Please, my lord, I have questions about how this all works— like, do I pay rent for my room? What about the food?"

All three of them stared at me.

"You wish to barter for what is given freely?" the Princeling asked.

The Crone chuckled.

"Uh, no?" I said, blinking away a fresh flush of tears.

"Good. Barter wisely, Lady of the True Dreams." This time, he pushed away from the table and stood up.

"Why do you call me that?"

The Crone chuckled again. The sound felt like a nerve pinching in my neck. The Princeling held out an arm for her and lifted her to her feet.

He inclined his head toward me and led the other two away.

—————————— • ——————————

In my room, I curled up on the floor to cry again. I imagined my Tinder profile in a few years: *Thirty, flirty, and trapped in a pocket dimension.* Doctor Kitten sat on the bed, looking down at me with his implacable green eyes. Doctor Kitten was used to my bouts of crying and seemed relieved not to be conscripted as a tissue.

I stayed that way for a long time, but I was a bit more alert than the night before and eventually the floor felt too hard beneath the padding from the blankets. Taking some calming breaths, I tried to reanalyze my situation with cold logic.

I was here in Faerie for ten years.

I had made a bargain with a Prince of Faerie.

If I completed my "mission" to teach faeries about humans, I'd get some kind of reward in the form of magical resources.

And, most importantly, this meant that I'd be in the same role for the next decade. Working with a likely rotating cast of young investment dudes. Under *Jeff.*

Not a great situation. But I'd panic later.

Standing up and shaking my limbs to get some blood flowing, I logged back into my computer. There were forty-three new emails waiting for me in my inbox.

The first read: *Send the most recent version of the presentation.*

My heart stuttered in my chest. 1:33, three minutes after I had closed the computer. I looked at my phone screen. 2:18. I'd been gone forty-five minutes. I went to the top of the chain and read the most recent message.

Miri, this is not a complicated request. It doesn't look good when you take too long to do simple things.

I tabbed over to the shared file drive and dragged the file into a response box. Then, for good measure, I attached the email I'd sent to him with the deck—had it only been two nights before?

Attached, and for reference it is in the cloud as well! I typed. Maybe the exclamation mark would make it friendlier.

I sent before I could think too hard about it.

I needed my to-do list.

Out of habit, I glanced under my desk for my backpack and almost wasn't surprised to find it lying there. Either I had put it there and didn't remember, or…magic.

I hooked my foot into a strap and pulled it toward me. I found my hot pink daily planner and a pen in the bottom of my bag, both coated with unidentifiable crumbs.

Flipping the planner open to the bookmark, I stuck the pen in my mouth. Yesterday's to-do list stared up at me.

Must do:

1. *Make a list*
2. *Model updates*
3. *Meeting notes summary*
4. *Map competitive landscape*
5. *Gym*

I had not gone to the gym.

Should do:

1. *Set up mentor meeting with Levi*

2. *Read daily newsletters*
3. *Last 12 months pitches—update*
4. *Change cat litter*

Balls. What should I do about my gym membership?

My computer pinged. Jeff had sent me a new email. Subject line: *I KNOW ABOUT THE CLOUD, MIRI. SEND DOCUMENTS WHEN I ASK FOR THEM. THANKS. JEFF.*

The body of the email was empty.

I fought back the wince that usually accompanied Jeff's emails. I hadn't done anything wrong.

I should cancel my gym membership.

I flipped my notebook to the next page and started a new list.

1. *Make a list*
2. *Model review with Levi*

I stopped writing midsentence, pinching the pen so hard it hurt my middle finger. What was the point? What did any of my reviews matter now that I had to stay in the same damn position for the next ten years?

Sighing, I pondered what I *actually* needed to do—I needed to tell my friends what had happened. But I'd do that later, when I had a good amount of free time to vent.

I needed to do boring logistical adult things, like figure out if they had mail forwarding to Faerie and what to do about my apartment. But that was like giving up too soon. So all that left was: I needed to call my mom and tell her what had happened with the Princeling.

Before I could think further about it, I dialed her number.

"Honey?" she said, picking up on the second ring. "Miriam? I was getting worried."

"Hey, Mom," I croaked. "Sorry." Unable to take it any longer, I stood up and started pacing around the room.

"I'm on a walk with Grandma," she said. "We've almost made it around the block." I walked past the foot of the bed.

"Oh, Grandma," I said. "Tell her I love her." I passed the door. I tried to imagine never getting another hug from my grandma, who was soft and warm and said *I love you I love you I love you* in a hoarse litany whenever I called. Something caught in my throat.

"Miriam loves you," my mom said. I could hear Grandma saying "Oh, Miriam?" through the line. I rounded the waterfall shower and passed the open-air toilet.

"Mom, let's chat tonight, okay?" I said.

"No, tell me what happened," she said, her voice closer to the phone now. She must have taken me off speaker. Now the desk, on my right. And the bed again.

"We made a deal." I started biting my thumbnail. "If I teach faeries about humans for ten years and manage to keep my job, he'll give me resources to find a way out." I sat down on the bed next to Doctor Kitten. Whatever style the bedspread had been in the morning, it was now cat fur chic.

"Did you get a copy of the contract?" my mom asked. "You need to define 'resources.' In fact, you need to make sure every term is defined. Otherwise, he has wiggle room."

Doctor Kitten nibbled at my ring. I took it off and put it on the bed for him to bat at.

"I was planning to do that," I said irritably to my mother. I had not been planning to do that, but it was a fantastic idea.

"Ten years is too long. Didn't you negotiate?"

"Yeah, down from thirty," I said, fuming.

"Send me the contract and I'll take a look." In the background, I could hear my grandma saying something about dinner. "No, Mom, we won't have oatmeal for dinner," my mom added. "I'll make us tomato soup."

"Is Grandma sick again?" I asked, sitting down on the bed.

"No," my mom lied.

"Okay." I patted Doctor Kitten on the head. "I'm going to hang up and get that contract."

"Okay! I love you," she said.

"I love you, too," I said. I hung up before she could say anything else.

I glanced at the clock. 3:14 p.m.

Stood up and returned to my desk.

Glanced at my inbox. Forty-five unread emails.

Started an email to Levi requesting a video call for the model review.

But I couldn't do it.

I opened a blank Word document and typed out what the Princeling had said.

You will teach my people of humans, whenever they ask and whatever they ask, for ten years. For that period, you will also retain your job—this should be manageable for you. And if you can complete both of these tasks to my satisfaction, then all of my resources will be laid at your feet.

I started a new Excel spreadsheet and added all of the words we needed to define.

- *Teach—Miri will provide accurate information to the best of her knowledge and within reasonable expectations; Miri will provide a set number of classes for a set number of hours, to be defined by both parties*
- *Retain—Miri will not resign from her job; if she is fired or laid off, that is still considered fulfillment of this term*
- *Ten years—ten human years based on the Gregorian calendar starting at 9:00 a.m. Eastern Standard Time on August 25, 2022*
- *Princeling's satisfaction—Miri has met all reasonable demands set forth in both the "Teach" and "Retain" definitions*
- *Princeling's resources—All information, written and oral, and all people, which may provide additional context about human imprisonment in Faerie, and any other documentation or information which may assist Miri in leaving Faerie without dying*
- *Laid at your feet—Accessible to Miri in a way that she can be reasonably expected to use based on her human limitations (e.g., no tomes written in dead languages or extended quests involving the obtention of documents from a dragon's hoard, etc. etc.)*

I sent this document to the Gray Knight, with a quick note requesting any edits within the next few hours.

Then I resumed my email to Levi. And tried my best not to look out the window, at the too-green grass and sunless blue sky.

———————————•———————————

The Gray Knight sent me a note that said *Received and revising.* She didn't send any further information.

Around seven p.m., I gave up on work and opened YouTube on my cell phone. I found a humor video from my favorite satirist and clicked on it.

The requisite pre-video advertisement popped up, a retro Elf off the Shelf replay. I couldn't help it—I let out a laugh. Of all the videos to be showing me right now, I couldn't believe the algorithm chose *this* one. Instead of skipping it, I watched as the too-bright swirling shapes danced behind the industrious elves in the foreground.

In 2017, an advertisement for a kitschy brand called Elf off the Shelf went viral on YouTube. The premise was simple. Some guy with CGI and a great props budget had photoshopped Santa's helpers into a thirty-three-second clip advertising higher-quality and less-expensive household goods.

People loved Elf off the Shelf. Until the founder, Oboe Micknickelstein, showed up on the *Today* show standing three foot six and claiming his pointy ears were real.

And that was how Humanity, capital *H*, discovered that the supernatural really existed.

Everyone was enraged. Some people claimed it was insensitive, racist, or absurd. Others felt this was a hoax propagated by their political enemies to "normalize weirdos." And a third group was immediately convinced that elves existed, they'd been right all along, and industrialization was a horrifying blight corrupting a once-pure species. Then a reactionary group called the third group infantilizing, and the discourse degenerated from there.

Doctor Kitten, hearing the familiar opening notes of the web video, came to my side and pawed at my leg. I hefted him under the ribs and slid him into my lap, much like a slab of pudding. He twisted in my lap to sit facing the phone screen. I scratched under his chin.

As it always did, his weight on my legs calmed me slightly. I hadn't realized how hard my heart was pounding.

"We will get out of this," I told him. "We'll get home."

I stared down at the inky black area on his head, where it went pink at the delicate skin of his left ear. I supposed it didn't matter to him if we got home or not.

We'd barely started the video when the first knock came. The pounding on my door was almost unsurprising. Doctor Kitten looked up at me, as if to say *This is a you problem.* Then he hopped off my lap, landed with an unbecoming thump on the floor, and launched himself into my bed.

"Coming," I said, sparing one glance back at the Doctor, who had curled into a cat's equivalent of a Fibonacci circle and tucked his eyes under his own back paws. Sahir opened the door before I could cross the room.

His suit was torn, and in addition to the cat scratches from earlier he now had a black eye.

"Holy cow," I said as I stepped into the hall, closing the door behind me. "Did you fall down the stairs?"

"Your colleagues accosted me on a smoke break, actually," he said, showing me his wrist, which had a circular burn mark on it.

My intestinal system did a weird thing. It felt like my kidneys tried to jump through my esophagus at the exact second my stomach made a determined dive at my left foot.

I stumbled, having been successfully unbalanced by my stomach, and Sahir grabbed my arm.

"My *who* did *what*?"

"The short smart one and the tall stupid one were outside when I left the office and demanded your return."

"My return?" I asked, shock making my face blank. And then, "Did they get fired?" A few faeries passing by turned to look at me with unabashed curiosity. "Sorry," I said out of habit. "I didn't mean to be so loud."

"Fired for fisticuffs?" Sahir snorted derisively. "Has the madness afflicted you? The attack was honest and returned in equal measure. Then I left them, for I had business to attend to here."

Sahir started walking down the hall and motioned for me to go with him; still in shock, I let my feet follow his. He kept his gaze forward, clearly ignoring my horror.

Around us the other faeries had formed a sort of herd. I felt like the middle penguin in a waddling flock, but a generally unhappy middle penguin full of ennui.

Sahir maneuvered us to the edge of the group, his right arm outstretched. People seemed to recognize him, or maybe nobody wanted to touch me—they parted when we got too close. He opened the cafeteria door and gestured several others through. He and I followed last.

The cafeteria was much fuller than it had been at breakfast or lunch, almost every seat taken. I stopped, startled by the cacophony of howls and hoots and clicks, and the forest of curling horns and inhuman heads and even a few tucked wingtips.

Sahir took my hand, pulling me along in a gesture so

seamless that it felt almost natural. His hand was warm on mine, the calluses on his fingertips brushing my knuckles. My eyes slid shut at the raw-silk feel of his thumb rubbing a circle into the back of my hand. I blinked until the jelly of my knees solidified, and followed him toward the serving area.

"You should know, Miriam," he said slowly, as though he wasn't sure he wanted to share whatever came next. "I swore your health on my life. It was all that would appease them."

I could barely hear him over the din. "What does that mean?"

It had gotten louder, a lot of scraping chairs on the floor. We were in the center of the room now, surrounded by tables on all sides.

"I bound myself to you in fealty," he said, louder, just as a hush fell across the room. Everyone had stood, and they were all staring at us. "I am your knight."

"Well, then," someone drawled behind us. "If you are already hers, I gather you will not become a knight of mine, Sahir."

The Princeling had arrived.

Chapter 6
In Which We Experience Community Theater

Sahir flushed.

"Has the madness afflicted you, Sahir?" the Princeling asked, in a way that destroyed any lingering hope I had that he wasn't listening in on my every conversation. Did he have nothing better to do, really?

I glanced around the room again. Everyone was staring at us. Oh good, another dinner show put on by the Faerie Players, featuring One Scared Human Girl.

"My lord," Sahir replied, bowing his head. "I do not believe myself mad."

"They never do," the Princeling mused. He had that same little half smile on his thin lips.

He had his usual cohort with him, the knights Gray and

Red and Blue, and the Crone in her blue cloak. They all stood by the cafeteria door, in the wide center aisle that ran the middle of the room.

The Crone leaned on the Blue Knight's arm and he supported her. Her cloak fell in folds that seemed to suck the color from Blue and Red both.

The Crone pushed her hood back, her black eyes burning in her head. "I saw it all," she said in a voice likely meant to be menacing. She sounded more like a gleeful teenage girl about to recap the plot of *Blood, Guts, and Pizza Huts: How We Found Friendship at Our High School Reunion and Then Died.*

Without looking at her, the Princeling jerked his head in acknowledgment. "Show us then, Crone, what has made this wretch forsake his future in my Court for a mortal woman."

The words made me uncomfortable, and I tried to pull my hand from Sahir's. But he held on.

The Crone raised both her hands—the knights Red and Blue each held an elbow—and spread her gnarled fingers wide. Between each finger a web of blue spread, joint to joint and then hand to hand, the color of night in my parents' backyard when I was a child and went out to stand under the stars, feet cold in the wet grass.

I wanted to fall into the color, but it fell toward us instead and lightened, until the room had transformed into the dull lonely gray of the courtyard between our office building and the next one over, the sort of gray that has heard of sunlight but isn't convinced of its relevance.

I shifted my weight. I knew this was vitally important, but it had started to feel like the time I went to Shakespeare in the

Globe Theatre and it was standing room only. My knees hurt. No one else in the room seemed like they wanted to sit.

The Princeling and the Gray Knight moved off to the side, leaving the other three in a place of prominence. There, leaning against the illusory wall by the building entrance, stood the Red and Blue Knights, the Crone between them. They each held a cigarette and wore the illusion of a black suit.

The Red Knight opened his mouth, and Matt's voice came from the Crone's lips. "Where is that stupid prick?"

"Calm down," said the Crone, as Corey. The Blue Knight moved his mouth in time.

"Calm down? This is so fucked up," Red Matt sputtered.

Between them they still held the Crone upright, and as they moved their mouths she spoke.

"It's probably a misunderstanding," Blue Corey said, flicking his live cigarette butt onto the pavement for dramatic effect. I glared. I always told him not to litter.

"Everyone sit down," the Princeling cut in, lazy and commanding. The Red Knight and Blue Knight paused midmotion as weight shifted around the room, faeries resting in their chairs.

Sahir stirred and slid his hand from mine, which left me standing in the middle of the room like an idiot.

He walked through the illusion—it parted like mist beneath his outstretched hand. When he'd passed through the revolving door, he turned and pushed it. It spun this time, like a solid object under his hand, and he walked "outside."

Red Matt called out to him. "Hey, fairy-boy!"

Obviously there are no subtitles in life but I felt fairly

confident that Matt had intended it as a callback to insults used for homosexuals, and would have spelled it with a *Y*.

Blue Corey elbowed Red Matt. "Sahir, we wanted to talk to you." He pulled another cigarette from the pack in his pocket and dangled it between his lips.

Around them the indistinct impression of people rushing by; between them the Crone with her web of magic. The illusions crackled at the edges by her fingertips, a glimpse of the Red Knight's shoulder plate visible where the faux suit splintered into her pinky finger.

Blue Corey lit the cigarette.

I glanced around the room. Like me, the faeries were transfixed. And we all hung suspended in the illusion, the gray of the courtyard extending on into infinity; a cracked, uninhabited pavement on which the wooden tables seemed to hover.

"Of what did you wish to speak?" Sahir was permitted his own voice, it seemed, though the Crone voiced Matt and Corey.

The Crone sagged slightly to the left; the Blue Knight hefted her straight again.

"Where's Miri?" Blue Corey asked. "We heard there might have been a misunderstanding, and she thinks she needs to stay in Faerie."

"The lady's intellectual capacity far surpasses yours," Sahir said, a surprising note of anger in his voice. "And she has understood well what must be."

Red Matt let go of the Crone to crack his knuckles. "Miri needs to come back."

"Clearly not." Sahir had recovered his composure and

clasped his hands behind his back. Red Matt took the Crone's arm again.

"*Clearly*, she does," Red Matt argued. "You twat." It was certainly something to watch the wizened Crone say the words *you twat* as the Red Knight mouthed along.

Matt had spent a semester in England, and it showed.

"The lady will remain in Faerie, as is our right. She partook of our fare and slept in our bowers."

"What are you insinuating about where Miri slept?" Blue Corey snapped, the faerie's face contorting into a passable imitation of a human's menacing glare. I felt my own face redden. What sweet, sweet morons. Blue Corey still had the lit cigarette between his lips. I kept looking at it, waiting for him to hold it against Sahir's wrist.

"I insinuate nothing," Sahir said, taking another step closer.

And to my utter shock, Blue Corey let go of the Crone and swung a fierce right hook at Sahir's face. The illusion fractured for a moment, hanging in the air like the shards of ice in a storm. I *felt* the stillness in the room as everyone stopped breathing.

Corey, really?

Blue Corey stepped back again and took the Crone's arm. The illusion knit back together, the grays and blacks and fabric and concrete. I wondered how it must look to the faeries, so unlike their brown and green and blue.

Sahir moved too fast for me to see, slamming his fist into Blue Corey's jaw. The crack sounded real, and Blue Corey recoiled, mouth gaping. The cigarette dropped to the ground.

In the crowd a few faeries cheered.

"Cease," Sahir said, sliding his hand back to touch the wall next to Blue Corey. "What is done cannot be undone." The motion was intimate, dangerous. He leaned in close to Blue Corey's face, their noses nearly touching.

Red Matt stooped next to them, one hand on the floor. Somehow the Red Knight managed not to lose his grip on the Crone.

Blue Corey didn't flinch from Sahir's nearness. "What will you do to her?"

"I will do nothing," Sahir breathed, though by some magic his voice carried through the room. "She is not my responsibility."

"Then make her your responsibility," Blue Corey said, his hand coming up to grasp Sahir's sleeve.

Sahir tried to pull away, but Blue Corey held him.

"Why would I do that?"

"I could go to the press," Red Matt said, "or HR."

"Human Resources," Sahir repeated, incredulously.

"You don't want to get fired, do you?" And then Red Matt opened his hand, the still-red stub of Blue Corey's cigarette pinched between his thumb and forefinger, and brought the hot end down on Sahir's wrist.

"And what is stopping you from going anyway?" Though he didn't wince, Sahir finally pulled away from Blue Corey, who hadn't let go of the suit, and the Crone imitated a ripping sound. Sahir held his arm out straight—showing the audience the tear in his suit?

"We could give you our word," Blue Corey said.

"The word of a mortal means nothing. You treat with me and burn my flesh in one breath."

Blue Corey stared at Sahir. "Please."

Sahir sighed. "I give you my word that I will do my best to keep her alive."

"Healthy," Blue Corey corrected. "Keep her healthy, not just alive. And swear on your life."

"Why would I do that?" Sahir snapped.

"Please," Blue Corey said again. He sounded genuinely devastated. I stared at the foreign face of the faerie, trying to imagine my colleague, who had never been anything but simply fine to me before, assuming that expression.

Sahir straightened, his jaw tight. I watched the muscle work there, the bob in his neck when he swallowed.

"Fine, if it means you will cease to accost me." He put his shoulders back, haughty, and brought both hands together in a long twisting gesture, an impossible sweep like a tangle of vines off a trellis. "I shall keep Miriam healthy, to the best of my ability, and protect her from foreseeable harm, until she dies of natural causes. I shall be her sword in conflict and her pen in peace, and I swear this on my own existence; may it not continue if I fail her."

There was a low hum of noise around the room, a startled incessant mumble.

Even I could tell this was more than he'd needed to do.

The image cracked again, and fractured into flakes and webs and shards, and clattered onto the floor. After the false cold light of the New York afternoon faded, the muted glow of the darting creatures by the ceiling and the flicker of torches on the walls felt gloomy and dull. The Crone sagged between the Red Knight and the Blue Knight, her head lolling.

Before the voices around us crescendoed, the Princeling spoke. "Odd," he mused. "The humans showed bravery and loyalty." He looked out among the crowd. "Did any of you know them to do thusly?"

Laying it on thick, buddy, I thought.

More silence.

I glanced from the Princeling to Sahir, expecting some sort of punishment.

But the Princeling seemed to have forgotten his anger— or he'd never really been angry. "It is done, then," he said, nodding once at Sahir. He looked around the room. "I have ridden out today, and visited my people on the river reaches. My Red Knight has letters and news, from those who wished to share messages."

The Princeling swept forward, the others behind him like a flock. Still in disbelief at seeing my coworkers actually worried about me, I tried to reset my brain with something else. My eyes landed on the Princeling's legs; his leggings hugged his calves. *I bet that guy can ride a horse,* I thought, because I grew up with internet access and Regency romance fan fiction. I followed his legs up to his muscular thighs and the edge of his tunic. Maybe faeries chose their rulers based on who could throw a log the farthest. He definitely had the thighs for it. And oh my god, my brain needed a muzzle. I looked away as he passed me.

The Gray Knight, who had caught me looking, smirked.

As the Princeling passed each table, faces turned to follow him. The Red Knight left the group and stationed himself by the door, a stack of papers in his hand. A few of the faeries at the near tables stood up and made their way toward him.

The Princeling's retinue approached the buffet counter, and Sahir came up beside me.

"What—" I started, but he took my wrist and squeezed in a way not conducive to my health.

I yipped. He stared at my face with such intensity I almost thought I could read his mind. *Later,* his eyes said. Or *I want soup.* I couldn't entirely tell.

Though I was tempted to ask anyway—it couldn't get *more* dangerous for me, right?—I held off. Instead, I jerked my head toward the food. His fingers loosened on my wrist, a bracelet instead of a manacle. We walked together to the buffet.

This time, the first faerie gave me a plate of stew over a ruffled brown grain that might have been rice, if I squinted. The second pushed a bisected bowl toward me: half roasted vegetables, half salad. And the third, grinning with those blue eyes like lamps in his golden face, plopped a slice of cake as big as my forearm onto my tray. I stared at him. He stared at me.

"Lady," he said, in what sounded like a southern brogue.

"Thanks," I said.

"Do not thank people," Sahir snapped, and led me to a table full of strangers.

When we approached, the table went silent. Sahir and I slid onto the last two empty stools. He slammed his tray down so hard his stew slopped into his salad. This was remarkably restrained, given the day he'd had.

I looked away from him, at our other tablemates: a cluster of sharp-faced people with naked curiosity in their eyes. Most of them had a humanoid skeletal structure, but there was at least one faerie with six limbs, another who looked like a giant sea squid, and one who was most definitely on fire but calmly eating the salad.

"Hello," I said, because everyone was staring at me.

This sent a wave of titters and squeaks around the table.

I glanced at Sahir, who had gripped a fork with fervor and was trying to eat his stew with it.

Instead of picking up a spoon, he flicked his pointer finger down the stem of the fork, and the wooden tines wove together into a teaspoon-sized basket.

"You have to teach me how to do that," I said, awed.

"Humans cannot do magic," one of the faeries at the table said. "Except for witches, but they have been gone a long time." I looked up. She was smaller than most of the others and had reflective feline eyes with slit pupils. Her face was furry. "Did you really ask for your cat?"

"I'm Miri," I said, refusing to eschew good manners in the face of adversity. "It's nice to meet you."

"Why," groaned Sahir next to me, in the tones of a man having an unmedicated appendectomy, "why must humans *lie* in greeting?"

"It's not a lie," I said, looking at the cat lady. "It's a pleasantry. It's a way of expressing gratitude for your time and conversation." I almost asked for her name but remembered the Gray Knight's explanation. "How should I address you?"

"You may call me Lene," she said. "But tell me truly, for you have been here but one rotation of the Earth upon its axis. Did you ask for your cat?"

"Yes. I was worried no one would feed him," I said, looking down at my tray. I stuck my fork in the cake, ignoring the healthy-looking options. How many times is a girl kidnapped into Faerie, anyway? I deserved cake.

"I had heard humans could not eat cake," said the man next to Lene. "Or they would grow horns."

I paused, fork in the air. The man next to Lene was on fire. I took my cue from the other people at the table and didn't worry about it.

"You will not grow horns," Sahir said to me, "as that is anatomically impossible." My fork resumed its course toward my face.

Lene stretched a hand out and touched my forearm, stilling me. "It is unusual to grow horns," she said.

Since faeries couldn't lie, either they'd been on the receiving end of a baffling disinformation campaign or I was about to be the coolest human I knew.

"Gaheris," Sahir said to the cake-horn-man who was on fire, "even you, who remember no sciences, should know it is anatomically impossible for a human to grow horns from eating cake."

"I do magic," Gaheris said, and wiggled a bone-white hand in my direction. Even with only that gesture I could tell he had an inhuman number of bones. "I could enchant the cake."

I couldn't help it. I smiled at Gaheris, who looked as pleased as a man who looks like two bushfires had a baby with a beech tree could possibly look. The flames licking up the sides of his head shot out as he smiled back at me, and Lene yelped, her claws digging into my forearm.

"I did not enchant the cake," Gaheris assured me.

"Thanks." I pulled my arm out from under Lene's hand, in no small amount of pain.

I stuck a forkful of cake in my mouth. It tasted fresh, and more like a sweet bread than a dessert. No one said anything. I took another bite.

Silence. Every eye remained focused on me. My cake consumption continued apace.

"So, what do you do? All of you," I added around a mouthful of cake, because the entire table was motionless.

"This is another human question," Sahir said, like my own personal and worse David Attenborough. "A greeting like the first, which assumes employment in some meaningless repetitive task or debauchery with wine and dancing to be the only options."

Too tired to argue, I ate a bite of stew. Despite a startling variety of shapes and colors, everything had the texture of a boiled potato.

"We are Fae," Lene said. "Sometimes I sit in the trees and watch below me for those that come and go."

"I sing to the rivers," said Gaheris, which didn't seem to mesh with his appearance. *Don't judge a book by its cover*, I reminded myself. When he saw my raised eyebrow, he added, "So they do not forget their path." As if that were the explanation I required.

"I scream in the courtyard at irregular intervals," offered a third—the one with two extra arms protruding from his midsection.

I blinked. "Why—what purpose does that serve?"

"Purpose?" The faerie had a very human face, a snub nose and brown eyes and brown hair, and behind his back long green wings folded down like a cicada's. "I like to do it."

We blinked at each other in mutual bafflement.

"Eat," Sahir muttered to me. I shoveled another huge bite of stew into my mouth. Though texturally deficient, it was warm and thick and very comforting.

"We will leave you, Lady of the Cats," Lene said. She rose, as did several of the others. "But if I may, I would like to visit you."

"Please do," I said, "but please don't call me Lady of the Cats. It's not, uh, it's not got great context."

"Apologies," Lene said. "I hope I did not give you the name of some great sorceress, dead for her misdeeds but much feared in life. Please tell me if I did this."

Since this seemed oddly specific, and also to give her great joy, I didn't say anything else.

Our table was depleted but not empty. None of the remaining faeries seemed interested in engaging with us.

"Sahir, I have a lot more work," I said, sticking my fork into the stew. "Can we bring the rest back to the room?"

"We do not eat outside this hall," Sahir said. "Roaches," he clarified when I stared at him. "They're better than most at getting beneath the hill."

With that reassuring thought, I plowed through several bites of stew, shoved the tray away, and stood up. "I'm going back," I said. "I'll see you tomorrow, I guess."

Sahir grunted and didn't look up. An auspicious start to our relationship as a knight and his lady.

———————————— • ————————————

Four hours later, I knelt on the cold stone of the bathroom, one hand on my work computer keyboard and the other clutching the rim of the toilet. The noise of the constantly running waterfall shower—which I'd come to find soothing—was an unyielding soundtrack to my pain.

I retched again and then tapped the spacebar so the computer didn't lock, turning my head to look at the PDF open on the screen.

Food poisoning on day one didn't bode well. Nor did the little voice in my head whispering *poison, yes*. I wondered if the Princeling would consider food poisoning harm, and if this meant he had broken his promise.

Doctor Kitten had perched on the toilet tank to supervise proceedings.

I gagged against the imagined feeling of hands clawing up my diaphragm but made myself read another sentence.

Vampire founders are performing well in the lifestyle sector, I read, and vomited so violently it came out my nose. *Blood-based health and wellness treatments are wildly popular, and the new ruling that the FDA won't need to approve them will only accelerate this trend.*

The bile burned my nostrils as it dripped into the toilet. It smelled like cake. I took a shallow breath through my mouth. The shower continued to tinkle musically.

We are following 8 of the most promising vampire-founded startups and have reviewed them below.

I heaved again.

Jeff wanted a report by midnight. I had no idea how I would type. I couldn't stand. But his email had been clear.

Miri, read the latest equity reports and come up with 2-3 targets for origination by end of day. Jeff.

Why he'd asked me and not Corey, who had absolutely nothing to do, I couldn't say.

I slid onto my stomach on the floor and opened the email reply box.

Jeff, it looks like there are three targets that haven't worked with a big bank yet, I started, and had to lever myself up to vomit again. What had *happened*?

Unbidden, the cafeteria workers' faces came to mind. Had one of them poisoned me? The angry one, or the friendly one, or the indifferent one in the middle?

I sagged back to the ground and tapped out a few sentences.

1. *Bloods and Bruises—EV 400m, EBITDA 22E 508m, multiple range 7-9x*
2. *Bitter Bites—EV 580m, EBITDA 22E 50m, multiple range 11-13x*
3. *Visshhush—EV 200m, EBITDA 22E 20m, multiple range 9-11x*

I hit send and threw my head back into the toilet with such force that I banged my forehead against the rim.

My computer dinged. I looked up.

Miri, let's circle back in the morning to review priorities. Visshush is too small for us.

I felt rage and misery swirling in my chest and burst into impotent sobs.

The part of me that was still a child thought someone might come for me. But I cried and cried, neck bowed, arm flung along the toilet seat, and nobody came.

So, sick and sobbing, I went back to the computer and tried again.

Jeff, sorry about that. Visshush is removed.

Again the immediate reply, like he was sitting with his phone refreshing his email.

Miri, why didn't you add any new companies? I can think of at least three I would like to see.

I stared at the screen, incredulous.

Jeff, please let me know what companies you have in mind. Happy to add them! I typed, wet snot mixing with vomit stains on my upper lip as my chest heaved.

This time the response wasn't immediate. I hefted myself upright, using the toilet bowl for support. I felt a rush of affection for the toilet, worthy of a refrigerator magnet poem (ah, my intimate acquaintance, your tender caress; ah, my companion in misery). But I needed to clean up quickly, before Jeff replied. I put the toilet lid down.

Doctor Kitten, who had watched this entire thing, scrunched his nose at me and started toward the bed.

I went to the running shower and stood before it, staring. There was a low rim around the outside of the stall, but no walls on the sides to prevent water from ricocheting off my body. There were also no dials to adjust the temperature, as far as I could see. The water fell from a lip that jutted out of the rock wall above my head in a melodic stream. I put my hand into the stream. A bit cool, but nothing unmanageable. I shucked off my clothes—had I been wearing my work pants for thirty-six hours?

As soon as I put my face under the running water I felt

better. I pushed my hands through my hair, letting the water soak my scalp. I reached for the bar of soap on the low ledge and scrubbed my arms with it.

The computer dinged. I rinsed off and stepped out, realizing only then that I hadn't seen a towel. I frowned, stepping out to see if there was one in a closet somewhere—or even a closet somewhere—when I was hit with a concentrated stream of warm air. I jerked to a surprised halt. Within seconds I had been thoroughly dried.

Well then.

I went back to my computer, picked it up, and took it to the bed. My suitcase still lay there. I pulled on clean underwear and a giant sleeping dress, breathing in the familiar scent of my own detergent.

How much longer would it be familiar?

I unlocked the computer and looked at Jeff's email.

Bloodburger, Vamp-moose, and Red Rims.

Scrunching my eyes, I opened a new browser window and started to type.

Chapter 7
In Which New Friends Renovate My Room

A woman in a golden diadem sat before a blazing fire. The rising smoke shifted into rotating planets around a flickering sun.

She looked up and met my gaze. Before I could speak, she'd moved—uncanny, graceful—and stood before me. I felt her gaze on me. Weighed and divided. Found wanting.

Her right arm came up, the rotation of her wrist sketching the curve of a ship's bow. She extended her hand, palm down, and pressed a single finger to my forehead. I felt my skin start to burn, radiating outward from where she touched me—

I woke up screaming.

No one came to take me to the cafeteria for breakfast, which was fine since I still felt aches in my stomach from the heaving of the night before. So I skipped breakfast. I skipped clothes, too, and logged into our morning meeting, camera off, wearing my baggy nightdress.

Was it only Thursday?

Good lord.

Jeff didn't call in to our morning meeting, so it was truncated and unexciting.

After the meeting, I messaged Corey.

Miriam Geld: Hi.

Corey Tucker: Hi

Corey Tucker: what's up?

Corey Tucker: busy day for me

Miriam Geld: just wanted to say thanks . . .

Corey Tucker: nothing to thank me for. Same team, remember?

I sat back and stared at the chat. *That* was all he planned to say about punching a faerie in the face and then bullying him into offering me lifelong protection?

Miriam Geld: Sure. Same team.

My head was pounding. I needed to talk to someone, so even though the workday had already started, I called Thea.

"Miri?" she asked when she picked up. "Is everything okay?"

"Yeah," I croaked, surprised by the sudden pressure behind my eyes when I heard her voice. "I was just . . . calling to say hi. What's up?"

"Oh," she said. I could picture her leaning back in her chair, one foot pushing against a desk drawer. "Nothing really. I'm going to a ping-pong bar after work. Apparently, there are just thousands of ping-pong balls, and you never run out."

"That sounds really fun," I said, staring out my window at what appeared to be one faerie teaching another how to fly a kite.

"Yeah, it should be," she said. "Do you wanna come with? Jordan will be there." She paused. "Please come, Miri. I know I just saw you, but you ran out on dinner, and I miss you."

"I miss you, too," I said. This was my opening. *I would love to come to the ping-pong bar, but I relocated. I relocated permanently. I live in a magic Renaissance faire.*

"I'm not sure yet," I said. "Work is really busy."

Why couldn't I tell her?

She sighed. "This job is eating you alive, Mir. I'm glad you're passionate about it and all, but make sure they value you, okay? Because you're smart and amazing."

I didn't feel smart and amazing. I felt like a sand castle in the middle of a dog park: uncomfortably damp and falling apart.

"I know," I lied. "But you forgot something. I'm *lucky*, too. Because you're my friend."

She snorted, and I closed my eyes, trying to remember what it felt like to sit next to your best friend while she laughed. Somehow, it was already slipping away.

———————— • ————————

Around midday, someone knocked on my door. I stood, not sure who to expect: Sahir would be in the office. Would the Gray Knight come to go over the contract in person? I couldn't stop the butterflies in my stomach at the thought. And then I hurled myself at the suitcase, which I'd relegated to the floor, and started a frantic search for clothes.

"Who is it?" I called, flinging my nightgown into a pile of clothing and yanking a gray cotton dress over my head.

"Lene," the reply came.

I froze, and breathed in. Lene?

Oh. Cat lady Lene. Why was she here?

"Coming," I said, starting for the door.

She, in the grand faerie tradition, opened it and entered.

"Hello—" I said, but she wasn't looking at me. She'd gotten onto her knees and started crawling toward the bed, over heaps of shirts.

"Pssssst pssssst pst," she said, crawling past me, and then "Tsk tsk."

"I'm sorry, are you looking for something?" I asked, nonplussed.

"Of *course*," she exclaimed, and stood. "The cat who inspired such affection! I must see this creature."

"Oh…uh, Doctor Kitten is by the window," I said, pointing.

I stared over her head at Doctor Kitten, who sat in a loaf on the windowsill, staring back at me. Doctor Kitten is a cat and doesn't have telepathy, but from the look he gave me, I knew in the depths of my soul that he suddenly despised my existence.

Lene leapt over the bed in a ballet split and landed on all fours on the far side.

"Hello, cat," she said, and followed it up with a torrent of sounds that I could neither describe nor transcribe.

Doctor Kitten stood up, his back arching, and hissed at her.

I started toward the two of them, bumped my thigh into a bedpost, growled a curse, and stepped between them.

"Lene, I don't think he likes that," I said, putting my hand palm down toward his nose.

"Shush," she said, and made another type of sound. I watched her face; her reflective eyes were intent on him.

Doctor Kitten unbowed his back and straightened his ears. Then he opened his mouth—so wide I could see all of his teeth—and yowled.

I put a hand on his back. "It's okay," I said.

Across from him Lene had opened her own mouth and started yowling, too.

"Please, Kitten," I started.

"Shush!" Lene said again, somehow without ceasing her own yowl or closing her mouth. I scooped Doctor Kitten into my arms but the noise didn't stop.

"Please, what are you doing to him?" I gasped, hugging him to my chest.

They both quieted.

"We're talking," she said, frowning at me.

"At the same time?"

Lene sighed. "Obviously at the same time. May I?"

She held out her hands for my cat. I didn't move. Doctor Kitten wriggled in my arms.

"What, you want to go to her?" I asked. Lene came closer, and I carefully tipped him toward her. He calmed down.

"What did he say?"

She blinked slowly at me. "He likes chin scratches," she said. "There are many birds here. He wonders how they taste. He told me that he exposes his stomach and you try to pet him and he bites you."

"Oh," I said, and stared at Doctor Kitten. "Does he do that on purpose?"

Lene appeared not to hear me. "And he likes the window. I will provide him with a larger window."

What? I didn't say, because she had already gone back to the door and opened it.

Gaheris, the fiery guy from last night, stood there, lurking.

"Bigger window?" he asked, in a voice that indicated he often trailed Lene, widening apertures for cats.

"A comfortable window seat as well," she said. "And perhaps a long hallway to run up and down? And a few crinkle balls?"

Gaheris stepped inside and closed the door.

"A long hallway," I repeated.

Gaheris glanced at me. "We can borrow space," he said. "The land above the hill will not miss a few meters of forest. The humans do not use it anyway."

"You're going to borrow space from a forest and put it in my room?"

He shook his head. "No, we will put a small passage into the mortal realm here."

He must have interpreted the look on my face as one of annoyance and not one of disbelief. "It will be self-contained," he added. "Like those shark tunnels humans love at the aquarium. Two entrances, here"—he pointed, and a golden flame shot up along the inner wall—"and here." Another flame, about a foot farther along.

Then, misinterpreting my expression, he added reassuringly, "They will dim at night!"

I stared at him. He stared at me. Doctor Kitten stared at Lene. Lene stared at Doctor Kitten.

"Aquarium?" I said.

Gaheris shrugged. "My sister works in a human hospital and took me to an aquarium a few years ago. I like them a lot."

"I just—I have to do work," I sputtered. "Will this take long?"

Lene carried Doctor Kitten to the bed and curled around him, her bushy brown tail flicking. "We will nap," she announced. Doctor Kitten had lain down in the decadent pose of an emperor, on his back with his legs splayed.

"You look like a possum," I muttered, but he chose to ignore me.

I sat down at the desk, hooking my legs outside the legs of the chair. My computer was still unlocked, the Excel model on the screen.

I looked over at the second screen, with the latest comments from the Gray Knight, and found the line where I had stopped.

Inputs, B36: change "operating expense" to "operating expenditure."

Behind me there was a noise like a sheet of paper going up in flame. I glanced back, unconvinced that anyone would warn me if there was danger. The left portal now looked like a crack in the wall of the bedroom, and through it I could see a tangle of roots and grass. Had he really just opened a way home? Would a new portal still kill me?

I forced myself to take a slow breath. I couldn't mess up this chance—there might be a portal in my bedroom that could take me back to New York. But I had to play it cool.

I unhooked my legs from the chair and stood up. Lene and Doctor Kitten didn't move on the bed.

Doctor Kitten. I was an idiot. They'd trapped me *with* my cat. If I took him through the portal and exploded in transit, then he'd be trapped outside in some godforsaken forest and covered in viscera.

Doctor Kitten, bless him, was a very spoiled indoor cat. He didn't like the decorative fern in my apartment and would strongly dislike a real forest.

I sat back down, clicked into cell B36, and made the change. Then I tabbed back to the Word document where I kept my notes, tabbed until I had selected the line, and struck through the line so I knew I'd completed it.

I'd keep an eye on this potential portal, but it was too soon to make any moves.

Another knock at the door. I looked up, but this time Gaheris answered.

A moment of complete silence and then, "My lady."

I stood up and turned to see the Gray Knight in the doorway.

She raised an eyebrow, taking in the room. I glanced around, too: Lene and Doctor Kitten on the bed, her brown fur against his white; Gaheris, frozen before her, and apparently in such distress that his head-fires had gone out, leaving him looking a little bit sad in his too-red tunic; and me, half-turned by my chair, hands clasped nervously in front of me, biting my lip.

I should note that when I bite my lip, I do not gently take the center of my lower lip between one upper tooth and my lower teeth, making an alluring red dent and drawing focus to my mouth. No. I gnaw the entire right side of my mouth until the skin is taut, drawing my jaw forward like an off-ramp.

"Lady of the True Dreams," she said, inclining her head. She walked past Gaheris and came to stand by me at the desk. "I assume you received my email."

"I was incorporating the changes when you walked in," I said, gesturing to the two screens. She smelled like…synthetic vanilla? Had the Gray Knight put on perfume? I felt myself sway closer to her, sniffing.

"Does it require clarification? I have come to assist you, if needed."

I stopped myself, nostrils dilated, and met her eyes.

"We can go through them together," I said, "since you came all the way over here."

On the bed, Lene rolled away from Doctor Kitten and opened her right eye to stare at me. I frowned back, in a way that must not have been menacing. She smirked and then raised her very human-looking hand to her own mouth and started grooming it. I wondered if her tongue felt like sandpaper.

The Gray Knight closed her eyes and brought her hands together in a complicated twisting gesture. When she pulled them apart, an acorn hovered between her palms, covered in sparkling gray filaments.

The gray filaments were connected to her fingers, too, like a cat's cradle. The farther she pulled her hands apart, the more they stretched the sides of the acorn; it grew until it was wider than her torso and as high as her waist. She flicked her left hand sharply, and the acorn spun to the floor; when it stopped, it had a seat carved into one side, and supporting legs that kept it upright.

She settled into the seat, hands on her lap, and stared up at me. I gaped back: The acorn had stretched between the fibers of her magic, pulled wider like taffy at her touch. My heart pounded.

She jerked her chin, indicating that I should sit.

I thumped into my chair next to her and grabbed the mouse, brightening the screens. I moused over to the Excel file, but the Gray Knight's hand covered mine to keep it still. I stared down at her hand where it covered mine—satin-smooth brown skin, without the ridged texture of prominent veins. She had a little scar on her ring finger. The backs of my fingers tingled where her fingertips brushed my knuckles.

"Before we review the financial model, we should discuss the definitions for the contract you sent over yesterday," she said, releasing my hand and gesturing to my Outlook icon.

Shaking off the discombobulation from her touch, I nodded. I pulled up the email I'd sent her and opened the draft agreement.

Understanding my purpose in Faerie would be far healthier for my cortisol levels than exchanging lingering hand touches with the Gray Knight. I highlighted the first point, *Teach*, and looked at the Gray Knight expectantly.

"You will provide six one-hour lessons per human week," the Gray Knight said.

I stared at her.

She stared back.

"This is the beginning of the negotiation process," Gaheris prompted, from somewhere behind me.

I turned to stare at him instead. I'd honestly forgotten that he was there. Had he created a portal? But when I glanced past him at the area he'd demarcated, there were lightly pulsating gray vines pouring from a sliver in reality. I looked away, because if you can't see something, it isn't happening.

"Sahir told me you would need guidance," he said, by way of explanation, while I stared determinedly at my computer screen. "You must negotiate the terms of your bargain."

"One lesson per human week," I said to the Gray Knight, who I assumed would protect me from the . . . portal situation . . . if need be.

"Four."

"Two."

"Two lessons for two hours each."

Shit—was Doctor Kitten safe? I glanced over my shoulder at him and found Lene curled entirely around his body.

"Fine," I said to the Gray Knight.

It was a win: four fewer lessons to plan out per week.

I couldn't help it—I looked at Gaheris again. He'd returned his focus to the portal, which was no longer oozing tentacle-vines but had turned pitch-black.

"If you are fired from your job at Tartarus, you have failed in your agreement." I whipped my head around to where the Gray Knight was pointing to the next line.

So much for my cortisol levels: The Gray Knight was going to give me anxiety with or without touching me. "I can assure you if I am fired I'll feel like a failure," I said. "But I don't have control over that."

"Is that the Princeling's concern?" She leaned back in her chair, eyes on Lene and Doctor Kitten.

"It wouldn't be a terribly fair term if there were something like layoffs happening, right?" My insides whirled around my abdominal cavity like frozen bananas in a blender. I probably would have puked if I had anything left.

She inclined her head, thoughtfully, and my panic started to ease. Without an actual commerce or work system, she'd likely never thought about the possibility of not having a role in society or being able to provide for herself. At least the Gray Knight was realizing what she didn't know.

"We can amend the term to state that you cannot take any action which you reasonably should have known would lead to your termination. So you must continue to attend work and turn in deliverables."

I sighed. I hadn't been *actively* planning to give up on my job in order to get out of this ridiculous situation, but I didn't relish the thought of losing the option.

The Gray Knight examined her slender hand. "And, for the last terms"—she nodded at the collective few about me finding a way out of Faerie—"we may consider any quests under three days' length."

"Um—" I twisted the gold ring around my index finger. I tried to channel my mom, who'd given me the ring when I graduated high school. "There shouldn't be any quests."

"Knowledge is earned, not given. You, of all the humans I have met, are most likely to understand the value of knowledge earned," she said, and if the Gray Knight were capable of coquetry, she would have fluttered those thick lashes at me. But the Gray Knight merely stared at me with those fathoms-deep eyes, with the unshakable expectation that I would see the justice in this.

I groaned. "Fine," I said, making the edit.

"Then your ten years begin today." She stayed in her chair, looking at my computer screen. "I will provide you with more information on your human classes tomorrow. Turn to your other work."

I tabbed back over to the Excel model, a bit too dazed to process what I'd just agreed to but still relieved to have some sort of plan in place.

"The next note is to update the inflation assumption," I said. "You said you didn't want to use our curves at two percent, and instead wanted…this." I gestured to the screen, where a series of numbers from 1.3% to 7.6% were arranged in an incomprehensible nonpattern.

"The Crone says there will be continued inflation for the next ten months," the Gray Knight said, sanguine.

"O-okay," I said. "Um, did she guess that or can she actually see the future? Because that might be uh, insider trading?" I frowned. Magical fortune telling was definitely not listed in the definition of "insider trading."

"That is not *insider trading*," the Gray Knight said. "Did you not study for your licensing exam, lady?"

"Of course I studied," I said, thrown violently back into the feeling of being scolded by my dad before a chemistry test.

"I suppose you cannot help it if you have only human retention," she said, completely disregarding the point that using concrete knowledge of the future was probably unethical.

I stared at my knees under the gray cotton dress. "I don't think that addresses the issue," I said, twisting my fingers into the fabric at my thighs.

She put her hand on my shoulder. I froze. "A careful advisor is a boon indeed," she said. "And I have spoken often with the Princeling about how fortunate we are to have you advising us."

Her hand was so strong. She squeezed the top of my arm.

"Thank you," I said. "I appreciate the compliment."

"Let us move on to the next item, then." She jerked her chin at the screen.

A minor explosion suddenly went off behind us, causing the Gray Knight and me to jump out of our seats.

"I will fix that," Gaheris called, breathless. He was shoulder-deep in a self-contained stretch of water, like he'd somehow brought a 3D projector into my bedroom to display a patch of ocean. There was half of a fish next to him, the other half presumably swimming happily through the Atlantic.

"How did you…" I started, but trailed off, not sure what the question would even be.

"Coordinates," he moaned, his feet kicking as he treaded water. "I mixed up coordinates. Latitude, longitude—why did you humans pick two words that sounded the same?" He flapped his hands for emphasis, causing water droplets to splash up into his hair, which remained aflame.

Having always struggled with latitude and longitude myself, I didn't feel qualified to answer that question.

"Should we help him?" I asked the Gray Knight, already moving to grasp his hand. I hadn't touched Gaheris before, and his skin felt strange beneath my fingers—like a poreless stone. I tried to pull him through the water, but no matter how hard I tugged, he came no nearer.

"I need to dissolve the spell," he said, gasping a bit for breath. "Or I will not be able to get out. My legs are somewhere in the place you call Greenland, I think."

And indeed, the water splashing onto me felt icy and miserable. Could faeries experience hypothermia? Even ones that were constantly on fire?

"Come back to work, Lady of the True Dreams," the Gray Knight commanded.

I looked at Gaheris, who nodded that it was all right to leave him. Tentatively, I sat back down at the desk. I glanced over at Lene and Doctor Kitten. Neither had so much as moved because of the sound.

The Gray Knight directed me through the next several points on the document. Most were relatively simple. At some point I heard a gurgling sound like water draining, but I resisted looking.

When we finished, she sat next to me as I emailed the updated model to Levi for review. "Why do you not send it to me?" she asked.

"I need Levi to approve it so I can send it to the client," I explained.

She stared at me. "I am the client," she said.

"Yes."

"I asked you to make these changes."

"Yes."

"I sat with you and made these changes."

"I don't know," I said. "I didn't come up with these systems. But Jeff's my supervisor, and he wants Levi to review it, so that's what we do."

She shook her head. "In Faerie, if you cannot accomplish a task without supervision, you are not assigned it."

"Well, don't you need supervision while you learn?" I looked out the window, at the wide lawn and the winding pathways.

"We apprentice and then we perform." She wove her fingers together, an idle gray glow playing between her palms.

"And what do you do?" I asked. "Gaheris talks to rivers and Lene spies on people from trees. What's your task? Financial modeling?"

She spoke seriously. "I am the Princeling's to direct. But in the Court, we all have different functions. The Crone watches, and listens, as well you know. The Red Knight and the Blue Knight will take positions, and debate them, so that the Princeling can understand the issues facing his people. They go out into the countryside and speak to our citizens, and bring back concerns for him to address."

She fell silent.

"And you?" I prompted.

"The Crone knows, and the knights Red and Blue listen, and I learn," she said. "When we decide upon a course of action, I execute."

"Like an operations manager!" I said, too excited. But she smiled at me.

"Perhaps, like an operations manager."

"Thank you for providing insight," I said, bowing my head.

She shifted in her chair to look at me more directly. "You went to his aid," she said.

"What?"

"The faerie. You went to his aid."

"Gaheris?" I asked, glancing at him where he'd finagled himself a space on the bed next to Lene. Whatever magic he'd been trying to do must have taken a lot out of him—he was fast asleep and snoring, little curls of smoke coming out of the higher nostril. No one had *asked* to sleep on my bed, but that was pretty low on my list of concerns.

"Yes."

"So?" I crossed my arms, bracing myself for some reproach.

"You did a kindness, unbidden and without request of fair return."

"He looked like he needed help."

The Gray Knight nodded. "And this was sufficient for you," she said. "He needed it and was therefore worthy of your aid."

I sighed. "A guy was drowning in a magic bathtub in the middle of my bedroom. There's no mystery here."

She stood up, her gray eyes locked on mine. Without looking away, she put her hands on either side of her chair. The gray magic sparked in my periphery—I could see the chair shrinking out of the corner of my eye as we looked at each other. "There are more mysteries than you see, Miriam Geld."

I stood as well, suddenly tired and longing to be alone. "Thank you for your assistance. It sped my review greatly."

The acorn chair had shrunk back to size in her hands, and she pocketed it. I glanced at the lump it made against her leggings.

"We can work together again, if you are inclined," she said, bobbing her head. Without waiting for a response, she turned and strode from the room.

Chapter 8

In Which I Have an Enchanting Encounter

I watched the Gray Knight leave, her silver hair flying behind her like a pennant, and then finally let myself look at my bed. Gaheris lay at the foot of the bed, one leg bent at an awkward angle. Lene and Doctor Kitten sprawled in the middle, taking up the bulk of the space.

Lene had considerately left a triangle of free space the size of my torso at the top right-hand corner, closest to me.

My room was trashed. Gaheris appeared to have opened at least four different portals and closed none of them. A hole in the floor near the foot of the bed was spouting periodic gouts of ash, and the two initial portals near the door kept flickering between the appearance of flames and thin slivers of roots and decaying leaves.

None of this made me excited about the idea of stepping through a portal Gaheris created.

He hadn't yet made it to the window, so the outside-facing wall was at least still unscathed.

Something glooped through the fourth portal, but it didn't seem imminently harmful. I glanced at the bed again; Doctor Kitten was safely ensconced between the two faeries.

This chaos was not mine to deal with, I decided. I was going to go for a walk instead.

I checked once more for any emails, grabbed my cell, and left through the door, closing it gently behind me. Lene seemed like she'd take good care of Doctor Kitten, and I had reconnaissance to perform. For the first time since I'd gotten to Faerie, I was both fully composed and fully unsupervised.

This time, I turned right down the hallway, heading in the direction we'd come from the first night. I counted doors and came to twenty-seven before the light changed. Most had numbers on them, but a few had titles or names. I came across *Sun Guardian*, *Charlene*, *Pogo the Proud*, and my personal favorites: *King of Thieves Who Do Not Steal Material Goods* and his next-door neighbor, *Lord of Omission*.

There were a few corridors off the main hall, too, like the one that led to the cafeteria. I decided against exploring those for the moment. I kept my right hand on the wall, which felt like packed dirt but didn't crumble away against my fingertips.

Seven doors later, I came to the archway that led into the Court. It was as I remembered it: as tall as the corridor, open to the sky outside, and hewn into the dirt side of the mountain. I wondered how it stayed up—whatever it was made of didn't seem sturdy enough to survive centuries.

But I didn't wonder for long, because then I was outside,

standing in an opening a little way up the hill, staring down at the clearing where we'd had our client dinner only two days previously. The sight made my stomach churn, but it was nice to have fresh air.

I hadn't anticipated so many people outside. A small family was using the side of the hill to teach a child to fly—their black raven's wings glittered as the two older ones jumped, showing the little one how to flap to get airborne. Beyond them, some sort of circle dance had sprung up, and a cadre of laughing Fae spun in whirls of unbound hair and fluttering cloth; loose feathers drifted in their wake.

Nearest the entrance, a trio of tall, slender faeries with willow bark skin stared at me. I stared back: They had long branches sweeping from their scalps and shoulders, covered in thin oval leaves.

No one moved to usher me indoors. I surveyed the landscape for a few moments, trying to understand how—or if—it related to the human world.

Most of the nearby area was open, a series of low hillocks and wide plains full of grass and wildflowers. It was cut with stony paths and bare gray outcroppings of rock. It stretched out into the middle distance, where the edge of a wide forest encircled us for as far as I could see.

I stepped out onto the path and came upon another group of faeries—five people lying in the grass together, sans blanket, with their heads on each other's stomachs. They looked like the contented aftermath of a game of Jenga. One of them was reading, but for the most part they appeared happy to lie beneath the sky and do nothing. I glanced overhead for the sun; I'd begun to suspect that Faerie didn't have one.

"My lady," one of the faeries in the grass said. He disentangled himself from his companions and stood. It was the faerie from the cafeteria who'd served me cake last night and looked like a twenty-seven-year-old actor portraying a heartthrob in a teen movie. He came across the lawn to me and stopped a respectful distance away, bare feet in the grass. "I didn't see you at breakfast this morning."

I touched my own stomach, realizing how hungry I actually was. "I woke up too late," I said.

He inclined his head. "Are you hungry now?"

I nodded. I found myself looking for something Fae or inhuman about him. He was taller than the average human man and had perfectly symmetrical features, like a butterfly's wings. Even his light hair parted evenly right down the middle. Beyond that and the sun-maddened blue of his eyes, he felt comfortingly familiar.

He bent down to a brown picnic basket that I hadn't noticed and pulled out a sandwich. I didn't see what kind of sandwich, because I was too busy gazing at the picnic basket. It lay fetchingly on the grass, one inviting flap open to reveal a blue gingham blanket and artfully arranged rows of sandwiches. The corner of the blanket hanging over the wicker side winked into a suggestive triangle for a moment before unfolding.

I gaped at the basket. The basket—there was no other word for it—smoldered back at me, even without eyes. Every strand in the wicker gleamed, a voluptuous weave that mesmerized me. I wanted to reach into it, to feel the soft fabric of the blanket, to help myself to all the delightful comforts within—

"Woah," the faerie said, as he kicked the flap closed. I blinked and looked down, realizing I was midstep, hand outstretched. "Sorry, she'll seduce anyone."

"*She?*" I repeated, jerking my arm back.

He held the sandwich up between us, and I took it from him. He started walking and I followed without thinking. "Been a few close encounters, if you know what I mean. It's hard with enchanted objects. You just have to remember, they don't mean any harm."

"Close encounters," I repeated, lifting the sandwich toward my face. I stopped, remembering the extremely close encounter with the toilet the night before. "Is this…poisoned?" I asked.

He frowned at me. "No. Do you want a poisoned sandwich?"

"What? No!" I said. "Did *you* poison my food last night?"

He looked even more confused. "No," he said again. "Was your food poisoned?"

Faeries couldn't lie. Satisfied that he wasn't the culprit, I took a bite. It was delicious, with the signature creamy purple spread, and neat rows of crunchy green vegetables on top. "I'm not sure," I said. "I was really sick after dinner last night. But more importantly, are you saying—"

"That I've had a close encounter with the picnic basket?" He laughed, though there was still a line between his brows. "I'm saying it's quite an enchantment, my lady, and you shouldn't feel bad for being susceptible." He'd put his hands behind his back and strolled along with an easy grace, his chest puffed. He wore a simple white T-shirt and gray leggings.

Behind him, several rows of people lay on the grass, bodies absolutely bare. "There are sunbathers," I said, trying not to look too closely. "But there's—"

"No sun," he finished. "They probably like it better that way."

I looked at him.

"Vampires," he explained.

"Vampires can live in Faerie?"

"They often do. It's easier for them here than on the mortal side. No sun to burn them, and no—er, less—prejudice."

Fascinating.

"Thank you for the sandwich." I raised it up for emphasis and took another bite.

He nodded, a little smile on his lips. Good—it was nice to feel like some of the faeries were already on my side, especially when I'd be seeing him three times a day for the foreseeable future.

"I don't know what to call you," I said. "Is there a title you prefer?"

He laughed again. He had such an easy laugh. "You can call me Milo, my lady."

"And you can call me Miri," I replied.

"Where are you walking, Miri?" he asked. "I'd like to escort you, if you wish."

I looked along the path. We'd almost reached the ill-fated dinner table.

"Can we—" I broke off, not sure how to ask.

He nodded. "Yes." He led me to the flat, packed-dirt tableau, the long wooden table and three-legged stools still there. At the other end of the expanse rose a shimmering column of slightly distorted air.

"Is that—" I started.

"The portal back to the mortal realm?" He crossed to the portal so quickly that I nearly tripped keeping up with him.

As we approached, I saw a tiny circle of toadstools in the grass. I stopped abruptly. "Milo, I'm—"

"Not ready to see it," he interrupted. He turned on his heel and walked back toward me, his bulk blocking the shimmering air from view.

I wasn't sure if Milo was a mind reader or just incredibly irritating.

"Where would you like to go instead?"

"I'm not sure."

Milo held his arm out for me. "Then let me lead you."

In the strange sunless light of the Faerie sky, the golden hairs on his arm glinted like metal. I felt a flash of discomfort—but he was being kind to me.

I put my arm in his. "All right, then."

He turned us back up the path. "You should know the Court," he explained, as we walked past the sunbathers to the Court's entranceway. "So you can navigate it."

It was a good idea, and so of course no one else had suggested it. I nodded at him.

As we approached the tunnel in the hillside, he took on a voice like a sports commentator or a particularly enthused tour guide. "This is the entrance to the Princeling's Court," he said. "It's very old, and carved with arcane magics. Every one of his predecessors for the past six hundred years at least have sat in this Court."

"Predecessors," I said. "I thought faeries are immortal."

He shook his head. "No, ma'am," he said, like a good southern boy. "They just live much longer than humans."

"Did you spend time in the—in the US?" I asked. "Your accent—"

Milo nodded, steering us into the hallway, and cut me off again. "This is the central hall," he said. "It runs through the Court, and if you follow it all the way up, you come out on the other side of the hill, where the river runs. And yes, in Texas. But I've been in the Court for ten years now."

As soon as we stepped into the hallway, the temperature cooled—something I hadn't noticed previously but that made me shiver now. Milo caught the gesture and slid his arm out from under mine. He slung his arm around my shoulders, pulling me against his side.

I stumbled a step. This was a lot of touching. A twist of fear caught at my throat, an almost animal panic that hurt my teeth. It threatened to paralyze me.

I pushed it down. Faeries seemed to be touchier than humans. I modulated my steps to match his and let his arm hang heavy across the back of my neck.

"What did you do in Texas?"

"I coached kids' football," he said. "Nothing as nice as tossing the pigskin with the boys."

"Maybe for *you*," I muttered. He didn't say anything. Instead, he ran one fingertip up and down my arm.

"This," he said, pulling me down one of the hallways, "is the area designated for Court business. You've got the scribes' rooms"—he gestured to a door on the left—"the throne room"—the wooden door inset with jewels, which I recognized from the day before—"the meeting rooms, a bathroom. And finally, down here is the courtyard."

This corridor was very short and ended in another open archway; this one led into what I thought might be the heart of the Court. When we stepped through it, we were greeted by the same sunless blue sky: a little disk of blue peeking at us as we stood in a well of light several stories down. Windows looked in at us from every direction. In the center of the courtyard, I recognized the cicada-adjacent faerie from dinner last night. He nodded a greeting, opened his mouth, and shrieked.

"Oh, *that's* the guy who screams at irregular intervals," I said.

Milo nodded. "I know what you want to ask." He started us back along the corridor. After a few awkward beats, I fell into step next to him.

"You do? How?" *Definitely a mind reader.*

"Because it's the human question," he said.

"Okay, sure. What do I want to ask?"

I tilted my head to look up at him, at the long line of his jaw and the golden stubble that coated it.

Milo shrugged. I felt his arm shift against my back. "Why he screams."

"Are you saying a faerie wouldn't ask that?" I wasn't sure what to do with my own arm, and settled for holding it behind my back.

When Milo looked at me, his blue eyes were twinkling. "Definitely not at first."

I pretended to frown. "Fine, I'll bite," I said, in the best bored voice I could muster.

"Please do," Milo interjected, smirking at me.

"What would a faerie ask first?" I continued, steamrolling over him.

"Why he screams *in the courtyard*," Milo said, and grinned at me.

I laughed. "I didn't know faeries had a sense of humor," I said.

"Everyone has a sense of humor," he said, looking confused.

We turned down another corridor, but this time he didn't say anything. I looked at the names on the doors as we passed, the tiny wisps that floated near the ceiling, providing shifting flickering light.

When he stopped in front of a door with the name *Milo* on it, I wasn't entirely surprised.

"I stay here," he said. "So you can find me, if you need anything."

"Thank you," I said. "I appreciate it." I wiggled out from under his arm and put my back to the wall next to his door, trying to give myself a bit of breathing room. He half turned, so that he faced me fully. His eyes were blue like lightning, mesmerizing, and I couldn't look away. He took a step toward me, one hand coming up to rest on my shoulder. His thumb brushed my collarbone where the dress left my skin bare. It was too heavy, a bruising weight. I could hear my own harsh, shallow breaths. He leaned down so that our noses were almost touching.

Was this faerie about to kiss me?

"Miri," he said, "I'd like to be kind to you. You deserve kindness."

I flushed. There was something intimate and painful about hearing those words from someone who couldn't lie.

"Milo—" I started, as the sound of pounding footsteps came down the corridor.

To my utter shock, Sahir flung himself around the corner and careened toward us, wearing a gray suit and panting. "Miriam," he called, and threw himself at me, tackling me to the ground.

We fell in a tangle of limbs, his arms coming up to cradle my skull. I landed under him, my hands against his chest as he pressed me to the wooden floor.

"Ow," I said.

"I sensed you were in danger," he said, curling into a protective shell around me. "I came to save you." He scooped me so that I was trapped in the place where the wall met the floor, pressed down by his body.

We stared at each other, nose to nose. His breath smelled of cinnamon, hot against my lips.

"What on earth is *this* doing against a potential threat?" I shoved my hands into his shoulders, and he shot to his feet, remembering himself. I stayed sprawled on the floor, dress around my knees, glaring up at him. "And where were you last night when I got poisoned?"

"Poisoned?" Sahir repeated.

Milo held a hand out to me. I reached for it, and Sahir slapped it away. *"He's the danger!"* he exclaimed, animated.

"Milo?" I said. "Milo's just been showing me around."

Milo and Sahir stared at each other for a second. Milo blanched, the color leaving his ruddy cheeks in a rush. "I should really be"—he glanced around for inspiration—"going to sleep," he said, jerking his thumb at his bedroom door. Looking mildly ashamed for abandoning me, he slunk inside.

Sahir whirled on me, wild brown eyes and wilder black curls haloing his head. "What did he tell you?" he growled, pulling me upright by the upper arms. His long fingers curled into my biceps, pressed the meat of my arm sharply against his palms.

"Ow, Sahir, I don't like it when you grab me like that," I said.

He froze. "Have I hurt you?" His grip loosened slightly, a solid touch instead of a squeeze.

"No, but I don't want to be yanked around." I brushed down the front of my dress. After an uncomfortable silent moment, I looked up at him between my lashes, like they would offer some protection against the intensity of his earthy brown stare.

He nodded, a sharp jerk of his head. "I apologize, Miriam. But that human is dangerous," he said. "Stay away from him."

Chapter 9

In Which Sahir Demonstrates Startling Versatility

"Human?" I said, blankly. I stared at Milo's door. There was no label underneath his name that said *Human* or *Can lie*.

This would have been a handy label.

I realized four things in quick succession.

First, Sahir thought that Milo had information to share with me—maybe about the Court or my captivity.

Second, Milo was a human.

Which meant that, third, instead of performing espionage like Sahir thought, or flirting with an interesting and very attractive faerie like I thought, I had been happily traipsing the corridors of the Court with some dude who grew up in Waco, Texas.

Who, fourth, could lie to me.

Sahir took me by the elbow and led me up the artery to the main hall. He didn't say anything else.

The silence stretched and snapped. "You don't tell me what to do," I said, exasperated. "I do whatever dangerous things I want to. And Milo isn't even dangerous, unless you mean dangerously hot."

Sahir did not dignify this outburst with a response.

We proceeded in angry silence. I tried not to think about how uncomfortable I'd been with all of Milo's touches.

"He's a *human*?" I said, still reeling.

"Mostly. He claims some Fae blood, and I think a grand-mother who was a banshee."

I glared at him. "I'm sure he was going to tell me that."

Sahir tilted his chin up in a very supercilious way, like an eleven-year-old boy preparing to explain an exciting bug fact to his friends. "I thought you cannot see the future, Lady of the True Dreams."

I groaned and wrenched my elbow out of his grasp. "Aren't you supposed to be at work?"

"Aren't *you*?"

"I was working. I took a break." It sounded more defensive than I had intended. Sahir wasn't my boss.

"I sensed your danger through our bond."

"Bond?" I sputtered. And, "Danger?"

"Yes, for I am your knight, and sworn to defend you," he said, sounding irritated at having to explain this, and not very knightlike at all.

"I don't even think you're a real knight," I snapped. "You don't wear armor."

Sahir stalked ahead of me, his shoulders tense. "Who would wear armor to an office building, Miriam? An idiot. And am I an idiot?"

I growled and chased him down the hallway, running to catch up. "Just tell me what happened and why you thought I was in danger."

"I was in a meeting about the release of a new green bond," he started, "and I felt an abyss open in your soul, so I left the office and came to find you."

"An abyss," I repeated. "Sahir, I don't—" I started, but he cut me off.

"I went to your room, and saw Gaheris and Lene on your bed with the cat. I was delayed in finding you because I had to close one of Gaheris's portals, which had unleashed two-thirds of a swamp into your bedroom."

"How do you know it was Gaheris's portal?"

He gave me a withering look. "You think you have the only cat in this entire Court?"

I stared back at him, uncowed. "How do you know it was two-thirds of a swamp, and not just half?"

He sighed. I thought Sahir should probably just record himself sighing so he didn't destroy his lungs, what with all the deep breaths and audible exhales. "Gaheris is so bad with coordinates that I sometimes wish somebody would invent a new type of portal magic for him."

"That's not very nice," I said.

He rolled his eyes. "We all have strengths and weaknesses. Gaheris is a fire faerie with death magic in his blood. If he persists in his architectural pursuits, he will undermine the integrity of the building."

The smug superciliousness in his tone made me want to punch his other eye so he would have matching bruises.

And then I felt a wave of guilt. His eye was black because of me, and he apparently also felt random and disruptive emotions during the workday because of me. "Why do you think you sensed danger?" I asked. "At least I can try not to set it off again."

Sahir pushed my door open, revealing the two faeries pretty much where I had left them, sitting up against the headboard with Doctor Kitten between them. Gaheris had extended his left arm as a sort of pin-cushion-slash-teddy-bear, and Doctor Kitten hugged it, claws out. I winced.

"Miriam," Lene greeted me, sounding cheerful, if slightly surprised, to see me in my room.

"What's up, Lene?" I said.

"The roof," she said, pointing up. I glanced up at the striated rock and dirt on the ceiling.

"That's a good point," I said. "Thank you." Doctor Kitten lifted his head and looked at me, his eyes slits. His loyalty had apparently shifted.

"Miriam—" Sahir started. I cut him off, shamed by my cat.

"Lene, when humans say *what's up*, they mean *what are you doing* or *how have you been*," I explained. Doctor Kitten blinked once in slow approval.

"Please," Sahir said. "We have much to discuss."

Gaheris nodded from next to Lene. "If I had known this, I would have explained it," he said.

Sahir lost what remained of his composure and exploded

into tendrils of brown smoke, tangled like the branches of creeping wisteria.

"*We need to talk, Miriam,*" the vaguely human-shaped smoky mass of vines said. I saw an arm try to coalesce and fail.

"Okay! Of course," I said, pretending not to be terrified. *My dad says I'm good in a crisis*, I'd told the Gray Knight. And I *was* good in a crisis. I kept my voice steady and calm. "Let's talk." I reached toward him, palm up. "Just…just hold my hand, and we can sit down and talk."

One tentative vine crept toward my hand, and then around my palm, solidifying as it did so. The smoke tickled, and it was a relief when it coalesced. Within seconds, I had a living wooden glove. I exhaled, a loud, steady sound, as the tip of the vine crept over my wrist, at the pulse point. I lowered myself to the floor, and the vine came with me.

"I have not seen him sublimate in decades," Gaheris said, peering down at us. "Not since he had just come to Court."

"That's a great vocabulary word," I said, keeping my tone even. "Sahir, what do you want to talk about? It seems like you're a little overwhelmed."

The disembodied voice came again. "You cannot just trust anybody who speaks kindly to you, Miriam. People will want to take advantage of you, of your naivety. The Princeling has raised you up, but there are faeries who want him to fail."

"Fail as in, *people don't like me?*"

"Fail as in, faeries kill you," Lene chimed in, helpfully.

"Which is why my friends came to spend time with you today," Sahir said, his voice remarkably stern, given its source.

I stared at the mass of half-corporeal vines that was Sahir.

A few more vines solidified. The one holding my hand had started to sprout leaves.

"Well," I said, "they were fantastic company."

This didn't mollify him. "And yet you fell into danger the moment I left," he said, sounding as melancholy as an indescribable vine monster can.

He paused for effect. "There is even a betting pool."

"A what?"

"A bet, for the remaining days of your life."

I filed that horrifying thought away for later. I immediately unfiled it and examined it again because it was highly unpleasant but also a little bit interesting. Who was participating? Would people try to protect me so that I'd live until their chosen day? Then I shook my head, like that would make it go away.

"What do faeries even bet? It seems like everything is socialized," I said, because the financial system and associated social safety nets of Faerie were apparently things Adult Me cared about more than my safety.

"Favors," the vines intoned darkly.

"Okay, well, I appreciate the warning, Sahir. You've done me a service in letting me know."

The solidity crept up his arm, the vines wrapped around my hand taking on the shape of human fingers.

"What else do we need to talk about?" I asked, forcing my eyes away from the transmutation.

"We must manage our bond. I did not know my oath would have these consequences." One of the vines near his shoulder started to writhe, and I put a hand on it, trying to channel soothing thoughts.

"Haven't you made an oath like this before?" I asked.

"You can only make that oath once," Lene chirped. I nearly jumped; I'd almost forgotten the two of them on the bed. "And most of us never make it."

Doctor Kitten jumped off the bed, apparently interested in the swirling shadows on the ground. He swatted at the nearest one, and vines twisted into existence there, too.

What I wanted to say was *Why in the sweet barbecued hell did you do this, then?*

But the guy was literally made out of vines, and I couldn't make myself reprimand him further.

Instead, I looked at the place I imagined Sahir's face to be. "Thank you for honoring me with your oath, Sahir. I would repay you in kind, if I could."

At that moment, to some extent, I meant it.

He seemed to realize that as well. The rest of his torso coalesced, and he sat on the floor, still twisted and knotty, but human-shaped. I looked into his eyes, deep-set under bark brows. Doctor Kitten climbed into his lap.

"I must apologize, Miriam. It has been a stressful few days."

"Is this, uh, your normal form?" I asked. I glanced over at Gaheris and Lene. I'd thought *they* looked inhuman.

He sighed, which meant he'd recovered his composure enough to engage in his favorite hobby. "Faeries have pre-ferred forms, Miriam, but our appearance is tied, to some extent, to our mental state."

"Cool," I said, and lay down flat on the floor, our hands still entwined. "I think I'm done for the day."

"We have resolved nothing," he said. His skin looked rough and cracked but was starting to knit into something more fleshlike.

"I know," I groaned. It felt so good to lie down. We disentangled our hands.

Sahir looped his arms around his knees and looked down at me. His nearer elbow had a little pink flower sticking out of it. "You said you were poisoned last night? Were you ill?"

"I had food poisoning, I think," I said. "But it wasn't Milo," I added, when he opened his mouth. "He gave me a sandwich today and I was fine."

"If I were attempting to poison you, I would not do it every time I saw you," Gaheris offered. "So we cannot know he did not poison you."

What were he and Lene still doing here? I raised an eyebrow at Sahir, who shrugged. "Gaheris, Lene, and I have been at the Court for roughly thirty human years together," he said. "We share much of our time."

I levered myself onto my elbows and caught Lene's eye.

"I need to get back to work," I said, standing up.

Sahir stayed on the floor, Doctor Kitten in his lap. "Can I move the creature?" he asked, though he didn't sound hopeful.

"No!" Lene and I both said.

I sat at my desk and turned my computer on to see fifty-seven unread emails. I stared out the window. "So vampires can live here? In Faerie?"

"Yes, many reside here," Gaheris said. "They like it because we have no sun. But I do not have many vampire friends." He sounded so sad it made my own heart ache.

156

"Which is very understandable," Lene said. She did not sound sympathetic in the least.

Sahir, in his signature move, sighed. "If you had ever paid attention in a science class, Gaheris, you would know that vampires have a moisture content of fifteen percent. If you had a moisture content of fifteen percent, you would not like fire faeries either."

I wanted to ask about faerie science class, but then I would never get my work done.

After a few minutes, their conversation became a pleasant hum in the background as I slogged through my emails, routing requests where they needed to go and answering questions when I could.

When we went to dinner, we sat in a group; it was better having them around me. We didn't see Milo or the Princeling, and on the way back to my room, Lene told me she was only three doors down.

It was almost a nice evening. But when I looked at my phone, I had missed a call from my dad, three from my mom, four texts from Thea and Jordan, an Instagram message from a guy I dated a while ago, and a dinner invitation from my Games Games Games group.

I couldn't stop myself from imagining the months and years ahead, as the messages slowed to a trickle and then stopped.

I scrunched my eyes shut against the other low, insistent thought thrumming underneath. When that didn't stop it, I pressed the heels of my hands into my eyes. But the thought pounded through, rising up the way it did in the most vulnerable moments.

You aren't helping anybody.

So I got ready for bed and then slipped under the soft duvet, well aware I had hours of work left to do and unable to make myself care.

That night, my dreams were full of unfamiliar Fae: a faerie who looked like a young man with wide white angel wings, staring down at me with desperation on his face; the snake-eyed cafeteria worker standing in a wooded clearing with a drawn dagger held aloft, her face contorted in a snarl; a faerie with a ridge of horns around his face like a triceratops.

I slept restlessly.

————————————•————————————

One week after I agreed to the Princeling's bargain, I stood in the middle of the cafeteria, looking at the faces of the seven participants who'd shown up to Faerie's very first human class.

I wasn't sure whether to be relieved or offended by the poor attendance: Two nights before, Lene had made me take a half hour away from work to trail the cicada faerie (his name was Schubert) around the Court while he screamed at irregular intervals. We'd been part of a crowd of at least eighty people.

Sahir, Lene, Gaheris, and the Gray Knight made up four of the seven. The other three were Milo, an oddly familiar guy with white wings named Kellen, and Kellen's unhappy horned friend Caraya.

Schubert had not reciprocated my proffered support. I vowed to never again listen to him shriek.

"Hi, everyone," I said. "Thanks for coming."

Since everyone sat at one table, I decided to join them. I pulled out a stool and sank down at the head of the table.

"I don't have an agenda today. Does anyone have any questions?"

Milo raised his hand.

"Anyone else?"

Milo shot me a look of betrayal.

"Milo," I sighed.

"Why did the chicken cross the road?" he asked, his gorgeous blue eyes twinkling. And then he doubled over in hysterical laughter.

"Thanks, Milo," I said. "Moving on."

The Gray Knight glanced sharply at me. "You are to answer all questions, lady," she said. "To the querent's satisfaction."

"All questions from the *faeries*," I said, exasperated and thinking about the presentation Jeff wanted me to edit later that night. "Milo's a human."

Milo's face fell. He looked away from the table, at the buffet station where he stood every day and served the Court.

"Milo is of our Court," the Gray Knight snapped.

I stared at my own chipped, unpainted nails, fighting a wash of guilt.

"The chicken crossed the road to get to the other side, Milo," I said. "And that's a good segue into jokes, so thank you for the suggestion."

"We understand jokes," Sahir said, his face in his work laptop.

Only nine years, eleven months, and three weeks, I reminded myself.

"Okay, sorry," I said aloud. "Does anyone have other questions?"

Caraya tapped sharp black talons on the wooden tabletop. "What is a human's mortal weakness?" she asked, in the tone of a teenager trying to scare a substitute teacher out of their county's school system.

"What did the chicken want to do on the other side?" Gaheris asked, in the tone of a teenager puzzling out a stoichiometry problem.

"Was the chicken edible?" Lene asked, in the tone of a teenager who wanted dinner.

I locked eyes with the Gray Knight. Her eyes were so beautiful, silvery and reflective, dazzlingly bright. I could see the challenge in her set jaw, the quirk of one eyebrow. Could I answer all of these questions satisfactorily?

"In reverse order: probably, he was visiting a friend, and most things."

"*Most things* is too vague," Caraya said.

Neither Gaheris nor Lene had follow-ups.

"Well, you can stab a human with almost any sharp object in a wide range of places on their body. You can suffocate, drown, or poison them. You can starve or dehydrate a human. I'm not really sure what you're asking, Caraya."

She tossed her head, curls bouncing. A ringlet got stuck on one of the curving black horns protruding from either side of her head. I stared at it, mesmerized. "Perhaps a food that humans cannot eat, or a metal they cannot touch."

I shook myself. "I have a nickel allergy," I volunteered. "But it just gives me a rash."

Sahir groaned.

"And I guess humans can't eat sulfuric acid," I said.

This at last mollified her. She nodded and snapped her mouth shut with finality.

"Is there a food faeries can't eat?" I asked, wondering why she'd pushed the issue.

"Yes?" Caraya looked confused, brow furrowed. "It is why we had to—"

"Adjourned," the Gray Knight intoned, standing with alacrity.

The six others shoved their chairs back from the table in one motion, silent. She watched as they filed from the room. Sahir lingered by the saloon doors.

So much for two hours. I didn't think it'd been two minutes.

The Gray Knight looked at me. "Next time, come prepared," she said, and stalked out.

———————————•———————————

Two days later, fresh off a fire drill at work where I'd created a frankly spectacular, flawlessly researched, and completely errorless pitch deck in under thirty-six hours, Sahir reminded me that my next human class was in approximately one hour.

I was in a sour mood, because no one had told me that the pitch was for a potential client who'd never forgiven Jeff for hooking up with his daughter at a Christmas party two decades back. *Why* the man had even agreed to the meeting, I couldn't say. But I felt sure that if I ever had to sit on another video call watching two adult men shout until spittle flew into their camera lenses, I would become fully insane. The sentence "My daughter's flower of youth was plucked in its prime by a man who only wanted to add it to his wilting bouquet" was uttered.

The sentence "I didn't pluck anyone's flower that night, you pompous shitbag" was also uttered.

When I figured out that they were arguing over the virtue of a married forty-five-year-old woman with three children, a dog, and a summer house in the Hamptons, I came off mute. "Hey," I interrupted, so gently that neither of them stopped speaking.

"Hey," I tried again, and they both quieted. "Do you want me to start the presentation?" I asked.

"Just a minute, Miri," Jeff said, flapping a hand at the screen. "And *you*, Ronald, have no leg to stand on here!"

Berating the potential client was an interesting new sales strategy. It proved ineffective.

By the end of the hour-long call, in which my perfect pitch deck stayed on its perfect title page, I pitied the daughter more for her father than for her brief carnal entanglement with Jeff. And that was truly saying something.

So when Sahir reminded me about my next human class, I snapped at him. "Just move it," I said. "I don't have any time." I was still sitting in my desk chair, which I'd turned to face him where he sat on my bed. He had his hands on his knees, his posture as upright as ever. Lene and Doctor Kitten, who'd napped through most of that meeting, lay on the bed behind him.

He only stared at me, soulful brown eyes wide and guileless. *Like a cow's*, I thought uncharitably.

"Fine," I muttered, well aware that Sahir couldn't move my human class. "I don't know what to talk about, but I'll wing it." I stood from my seat and snatched my hairbrush from my desk. Doctor Kitten stood up and padded over to Sahir. He butted his head against Sahir's hand.

"What is 'wing it'?" Sahir asked, looking intrigued, as I yanked snarls of brown hair through the bristles. Doctor Kitten butted his hand again. He still didn't pet the cat. "You do not have wings."

I sighed. "It's an idiom." I dropped the brush. The plastic handle bounced once, forlorn. Doctor Kitten mewled. Sahir relented and ran a hand down the cat's back.

"An idiom," Lene repeated, blinking sleep from her eyes.

"A...a saying that is so common everyone understands what you mean, even though it isn't what you said."

"You could talk about those?" Sahir suggested. Doctor Kitten hopped onto his lap, shedding white fur on his black suit pants.

"I don't know enough about idioms to explain them right now." I watched Lene swing her legs over the side of the bed. She nudged her head into Sahir's shoulder, in exactly the same way Doctor Kitten had just done to his hand. Sahir, who was occupied in petting Doctor Kitten, rested his head on hers.

"You could discuss human greetings," he mused. "I struggled with human greetings when I first joined the bank."

I stared at him with new eyes. "Sahir, you genius," I said. "You're the best person to talk to about these classes, since you've experienced the human world from a faerie's perspective." I resolved to lesson-plan with Sahir going forward.

He tilted his head. "Just so," he said. "You may refer to me as a genius whenever it pleases you."

I snorted. "Come on, let's get down to the dining hall and set up."

We left Doctor Kitten in the bedroom because Lene said he had found the pitch meeting "so disturbing to his rest that he required an additional nap to find composure." I told him he was a weenie and a whiner, because he hadn't even been on camera. He then apparently told Lene that I was empowered to hang up at any time because the arrangement of my human phalanges meant I could easily hit the correct button on the keyboard or mouse, whereas his limited dactyl range meant that he could *not* hang up for me without significant trial and error.

Before I could ask *a lot* of questions about my cat's knowledge of biological terminology, Sahir said we needed to leave for the lesson. We left Doctor Kitten lying smugly in a nest of pillows at the head of the bed, the black patch on his side glistening in the twinkling light of our resident will-o'-the-wisp.

"Lene, did you make up the dactyl range thing?" I asked as we made our way down the hall. The tail end of the dinner rush was coming toward us. I knew from watching at my window like a tower-bound princess that many Court denizens would go outside in the evenings to enjoy the cool night air.

"No," she said, sounding a bit offended. "I cannot lie, Miri. And 'making up' things, as you say, is just another way to lie."

"Oh yeah. Sorry." I pushed on the dining hall doors, gesturing for her and Sahir to enter. "I just don't know where he learned that."

"We can ask him later," she said.

I followed the two of them inside and glanced around. A few stragglers were picking at trays of food. By the far wall, the cafeteria staff stood cleaning up their workstations. Kamare, the snake-lady, glared at me. Milo hadn't noticed me yet.

"Begin with greetings," Sahir advised, leading the three of us to the same table as the previous session. He sat to the left of the head of the table; Lene sat to the right. I knew where that left me, and took the seat reluctantly.

"What should we do for the rest of class?" I asked.

Sahir gave me a look that said *You are not yet privy to the great mysteries of the Fae, but you're about to be, and you won't enjoy it.*

"There will not be a rest of class," he said, with perfect confidence.

Caraya and Kellen came in through the cafeteria doors together, Kellen's angel-white wings tucked against his back. Caraya wore a sparkling golden cape that draped from the points of her black horns down to the floor. It blew out behind her in a *clearly* magically manufactured breeze—but the effect was stunning.

They sat together on Lene's left. Neither of them said anything to me—which I supposed was Sahir's point, actually. The Fae didn't *have* greetings.

I had a fantastic view of the dining hall doors, which swung open again with force. The Gray Knight stood between them, a glittering silver vision against the darkness of the hallway.

Beside her, the Princeling stood at parade rest. She stalked into the room, her clothing glimmering with every step. He followed, a menacing solidity wearing a simple green tunic and made broader by the slight flare of his wings behind his shoulders. The doors didn't dare swing shut until he'd seated himself at the foot of the table.

Though the table had only had backless stools when he walked in, by the time he situated himself on his chair it had become the silver throne he favored. He shifted on it until he'd assumed his menacing lounge, one knee hooked over an armrest and his lower back pressed to the other.

I watched the way his iridescent green wings hung down and wondered for the first time if he sat that way for comfort as much as for how cool it made him look.

The Gray Knight remained standing behind him, hands clasped. Her tunic had flared sleeves that ended in a tight cuff at the wrists. Her mouth was thinner than usual, a grim unobtrusive line beneath the sharp slash of her nose.

My eyes flicked between them: He hadn't come to the last class.

"Proceed," he said, waving a careless hand. Emerald sparks flew when he gestured. He didn't need to wear jewels when he dripped magic like gemstones from his fingers.

The door swung open again: Gaheris stepped through, the flames on his head slightly subdued and his hand clamped around Schubert's wrist.

"I had *planned* to scream tonight," Schubert informed us all. He then sat with great dignity and absolutely no deference to the Princeling.

Milo, having finished his food-related work, joined us at the table.

"Hello, everyone," I said. "Today we're going to talk about human greetings in America, the country I'm from."

The Princeling raised an eyebrow but didn't comment. I didn't enjoy having him at the foot of the table, eyes intent on me.

"Right," I said, realizing I'd expected some kind of response. "So, greetings are the way that humans…" I fumbled. "Greet each other." I glanced at Sahir, hoping for a knight-in-shining-armor rescue.

He—unsurprisingly—sighed. "Humans cannot begin an interaction until they have signaled acknowledgment of each other," he said. "They have devised an array of incomprehensible rituals, which can be altered and adapted to declare mood, conversational intent, and even level of intimacy. If you do not greet a human in a way that they expect, they take it as a sign of rudeness or disrespect."

"I do not believe I asked Sahir to lead this class, lady," the Princeling said. He'd conjured a thin green vine, which he coiled and uncoiled around his fingers as he spoke.

I glanced at Sahir, who rolled his eyes.

"Thank you for that summary, Sahir," I said. I wanted the Princeling to go away. "So, as Sahir said, we signal acknowledgment at the start of every interaction. That's a *greeting*. I'll teach you a simple one to start."

I turned my attention to the Princeling. "May I involve Sahir in a demonstration, my lord?" I asked, a bit of bite in my voice.

He inclined his head. "As you wish."

"Great. Sahir, let's stand up." I pushed my stool from the table and stood. Sahir stood, too, making the face that meant *I regret giving you any support, moral or otherwise.* I held my hand out to him and he shook it, once, like I'd handed him a dead fish.

"Hello, Sahir. How are you?" I glanced back at the table. Lene and Kellen were both watching with lively interest. Caraya had engaged Schubert in what appeared to be a thumb war, though it didn't look like either of them had exactly five fingers. Gaheris was staring dreamily into the middle distance.

"I am well, Miri, thank you for asking. How are you?"

The Princeling was also watching his subjects intently.

"I am well, Sahir." I turned back to the table. "So that's how you greet someone. Once you've done that, you can start whatever conversation you want."

Kellen, Lene, Caraya, and Milo all spoke up at once—

"But why would you do this?"

"What if you cannot say you are well?"

"Why did you touch hands in this strange fashion?"

"Do you use the greeting if you are challenging the human to mortal combat?"

My eyes met the Princeling's. He inclined his head, indicating I should answer.

Sahir had been completely right: Greetings filled the entire two hours, and then two more class sessions after that. If *this* was all the Princeling required, maybe this wouldn't be so bad after all.

——————•——————

The next two weeks blurred. I skipped breakfast, rolling out of bed bleary-eyed to be on the morning call. Lene lay on my bed and kept me quiet company, sometimes with Gaheris, and sometimes alone.

At lunch and dinner, I prioritized dessert and never finished my food, afraid to be away from the desk in case an email came in. I was sick a few more times, probably from stress, though never as badly as the first night. Maybe a faerie hadn't poisoned me after all. Maybe it'd been psychosomatic.

At some time between midnight and two a.m., I rolled back into bed, asleep before Doctor Kitten could even curl into my side. Once I dreamed of Thea and Jordan, sitting together on Thea's blue couch.

"Have you seen Miri since that dinner we had together?" Jordan asked.

"No," Thea said, holding a glass beer bottle to her chest, her brow furrowed. "I think she might be mad at us for what we said about her job."

I shot bolt upright, scrambling for my phone, and it took me several seconds to understand it had only been a dream.

I dreamed of my mother once, clutching her pillow and crying out for me. In the morning, my dad called and told me she'd woken him in the night with questions about me.

"Weird," I said. "Maybe she's also a Lady of the True Dreams."

The title had begun to amuse me: I dreamed of stew for lunch and then laughed when a cafeteria worker plopped a bowl of stew onto my lunch tray. Three nights in a row, my dreams accurately predicted the type of cake Milo would serve me the next day. True dreams, indeed.

And every day, my mom called to ask if I'd taught human class, and if I was fulfilling the terms of my bargain.

One night, I told the Games Games Games group chat that I probably wouldn't be playing with them for the foreseeable future. I had too much work to do.

I received and ignored a barrage of phone calls in response. Jordan sent me a series of Venmo payments labeled *Emergency Cheese* and *Comfort Bagels*.

I called Thea, and she told me a very involved story about a coworker's misadventures while purchasing donut-themed socks. I cried until I laughed.

Every day that passed, it became harder to tell my friends that I wouldn't ever see them again. So every day that passed, I didn't.

Chapter 10

In Which I Am Forbidden from Eating Toast

One night, Sahir knocked on my door still in his suit, his laptop under his arm. When I called, "Who is it?" he opened the door and entered.

"Hi, Sahir," I said, leaning back in the desk chair. "How are you?"

Sahir hated human greetings more than anyone else in the class, probably because he was the only one who actually had to use them regularly.

He looked around, frowning. "Are you working?"

I gestured to my computer screen, where an Excel model was running through twenty-four data tables. "Of course."

"I thought I might work here, with you."

I looked around my room for a good spot. Bed, desk, yards

of bare wall. I waved vaguely into the air. "Yes, sure. Sit anywhere."

He went to the unmade bed and stared down at it like a drill sergeant preparing to ream out a recruit. But he didn't say anything, just grabbed a corner of the quilt and pulled the coverlet up the bed. Then he slid out of his suit jacket, revealing a white button-up shirt, and hung it on a hook by the night table. I did not recall the existence of this hook. When he reached out, his button-up strained at the shoulders but didn't tear, thus failing to perform a public service.

I propped my elbow up on the desk and watched him settle onto the bed, his long legs out in front of him and his back against my pillow. I thought about asking him to add a throw pillow into the mix, so his shirt wasn't on my sheets.

He looked up and caught my eye. "Do you want to sit with me?"

What, *on the bed*? My mouth went dry, and then watered, and then I choked on my own saliva and coughed unattractively. Sahir sat impassively through this completely wordless and unutterably mortifying ordeal.

"Sure," I said, once I was reasonably sure I wasn't choking anymore. I unplugged my laptop from the docking station and joined him on the bed. We sat side by side, my shoulder against his upper arm. He smelled comfortingly like cinnamon, warm and earthy.

I felt myself melting into his side, my piano-wire-tense muscles relaxing as the adrenaline faded from my bloodstream. I waited for him to inch away, but Sahir had already proven himself very touchy. He put his arm around me and pulled me against him, his eyes still on his work.

I glanced at his screen to see one of the bank's newest climate change campaigns, centered on the reuse of the provided single-use plastic utensils stocked on every floor. It was called *Pla-STICK It in a Drawer*, and I couldn't decide if the responsible copywriter should be fired or promoted. I ran my thumb along the gold ring on my index finger, and then twisted the ring from one hand to the other.

"Has that campaign had any impact on our office's waste?" I asked, jerking my chin at his lap.

He rubbed his fingertips along my elbow, dragged the rough fabric of my shirt across my forearm in a soothing circle. "None whatsoever."

I leaned my head against his shoulder, relieved to have some kind of contact with another person. The hours passed, the two of us tapping away at our keyboards, and by the end of the night I'd become inured to his presence on my bed.

After that, he came and worked next to me most nights. We sat in silence and typed on our computers. Sometimes I felt him looking over my shoulder at my email exchanges.

Usually I fell asleep next to him before he left, sliding down the pillows with my laptop still on my lap. Doctor Kitten always lay between us, the world's hairiest chaperone.

Another week passed this way.

———————————— • ————————————

The Gray Knight sat on the edge of the bed, staring at me.

"You are someone special," she said, "and I cannot stop thinking about you."

She changed, lengthening and darkening, and was the Princeling. "Your mortal mind cannot comprehend my plans," he told me. "And there is no reason to try. You serve me best here. Isn't that what you always wanted?" He smirked, cruel and so, so beautiful. "To serve your faerie lord?"

His shoulders hunched and he became the Crone. "A strand of yarn does not know it is part of a cloak," she said, in a voice like my father's.

I woke up and grabbed my phone from the pillow beside me. I'd dialed my dad before I even checked the time, but it didn't matter. He was on his way to work, of course.

"Miri?" he asked. I heard the rush of air and the whir of his tires on the cement. He was on the highway.

"Dad?" I said. "Can you hear me?"

"Yeah. Are you okay? Your mom's getting worried."

I pictured him sitting in his car, his left arm on the window and his right on his thigh, hands loose around the wheel.

There was a loud noise from the hallway.

"I'm fine, Dad." I stood up and went to the door. "I've just been busy with work stuff." A technically true statement.

"And with your pedagogical responsibilities?" Dad sounded amused.

Of my parents, my dad was the less concerned about my relocation. He found the Princeling entertaining as a concept, and he seemed unshakably certain of my ability to finagle a way out of Faerie in time for the holidays in three months.

Another noise from the other side of the door, like a ball bouncing down the corridor. I sighed, opened the door, and stuck my head out into the hallway.

"Mostly busy with my regularly scheduled poisonings,

actually." I swung my head around, but I saw no potential source of noise. "I was sick again last night, and I'm pretty sure it's the food." This fact hadn't impacted my staying up until two a.m.

One last glance around the hall yielded no evidence of a perpetrator. Maybe Schubert was getting some rounds in. I closed the door and went back to bed.

"You probably just aren't used to magical food," my dad said dismissively. My dad was a surgeon and consequently believed that if he couldn't operate on it, it wasn't a problem.

"Maybe…but I don't really want to talk about it. How's stuff at home?"

"Same old," my dad said, and didn't elaborate.

"Is Mom okay?"

"She's fine."

I wondered what he wasn't telling me—probably that she was waking him up every two hours to propose some new harebrained scheme to spring me from Faerie. Probably that they were falling apart at home, worried and terrified.

My dad cleared his throat. "How's my grandcat?" he asked.

"Delightful," I said. "And chaotic. He's made friends with a few birds."

Doctor Kitten had quickly become a favorite of the birds, who liked to sit on the other side of the window and taunt him until he stood up on his hind legs and scrabbled uselessly against the magic barrier.

"We miss you," my dad said. He sounded uncertain.

I stared across the room, at the waterfall shower. "I miss you, too," I said. "I have to go. I love you, Dad."

"Love you, too," he said. I hung up and got out of bed, crouching over the suitcase still on the floor where I'd left it. It seemed that nobody intended to give me a closet or any sort of dresser, so I'd be living out of my suitcase for the rest of my life. I pulled out a pair of jeans, stared at them, and threw them over my shoulder. Why did I need to look nice? It didn't matter. I grabbed black sweatpants covered in white cat hair and pulled them on.

When I used the toilet, I looked at the shower but didn't get in. And at the sink, I glanced at the makeup bag but didn't open it. I did take Doctor Kitten's water bowl, empty it out, and refill it. The food stayed full no matter how much he ate. I kicked the litter box, but there were no clumps.

There never were. It must have been faerie magic, because I'd started watching to make sure he went, and he definitely went.

"Breakfast?" I asked Doctor Kitten, who'd sat down in the warm spot I left on the bed. He looked up from his grooming. "Lene will be there," I added.

He raised a cat eyebrow. "Fine," I said. "You stay here."

I knocked on Lene's door, and she opened it immediately. "Breakfast?" I asked, feeling a little shy.

"Of course!" she said, stepping into the hallway. She wore a jumpsuit, a loose, sleeveless blue thing that didn't restrict her movements. Her tail stuck out a hole at the back. "I knew you would retrieve me, so I waited."

"You waited to eat breakfast with me?" I asked, touched.

"Yes," she said. "I am good at waiting." She stopped in front of the dining hall doors. I pushed one open, and she stepped through in front of me.

I'd decided that this was an opportune time to revisit my questions about different types of faeries.

"So if Gaheris is a fire faerie, and Sahir is a dryad," I started, but she giggled.

"Sahir is not a *dryad*," she said. "Oh, that is so funny. You should call him a dryad. He's a woodland Fae." We went to the buffet line. I scanned the three people working it—Milo was on the end.

"Ah, I'm sorry," I said to Lene. "Is it rude to ask people what type of faerie they are?"

"Well, usually we can tell," she said. "So I have never thought about it. But you can ask me." She held her tray out and the first faerie—the one with snake scales on her face— put a bowl of hot cereal onto it.

I did the same. The faerie gave me a single piece of buttered toast.

"Okay," I said, choosing to ignore this—she gave me something boring and bland whenever she thought she could get away with it. And anyway, I loved toast. "What type of faerie are you?"

"Well, some call us therianthropes, but we are just faeries with a particular affiliation for a type of animal. We tend to become more like them as we age." The second faerie served us both, some type of quiche thing. Milo put a bowl of fruit on Lene's tray. I stopped in front of him.

"Good morning, Milo," I said.

"Good morning, Miri." He put a bowl on my tray as well: Today the fruit salad was composed largely of slightly spiky fruits that looked like rambutans but had no peel. I didn't enjoy them at all; the fibrous exterior caught in my throat.

Lene and I went to the usual table. I wasn't entirely surprised to see the Gray Knight sitting there, eating something that looked suspiciously like a normal human-world banana. She had popped in and out of the rotation a few times over the past few weeks, usually to criticize my interpretations of human behavior during class.

"So you believe you were poisoned," she said, by way of greeting.

It took me a moment to understand what she was talking about.

"Good morning," I said, still clinging to my manners. "It's lovely to see you. Yes, it's rude to eavesdrop on people's pre-dawn phone calls with their parents." I stared at her severely, to see if she would apologize.

An apologetic frown didn't mar her delicate features. She stared back, imposing even lounging splayed-leg on a wooden stool. "It is not eavesdropping when you shout it down a hallway."

Touché. Perhaps not my subtlest moment.

"No, I don't think I was poisoned." I sighed. "I've been sick a lot, but I'm sure it's just stress."

She thrust her hand toward me, thumb pressed to her pinky, and her three middle fingers curled. A bolt of gray magic hit my tray and settled in a fine mesh over the buttered toast.

"You *were* poisoned," she said, standing. The noises around us cut out; a buzzing filled my ears as I stared down at the bread on the plate.

Magic dusted the whorls and crevices in the crumb in a fine gray powder.

"Wait, what?" I pushed the tray away from me, but the Gray Knight had already stridden away, to the serving line.

"Kamare," she said, in a booming voice so loud the entire room turned to stare. "You dishonor our Princeling with your treatment of his guest."

"The Princeling dishonors us with his choice of guest," the snake-scale lady countered, so smoothly she must have been preparing for this confrontation for weeks.

I stared at the toast, waiting for the poison to jump off the butter and down my throat.

"Do you serve the Princeling and his Court?" The Gray Knight stopped in front of Kamare, the table between them.

As it had once before, a weapons belt appeared at her waist, slung low over one hip. Instead of a gun, she had her hand on the hilt of a long thin saber. Its pommel glinted like diamonds in the flickering lights of the room.

"Does the Princeling serve his people?" Kamare countered. "Will a factory serve us, who do not need mortal money and do not value gold? What can they give us, if we open the winding ways to our kingdom and let the humans in?"

"The Princeling has brought choices, Kamare. The opportunity to stand beneath the sun and the moon. That was his promise and it will be his gift. But not for you, I think," the Gray Knight said, drawing her sword.

I stood up, stumbling over the stool, and started toward her. "No, wait—" I said, sprinting past a table full of startled faeries.

She brought the sword up in a sharp slicing motion, and down—I hurled myself at her, catching her arm.

She stopped. Not because I was strong enough to hold her. That much was immediately obvious. She stopped because she wanted to.

I panted, my left hand clutching her right wrist, my body pressed to hers. I leaned up to look into her face; she stared over my head, at Kamare.

"The human spares your life, though you would not have spared hers," she declaimed, in the tones of a particularly dedicated town crier at a Renaissance faire.

Son of a bitch, I thought. She'd baited me into it. She wanted the other faeries to see me stand between her and one of them.

I glanced past her at the other people in the room. A few had their mouths open in shock. As I watched, one faerie with blue skin and gray eyes reached over and pushed on his companion's jaw.

"The human is weak," Kamare snarled. "And when my Queen takes your Court, she will wear a necklace of the human's teeth."

In the rush of the past few weeks, I'd nearly forgotten the Queen and the threat of potential invasion. This was *not* the way I'd wanted to be reminded of her.

I let go of the Gray Knight and whirled to look at the woman who'd tried to kill me. Her face was twisted with hate.

"Perhaps the human is stronger than you," the Gray Knight countered. "As our guest requests it, I will not kill you."

I sagged in relief. Murdering people who didn't like me seemed like a bad PR move.

"By the authority of the Princeling, Kamare, you are banned from the Court," the Gray Knight finished.

I waited for somebody to say something. No one did.

Seconds passed as we all stood there, Kamare behind the table, the Gray Knight and me in front of it. The two of them stared at each other.

"Fine," Kamare said, like they'd been having some kind of conversation. "But when my Queen brings her army upon your Princeling's Court, you will remember this day." She took off her apron, threw it onto the bowls of porridge on the table, and stormed out of the room.

The Gray Knight put her arm around my shoulders. "That was brave of you, to come between my sword and its target," she said loudly at the air above my head. I stood stiff beneath her, trying to ignore our audience.

"Could we be less dramatic next time?" I whispered.

She smiled a smile that said *Absolutely not* and steered me back to the breakfast table.

Lene, who'd apparently lost interest sometime during the confrontation, had finished her breakfast. "Sahir will be angry he missed this," she said, and sounded positively delighted at the thought.

I was also wondering why Sahir hadn't come running. Surely finding poison in my food and stepping in front of an actual weapon was more dangerous than almost being kissed by a lying human?

"Do you think the bond only activates when *I* think I'm in danger?" I asked, trying to understand. I looked at the toast again. Oh man. I wanted toast so badly.

Maybe someone would make me a new piece of toast.

"A knight's bond is shaped by his liege," the Gray Knight

said, watching me stare at my plate. "It is based on the liege's emotions. We cannot sense your environment, and we cannot tell threats real from imagined, nor fear from shock." She flicked her fingers and the toast disappeared from my tray. "Perhaps he will learn to manage his response."

"Poor Sahir," I muttered. "Can it be undone?"

She shook her head. "He did an unusual thing, Lady of the True Dreams, but a brave one. Now, I believe you have a meeting to attend."

I ate a few bites of the fruit bowl from Lene's plate—which lacked any spiky bits—and then stood up. "Coming with me?" I asked.

Lene frowned. "I scheduled a nap with a few friends on the river side of the Court," she said. "I can visit your chambers later, though."

I felt disappointed, almost afraid at the thought of working alone in my room.

"Your room is on the way to my office," the Gray Knight said. "I can walk you there."

We left the dining hall in silence, with a small crowd of other Fae. "I think you saved my life," I said, when we'd turned away from the group. "Or at least my morning. Thank you."

She inclined her head in acknowledgment. "I regret that there was a threat to you in our Court." The tip of her pointed ear poked up through her silver hair. It looked soft, so light it shouldn't have lain flat. But maybe faeries didn't get frizzy hair.

"There will always be threats," I said softly, not thinking about the Court.

She looked at me, a little furrow in her brow. "You are a bit odd, I believe. Though I have not met many humans," she said. "And neither has the Princeling."

"But don't the Courts trap us, for sport?" I wondered if that was why Milo's eyes sometimes looked like cracked shards of sky, if he'd been tortured once—he was definitely not being tortured now. We stopped in front of my door, two upright pillars in the long hallway. She stood closer than she needed to, her toes nearly touching mine.

"Our Court does not." She glanced down and touched my ring, almost absent-mindedly. Her fingertips skimmed along my knuckle. "Except for the Queen's Court, most have not, for a long time."

Thoughtlessly, I flipped my hand so our palms touched. "So humans aren't amusing anymore?" We looked together at the press of palm to palm, watched the dry brush of her fingers across my wrist as she pulled away.

I followed her hand as it slid up my arm, mesmerized by the warm walnut brown of her fingers against my waffle-knit Henley. Then she smiled and squeezed my shoulder. "You are still amusing. But our tastes have evolved."

I touched the bottom of my name, carved into the wood. "You knew you trapped me," I said. "You gave me the food."

She met my gaze, her silver eyes hard. "I knew."

I realized I didn't actually have another thought. I had expected her to apologize. But of course she wouldn't; it had been a direct order from her lord.

We looked at each other for another minute, and then she nodded and walked away.

My next human class was scheduled for that night. I picked Lene up on my way down the hall to the cafeteria. The route had become so familiar it was automatic.

When I pushed the doors open, I stopped in shock. The room was completely full. Crammed to the point where people stood along the walls.

My usual seat at the head of the center table was occupied by the Princeling. Behind him stood the Gray Knight, who jerked her head toward the front of the room—the serving area where she'd stood with Kamare that morning.

The Gray Knight was a budding dramaturg.

Lene split off from me to stand next to Gaheris. Sahir stood up when I walked past him, and stalked three steps behind me on my left flank.

At some point, I'd need to tell him I was left-handed so he could bodyguard on my right side instead.

Sahir and I turned at the front of the room.

"Hi, everyone," I said. "How are you all doing?"

After a moment of confused glances, a new student spoke up.

"Do you mean, *what* are we doing?" she asked. "We are attending your class."

"Um, no," I said. "And please raise your hand before asking a question here. As for your question..." I glanced at Kellen. "Kellen, what do I mean when I ask how someone is doing?"

"It's a greeting!" Kellen exclaimed. Kellen was a fantastic

student. "Humans use it as part of a formulaic exchange when-ever they meet."

He turned to Caraya, who joined him with increasingly feigned reluctance every class. "Caraya, how are you doing?" he asked, tilting his head.

"Thank you for asking, Kellen," she replied, affecting a British accent. "I am well. And how are you, Kellen?"

The British accent was my only guilty pleasure.

"It is well that you are well," Kellen concluded. Since they were mimicking me mimicking a posh London accent, he sounded like he had a mouth full of cotton. "I, too, am well."

Kellen stopped and looked out at his bewildered audience. "After this exchange, you may discuss whatever you please," he said in his normal voice. "However, humans will not be receptive to your communications if you do not begin in this way."

Someone else raised a hand—a very tall woman wearing a dress made out of cobwebs: gossamer-thin and so gray it seemed to suck the light from her corner of the room.

"Please say your name when I point to you, and then ask your question," I said, pointing to her.

"My name is Triathe," she said. "What does this exchange mean, though?"

"Nothing!" Caraya said, exasperated. "Nothing the humans say means anything."

"Well, no, it's kind of like...an opportunity to let them tell you if something is wrong, before you start asking them questions."

"But you said we have to say we are well," Kellen interjected.

"And if we cannot say that, we must say good, and if we cannot say good, because it is a lie, we must smile and nod noncommittally."

"The humans do not want to know if you are not well," Sahir added.

Several faeries nodded, as though that were expected.

"We do!" I said, feeling defensive. "Just not right away. We like to ease into it."

This declaration set off a fierce storm of muttering.

"Why are all of you here today?" I asked. "It's more crowded than usual."

Caraya raised her hand and then spoke without waiting for me to call on her.

It had been such a battle to explain hand raising that I wasn't inclined to belabor the point further.

"They want to know why you stopped the Gray Knight from killing Karame," she said. A few feet away from her, the Gray Knight looked smug. She was probably just pleased that her performance this morning had made my life so much more difficult.

Seated next to her, the Princeling also looked smug, though he was doing a much better job maintaining a solemn expression.

Explaining humans to the satisfaction of seven querents had been painful enough. Another eighty were unlikely to simplify my task. I needed to talk to the Princeling; it had been a month. If he expected my class size to keep growing, he had to show me some sort of proof that he could help me find a way out of Faerie. As it was, the four hours I spent a week on this were already eating into my sleep. And, because he'd been unable to find any errors in my recent decks, Jeff had sent me several increasingly rude emails about my inability to create compelling PowerPoint footers.

I glanced at Sahir, who shrugged. He stood with his hands clasped in front of him, face expressionless. He still wore his suit from the workday.

"I . . . didn't want someone to die because of me?" I said, but it was a question and not a statement.

Someone else called out from the side of the room: "Death was fair return for the attempt on your life," they said, hummingbird wings trembling behind them. "Kamare expected to die."

"Rhesus did not raise his hand!" Caraya exclaimed, flinging her own hand up a second time.

"Ah, yeah, Rhesus, again, we try to raise our hands when we speak," I said, scratching the back of my neck. "But thank you for your contribution to our conversation. I didn't know that death was the fair return for the attempt on my life . . ."

Everyone was silent.

"So, yeah, thanks for . . . enlightening me," I finished, dropping my hand and then violently twisting my ring around my finger.

"Perhaps death was not her expectation," Rhesus's pearlescent neighbor argued, thrusting their own hand skyward. "Kamare was not truly of the Princeling's Court."

"Kamare was born in the Princeling's Court!" a third person said from across the room, both many-fingered hands in the air like an emphatic sea anemone.

"Her fealty shifted!" Rhesus said, flinging his second hand up and then hovering a few inches off the ground.

"How could her fealty have shifted?" I asked.

"Is this human class or faerie class?" the Gray Knight interjected, her silver eyes flashing. She hadn't raised her hand, but none of the other faeries pointed this out.

Anger bubbled in the yards of negative space between us. I clenched and unclenched my fist, flexed my fingers to shake out the phantom feeling of her hand on my palm that morning. Instead, I tried to concentrate on the Princeling's mask of a face, staring at me implacably from that damned silver throne.

He quirked his brow at me, startling me out of my reverie.

"Sorry, right. Well, the reason I didn't want her to die is…" I trailed off. "Her feelings were valid?" I tried.

This set off a storm of raised hands and raised voices. I couldn't understand any of them, so I looked back at Sahir.

"The general tenor of the commentary is confusion," he explained.

"Look, Kamare is right that humans could fundamentally alter your way of life," I said.

The expression on the Princeling's face could've pulverized stone. But I wasn't stone. I was a human, and squishy, and really fucking annoyed right now.

"Faeries prize honesty, right?" I said. "Faeries must be honest."

"We prize deception," Kellen called out, waving his left hand like a stoner at a concert. "We prize lying through truth."

I turned and thumped my forehead against the wall next to Sahir.

"Why is she doing that?" someone asked—I obviously didn't see who.

"I'm expressing frustration," I said to the wall.

"What if I don't have hands?" someone else called out. "How can I raise my hand and speak?"

"If you can put an appendage upward, please do," I told the dirt in front of my face. "And if you can't, you may just call out."

This emboldened all of them. I shut my eyes tight as a swarm of voices rose up.

"Do all humans express frustration by hitting the wall with their faces?"

"It must be a way of connecting to the earth and recentering themselves."

"I do not understand."

Sahir cleared his throat, and everyone quieted. "The lady will explain why she spared Kamare, if you let her speak."

He touched my shoulder, spun me gently around. He left his hand on my elbow, providing small support.

I opened my eyes to a sea of faces staring at me.

"I didn't want Kamare to die for trying to protect you," I said. "She believed she saw a real threat to her people and tried to eliminate it. I won't hurt you, but I can't promise *no* human will hurt you. Humans are like you—we aren't all one thing. To me, Kamare did what she thought she needed to do." I paused, and then realized perhaps I should expound further. "And if you're worried about me altering your way of life, you can talk to me about it, and we can resolve it peacefully. Without killing, maiming, or incapacitating me. But I understand her motive."

The Princeling stood up, giving me an hour and forty-five minutes of my night back. "That is all the time we have today for human lessons," he said. "If you have more questions for the Lady of the True Dreams, you may come back three days hence for another lesson."

Masterful. The faeries filed out reluctantly, and I suspected I would see many of them at my next class.

Chapter 11

In Which I Learn Applicable Construction Techniques

My dreams were full of blinding blue magic, sheets that rained from the sky and settled in the dust like fitted carpets. They left me groggy and bewildered, dazed so that my eyes hurt before I even opened them.

I logged into the morning meeting three minutes late to the middle of an argument between Jeff and Levi.

"If we keep giving away free work, no one will hire us for anything," Levi said.

"If we don't give away free work, we'll never meet any potential clients anyway, Levi," Jeff said. "We don't have a strong enough reputation. And if this faerie deal falls through, we are fucked like a bowl of mashed potatoes. Speaking of, thanks for showing up, Miri." He added the last bit having seen my name pop up onscreen, I supposed.

"Hi, Jeff," I said. I went on mute.

"Jeff, we need to start going after smaller clients," Levi said. I stared at Corey's and Matt's initials on the screen. "That's the only way for us to build credibility."

"We need prestige. We need more big names."

"We keep losing to other banks on the big names!" Levi snapped. I wondered if he was in the office today or at home; if other people on the floor could hear him as he shouted into the phone. "We don't need more big names. We need *any* names."

I wondered if my job was at risk. The thought had a laugh bubbling up in my throat, a hysterical keening giggle. Was I really going to lose the Princeling's bargain because of my manager's incompetence?

And the other thought, always underneath, begging me to examine it—was being trapped in Faerie the worst thing in the world?

Yes, I reminded myself. *I miss my friends. I miss my family. I miss paying a quarter of my salary for a gym membership I never use.*

I shoved that back down and refocused on Jeff and Levi.

"If you have these relationships, Jeff, start using them!" Levi said. I held my breath. People didn't talk to our boss like that, generally.

"If you think you can find a better job elsewhere, Levi, you're *welcome* to leave," Jeff said. "People leave. You need to do what's best for you. I personally couldn't care less."

No one spoke. I wanted so badly to be in the office, to be

able to look over and see Levi's face, or Corey's reaction. I stared at the screen, mostly black, except for the bubbles where their initials indicated their presence on the line. And surprisingly, there was a bubble on the screen I hadn't seen before.

"Thank you for that feedback," Levi said. "In other HR news, everyone, say hi to Kayla. She's an internal transfer, provisionally on our team so, you know, test her out. Give her a go. Hop on that ride." He chuckled. "We can always get rid of her."

"Are there any client issues to discuss?" Jeff asked, having not said hi to Kayla. "Miri, you're on the ground. What's going on with the client?"

I pondered for a moment.

"Seems pretty quiet here," I said.

"I'm sending you to the client site today," he said while I was talking.

I'm on client site, I thought.

"The Princeling will take you to the factory construction site so you can look around. That way, when our investors go, we can give them a sense of what to expect."

"Oh, okay." I hoped he heard bland indifference in my voice, and not immense irritation at the fact that he felt he could move me around like a pawn on a chessboard.

"So, bye," Jeff said. Was he hanging up, or just telling me to get off the line? I stared at the screen, my hand on the mouse.

"Miri, you can hang up," Jeff added. "We have some other stuff to talk about."

I exited the meeting, feeling anxious.

The Gray Knight opened the bedroom door behind me, like she'd been listening in. Which she probably was.

I stood up and turned toward the door. "So everyone except me knew that I would be going to the construction site today," I said flatly. Doctor Kitten hopped onto the desk and pawed at my hand, as if to say *Chill out, homie.*

"I do not control what Jeff shares with you," the Gray Knight said, shuffling the papers in her hands.

"You control what *you* share with me."

She looked up at this. It was hard to read the sharp angles of her expression, but she seemed almost surprised.

"Indeed," she said. "Well, I will share that these are papers. They will help our Builder design our factory." She flapped the papers about. Then she made a weird twisting gesture and they disappeared. She looked me up and down, appraising. Her eyes lingered on my bare throat. "And I will share that you may wish to ask the Princeling about Roman today, Lady of the True Dreams."

I frowned. Was this a trap or a hint? Who, or what, was Roman?

"We should get you some new clothes," she added, before I could ask for clarification. Now she was staring somewhere around my navel, with a slight curve to her lips that I would've called a leer on a human. On the Gray Knight, it was probably disdain.

"Oh, I'm good," I said, choosing with immense dignity not to eye her up in return.

She raised an eyebrow. "Your goodness has nothing to do with your clothing," she said, and brought her two hands together in a motion like twisting a cap off a jar. I felt a slithering sensation along my skin—it drew in from my wrists and ankles, an uncomfortable tingle on the sensitive underside of my arms. The sensation continued inexorably upward, a brief vise grip at my elbow, a pressure on the wing of my collarbone. Behind it came a soothing softness. When I looked down, my old clothes were on the floor in a heap and I wore a tunic and leggings like hers, only green instead of gray.

"I like green," she opined.

"'I'm good' is a human way of saying 'no thank you,'" I said. "Just, you know, for future reference."

She inclined her head but didn't answer.

With a sigh, I patted Doctor Kitten on the head, checked his food and water, and followed her out of the room. "Does Roman have anything to do with my leaving Faerie?" I asked.

"Yes," she said. She turned left down the hallway, which meant we were going out toward the river. I hadn't been that way yet.

"Why didn't you lead with that?" I burst out, exasperated.

"A person must divine some truths for themself."

I glared at her, but if she noticed, she didn't say anything. We passed the turnoff to the cafeteria and continued along the hallway. It remained identical to the hallway outside my room, except for the names burned onto the doors. *Elsie the Eviscerator, Tomlischai, Emeris the Expunger, Ophelia the Organized,* and so on. Was it better to be expunged or eviscerated? Probably expunged.

A few Fae passed us in the hallway. I recognized one or two of the faces from the big class the other night. I waved to them, and they raised their eyebrows at me in return.

Did she mean *Romans*? Like, ancient Romans? Or modern Romans? Was there a Roman road out of Faerie that would pop me out in Italy?

When we left the Court, the sunless blue sky greeted us. We stood at the top of a hill, and below us a wide, slow blue river wended its way off into the horizon. On the other side of the river were low gray cliffs, topped with tangles of trees.

The Princeling, the Crone, and the knights Red and Blue sat on four horses by the entrance. Two more waited: Sparkles, and the Gray Knight's silver horse.

"Does it rain here?" I asked.

"Sometimes," the Gray Knight said. "When it needs to." She hoisted me onto Sparkles, her thumbs fitted into the dent of flesh at my waist. The saddle appeared underneath me as I settled onto Sparkles's back.

I looked over at the other two knights. I hadn't ever paid much attention to them. They sat astride matching yellow horses and didn't look at me.

"Let us depart," the Princeling said, and in unison, the horses started down the path.

———————————•———————————

We didn't speak on the way down the hill. When the ground steadied out beneath us, we turned to the right—I would've called it north, if we were still in New York and this was the Hudson. But the topology was slightly different here, and the air full of magic. Who knew where we actually were, or what cardinal direction we faced?

The Princeling fell back, letting the Red Knight take the lead, and waited until I'd ridden up next to him.

"Good morning," he said, only the barest hint of mockery in his tone. "How are you? Did you sleep well? Did you have interesting dreams?"

I absorbed this for a half second. "I dreamed about blue magic," I said, unable to keep the irritation from my voice. "But, my lord, what do you know about Romans?" I asked.

"Roman's what?" He seemed a bit befuddled.

"The Gray Knight told me to ask you about Romans." I glanced back at her. Maybe it was a prank. Did pranks count as lying in Faerie?

"My lady, I do not know much of Roman. I can tell you only that his father helped construct the First Ways into our realm, and that he knows more of our tunnels and pathways than any other. If you fulfill the terms of our bargain, I shall commission him to hunt a safe path back to the mortal realm for you, if such a thing can be found."

I facepalmed myself so hard that my ring made a dull *thwack* against my forehead.

"Roman is a *dude*?" But the Princeling's gaze had caught on my hand.

"Where did you get that ring?" the Princeling asked, leaning toward me with the most intensity I'd ever seen in his eyes.

"What?" I glanced down at my ring. Dull, boring, gold. "My mom gave it to me. Her mom gave it to her. It's a family heirloom."

"May I," he said, holding out his hand.

Clearly, he may.

I twisted the ring off my finger and dropped it into his palm. He closed his fingers around the ring, and sparks of green danced off his nails. I stared, mesmerized, until Sparkles took a particularly uneven step and I almost fell off my horse.

"What's wrong with my ring?" I asked, uncomfortable. My finger felt too light without it.

When he looked back at me, the expression in his eyes had changed.

"Nothing," he said, opening his palm and proffering it to me.

"What did you do?"

He frowned, considering. "I want to be honest with you, Lady of the True Dreams," he said. "To give you a favor freely, in deference to the freedoms I have taken from you."

"A favor would be a great start," I said, taking the ring from him and sliding it back onto my hand.

"It's an old ring, of value beyond your ken. The enchantment upon it could not have been wrought without true moonlight. It is likely older than our realm, and very precious. If it has adorned the fingers of your mother and grandmother, then you are not the first friend of the Fae in your family."

There was something so odd about the way he said *friend*. I opened my mouth, but he steamrolled over me.

"When will we release the presentation to the buyers, lady?" the Princeling asked. I looked at him, easy and tall in his saddle.

We should have released it two weeks before, and the Princeling knew it. I spun the ring around with my thumb as I spoke.

"Jeff and Levi think next week," I said. "We're just waiting on a few more potential investors to sign nondisclosure
agreements."

"Do you think this is the best strategy?"

This was the most transparent attempt to distract me since
I was six and my mom baked me cookies before I got my ton-
sils out.

"Oh, well, Jeff and Levi have done this a lot more than
me," I said.

"That is not what I asked, as you well know." The Princeling didn't sound annoyed, though. More amused. I looked at
him. He had such a clear face—no blemishes or wrinklage of
any kind. Our knees brushed, and I glanced down.

"You dissemble quite well." I heard the smirk in his voice.

"No, I don't," I blurted.

He shifted in his saddle to face me. The horse didn't seem
to notice or care. "Do you know what *dissemble* means, lady?"

"Yes," I muttered. "I don't need a vocabulary lesson. My
lord," I added.

He laughed, a surprised sound that echoed against the hills
that seemed to follow us, rolling along to our right. "I have
always found your tongue sharp," he said. "I have been keen
to feel its bite."

I blushed. I knew his eyes caught it, could feel them on
my cheeks. I wondered what he saw, with his keen eyes. My
pores, my blackheads?

Did faeries have better eyesight than humans? I'd just
assumed...

"Why do you really want to open this factory?" I asked.

"Seems like it isn't popular among your people. And even if you manage it, I'm not sure how it's going to help in your… culture war with the Queen."

He laughed again. "Very true, lady." He looked forward at the Blue and Red Knights and the Crone. Then back, where the Gray Knight had given us a respectful bit of room.

"My people are divided," he said. "Some long for the human world, where our ancestors roamed, and for the sun, which many have never seen."

I felt a brief unwelcome wash of understanding for this man, who was only doing what he thought would help his people.

He glanced down at my ring again. "And for the magics that we have almost lost," he added, though he sounded reluctant.

"I thought Faerie was your home?"

"Faerie is where we live." He ran a finger along his lip, thoughtful. "In some ways, we are trapped here, like you."

Probably not like me.

"Why? You can leave Faerie whenever you want, right?" I asked. I leaned forward to pat Sparkles on the neck, because she was doing a good job and because I wanted to touch something warm and solid.

He sighed. "Faeries have weaknesses, which make us more susceptible to human cruelty than the other supernatural creatures you know of."

I frowned. "Faeries have been cruel to humans," I started.

"Yes, yes." He cut me off, waving his hand in a vague gesture. "We cannot tally each individual hurt, or go back seventeen centuries to see who struck the first blow. Suffice it to say, we have made ourselves a prison that is a home, but some of my people want to dance under the sun and moon. And so, as their Princeling, I must help them do it safely."

He looked into my eyes, as if trying to gauge my understanding. I stared back, lost in the dappled greens of his.

"So, to do it safely, you need to start a company?" I asked. He'd lost me.

He laughed again, though I wasn't sure what was funny. "To do it safely, I need to integrate us in a cautious, specific way. In a way that protects my people and our secrets. In a way that makes us more valuable to humans alive than dead."

We looked at each other.

"No, Lady of the True Dreams," he said. "I am not afraid that you will betray me."

"Can you read my mind?" I asked.

Another laugh. Was he always this easily amused? "No, but I can read your face."

"You're spying on me a lot, for a guy who thinks I won't betray him," I retorted, indignant, and straightened my shoulders.

"Why did you take this job?" he asked, still staring at me. I felt very grateful that Sparkles had a good sense of direction.

Money was the correct answer, the answer Jeff expected me to give.

"To make a difference," I blurted.

The Princeling raised an eyebrow.

"Um, whenever there's someone different, people can be afraid," I said. "I used to work in the human government, trying to make sure there weren't any discriminatory regulations passed against supernatural people. But regulation is cautious, and slow. And I thought that maybe the fastest way to get past the prejudice would be to integrate you into our economy. So that's why."

"And that is why I do not think you will betray us," he said, inclining his head.

I stared down at the stony path beneath us.

"I do feel sorrow," he said, so softly I almost didn't hear him over the clack of hooves on the ground. "I cannot regret your...relocation. But I apologize for the inconvenience."

Bone shards and blood mist.

"Why did you do it?" I asked, still not looking at him.

"Whenever there is someone different, people can be afraid," he said. "That is not true only for humans. Familiarity reduces fear."

I stared over his shoulder, flushing and confused. But I couldn't keep my eyes on the wending river for long.

"What's wrong with Milo? He's a human."

He said nothing.

"Are there other humans here?" I chided. "Why couldn't you use him or one of your other human pets to get faeries more comfortable with my kind?"

The Princeling tilted his head consideringly. "We take in madmen and wanderers, for madness is a specialty of the Fae."

"So you wanted a *sane* specimen?" I snapped. "You chose wrong there, buddy."

"For some, Faerie is a refuge." He frowned. "I understand that it may not feel that way for you."

I turned away fully, so he wouldn't see the frustrated tears in my eyes. He seemed to take the hint; he urged his horse forward, leaving me to Sparkles's sedate clomp.

Another half hour passed in silence, the rolling green hills and sparkling water bookending the perfect tableau of the idyllic road stretching on into the distance.

In front of me, the Princeling, the Red Knight, the Blue Knight, and the Crone stopped like four pigeons in a synchronous flying competition hitting the same glass wall.

"We have arrived," the Princeling called back, though the landscape wasn't discernibly different in any way. As Sparkles stopped, he slid off his own horse. I looked around for the Gray Knight. She was still behind us.

The Princeling came to stand next to Sparkles and held his arms out. I slid my leg over the horse and he caught me as I dropped down. He put me on the grass next to him.

The Red Knight strode up beside us. "Have you been to many factory construction sites?" he asked, startling me. I didn't think we'd spoken before.

"This will be my first," I said, and then wondered if I should have lied.

He examined me for a moment, a hard set to his rugged jaw. "It would not matter if you had," he said finally. "No human building can rival the construction of the Fae."

"I'm sure," I replied, meaning it.

"Though I would rather not give the humans an opportunity to compare," he added lowly, the tendons in his throat in bas-relief. I blinked at him, startled. I knew the Blue and Red Knights *had* opinions; they'd just never yet deigned to share them with me.

The Gray Knight joined us. "I shall alert the Builder to our presence." She stalked off toward the side of the nearest hill.

I checked my cell phone. There was no service.

The Gray Knight knocked on a piece of empty air. A hollow reverberation sounded.

"What?" someone snapped, and then the air opened, revealing an irritable-looking man with curling ram's horns and a patchy red flush across his cheeks, holding a small hammer in one hand. I could see his other hand, *curling* around the edge of the sky.

Behind him was…more air. It looked the same as the other air. I blinked, which changed nothing about the landscape.

"The Princeling has come to assess your progress," the Gray Knight said. "Will you allow us to pass?"

The faerie grunted acquiescence and stood back, pulling the air doorway open enough for us to pass through. The Gray Knight led the way, and the five of us followed her.

We just left the horses outside, which was bold. But no one seemed to be around this area anyway.

On the other side of the doorway was something that looked much more like a construction site, though a very odd one.

Nearest to us stood a small cottage with a thatched roof, like one you might see in a fairy-tale storybook, with a stone chimney and flowers in the window boxes. Outside the cottage, an old woman sat at a loom, weaving fine gray thread into long panels. *Cobweb curtains*, I realized with a start. Beside her sat a workbench, recently vacated, and several acorns.

Behind the cottage sprawled the imprint of a giant building, carved from the dirt. There were no trucks or diggers, and no other people.

"How—" I started.

"Magic," the Gray Knight said, anticipating my question. She pulled her documents from thin air and handed them to the Builder, who grunted in acknowledgment.

"Builder, this is the Lady of the True Dreams," the Princeling said.

"Lady." The Builder inclined his head with more respect than I merited. I wondered then if the Princeling had given me the title as protection, as a way to elevate me in the Court so that I could be seen with him.

"Will you show us your progress, Builder?" the Princeling asked. But he stood at a respectful distance, his hands clasped before him demurely, as though he would turn around and go back to the Court if the Builder said no.

The Builder looked at me. I smiled at him, hoping I looked friendly and not pained. There was something incredibly jarring about his furred hind legs, which were hidden at the upper thigh by the bottom of a flannel tunic.

"Yes," he said. He jerked his head, and we followed him past the cottage. I waved at the old woman at the loom, who stared back at me like I had three heads.

Or maybe like I only had one head but she was used to people having three.

"Where are the workers?" I asked. "Aren't construction sites of this size supposed to have around a hundred people, usually?"

"Magic," the Gray Knight said again, her hand flexing at her side. Her silver belt had reappeared, sporting a crossbow. I took a half step closer to her; the belt only materialized when she was feeling threatened. Though I wasn't sure about the weapon—based on my extensive reading experience, I *personally* wouldn't have used a crossbow for close-range combat.

"Oh, okay," I said. I gathered that "magic" was going to be the answer to a lot of my questions.

The Builder stopped at the near corner of the site, where two deep trenches met. "We plan to add a moat," he said.

The Red Knight glared at the Blue Knight. The Princeling looked from one to the other, and then at the Builder.

"A moat." He brought a hand to his jaw. "Interesting."

"If this is our first chance to show humans our workmanship, we want to display waterwork as well," the Blue Knight explained. "We should show them the full capabilities of the Fae."

The Princeling nodded. "Proceed."

The Red Knight, who had the Crone on his arm, flushed but didn't speak. Instead, he shot a glance at me, as though expecting commiseration. Two wolves warred inside me: One wanted camaraderie with anyone willing to give it, and the other wanted to be in constant agreement with the Princeling, who scared me. A lot.

In the end, I smiled at the Red Knight with all the conviction of a flavored sparkling water. He seemed satisfied enough, though, and actually *smiled back* in my direction.

We followed the Builder along the perimeter. I couldn't really understand some of what he talked about—magical reinforcement spells for the foundations and the casting technique for adaptive climate control spells.

"You kind of just pile materials up and hold it together with magic?" I asked the Gray Knight, whose fingers were twitching toward the handle of the crossbow at her hip. Did she look *nervous*?

She made an exasperated noise. "How else would one construct a building?"

"Well, humans don't have magic," I said mildly. "So we use complicated mathematical principles and innovation. I can't do it, but it's really quite clever."

"That sounds tedious," the Builder said. He raised his hands above his head. The Red Knight let go of the Crone and stepped in front of the Princeling.

The Builder cackled, a sound like a dryer full of pennies, and turned to face the construction site. "Cower, then," he said, and brought both arms down in a slicing gesture that gathered the sky between his palms and flung the entire atmosphere forward before him, an unfurling carpet. He followed the motion like a man in prayer, onto his knees, until he lay prostrate on the ground and streams of blue light shot down across his back, along the tops of his horns, and into the dirt before us.

I fell to my knees, too, gasping as the sheets of blue light fitted themselves into the dirt imprint and solidified, until they looked like gray concrete foundations in the earth.

The Builder sat up on his heels and looked at me over his shoulder.

"That is magic, lady," he said, panting.

"Thank you," I whispered, my eyes damp.

The Gray Knight took my shoulder and lifted me. "Stop fussing," she said, but she didn't sound angry.

"Will the humans all react like her?" the Builder asked, getting to his own feet and looking at the Princeling.

"You know our magic is stronger than that of any other species." The Princeling glanced at me.

"And our weaknesses proportionate," the Builder muttered. But he inclined his head to me. "Your joy has given me joy, lady. Thank you."

The Princeling sighed. "I imagine it will be a few days before you can continue construction."

The Builder rubbed his upper arm. "I intended to build the foundation over several days. This did not alter my schedule."

"The Blue Knight will come back three days hence," the Princeling said. I caught the look the Red Knight gave him and promptly filed it in the part of my brain labeled *Somebody Else's Problem*.

As we left the site and the Builder closed the door in the air, I kept seeing the sky come down across his back and lay itself in the dirt for him.

Chapter 12

In Which I Receive a History Lesson from the Gray Knight

The Gray Knight put me back on my horse, and the rest of the retinue rode ahead, much faster than us. "They have other councils to attend," she explained.

The sky flushed pink and gold, night setting in.

Our horses slowed further, and we rode next to each other at an easy pace, our knees bumping every few strides. I couldn't look at her, embarrassed by the closeness but unsure how to move away.

"Would you like to stop here, with me?" the Gray Knight asked. She sounded more unsure than I'd ever heard her. I glanced at her, but she had her eyes fixed on the road ahead of us. "There is something I would show you."

Her tongue darted out to wet her lips.

My stomach rumbled. If I said no, she would take me back to the Court. And I was hungry. But...

"Sure, I will stop with you," I said carefully. "And see what you want to show me."

She leaned forward and said something to her horse, who stopped and turned off the path. Sparkles followed.

We rode for several minutes, the way grassy and easy for the horses to traverse. The sky had deepened into a velvet blue and stars twinkled overhead, swirling into new patterns like our own personal pictographs. I'd grown used to Sparkles's even gait, and it was becoming natural to shift with her as we moved. Thick-trunked trees dotted the area, branches swaying in a breeze that felt exactly calibrated to cool my temples without mussing my hair.

The horses stopped on the riverbank, where a cascade of smooth stones in descending size order sloped at a perfect angle into the clear shallows. The Gray Knight dismounted, then lifted me off the horse as usual. This time she lingered, holding me against her, her hands around my waist and my toes barely touching the ground. I put my hands on her shoulders. Our eyes met, hers silver and implacable in the night.

When she let me go, I stepped away, startled and flustered. I stared down at the rocks, searching for something to say. "Is everything in Faerie so...perfect?" I asked. "So beautiful and well-made?"

She shrugged. "It is all designed," she said. "So of course it is designed well."

I tried to think of this riverbank like that: a cage designed to keep danger out. But it was so difficult, with the streams of starlight in the sky and the birds in the trees.

"You said you wanted to show me something."

She pulled a basket from the air in front of her and set it on the ground.

I watched, too surprised to help, as she laid out a blanket on the largest stones at the edge of the grass and knelt, taking perfect plates of sliced hard cheeses and jam and bread and setting them on the ground.

After a moment, I knelt, too, and held out my hands. She glanced up and smiled. It hit me with the force of a swift fall, the moment where your stomach braces for impact before you've even hit the ground.

But she didn't appear to notice the way I knelt, laid bare by confused longing. "You are always offering aid," she said. "I desire only your company."

Swift inhale. Slower exhale. I pulled my last remaining thread of composure up my spine.

Then, affecting a level of chill I'd never once in my life actually experienced, I sat back, hands on my knees. "Well, thank you," I said. "I was getting hungry."

At this, she laughed. "You are often hungry, Lady of the True Dreams."

I couldn't help it; I smiled back at her. "That may be true, though faeries seem to eat as often as humans."

She handed me a glass and a bottle of something sparkling.

"Champagne?" I asked.

"I do not know what that means." She grasped the hem of her shirt. My breath caught. She rose up on her knees, moving like a cresting wave, and pulled her shirt over her head, revealing a thin white camisole. Her hair caught and then fell around her shoulders in a glittery spill.

"The drink," I said, my voice hoarse. "What is it?"

She saw me staring. "It's faerie-made cider."

I poured generously and handed her the first glass, reaching into the basket for the second. She took it, then stopped and pointed a finger upward. "Before I forget," she said, and rotated her hand clockwise, so quickly it blurred. Something spun out from her fingertip and shot upward, then cascaded down around us like a fountain of silver. "I do not think the Princeling would listen in on me," she explained. "But there is no reason to tempt the Crone."

"Can they just listen to anything that happens in Faerie?" I asked, pouring myself a glass of cider and trying to make a politely bored face, instead of a desperately curious face.

She shook her head. "It is much broader than that; they can listen anywhere unprotected." She read my expression. "Your bedroom is protected, lady. They grant our people that dignity. But I will share no more."

"Of course," I said. I put the bottle of cider down in front of us, next to a loaf of bread. "I don't want to put you in an uncomfortable position."

"I am in an uncomfortable position now," she said, and slid backward off her knees. She crossed her legs. She'd come closer to me in the process, her knee almost touching mine. I sank back, too, shifting my weight onto my thigh. That brought us closer still, two leggings-clad legs suspended in the minute space between us.

"Would you like something to eat?" she asked, setting her glass down.

"Yes," I said, watching the line of her throat as she leaned forward to pick up the plate of cheese.

"Sometimes I dispense with the bread entirely," she said, in a low voice like she was confiding some grave secret.

I giggled at the absurdity of it all. Her answering smile was brighter than all the stars above, brighter than the silver shield that fell like rain around us. "Me, too," I whispered.

She picked up one of the jams and dipped a piece of cheese into it, her eyes on mine. They sparkled, reflecting and refracting the silvers in the sky. She held the cheese up, and my lips parted automatically.

Slowly, she brought the cheese to my mouth, and I took a bite, staring at her. I barely tasted it—just a jolt of something sweet, and a note of something sharp. She brought the rest of the slice to her own mouth and bit into it. I watched her lips part, the flash of her teeth. I felt myself leaning forward without conscious intent.

"Try the cider," she said, picking up her own glass.

My heart was racing. Could she hear it?

I took my glass, and we tapped them together. "To a successful capital raise," she said.

"Agreed," I said, stomach dropping. She was my *client*. What was I doing?

I shifted away from her, into a cross-legged position. I felt her eyes on me and resisted the urge to pull at the waistband of my leggings, worried I had sat in an unflattering way. I brushed my hair back instead.

Maybe she caught the thought behind the movement; maybe she had brought me here for a purpose and intended to see it through. She reached for my free hand. "Do they tell you that you are beautiful, in New York?" she asked, her warm fingers tracing my knuckles. Every touch made me tense, like a ballerina in a wind-up box, waiting to spin free.

"I'm not," I said, out of habit.

She pulled away and took another sip of cider. I watched her lips on the rim of the glass. "We disagree, lady."

I copied her. The cider fizzed on my tongue, bubbled down my throat. "*You* are beautiful," I said, unable to stop myself. "Like moonlight. I go on my fire escape some nights and look at the moon, and it makes me long for something I can't describe. That's what you're like."

She rose to her knees again and set her glass down. "I do not think you are very common, are you, Miriam?" The silvery light caught in the hollows of her bare shoulders, the divot of her collarbone at the base of her throat.

I opened my mouth, but she cut me off. "It is no matter. You are rare to me."

She took another piece of cheese off the plate and settled herself once more, this time so close to me our shoulders touched, and her thigh rested under mine.

I took a smaller bite, and so did she. The tang of it stayed on my tongue. When she brought the cheese back to my lips, she smiled and pushed it into my mouth, her finger resting against my lower lip. "We have shared food," she said. "It is almost as if we had kissed."

I could feel the muddle of my own thoughts, the strain as

muscle fought mind. I wanted so badly to lean in to her, to press my lips to hers, to flatten our bodies together. Even just to tilt my head to her neck and breathe her in.

You know nothing about this woman.

I swallowed, hard. "You wanted to show me something, my lady."

"Ah. Yes." She stood gracefully and held out a hand to help me up. I took it, and she pulled me upright with ease. I watched the muscles in her arm flex.

We walked toward the edge of the water, the silvery dome keeping pace with us, and stopped at the edge, standing together on the smallest pebbles. "Take off your shoes," she said, kicking off her own. I toed out of my boots, then socks, following her lead. I dropped my cell phone into a shoe.

She stepped into the water, and I followed. It was cool but not unpleasant around my toes. She took another step. So did I. And another.

As much as I wanted to go along with this, unburdened by questions or concerns, a part of my mind wondered about the plan. Were we about to wade in up to our chests, ruining our clothes, and then splash around until we got hypothermia?

I stumbled.

She glanced at me and took my hand in hers. We waded in to our calves. Our thighs. Our hips, mine submerged before hers.

Some part of my brain screamed at me, *Stop, stop, are you insane?* But the water was lit all around with the glow of her silvery magic, and when she looked at me, I nodded. We took one more step together, off a ledge and into the depths. I closed my eyes as we sank.

My hair floated in fine strands around my head. I opened my eyes and looked around. We were submerged a foot or two below the water, her magic around us in a bubble: It stopped a yard or two below our feet. I kicked up, for the surface, but she caught at my hand.

"Breathe," she said, her voice burbling but comprehensible.

I stared at her. I could feel my heart pounding. I had known it was coming. But I couldn't—

I shook my head, my lungs burning.

She pulled me to the surface; our heads broke and I gasped for air. Her hair was plastered to her long cheekbones.

"You can breathe underwater so long as I hold you," she said. It couldn't be a lie, but I still had a very hard time believing it.

"So come with me." She tugged on my hand and I took another deep breath.

We submerged again, down and down this time. The water in our bubble remained clear, lit through by the silver of her magic. Everything outside was blurred, like a darkened street viewed through a window in the rain.

I tried to inhale but couldn't make myself. She must have seen something in my face—she directed a stream of bubbles toward me with a finger, and they formed an air pocket around my nose and mouth. I inhaled gratefully.

Our feet hit the sandy bottom. I looked down, not sure what to expect. There was a mosaic beneath our feet, partially obscured by the sand of the riverbed. Every tile glittered— I couldn't tell if it was constructed from precious stones, or just polished glass reflecting the ever-changing miasma of our light.

The mosaic shimmered far beyond the light of our bubble, little glints of light reflecting back through the shield of
magic. I tilted a little, until I floated face down above it. There
were clearly figures—faeries—being chased away by . . . other
figures?

"What is this?" I asked, not sure if she would hear me.

"They created the river much later," she said. "This used to
be an entrance to Faerie." I strained to understand her through
the mild distortion of the water.

She pulled me to one edge of the mosaic. It must have been
a road once. We floated together beneath a high rounded arch,
staring down at our feet. The keystone of the arch was beyond
the edges of our bubble, and columns loomed over us, bend-
ing toward each other and then disappearing into the rippling
silver of her magic.

"It tells the story of our flight and liberation in our own
world," she explained. "The mortals had discovered our
weakness—"

"Iron," I interjected.

"—which is now again lost to time," she continued. "And
not iron, obviously, or Sahir would not be able to work in
your building." Even muffled underwater she managed to
convey a startling level of contempt. But her gaze hadn't left
my face since we descended, and her expression was one of
fascination—almost longing. For a world lost to her? Or for
something else?

My face flushed; I wondered if a blush would be visible
underwater.

"Oh, yeah," I said.

She squeezed my hand again, or maybe she was just flexing out a finger cramp. I tore my focus from the great mystery of the Gray Knight's unfathomable thoughts.

I looked down at the figures, the fleeing faeries and the angry humans. With the undulating current and the shifting sand, it looked like they were running even now.

"I . . . thought you would want to see where it started," she said. "Because it is a piece of history."

"Thank you," I said, a bit awed.

The Gray Knight and I drifted along the road, images unscrolling before us. The faeries opening a door in a hill, and hollowing out a space. The faeries with their arms to the sky, sending stars overhead. The faeries crowning someone. The faeries shaping the landscape; raising hills and cratering valleys; sending flocks of doves skyward from the slender bones of their wrists.

It was eerie, and so oppressively silent, with the two of us in our silver bubble like a beacon under the waves. But no fish or Fae disturbed us, and we floated together down the road, hand in hand.

We spent a long time under the water.

When she finally tugged me upward, I went willingly. We waded to shore together, still hand in hand, and collapsed next to each other on the picnic blanket. I lay face down, breathing in the cool night air and the damp river smell.

She pushed on my shoulder, rolling me onto my back. The wet clothes clung to me, clung to her. Her shirt had rolled up, and I stared at the strip of skin above her hips. "You appreciate history and truth," she said, looking down at me. Her hair fell in sheets and the magic fell in sheets and I could see nothing except the silver glint of her eyes. *You appreciate history and truth* is a very unsexy sentiment, for what it's worth. But she had fine silver hairs on her navel, and water droplets slid down her collarbone and onto the blanket beneath us.

"I appreciate you," I whispered, smooth as always, propping myself up on my elbows.

Without another word, she leaned forward and kissed me.

Oh, I thought.

Her lips were so soft, impossibly soft, and hot. She tasted of the cider, of river water, of something indefinable and necessary. It was a million times sweeter than the jam.

She smiled while we kissed, one hand fisting in my tangled wet hair, the other keeping herself steady. I wanted to pull away and look at her face—I didn't think she'd ever smiled in my presence before tonight, and it was so odd to only feel it but not observe it. I gasped and grabbed at her shoulders, her arms, startled and yearning. I pulled her onto me, and she laughed. Her hand trailed down the side of my neck, along the divot above my collarbone. Her fingers curled under my collar, nails scrabbling against my bare skin. I shivered and pressed up against her, sliding my own hands down her back to her waist. She nipped my lip and I groaned.

I am kissing a faerie. A faerie. Oh my god. I mean, I don't know how I like, feel about her, but she's hot and I'm kissing her. Am I kissing okay? Should I do something different?

And then—*Am I fetishizing faeries?*

Which is not a sexy thought.

I jumped when she put her hand on my hip, and squirmed

away from her. She pulled back and looked at me. "Did I hurt you?"

"No, I'm just—self-conscious," I said, taking her hand.

She frowned at me. "Do you think I would kiss you if I did not want you, as you are?"

She dipped her head to kiss along the line of my throat. I stared over her head at the spill of silver magic above us, trying not to think. Her lips were cool on my skin, soft.

I felt hollow, afraid to mess this up and afraid to continue.

But she deserved my enthusiastic participation. I pushed away. "I'm sorry," I said, sliding out from under her. "I don't think I'm ready to be…doing this. It's been a stressful month, you know?"

She sat up, her still-damp hair in disarray. "I find physical distraction helpful," she said. "When I feel stress."

"I…don't think I do. Can we just hold each other?"

If she found the request odd, she didn't say so. She just lay back on the blanket and held her arms wide for me. I nestled into her embrace, staring at the little hairs that curled away from her temple. "Thank you," I said, still breathless and dazed.

The minutes passed. My heartbeat evened out, the warmth of her body against mine soothing and familiar. We breathed each other in, our legs tangling. I started to doze.

She smiled, kissed my cheek.

I nuzzled closer. "I need to get back," I said, and then sat up, a bolt of panic shooting through me. "Oh, god, I need to get back. What time is it? I might have missed some work."

I leapt to my feet, snatching at my wet clothing like that

would make it more comfortable, and yanked my boots on. "Can you zap us back to the Court?"

"Zap?" she repeated. She sat up, looking more baffled than a woman posing for a Jackson Pollock painting.

"Teleport us back to the—the Court—the castle—the—"

"It is not a castle," she said, pushing to her feet. "It is a warren. And I cannot teleport. What magic would that even entail? The displacement of living beings on a molecular level? That sounds like a fantastic way to die."

"Please," I begged, voice low and hoarse, "can we please go back?"

She frowned but waved her hand and dissolved the magic dome around us. We didn't speak again as she lifted me onto Sparkles, or as we rode back to the hill.

But when she helped me down from the saddle, she pressed her lips to my temple, a gesture so soft it nearly shattered me. I turned away from her and hurried into the Court, sodden clothes itchy and my heart pounding like I'd run a marathon. Or, more realistically, half a mile.

———————————•———————————

In my bedroom, I dashed to the computer and turned it on to the expected barrage of angry emails.

Levi and Jeff had gotten into a discussion about the valuation I'd sent over, and left me in CC.

Jeff had sent us a new email titled *SEND OVER COUNTRY COUNTESS VALUATION MIRI ASAP THANKS.*

Levi had replied:

Jeff, Miri's still at the site visit. She sent the valuation in the email Country Countess Valuation *at 1:23 this morning.*

Jeff to Levi:

I need her to send me the valuation.

And then Levi back:

The valuation is attached in her initial email to us. Reattaching it here.

Jeff again:

She needs to be online.

Levi:

When she gets back I will let her know she needs to bring her phone next time.

Jeff:

I'm not paying her to go on day trips.

Levi:

Can I answer any questions about the valuation?

Jeff:

No just tell her to call me when she's back.

I wondered why I'd been left in CC.

It didn't seem like there was anything actionable for me to do at this point except stew in impotent rage. I drafted a quick note to Jeff so he'd know I was online and not traipsing about with woodland creatures—or kissing faerie women.

Jeff, I just got back from the site visit. They are using magic to build. The foundations are in place. It takes about an hour to travel there via horse. Miri.

I logged off the computer and lay down to sleep next to Doctor Kitten.

But I didn't sleep. I lay awake, clenching my eyes shut,

rolling back and forth across the mattress with my left leg anchored in place so I didn't disturb the cat. I hadn't even done anything wrong. My work had been fine; Jeff was just upset I hadn't been online. And he was the one who'd sent me away to begin with.

When I finally did sleep, I dreamed of the Gray Knight, her silver hair and silver eyes and silver tail. She propped herself above me on her forearms and glowed brighter and brighter, until I shut my eyes against the light. She kissed along my cheek, my lower lip, the line of my jaw, until I was writhing beneath her. But when I opened my eyes, it was Sahir above me, his curls hanging down around his face, his lips red with kissing.

I woke up panting in the middle of the night, bolt-upright and wild-eyed.

It took me a long time to sleep again after that.

Chapter 13

In Which Jeff and I Discuss Marketing Tactics

I dressed with care in the morning, choosing clothes with less cat hair on them, and swiped mascara on my lashes before I left the room. Not for the Gray Knight, obviously. For me. I knocked on Lene's door, but she didn't answer, so I went to the dining hall by myself.

There were a few groups clustered around the tables. I went to the serving area, where my erstwhile poisoner Kamare had been replaced by a short man with wide cheeks and bulging eyes. He didn't look invested in my existence one way or another and put a bowl of porridge on my tray with a nodded greeting. The second faerie, as ever, said nothing. Milo dropped a fruit cup on my tray, grabbed a second one, and followed me to the nearest table.

I sat down, resigned to his presence.

"Hi," he said, sitting across from me. "How are you?"

Having now taught greetings in human class several times, I couldn't help but see the absurdity in the ritual. It was a nicety, a shared tradition, and a little bit inane.

"Still kidnapped," I said, intending to snap my mouth shut. But decades of lectures on politeness from my mother forced my tongue: "Otherwise, I'm fine. How are you?"

He nodded, spearing a vivid green melon ball with a two-pronged wooden fork. "I thought you might say that," he said. He waved at someone over my shoulder. I turned to look and saw another human-type person walking toward us.

"You thought I might say that I'm kidnapped?" I asked, my tone more baffled than I'd intended.

He rolled his eyes. "No, that you're fine, since that's what you keep telling us to do in class."

He popped the melon ball into his mouth and chewed openmouthed. His eyes were somehow…less shattered than usual today. The darker blue and gray veins that sometimes divaricated his irises had shrunk into themselves, leaving more pale blue.

I'd almost asked him once about the Princeling's claim. Had he wandered into Faerie a madman? Had he just wandered in, period? But his mental health wasn't my business, nor was his treatment plan relevant information for me. If some people did psychoanalysis and some people decided to live in pocket dimensions, I certainly wasn't qualified to determine which was more effective.

Milo finally swallowed his very well-chewed mouthful of

fruit. If he'd waited much longer, a will-o'-the-wisp might've swept down from the ceiling like a baby bird and—

Eugh. I cut off that train of thought.

He cleared his throat. "Do you think you're going to go to the press?"

I hadn't even considered trying to draw media attention since the first days in Faerie. Once I'd made my deal with the Princeling, any other actions felt underhanded.

So I picked up my own fork and bit into a similar green melon. "No." The melon tasted closer to raspberry than honeydew. "I don't want to make people even more prejudiced toward faeries," I told Milo, who probably didn't care.

The person he'd waved at stopped next to our table. I looked up.

"Hi, Chad," Milo said, nodding at the new guy. "Do you want to sit with us?"

Chad sat next to Milo and picked up his own fork. Milo looked back at me. "I heard you were one of those Faerie-lovers." He plucked a disc of blue fibrous plant matter from his bowl and bit into it.

I glanced at Chad, wondering whether I should be cautious. But I needed to talk to Milo. "That raises a lot of questions, Milo. Like who you heard that from, or what it means. But more importantly"—it wasn't more important to anything except my wounded pride—"why didn't you tell me you were human?"

It had been almost a month since his aborted tour of the Court, and I still felt embarrassed and confused when I saw him. I put the fork down and picked up the spoon, looking at the porridge now.

"I honestly didn't realize you didn't know," he said. "I mean, *I* know I'm human."

"Well, of course *you* know," I said.

He only looked at me, an expression of slight bemusement on his very handsome, very modern, very American quarterback face.

"Milo, how am I supposed to know something that you know without you telling me?"

Chad looked up at this, grunted in what might have been assent, and attacked his porridge with ferocity. Chad had even broader shoulders than Milo, and the most adorable snub nose I'd ever seen.

Milo shrugged. "I thought the faeries said you could read minds, or something. Don't they call you Lady of the Mind Reading?"

I put my spoon down. "Lady of the True Dreams," I corrected automatically. Then winced, even more embarrassed. "But Milo, I can't know something if you don't tell me."

"Well, *now* I know that!" he said cheerfully. "Honestly, what good is a true dream? Mind reading would be much more useful."

He wasn't *wrong* but he was definitely irking me.

He added as an afterthought, "Chad is human, too."

I looked at Chad. "Okay, then," I said. So apparently there were at least a few of us.

Sahir had intimated that Milo knew something about my imprisonment. Maybe Milo knew a way for me to get out.

Gritting my teeth, I tried to decide what to do: Should I let it be, trusting the Princeling to uphold our bargain (and Jeff not to fire me)? Or should I ask Milo what he knew?

As if my mother were reading my mind, my phone buzzed in my pocket. I pulled it out and glanced at her text. *Any progress on coming home?*

We sat awkwardly at the table, Milo's sun-faded blue eyes on my face. Chad had finished eating and looked at me, too, his eyes even madder than Milo's: so blue they were almost white, and irises shattered by those darker veins, like panes of leaded glass held together by iron filaments.

"Do you want some of my food?" I asked him because he kept looking at me.

He started, and then blinked. "Did you just offer me your food? Off your *plate*?" He had a surprisingly sweet voice, like the aftertaste from a Double-Stuffed Creme cookie. "You must be the nicest woman I've ever met."

I couldn't tell if this was a bit. I opened my mouth, but he kept talking.

"You must be an angel."

I shrugged and shoved the tray toward Chad, who pulled it to himself with fervor.

"This might be because I haven't seen a human woman in five years," Chad began—an auspicious start—

At this, Milo seemed to remember himself. "Chad," he said, putting a hand on the other guy's shoulder to cut him off, "stop while you're ahead."

Milo met my eye, as if to say *See? I helped.*

"Do you know how to get me out of Faerie?" I asked, having given up on conversational segues.

Milo shrugged. "Once you eat faerie food, you're stuck," he said. "Unless you want to be rearranged into nothingness."

"Have you ever *tried* the portal?" I asked.

Chad and Milo exchanged a look. "No—" Chad started.

"Is that a threat—" Milo said simultaneously.

"Are you so keen to leave our realm?" the Gray Knight asked, sliding into the seat next to me. She wore loose pants and a low-cut blouse today and had silver flowers threaded through her hair. A small, silly part of me wondered if she'd dressed up for me. "But things were just getting interesting here."

Milo looked from her to me. "Gray Knight," he said.

Chad, having said everything he'd needed to, looked back down at my erstwhile tray of food.

She smiled and took my hand, on the table, where anybody could see. I pulled away, not wanting the attention. "Hello, Milo," she said. "Your conversation sounded intriguing, so I wanted to join."

"I cannot take credit for that," he demurred.

I felt something on my knee and jerked away. It was the Gray Knight's hand. I frowned at her but didn't want to call attention to it.

"Milo was just telling me how a human can get out of Faerie," I said brightly. "Do you happen to know if there is another way?"

"I know that the Princeling has need of you, and so do I," she said.

I was done being polite. Something about Chad—who'd gone absolutely still and locked his eyes on my face—had beaten my obeisance out of me. "Even if that's a euphemism, my lady, I am not interested."

"It is a euphemism," she said, "as I've said one thing in place of another."

I sighed. "Please, for the love of god, let's not do this right now. I'm very tired and grumpy, and I want to go home."

The Gray Knight stood up, her jaw setting with the solemn finality of the tomb. "Then let me escort you back to your room," she said. "As that is your home."

I kicked the stool away and got up, too, my eyes still on Chad, who finally had the good grace to look down at the remains of my porridge. The Gray Knight and I left the room together, the doors of the hall swinging behind us.

She reached for my hand again as we started down the hallway, but I pulled away. All of the faeries were touchy—Sahir held my hand or arm all the time, and Lene curled into me whenever I sat nearby. Gaheris often sat at my feet while I worked, leaning against my knee while tearing tiny holes into the wall beneath my desk with the assurance that a portal there would be:

A. unnoticeable to the room's inhabitant (i.e., me);
B. unlikely to expel hungry tentacles, grasping hands, an animated mouth full of gaping shark teeth hungry for human toes, or anything else harmful; and
C. super fun for Doctor Kitten, once Gaheris got the magic right and stopped conjuring swamps by accident.

I had at this point determined never to try my luck escaping through a portal Gaheris created.

This to say, I often leaned on or cuddled my new friends.

The Gray Knight may not have meant anything by the touch. But none of my friends had kissed me, or taken me on a romantic date, or fed me cheese.

"I'm sorry," I said. "I need time to sort myself out before I start, um, anything."

She trailed a hand along the wall. "I do not take your meaning."

"I don't want to be your girlfriend right now," I blurted, feeling mortified that I might have misread the signals.

"Girlfriend?" she asked.

I would not say the word *lover* out loud.

"Partner?" I suggested.

And, of course, she looked at me, her gray eyes sparking. "I did not ask you to be."

I felt myself flush. I was a moron. Of course a faerie woman didn't want me to be her girlfriend.

———————————•———————————

Later that afternoon, distressed and demoralized, I logged into a two-hour meeting block on my calendar to review the presentation.

Jeff was in a foul mood. Levi was on but not talking.

"What is it, Miri?" Jeff asked, even though he'd sent the calendar invite.

"Oh, can we review the PowerPoint?" I asked, because it wasn't worth mentioning.

"Page three," Jeff said. "The footnotes are off. This stuff isn't hard, Miri."

I went to page three, where the footnotes were actually *not* off.

"Some of these mistakes are actually improbable," he added. "Like, you must have messed them up on purpose. How did you get every single color slightly wrong on page seven?"

The colors were completely right on page seven. "Jeff, did you check the saturation settings on your laptop?" I asked, trying to keep my tone neutral.

Neither of us had our videos on. I was sharing my screen, trying to keep up with the speed of his commentary.

"My saturation is perfect," he scoffed. "I might as well have just given this to the new girl. I would have, if she wasn't even more useless than you."

Jeff was a man of many talents, one of them being motivational speaking.

"I'm sorry," I muttered, feeling less *sorry* and more *deeply enraged*. I stared out the window, at the sunless blue sky and the revel on the lawn below me. Doctor Kitten was enthralled, his tail twitching as he watched the figures below us dance. The window seemed to sense that I'd lost interest in my meeting, and suddenly music drifted up, where it hadn't previously.

"Page eight," Jeff said. I listened with half an ear to the sweep and swell of the song outside. It sounded like a strings rendition of a Backstreet Boys song. I clicked over to page eight. "Miri, you aren't using any shortcuts."

Levi cut in. "You don't even have any shortcuts on the quick access toolbar. No wonder you're so slow."

I was certainly relieved to know that Levi had been paying attention.

"Change the header," Jeff said. "This isn't a marketing pitch; we don't need to say anything nice about the company or the client."

I had been under the impression that it was a marketing pitch, and in fact that we probably should be saying nice things about the company and client to our potential investors.

"Okay," I said, selecting the header and deleting it.

"No, why did you do that?" Jeff snapped. "Undo. I still want to look at it for reference."

I hit CTRL+Z, my eyes drifting back over to the window. Why did any of the faeries want to leave what was essentially a paradise for them? Was the sun really worth that much?

"Those boxes aren't left-aligned," Jeff said. I selected the relevant boxes and hit ALT+H+G+A+L. The boxes were, in fact, left-aligned.

"Well, they look weird," he amended.

"I think it's the drop shadow," I said.

"We always use drop shadows." Jeff sounded irate. "They don't usually look weird. You did something to them."

"I'm sorry," I said, instead of arguing. Maybe I had done something to them. God knew I didn't have immense levels of expertise in the specifics of drop shadows on a PowerPoint presentation.

I double-checked, but the shadows were lower-right, as always.

We'd made it through most of the deck when Jeff started commentating again. "Miri, this shouldn't have taken this long to review," he started.

"I'm sorry," I said.

"Is this a broader pattern?"

I gritted my teeth. "What do you mean?"

"It feels like things always take longer with you, Miri."

My eyes flicked over to my second screen, where Levi's initials indicated he was still online.

"I'm sorry," I said.

"You need to do better work and do it faster."

"I'm sorry."

Jeff sighed. "Just do better. Don't apologize."

"Okay."

"Clean this up, PDF it, and send it to the client."

He logged off. Levi followed a moment later. I stared at my screen, feeling frustrated and useless.

This was my job. I was literally hired to edit documents and put together slides and models. I had no right to feel so . . . angry.

I did as Jeff bade me and sent the document to the Princeling and the Gray Knight in PDF and PowerPoint formats with a quick note. Then I stood up and went to the window, staring outside at the dancers still spinning in wild widening gyres below. They tossed their heads up and let the blue illumination of daytime hit their cheeks—but, as ever, there was no sunlight to warm their skin.

Chapter 14
In Which I Educate Sahir About Wordplay

I planned to discuss taxes in this class. I'd put together a list of basic information about them—what they do (in theory) and the way they worked in the United States specifically. I thought if faeries understood how humans collectively pooled money for the kinds of resources that they could just build with magic, they might understand the monetary system a bit more. I sat in the cafeteria a few minutes before class, reviewing my list and keeping an eye on my emails.

Guess how much money you owe, my notes said. *You might be wrong.*

Kellen burst in, panting. His wide white wings vibrated at a speed better suited to a hummingbird, throwing gusts of air about the room and scattering the papers in front of me.

"Lady," he exclaimed, "I beg your assistance! In exchange, I will provide you with one service. Unless you do not want a service, because humans do not exchange favor for favor."

I looked up. "Hi, Kellen," I said. "Are you okay?"

"Okay?" Kellen shrieked. "OKAY? What is OKAY? I am *overwrought*." He flung his hands up and—I assumed accidentally—whacked one with his fluttering wing. He brought them back down, wincing.

"Humans actually do exchange favor for favor," I corrected. "We just—it's just not as explicit."

Kellen wrung his now mildly injured hands, beside himself.

"But that's not relevant," I added hastily. "Kellen, do you want to tell me what's wrong?"

While Kellen made a noise like a teakettle, the cafeteria doors opened again. Sahir, Lene, and Gaheris came in as a group. Sahir carried his work laptop; Lene carried Doctor Kitten; Gaheris carried nothing.

Momentarily distracted from Kellen, I said, "Oh, I didn't know you were bringing Doctor Kitten," hoping she'd note my displeasure.

"I have made an ERROR," Kellen said before she could respond, his face twisted in anguish.

The Gray Knight came in behind him, Caraya and a few new students in a gaggle at her back.

"Okay, what was the error?" I asked. The doors swung open a fourth time, and a steady stream of faeries settled themselves. Kellen stayed next to me, rocking slightly.

"I went through the portal," he said. "I still do not know what 'okay' is."

"Oh." I shoved down the wash of jealousy. It wasn't Kellen's fault I would explode if I tried to go home. "What happened when you went through the portal?"

"I SAW A WOMAN," he exclaimed, and sank onto the nearest stool.

"Okay." I stopped. "Kellen, I don't understand what the error was?" I said, more a question than a statement. His wings had calmed to sad, uncertain, occasional flaps.

"And I do not understand 'okay'!" he snapped, and seemed disinclined to continue.

I looked around the room. We were about half full.

The Princeling had come in and conjured his silver throne, looking uneasy. His wings hung over the side, drooping. He seemed tired.

The Gray Knight stood behind him, her expression unreadable and her arms crossed.

"Start the class," the Princeling ordered.

"Okay, just give me a second," I said. "Kellen and I were finishing—"

"Start the class, Lady of the True Dreams," the Gray Knight said, her voice colder than the Arctic wind. I glanced at her; her eyes were as remote as stars. *This* was the Princeling's enforcer, staring me down. For a brief moment I missed the smiling version of the Gray Knight.

"So . . . today, we can talk about taxes," I started as I headed for the front of the room.

Kellen's hand shot up.

"Kellen, I'm not—"

"I SAW A WOMAN AND SHE WAS HUMAN AND I GAVE HER A LEAF I FOUND IN THE PARK AND SHE MOCKED MY GIFT, FREELY GIVEN, AND I

SHALL NEVER RETURN TO THE MORTAL REALM AGAIN."

Sahir looked up from his laptop. I raised an eyebrow at him. He shrugged. This usually meant *Do whatever you want*. I shrugged back at him, which meant *I have no idea what to do*.

"Perhaps instead of taxes, you would like to explore human mating rituals," Sahir suggested. The tiny smirk twisting his mouth reminded me that he'd sworn fealty to me but he'd never sworn not to put me in mortifying situations he'd find hilarious. In the depths of my soul, something curled up and died.

"Kellen, do you want to talk about it?" I asked gently. "I don't think you made an error. I think maybe she just . . . didn't see how valuable the gift was."

"FREELY GIVEN," Kellen repeated, still at volume.

I glanced around the classroom. "Does anyone have any ideas about why the human woman might have laughed?"

A newer student threw their tentacle into the air, dislodging a good amount of viscous slime. I watched the slime reach its parabolic height and descend, inglorious, into the fires of Gaheris's head.

"What do you think . . . ?" I asked, trailing off so they would give their name.

"Herman," the student supplied. "I have spent time in the ocean. I love the ocean."

"The ocean is great," I agreed.

"I have watched many human mating rituals from the shallow warm waters by the shore. Kellen should have given her the shell of an Atlantic moon snail, the desiccated corpse of a proud mollusk for her to thread around her neck."

"Humans appreciate corpses?" asked Herman's seatmate, a faerie with rubbly skin like a starfish.

"Humans appreciate *necklaces*," another classmate corrected before I could jump in. "Herman has misunderstood the value of the gift."

"Humans appreciate a lot of different things," I interrupted. "But humans are like you. Everyone places different value on different things. Some people might like seashells, and some people might like leaves, and some people might like necklaces."

"And some people like corpses!" Herman chimed in.

"Then how could I have avoided my error?" Kellen asked, his voice sunken in despair. "Should I have brought her a corpse as well?"

I hesitated. "I think you need to learn what each person likes," I said. "I think you can't give someone a leaf until you know them."

I glanced over at the Princeling, who had pressed his lips together so tightly they'd all but disappeared. I couldn't tell if he was suppressing laughter or the desire to strike me where I stood.

We stared at each other. I realized I should probably address the corpse thing before it became a national incident.

"Also, Herman, I appreciate your contribution, but...people don't like corpses. Please never give someone a corpse."

And with that, I turned to the scintillating topic of the American tax system.

As I left two hours later, everyone more confused about taxes than when I'd started, I saw Sahir and the Gray Knight leaning against a wall and murmuring to each other. Sahir nodded as I passed, but the Gray Knight didn't meet my eye.

———————•———————

I woke to someone standing over my bed.

"Did you *lie with the Gray Knight*?" Sahir asked, ruining my middle of the night.

I groaned and rolled over. "You have been here *a month*, Miriam," he continued, in a voice depressingly reminiscent of my freshman-year college roommate's when she gave me the same lecture.

"Don't you have better things to do?" I asked, shoving into a seated position because he was clearly geared up for a speech. I stared at his silhouette, a deeper black against the darkness of the room.

He waved his left hand at the will-o'-the-wisp who liked to sleep on my bedside table. The wisp lit up accordingly. "I have many things to do, but I am your knight, and therefore, I have nothing more important to do."

"Why do you think I lay with the Gray Knight?" I asked, squinting against the light.

Sahir stood over the bed, arms crossed, wearing a loose shirt and black sweatpants. "Because she told me," he growled. "Do you never listen to me?"

I felt the pit in my stomach opening. "Of course I listen to you," I said. "But I didn't..."

"Did you think that because she was the Princeling's knight, she would not attempt to snare his human pet? You thought she would not want the clout? Of course she would! She is the Princeling's knight. You do not become the Princeling's Gray Knight by playing only one game, Miriam. She knows that humans are often monogamous. She wants your affection, and through it, your loyalty."

I made myself laugh. "Sahir, I don't have feelings for her. We kissed, that's all."

His arms flailed in the air. The last time I'd seen him this agitated, he'd turned into an incorporeal vine monster.

"Can you just like, sit down?" I croaked, scooting back until I leaned against the headboard.

He sighed but sat next to me on the bed, legs stretched out over the covers. He tucked his chin against his shoulder, frowning at me. The light gilded his ear, his jaw, the line of his throat.

"I don't know her, really," I said.

Let the record show that I had once imagined having a house and family with the guy who sat next to me in calculus, whose name I did not know. He had broad shoulders.

"And she's not very nice to me," I added. *Most of the time.*

Let the record also show that this had never, *ever* stopped me from liking somebody before.

"And anyway, my parents wouldn't approve," I finished.

Let the record end with the fact that this was a lie. My parents would not care if I brought home a masticated fish stick, as long as the fish stick treated me well and had ambition.

"Are your parents homophobes?" he asked, tensing. "Must I educate them? Do they not know that you are a lesbian?"

I put a hand on his arm. "That's sweet, I think," I said.

"But I meant because she kidnapped me, not because she's a woman. And I'm not a lesbian."

"You aren't?" He took my hand in his in a gesture that aimed for *casual* and landed somewhere around *calculated*. Doctor Kitten, who looked jealous, jumped onto the bed and strutted between our legs.

I had a quick but quite ferocious internal debate about explaining sexualities to a faerie. Then I remembered our earlier classroom discussion. No topic was off limits. "I'm bisexual, Sahir."

He dropped his head back against the wall. "What's that?"

"Aren't you in the LGBTQ interest group at work?"

"Yes." He squeezed my hand. His palm was soft against mine.

"What does it stand for?" I started tracing a pattern over his knuckles with my other fingertip. The contact felt safe, lazy and hazy but still charged with some undercurrent.

"Lesbian, gay, biracial, transmutated, and quantified," he said.

I pulled my hand away and stared at him. "Who do you think that interest group is for?"

He shrugged. "Shapeshifters, like me. And lesbians."

"Okay." It probably wasn't worth addressing that any further.

We sat there. I fidgeted with the gold ring on my pointer finger. He put his hands in his lap.

"Um, just so you know, it's actually lesbian, gay, bisexual, transgender, and queer, meaning anyone who isn't cisgender or heterosexual, which means they like people of the opposite gender."

Sahir and I looked at each other. He looked unimpressed.

"Sorry, what would 'quantified' even mean in that context?" I brought my hand to my mouth and started gnawing on the tip of my thumb.

He frowned. "I thought perhaps it meant mathematicians."

"A support group for gay people, shapeshifters, and mathematicians?" I raised an eyebrow.

"I signed up to get out of a weekly assignment I did not like," he admitted, sounding like a frat boy and not a faerie.

This was simultaneously endearing and rage-inducing.

"Right. Well, to level set, thank you for telling me. I did not have sex with her. I'm not sure how she said that sentence since she cannot lie." I patted his thigh. "I will probably survive, though, and I am bisexual, which means I like both men and women."

"We do not have all of these descriptors," Sahir said, sounding quite condescending for a man who thought *T* stood for *transmutation*. "We do not use labels here."

I sighed and made a conscious choice to disengage.

But Sahir wasn't done. "She said you lay with her."

My irritation bubbled over and I flung my hands into the air. "I didn't—" I stopped midoutburst, realization hitting me like a rotten tomato. My hand dropped to my knee. "I did lie with her. I lay down with her. On the ground. We lay down. *And* I slept with her. I fell asleep."

Sahir's mouth dropped open. His face looked like a birdhouse.

"Sahir, you handsome, unnecessary alarm clock. Not to be rude, but aren't you a faerie? Isn't wordplay, like, your thing?"

He stood up so quickly I unbalanced, sliding sideways like a seven-layered cake. "Apologies," he said, "and good night."

He left the room like he'd just remembered he left the stove on in another country.

But I lay in bed, remembering the spinning silver sky she'd built for me. It took me a long time to fall asleep; when I did, I dreamed of Gaheris creating a portal in the kitchen that let swarms of cockroaches come inside.

In the morning, my phone buzzed.

"Hi, Jeff," I answered on the first ring.

"Miri," he said. "Be quick, I have a lot going on today."

"Be quick?" I asked. "Jeff, you called me."

He grunted. "Tell me what you think of Kayla," he said, reminding me that we had a new analyst who I'd barely spoken to.

"I like her," I started.

Jeff cut me off. "Miri, never start a human resources conversation with the fact that you like someone."

"Sorry," I said.

"She's slow. She doesn't take initiative, and she doesn't talk to anyone."

I tapped my fingers on my desk, not sure why I was involved in this conversation.

"Maybe she's just overwhelmed," I said, "being the only woman left in the office."

"Corey said she does bad work."

I felt a flicker of frustration. "Corey has high expectations. She just started."

"We can send her back now, but we won't be able to later."

"Does she want to be on our team?" God knew *I* didn't want to be on our team any longer.

"She asked to be here."

I stared at my computer screen. The poor girl. "Give her a chance," I said.

"Fine. I'll give her a task to work on under you."

My stomach dropped. This was a suboptimal outcome.

"Don't you think it would be better if she worked with someone in the office?"

"No," he said, and hung up.

I sighed and sent her a quick email.

Hi Kayla, Jeff might be sending us a project to work through together. Let me know if you want to chat about it.

A few minutes later, the email came in from Jeff, titled *Valuation.*

Kayla, Miri, research six competitors for the Faerie Trade Goods endeavor and value each of them. Will expect your analysis as soon as possible.

I groaned and called Kayla.

"Hi?" she said.

"It's Miri. Let's talk about Jeff's email," I said. "Have you ever done a valuation before?"

Someone knocked on my door. I glanced at it.

"No, I've never done a valuation, but I'm excited to learn!" She sounded too chipper.

I stood up and went to my door. "Okay, give me a second,"

I said, and went on mute. I opened the door. The Gray Knight was outside.

I felt a flash of rage: She'd told people we'd lain together. "Yes?" I said.

"We need to go over the model now."

"One second." I went off mute and said, "Kayla, I need to hang up. Look through some old valuations on our server and see what you can learn. I'll reach back out as soon as I'm done."

She started talking, but I hung up on her midsentence. I stepped back and let the Gray Knight in.

"Are you working on another deal?" the Gray Knight asked. Something flashed in her eyes.

"No," I said. "We're looking up some comparable transactions for the faerie deal."

She pulled out her acorn and sized it up to a chair again. Doctor Kitten hopped up onto the windowsill and stared at her, his tail flicking. I sat in my own chair.

"Did something happen with the model?" I asked.

She shook her head. "We just need to update it and send it out to buyers today."

"Today?" I frowned. "We haven't even finished the presentation—"

"Yes, I edited that last night. We will be ready to send it out with the model in a few hours."

"I think I need to tell Jeff," I said.

She shrugged. "The Princeling has sent him an email."

I checked my own email. Nothing had come through. But I reopened the model and sized it up to fill the screen.

She pulled a crinkled piece of paper from some pocket, full of incomprehensible scribbles. "These are our new assumptions for expenses," she said. "Your human values were far too high. We can reduce many of the costs in the model, because the Builder can create the equipment more efficiently and for far less money."

"Okay." I hit CTRL+Page Down until I reached the Inputs tab and looked at her expectantly.

She cleared her throat, scanning her page. "First, the initial capital expenditures for the project. We're bringing that down to sixteen million dollars."

I changed the assumed hardcode and looked at her again.

"The materials costs," she said. "We can scavenge cobwebs and acorns easily. We are more concerned about ensuring we do not have an adverse effect on mortal habitats as we source our materials. So the cost will be primarily for an environmental study."

This had me raising an eyebrow. "Who will do this environmental study?"

"We will need to find a consulting company. Your team can help us interview them."

Doctor Kitten jumped down from the windowsill and onto the desk. I held up an arm to keep him off the keyboard. He rubbed his face against my hand, looking irritated.

"Fine. I'll put a plug in for now." I typed *$1,000,000*, just for fun, and then looked at her. "Do you want to separate out labor? Will you be paying your scavengers?"

"For now, we will not concern ourselves with wages for the faerie teams." She shook out her paper and ran a finger down the page. "Many of these will still require more information."

Doctor Kitten made another attempt at the keyboard, but I caught him before he started editing my Excel.

"It's better for us to write down what we can, at least," I said. "That way maybe the returns won't shift as much when we get better numbers."

She shifted in her chair. "We expect very high returns, lady. Our labor costs will be low."

I shrugged. "People might worry about exploitation. We need to be careful about things like that."

As I said it, I CTRL+Page Up'ed into the Control tab of the model.

"I will concern myself with the assumptions," she said.

An email came in from Kayla, popping up in the lower right-hand corner of my computer screen. The subject line read *A Few Questions*.

I glanced at the preview. *Hi Miri, I am having trouble—*

"My lady, Jeff has requested that I work with our new analyst on a valuation assignment for your company. It would be helpful if I could take a half hour to give her instructions."

The Gray Knight frowned at me. "The model updates are our priority, Lady of the True Dreams."

I glared at the sharp slope of her nose, intending to melt it off her face with the heat of my anger. But her nose stayed fixed firmly in place while my gaze melted into an appreciative stare.

I squeezed my eyes shut. "I just need to—"

"This task is urgent. Continue along the Inputs tab."

I did as directed, following her line by line down the Excel sheet.

Several minutes passed. Another email popped up from Kayla. Subject line: *Am Concerned.*

The Gray Knight caught me looking and *tsked.*

"Sorry," I said, out of habit, and immediately felt irritated with myself. It wasn't a crime to look at my own emails on my own computer.

She sighed and shifted in her chair. "As I was saying, please look at row 97. Our debt module assumptions require some refining."

A third email from Kayla entered my periphery. Subject line: *Please Help.* I made a mental note to explain to her the vastness and understated grandeur of our compliance department, who read every single email sent on our servers.

I looked around the room, shaky and a little desperate, and saw the toilet. "Um, I need to use the bathroom," I said.

She jerked her chin toward that corner. "You may," she said, very graciously.

"Humans prefer privacy," I said, fiddling with the mouse.

With a noise like an overburdened cement mixing machine, she stood up and stalked out of the room. I stood and took a few steps away from my chair.

The second the door closed behind her, I tiptoed back to my seat with absolute stealth and absolutely no grace. I slid gingerly down and tabbed over to my emails.

I opened Kayla's latest.

Hi Miri,

I am sure you're busy with the client but I don't know where to start with this and am sitting paralyzed with indecision and fear at my computer. Haha.

The previous email began similarly.

Dear Miri,
I don't want to bother you but I don't know what folders in the
server I should use to find this information. Or what information
I am looking for. Jeff is in the office but Stoneleys Gross got
the mandate for the werewolf food company this morning and
he doesn't want to talk. Levi is at home and won't answer my
calls. I don't want to ask Corey any questions in case he thinks
badly of me.

I bit back a groan.

Hi Kayla, I typed in reply, trying to tap lightly against the
keyboard. I pictured the Gray Knight standing outside my
door, ear pressed to the wood, listening for the sounds of uri-
nation or betrayal.

Don't panic. Google is your friend. So are PitchBook and Capital
IQ. Just look around for companies that manufacture household
goods—public companies or private companies with accessible
financials—and use those to set up a valuation spreadsheet. Please
ask Corey questions.
Miri

I sent it and tabbed back to the Excel model. "Ready," I
called out, and the Gray Knight opened the door posthaste.
She popped in like a Jack-in-the-box, only beautiful and
slightly less scary.

"You took a long time," she said, glaring around suspiciously as she returned to her seat. I checked the clock. I had not taken a long time, and she was being quite grumpy, really.

"It wasn't that long," I said.

"I felt the press of the eons upon my shoulders as I waited."

If she said it, it must have been true. So apparently she wasn't having a great day either. Doctor Kitten and I looked at each other.

"Sorry," I said. "I realized Doctor Kitten...needed me."

"You detained me in the hallway in order to engage with your cat?" Her voice had gone flat.

I flinched back in my chair. "No, sorry," I said. "I didn't do that."

We both shifted in our seats. Her unbound hair swung across her shoulder in silk sheets. I scratched at my hand, fidgeted with my ring. She didn't speak. Her profile was so severe, so rigid I almost couldn't remember her saying *You are rare to me.*

"Why did you tell Sahir we lay together?" I blurted.

She froze, eyes on the window.

"Why would I not?" she asked, and I thought I saw a tic, a jump in her jaw muscles. "Are you ashamed of what we did?"

Two questions for the price of one. I gritted my teeth.

"Sahir thinks you wanted me to fall in love with you so you would have more political cachet," I said. "He thinks you think humans are all monogamous and that you wanted power over me."

She scoffed. "I do not need more power in this Court, human," she said, sounding haughty and offended at the same time. "I did what I did because I wanted to."

Oh.

I'd been ready to have a confrontation, but I wasn't ready to have this conversation.

I gestured to the screen. "We can finish up the Inputs tab," I said. "We're almost done."

Doctor Kitten leapt from the windowsill to the bed in a cloud of dislodged cat hair, which floated across the desk and our laps in a majestic glimmer of sunless light from the window.

The Gray Knight opened her mouth, like she might say something else—but she clamped it shut and nodded once, that muscle in her jaw still jumping.

And we continued on.

———————————•———————————

An hour in, Kayla sent me another email. The preview showed the sentence *I think this company might be worth $18 billion.* This was almost certainly inaccurate.

A few minutes after that, Jeff emailed me and Kayla both, subject line: *WHERE IS MY VALUATION.*

I glanced at the Gray Knight, but she only shrugged. "Jeff is not your primary concern," she said. "I am."

We were in an operational tab of the model at this point, talking through probabilistic weighting. I was bored nearly to tears.

"Well, Jeff is my boss," I said, striving for a reasonable tone the way we all strive: with the best of intentions and absolutely no follow-through.

"That is a fact but not an argument."

"I need to keep this job for about nine and a half more years, as you know," I said. I was rounding down optimistically.

"You may have different jobs."

I hunched over, like her words were a physical blow. "I can't have different jobs. That's not part of the bargain."

"If you relinquish the bargain, you can have a different job."

I seethed. Relinquish the bargain? Give up, having barely attempted it?

"Setting aside for a moment the obvious objections, how would I get a new job if I can't get out of Faerie?"

"The Princeling would certainly employ you."

I choked out a laugh. "Yeah, he seems like a great boss." I paused, tried to bite down the next words. Instead, I bit my tongue, and they came out with even greater fury. "I guess it'd be very useful to have someone on the team who can lie. What's the monthly kidnapping quota?"

The room exploded into gray. She shot out of her seat so fast the acorn chair spun into the side of my bed and cracked in half.

"You do not speak of him this way," she intoned in a dark voice I'd never heard from her before.

I stood as well, my knees knocking against the back of my chair. I glanced at the bed, where Doctor Kitten had leapt to his feet, back arched in shock.

Another wave of rage swept through me, so potent I was shaking. I could feel my eyes burning with anger and hopelessness. "Your liege has ruined my life, lady. He trapped me here, and you helped. If I lose this job, he won't help me leave Faerie. I will never be able to do human things. I will not marry or have children. If I lose this job, I will lose my *life*. My friends and family will forget me as I rot away in silence and in isolation and in misery, and all because of your liege, who decided to make me a poster child for happy human-faerie relations. So if it pleases you, get out of my bedroom."

She ground her teeth audibly, clenched her fists. I braced for a blow. Instead, she spun so her hair hit me in the face, and swept out of the room faster than my mortal eye could follow. She'd left her weird angry gray magic tendrils behind, and they convulsed in time to a rhythm I could not hear.

I sank back into my chair, staring at Doctor Kitten.

But I didn't have time to cry. I opened my email again to find an exchange between Jeff and Kayla, wherein Kayla had emailed Jeff a table that I could tell from four seconds' review was vastly incorrect, with the sentence *Please find attached the work Miri and I have done so far!*

I was sure she was trying to cover for me. I wanted to puke.

Sure enough, my phone rang. I picked up.

"Hello?"

"Miri, it's Jeff," he said, like a man who hasn't discovered caller ID yet.

"Hi, Jeff," I said.

"This valuation is terrible."

I pondered the appropriate response. My choices were:

A. I know, I've been tied up with the client and Kayla did it all

B. I know, it's a work in progress
C. No, it's not
D. I'm sorry

I, of course, went with *D*.

"I'm sorry," I said.

"How on earth did you think that this was acceptable to share with me?" he asked, disregarding the fact that I hadn't sent it to him.

A. I didn't think this was acceptable to share with you
B. It's a work in progress
C. It is acceptable to share with you
D. I'm sorry

"I'm sorry," I said, ever a consistent test-taker.

"Stop apologizing and actually do something useful, Miri," he snapped. "I don't even know why I go through you. It would be faster to just talk to the analyst directly."

"Kayla."

"What?" He sounded like a blood vessel had just popped in his forehead.

"Her name is Kayla," I said.

"Miri, I'm giving this task to Corey since you're clearly not capable of it. We'll have a longer conversation later." He hung up.

I looked at my phone and thought about my mother. I'd been avoiding her calls. If she asked me one more time whether "the Prince/King/Duke/Baron" had "shortened the timeline" I would hurl my phone into a faerie dance circle.

I thought about Thea and Jordan, too. I still hadn't told them where I was. Jordan's latest text to me just said, *Are you alive?*

In the end, I didn't call anyone.

————————————•————————————

Weeks five and six went quickly.

My mother and I talked on the phone for three minutes every morning.

Jeff sent Kayla back to her old team. No one said goodbye. I called Corey and chewed him out for not making more of an effort to help her learn. He told me not to be such a busybody.

I called my grandma and told her I missed her. I called Thea and listened to her immensely distressing story about going on a date with a man who had a bedroom full of female Funko Pops and absolutely nothing else.

"We live in *New York City*," she said, her tone a mix of glee and horror. "His apartment was probably five hundred square feet *total*."

I don't live in New York City. The words caught in my throat. "Sounds dedicated," I said instead. "Maybe he'd be a dedicated boyfriend, too."

"Miri, he had a hundred square feet of Funko Pop dolls. They were *all girls*, Miri. He could never commit to me. His attention would always be divided."

We both cackled.

I called Jordan and we talked for over an hour about fan theories for the last book in one of our favorite trilogies.

I called my dad and told him about lunch with Lene and Gaheris, about avoiding the Gray Knight in the hallways, about my job—but never about how hopeless I'd begun to feel. One day, I told him another truth instead:

"I regret telling Mom I was trapped here," I said, staring at the ceiling.

"Mom's only trying to help," Dad said. I could hear the steady beeping of a heart rate monitor behind him. He was probably between patients.

"Mom's stressing me out by asking the same questions about it every day."

He sighed. "Miri, if anyone can fix this, your mom can."

"Mom can't accept when things are unfixable." I gnawed on my lower lip.

"You need to decide if you like that about her or not," he snapped.

"*You* married her," I said. "I didn't choose her."

"Don't talk about your mother like that, Miriam. She wants to protect you."

I sighed. "Can you ask her to lay off?" I asked, my tone bitterer than I'd meant it to be.

As always, my dad took pity on me. "I'll talk to her. But how are you otherwise?"

"I'm fine," I said. "Teaching a class on human methods of washing dishes tonight. The faeries don't really understand the part where we don't use magic to clean everything."

He chuckled, but it was tense. "You shouldn't be teaching anyone how to wash dishes."

"Et tu, Brute?"

My dad snorted. "Okay, I have to go see my next patient," he said. "Love you."

"Love you, too," I said, but he'd already hung up.

I stared at the phone screen. The Games Games Games chat was popping off, Jordan planning a new campaign.

I missed my friends. I missed them, and, as often as I could bear it, I ignored their calls. *What if I couldn't get out?* It was better to cut them off quickly than to watch them fade away over time.

———————————•———————————

Week seven was numbing.

Corey called again, to talk about Kayla.

"Miri, you know it's easier for women to get this job than men," he said. "You don't have to be as qualified as we do."

"Excuse me?" I put down the pen I'd been playing with.

"Because they're trying to even out the numbers," he explained, which was not the part I objected to.

"So you think that I'm not as good as you at our job?"

"No, no, you're good," he said quickly. "It was probably just easier for you to get hired. Lower bar, you know."

And I realized: It didn't matter how good I was. If I succeeded, I would be considered a fluke. If I failed, it would be expected. There would be no systemic change because I existed: I could only be an anomaly, or a data point proving why women shouldn't be hired.

Nine and a half years. I needed to make it nine and a half years. If I didn't rock the boat, if I kept my head down and pretended I didn't exist—

"Sounds like you think I'm not as good as you," I said, ignoring the blood rushing in my ears and the knowledge that I should just be quiet.

He huffed. "Miri, stop twisting my words, or I won't call you anymore."

My loss, I didn't say with biting sarcasm.

"Okay, sorry," I did say. "I didn't mean to twist your words."

Eventually, another month passed. I worked most days, so I didn't know the difference.

Our buyers list dwindled as more people withdrew from the process, or in one dramatic case emailed Jeff to tell him a series of increasingly creative things he could stick into his own anus, were he so inclined. I wrote some of those suggestions down for future insults.

I went to meals, led the twice-weekly human classes teaching about everyday human monotony, and otherwise stayed in my room.

I answered questions shortly. I stopped picking up phone calls. And slowly, everything became muffled around me.

It was quiet in my head, but I didn't mind. I worked from eight a.m. until I passed out at night. I traced a path from bedroom to dining hall and back. During the day, I let Lene sleep on my bed while I sat at the computer. Sahir came to my room after dinner and worked next to me, but we rarely spoke anymore. I didn't have anything to say. Doctor Kitten curled up at my side at night while I slept.

My dreams became more vivid, stranger. Vermilion landscapes where trees grew with mirrored trunks, and I sat cross-legged on the ground watching my face wrinkle like a raisin. The ruins of a hall that looked like it belonged to an Ent, rows of fluted pillars giving way to equally stolid rows of grasping oak.

Once I dreamed of chocolate milk, and the next day, Sahir brought me a plastic bottle of Fairlife. "Humans seem to like this," he'd said, dropping it carelessly onto the bedspread. I stared at it; I hadn't had chocolate milk in two decades.

It was delicious.

Sometimes I imagined quitting my job, once I'd won the Princeling's bargain. I'd call Jeff and let him have every piece of my mind.

"Hi, Jeff, you run-of-the-mill dingbat," I'd start. It usually degenerated from there.

Time passed, as time always does. It had been eleven weeks since my sojourn to Faerie at the end of August, and I had become, to be blunt, quite depressed.

Chapter 15
In Which the Scenery Changes

Sahir banged on my door. I assumed it was Sahir, even though he usually didn't knock with violent force, because nobody else visited me in the evenings.

I considered ignoring him. I lay on my back in bed, Doctor Kitten curled in the juncture of my head and neck.

"Get up, lazy human," Sahir said, unaffectionately. I almost retorted with the timeless gem: *I know you are, but what am I?*

But Doctor Kitten stuck his nose in my ear and snuffled until I rolled away from him, squeaking. "Okay, okay," I said. "I'll get up."

Sahir, apparently listening outside, flung the door open. "Make haste."

"Your mom should make haste," I muttered.

"What?"

"Nothing." I heaved myself off the bed and stood up.

"What am I making haste for?"

He made a show of looking me up and down. "You look disgusting. When did you last bathe?"

Since he'd seen me last night and not commented on my appearance *or* otherwise been remotely insulting, I bristled a bit. "What's the point of bathing? I'm trapped either way."

Sahir leaned against the doorframe and crossed his arms. "When we go to war and our enemies imprison us, our armies maintain our discipline. We rise early and practice our exercises. We sit quiet and when they torture us, we make no sound."

I had stooped and stuck my head under the bed, looking for a shoe.

"That sounds terrible," I said. "And your enemies shouldn't have imprisoned you in the first place."

My shoe appeared to have nested in a pile of old shirts covered in cat hair. I fished it out.

"Who should have done what is irrelevant," he snapped. He sounded close to the end of his tether—I wondered distantly if he'd explode back into a wisteria if I kept pushing him.

"Right, and so I shouldn't do anything," I said, because I am a florist at heart. "Anyway, are we going to dinner?" I stuffed my feet into my shoes one at a time. One shoe had untied laces, but I couldn't make myself bend to tie it.

"No," he said, "we will go outside. You have been in the Court for too long."

"Outside?" I repeated.

"We will visit a town in Faerie."

"Oh, good, so you're with the tourism bureau now," I said.

"Take your shoes off and clean yourself," he said. "I won't be seen with you like this. It reflects poorly on me, and anyone could interpret your appearance as a failure to fulfill my oath and stab me."

I considered arguing, but what did it matter?

"Fine." I kicked off my shoes again and stalked toward the cascading waterfall of the shower. I shucked off my sweater as I went, not even glancing back to see if he had left.

The door slammed shut behind me. I divested myself of my remaining garments and stood shivering in the cold air.

Doctor Kitten had come to stand on the narrow ledge of the shower stall, next to the rocky wall that likely held the pipes. He mewled when he saw me hesitate.

Without checking the temperature, I stepped into the water. It hit me with enough force that I almost staggered. But the water felt nice as it sluiced down my body, wiping away days' worth of grime and dander.

I took up the lavender soap and scrubbed my chest and arms with it, my heart pounding. Why had Sahir walked in so angrily? I lathered my hands up and massaged the suds into my scalp, my nails digging in. He'd pissed me off, storming in like that. But the lethargy reemerged before I'd even rinsed the soap away.

Doctor Kitten, having jumped back a step to avoid splashing water, started bathing himself, too. He sat decadently on the stone floor, one leg outstretched with ballerenic poise, licking his own phantom balls.

I stepped into the drying stream that came through the vent. Within moments, the water droplets beading my skin had been flung up and away into what I could only assume was the ventilation system for the entire Court.

After that I went to the bed, unsurprised to find clothes already laid out for me with magical precision. They were the usual fare: a simple brown shirt, a thicker overshirt in deference to the cold weather, and leggings with a woven belt. Doctor Kitten, doing his civic duty, had somehow beat me to the bed and covered them in cat hair in the past thirty seconds.

I nudged him onto the bedspread and pulled the clothes on. Sahir had laid out my soft boots as well, and thick woolen socks. I considered sticking to my sneakers but couldn't make myself care enough to defy anyone. Especially not in a gesture as hollow as my choice of footwear.

When I opened the door again, Sahir was sitting on the floor across the hall, typing on his work phone—which I recognized because it matched mine.

"Exciting day at the office?" I asked, sounding simultaneously snide and miserable.

"No." He stuck his phone in his pocket and stood up. "Quite boring. Several hours of meetings about a new bond issue, and then a very long and distressing discussion about a strategic initiative."

I stared up at him. "Where are we going?"

"Outside," he repeated, striding down the hallway—toward the river, not toward the clearing. I trailed after him, a small bubble of frustration rising in my chest and then deflating. It didn't really matter where I went, did it?

We stepped out of the Court and I shivered in the chill air. The faeries had replicated the seasons. It was a pure, crisp night, and it even smelled like fall: spicy and cold and exciting. It felt like an adventure. I couldn't stop myself; I looked around for *something*, the way I always had as a child. A magic carpet or a moving castle or a child flying in the sky.

No magic carpet popped up, but Sparkles did, along with another horse for Sahir.

I glanced at him. "Going for a scenic horseback ride is a very odd thing to do on a work night."

"I have reasons for everything I do." He wouldn't look at me, though. Instead, he gestured to Sparkles. I stared at her bare back, trying to pinpoint the moment the saddle appeared.

He hefted me, his thumbs under my armpits. I flopped onto her back, where the saddle was suddenly beneath my legs. I sighed and watched him mount gracefully.

"Let us depart," he said. The horses, who were much better listeners than me, started along the path.

———————————————•———————————————

We'd wended our way along the riverside for almost an hour when Sparkles began to slow. The horses' hooves clacked on the errant stones in the dirt path, and we wound upward and upward, the river falling away from us, until we'd crested a hill. We veered left, away from the river and the path, and I stared down into the cup of the valley.

It wasn't a town, at least not by my human standards. It was more like a street, a row of permanent structures set at a juncture in the winding road where it followed the river most closely. On the riverbank, a neat row of piers jutted into the water, set among the marshy shallows with waving cattails and thick reedy grass. Across the dusty dirt track the buildings squatted. They were not beautiful, but elegant in the way of old things, made of rounded stone set with mortar so ancient it had all but crumbled away.

There seemed to be a crowd of people standing at the entrance to an alleyway between two houses.

Sahir had dismounted before his horse even stopped, in a motion so swift I didn't follow it. He was at my side in another, his form blurred against the twilight into an indefinable smudge.

This time I slid into his arms without a flicker of emotion, too dull to feel shame or embarrassment. He caught me and held me in a cradle, saying something to Sparkles in a language I didn't understand. Both horses trotted toward a paddock situated a little way off the path, with a narrow structure jutting from one side.

I lay in Sahir's arms like a dead fish.

He dropped me.

I stared up at him. "Ow," I said.

Something flickered in his eyes. "Get up, mortal."

"This was your idea," I said. I could feel my brows furrowing. Everything felt far away, like I was watching us through a pane of glass. Like a badly directed film, where I knew the emotions I should be feeling but couldn't connect.

"You embarrass your kind."

I felt the smallest lick of irritation and shoved up onto my knees.

Almost like he knew what he'd done, Sahir smirked down

at me. His brown eyes twinkled. I hadn't looked at his eyes in weeks.

From a distance we must have looked a picture—a knight, supplicant, ready to receive benediction, and her lord above her.

"The Princeling did not bring you here to shame you or yours," he added. He held out a hand to me, and I shoved it away.

"I didn't ask to represent my kind," I burst out, roiling up to my feet. He held his ground, so we stood nearly toe to toe on the grass. He had bags under his eyes, and his hair was a little greasy, shining in the starlight. He looked tired, hunted.

"None of us asked to be what we are." He left his hand where I'd slapped it, at his side and palm up. I couldn't keep looking at his face; a flicker of shame heated my cheeks. He was my knight and I definitely wasn't making his life any eas-ier. I stared at his hand instead. He had scars in the meat of his palm, near where it connected to his wrist. My gaze traced them, up to the first joint in his long pinky.

"What you are is probably a lot better than what I am right now." My anger had cooled, and it sank in me like a hunk of basalt, cracked off and cooling in the embrace of the oceans.

"Do not presume to know what I am," Sahir said.

I only stared at his hand, still open toward me. "You'll for-give me if I don't empathize with you."

The silence stretched on long enough that I looked at him, not curious, exactly, but maybe a little impatient. And guilty. Definitely aware enough to feel guilty, and melodramatic, and frustrated with myself more than him.

Sahir jerked his head toward the village below us. "Let us go," he said. "I want you to visit my hometown."

I trailed behind him, my calves aching a bit at the slight declining slope of the path. I hadn't moved much recently, had I?

This felt like an oversight, given I might have to run from a horde of ravening enemies at any time.

Not that any level of training would prepare me, of course. Not that any amount of human strength or human cunning could protect me from my captors. It was like putting an average adult into the Olympics.

Run this race, you'd say. So they'd try, and they'd make it, maybe—in twice or three times as long.

Or *Go down this ski jump*. And they'd get over the slope, to land on their neck and crack their skull open.

I *felt* the viscera in the image, the amalgamated flash of fifteen violent movie deaths I'd witnessed coming together into splashes of red blood on white snow. My stomach roiled inside me. I missed a step and stumbled, righting myself before I fell.

"Are you all right, Miriam?" Sahir asked, looking over his shoulder.

"Yep," I said, short with frustration and breathlessness.

We'd nearly reached the base of the hill, and the town was not far. But the crowd of people I'd seen from the top of the hill had disappeared.

The first elusive strains of some sort of music reached us, increasing in volume as we started along the straight and level part of the path. I avoided the loose stones in the road, but Sahir walked with the ease of a man used to every uneven step. The river surged closer again. Over it, the music continued, a not-quite-piano playing a not-quite-melody.

We were close enough to see the details on the doors of the houses: flowers and vines carved into wooden mantels; flaking paint in muted greens and reds.

The town must have emptied as we walked down the hill—presumably they'd seen me stumbling down the road and remembered collectively that they had to do some washing up. The music continued, swelling discordant notes softening into a melancholic minor key. As we walked past the first house, I couldn't stop my body from shivering—a long, thorough shake that left me even colder than before.

Between the second and third houses we came upon the player. He sat in the open air, at an instrument that resembled a baby grand piano, positioned so he could look out over the water as he played. His body swayed back and forth, following his arms across the keyboard—which was longer than any piano I'd ever seen.

His eyes were closed, but he had long blond hair half piled into a bun at the top of his head, curls spilling around his shoulders and down his back. He wore a simple black tunic, and over it a very human-looking overcoat, black wool that tangled his hair. And he was broad, broader than a musician should be, and with the pinkest skin I ever seen—like the icing on a strawberry donut.

As if he sensed us, his eyes snapped open, though his fingers didn't even stutter on the keys.

"Sahir," he said, and he had pink irises, too, crenellated like the petals of a chrysanthemum. I could imagine myself falling into them, caught between the layers like a tiny silver star in a kaleidoscope.

"Aram."

I tried to feel vague surprise as Sahir slid between the almost-piano and the far wall and joined Aram on the bench.

Instead I mostly just felt annoyed, even as his hands joined Aram's and the melody redoubled. I leaned against the wall and couldn't manage to feel unnerved as it shifted beneath my weight.

"You bring her here," Aram said. I could hardly hear them over the swell of the music, the twining joy and melancholy. Which was probably Sahir's goal. "With our lord's permission?"

Unfortunately for Sahir, I had perfected the art of listening to my parents' conversations through bass-heavy pop music on long car rides.

"Little happens in his realm that he does not know," Sahir answered—a nonanswer. So did the Princeling not know I'd left? "And where are the others?"

"Inside." Aram jerked his head to the side, toward the wall of one of the houses. I found myself sliding between the not-piano and the wall to get closer to them. It was a tight fit, and my shirt caught on the edge of the semi-piano, but I got through. "They will come out if you wish it." Aram's eyes flicked toward me and then away.

Sahir turned his head to stare at me and spoke without breaking our gaze. "I wanted her to see some of our world. I thought it might help her adjust."

At this, Aram stopped playing, abruptly. Sahir continued

on for a few surprised notes and stopped, too. The silence rang in my eardrums. Aram swept his black peacoat out away from the bench and stood up, one hand already reaching for my chin.

Before I could duck away he'd grabbed me, and I squirmed for a second before giving up. I stood, pinned to the wall, and stared at his face. It didn't matter what he did, after all.

"Read her face, good-brother," Aram said. "Can you not see her thoughts there, plain as a tree against the sky? Mortals cannot live without the sun. They wither, or they snap. You were not alive before—you have not seen it. But I have watched them wither, like so many stems in glass vases, and dry, preserved but lifeless, under the hills."

"I thought—" And I could *hear* it, the catch in Sahir's voice. The pain. Did he sound like that because of me? "Why do you say these things, where she can hear?"

"Does she look like she cares?" Even this he didn't say cruelly. I felt his grip tighten on my chin, the dry rough scratch of his fingertips as he turned my head to the side. "Stay for the evening meal."

"Will my cat wither, too?" My voice shocked me, hoarse but urgent.

"Your what?" Aram dropped his hand to his side, wiped his fingers on the leg of his trousers like my skin was dirty.

Sahir cleared his throat. "She brought—I brought her cat here."

"If he'll wither, too, please let him go," I said.

Aram moved his piano-adjacent object to one side, the strength of the gesture at odds with the gentle way he handled the instrument.

"Cats do not *wither*," he said scathingly. "Cats are indifferent." And he headed farther back into the alley between the two houses, his skin gleaming in the dusky air. "You interrupted our evening concert, good-brother," he added.

Sahir grunted, apparently unimpressed. He took my arm and led me after Aram. It took me a moment to recognize what I felt as relief. Doctor Kitten would be fine.

Aram ducked under a low lintel a few paces back in the alleyway. Sahir followed, ducking as well. He pulled me behind him, but I didn't need to bow my head at all.

The room beyond reminded me more than anything of a kitchen in a seventeenth-century manor house preserved somewhere in Europe. It was long, low, devoid of modern technology, but comfortable and lavishly decorated. I stared at the fireplace that dominated the center of the room, with its red brick beehive chimney. On the hearth, a little girl sat playing with a cloth doll.

She cried out when she saw us and ran to Sahir, arms wide. He bent down and caught her up, smiling. "Little one," he said, pressing a kiss to her forehead. "You're taller than me already!" He held her up, dangling her above his head so that it was technically true.

She giggled, pink eyes huge, and grabbed at his arms. "Uncle!" she shrieked. "Higher!"

And he pushed her higher, tendrils of magic streaming from the palms of his hands, until she dangled suspended and shrieking with delight.

I hung back in the doorway, taking in the rest of the room. A woman rose from a chair by the hearth, a bowl of something in her hands. Behind her along the wall was a wide wood countertop, and open shelves built into the walls, which held earthenware.

There was a backsplash of sorts on the wall, in white porcelain with blue patterning, and a kitchen table in front of another door, which I guessed led into the rest of the house.

"Sahir," the woman said, "your visit is unexpected."

"But not unwelcome, I hope," he said, putting the girl down. "Hello, Rijska."

When she smiled, I realized they must be siblings. She had the same dimple in her left cheek, the twinkling brown eyes.

If I'd felt up to it, I would've felt awkward. As it was, I mostly felt bored.

Rijska held her arms open for him, and he swept her up in the same hug as her daughter. When they broke apart, he kept one arm slung around her shoulder.

"Rijska, I have brought a guest," Sahir said, gesturing to me. "Please bid her welcome."

I frowned at him. It sounded suspiciously like the sort of human formality that made him want to rip his own hair out. Was he—was he baiting me?

"I apologize for the intrusion," I said to her.

Sahir looked almost disappointed.

"You have brought my brother," she replied, "and this gift is greater than any disruption you may cause."

I felt something tugging on my shirt and looked down. It was the little girl, her black curls tied back with pink ribbons that matched her eyes.

"You look funny," she said.

"I know," I said.

"They would stay for dinner," Aram said. I had almost forgotten him, lurking in a corner like an imitation coat rack. He'd hung his peacoat up and wore only his tunic now, which was short-sleeved and showed the variegations in color along his arms to his fingers.

"Of course," Rijska said, and smacked Sahir. Then she glanced at her daughter, her lips twisting like she'd realized she needed to set a better example. "Everly, please set the table." Without waiting to see whether the girl listened, she turned back to Sahir again. "It has been months, brother. What has kept you away?" She began whacking him repeatedly on the arm in a way that made me ache for Jordan, whose favorite activity was gently hitting his loved ones.

"Ow," he said, grabbing her wrist. "Rijska, desist, please!"

Everly tugged on me again. "I set the table," she said, with gravitas. "It's my task. Would you like to help me?"

I smiled, because who isn't going to smile at an adorable child solemnly explaining her boring household chores? "Of course," I said. "I'd love to." I let her lead me toward the open shelves on the far wall.

"Brother, what has kept you?" Rijska repeated.

Everly pointed imperiously up at the shelves, her ribboned pigtails bobbing. "My pap gets the plates," she said, "but you can if you want."

I stood on tiptoe and pulled a stack of plates into my arms.

"Five, correct?" I asked Everly, meaning to put a few back.

"Seven," Aram said. I glanced back at him—he had taken out a cutting board and begun dicing vegetables.

"I was detained," Sahir said to his sister. "The Princeling has need of me."

"The Princeling will scheme for centuries," she snapped. "Everly is only a child once."

Everly, who appeared not to be listening, had taken forks from a drawer. She held them in front of her like an exciting multipronged weapon, her tiny pink fingers barely meeting around the bouquet of cutlery.

"Lead the way," I said to her, nudging her toward the kitchen table.

She chirped, skipped twice, and went right past the kitchen table, through the far doorway.

I looked back at Sahir, but he only waved me away. So I followed Everly into a cozy combination living-dining room.

There was what could only be described as a chesterfield sofa on one wall, framed by two tall, rickety bookcases and catty-corner with a simple wood bench. On the near side of the wooden bench was another table, nicer than the one in the kitchen, laid with a lace runner I was almost positive my grandma also owned.

The two short sides of the table had one large chair each, and the other long side had two smaller chairs. Everly, practically bouncing, started to divest herself of forks.

I followed her, laying plates down—three along the bench. "And Uncle Sahir will sit with me," Everly said. "And Pap will sit with me, and Grumps will sit with you, and Grumpy will sit with you."

"Grumps and Grumpy?" I repeated, convinced I had misheard her.

"My parents," Sahir said, appearing next to me with two stacks of glasses. "My dad, Grumps, and my mom, Grumpy."

"Is that…" I trailed off, glancing down at Everly. She'd turned to look at her uncle as soon as he walked in, mouth agape.

"Are the descriptions accurate?" he filled in for me. "You will have to decide for yourself." With a wink, he tossed the glasses in the air—I gasped—they hovered, unstacking themselves, then floated to sit at the right hand of each plate.

"Show-off," I muttered. But Everly squealed in delight.

"Again!" she crowed.

"Everly, where will Mamsie sit?" he asked her, having apparently heard her entire speech.

She shrugged. "Mamsie sits at the top," she said, pointing to the head of the table. "Mamsie is in charge."

It was hard not to smile at that.

"Very true," Rijska said, entering with a large tray. "Sahir, will you get Grumps and Grumpy?" They grinned at each other.

Sahir saluted his sister and went up a narrow spiral staircase I had not noticed, in the shadowy corner of the room.

"Mom! Dad!" he shouted as he went, which made me smile again, imagining him as a kid. I wondered what childhood was like in Faerie, and what Aram had meant when he'd said Sahir wasn't old enough to remember the last time humans had been in Faerie. There were at least three humans in Faerie right now.

I suppressed a shudder, remembering Chad and Milo.

Everly grabbed my hand and put me in one of the chairs

on the long side of the table, against the wall; then she went around to the other side and slid to the middle of the bench.

Aram—I hadn't noticed him come in—laid several dishes of food out and then joined his daughter, yanking on one of her pigtails as he sat.

She giggled. Everly appeared to be a generally delighted and delightful child. If I ever had a daughter, I wanted one just like her.

Except I would never have a daughter now. I stared, aching, at the staircase in the corner.

Sahir's boots were visible first, followed by two bare pairs of feet. The three of them spilled out into the room almost simultaneously and jerked to a preternatural halt as one.

"Grumps," he said, gesturing at the man, "and Grumpy"—with an affectionate clap on the woman's shoulder.

I stood up, unsure what to do, and knocked the chair over. "Oh, no—" I said, but Sahir had already righted it with a tendril of brown magic.

"This is my lady," he said. "In Court we call her Lady of the True Dreams, or Lady of the Cats."

"Nope, not the cat one," I said. "But really, Miriam is fine."

"We are not so determined to hide our names here," Grumpy said, giving Sahir a look. She had the same sharp brown eyes as her son, the same way of standing so she took up more space than her body. "Nor will we use yours ill, Miriam."

Since I doubted Sahir's parents had been auspiciously named Grumps and Grumpy and then found each other and started a family, this felt a bit ironic.

"Dinner looks delicious, Rijska," Grumps said, smiling at his daughter. His children got their riots of silky black curls and the broad strong angles of their faces from him. "Let us sit and eat, and we can discuss your query, Sahir."

Query?

But I dutifully sat again, looking around the table. I hadn't had a family dinner in months—it had been months even before I was trapped in Faerie, because I'd been so busy at work.

As Everly had said, she sat on the bench between Sahir and Aram, lolling side to side so her head rested on first one and then the other of them. Every time her head landed on Sahir's arm, he smiled down at her, his face so soft it sent a stab of unnamable longing through me. Or maybe namable but unwanted longing.

I sat between Grumps and Grumpy, not lolling at all. Grumps had taken the foot of the table and Rijska the head.

They all reached for the food in front of them, and so I did the same. There were six dishes—a salad of sorts with the purple veiny leaves I'd become accustomed to, a ricelike dish, a pressed protein that looked suspiciously like an extra firm tofu slab out of a package, soft dinner rolls, a thick brown sauce, and what appeared to be a tub of unflavored yogurt.

I gaped when Grumps handed me the yogurt. "You guys have this?"

Grumps grinned, one thick-knuckled hand still on the container, his eyes crinkling with crow's feet just like a mortal man's. "Sometimes our friends who walk the mortal world return with gifts."

I glanced around and saw that everyone had taken a heaping spoonful.

"We should discuss," Aram said, when everyone had filled their plates. "How to stop the mortal girl from withering." His left hand splayed out on the table; he tapped his fingers in restless staccato.

Sahir pretended to steal a bite off Everly's plate, and she squealed.

"Well, why is she withering now?" Rijska asked, intent on Aram's face. She stared at him with wide, trusting eyes— Sahir's eyes, with an expression I'd never seen on his broader face. Without any apparent conscious thought, she laid her right hand over Aram's left on the table. He flipped his palm up and squeezed.

"There is an answer," Grumpy said. She had filled her plate with heaping scoops of yogurt and nothing else. My chest tightened in anticipation. Who knew what Grumpy might say? *Faerie curses*, or *a lack of dopamine*.

Everyone turned to her, expectant. She stuck her spoon in the yogurt and plopped a dollop into her mouth.

"Well?" Sahir prompted.

"I do not know the answer," Grumpy said. "Only that there is one."

Grumps sighed, a heaving exhalation that put Sahir to shame. I glanced at Sahir, whose lips quirked like he knew what I was thinking. Sitting across from him at the table, I could see again the shadows beneath his eyes, the hollows under his cheekbones, and the unshaven stubble at his jaw. I'd never seen him so tired.

"Perhaps the Queen or the Duke will know the answer," Grumps volunteered, tearing a soft roll to pieces on his plate. He tossed a piece to Everly, who flinched under her father's arm and then giggled. Rijska glared at her father with enough force that I, personally, would have crawled under the table. He ignored her and continued, "Though I cannot advise you to ask them for it."

Now there was a *Duke*, too? Was he planning some kind of land invasion as well?

I stared at Aram. He had a faraway expression in his eyes, and I wondered what he knew. He seemed more alien than the others.

"Some of the humans do not wither," Sahir said. "Those who wandered into the Court through winding roads open only to them."

I looked around the table, struggling to process. Were they all trying to figure out why I was unhappy? Did *wither* just mean *experience crippling existential depression*?

"But it does not matter." Rijska ripped a roll in half. "No matter who you ask, you will have to travel the roads. And we know the Queen's soldiers have become bolder."

Sahir looked at her. "You have seen them?"

His sister shook her head. "No, but we have heard from others. They wait along the paths between the Courts," she said. "They waylay travelers and take them captive."

Aram put a hand on Everly's head.

Grumps stared at his son. "You will need a company for your journey, Sahir."

I couldn't stop myself, the sudden surge of rage. We didn't

need a magical mystery quest or another faerie to give us riddles. "I already know how to stop me from withering," I said, slamming my fork onto the table. "You need to let me go home *to my family.*"

Sahir looked from Everly to me. And I saw him realize, fully, what had been done to me.

He sagged onto the bench, limbs lengthening. His body started to flicker.

"Oh no, you *do not,*" I shrieked, shoving away from the table so hard that my chair fell over again. "No, you do *not* turn into a vine monster! This is *not your pain.*"

I was roaring by the end, hands flat on the table, hunched over and staring at him.

Aram cleared his throat. Everly had ducked under his arm and buried her face against his side. "The human is right, of course."

Just like the flash of a watch reflecting sunlight on a wall, the rage died. I felt foolish, and dull. I leaned back and picked up my chair. "I'm so sorry." I sat down again.

Sahir's arms remained suspiciously vine-y, but he managed to maintain a corporeal form. "Do not apologize."

"You cannot go home," Grumps said, staring at me. His eyes were so old, his features so subtly *off.* Just slightly too sharp, slightly too wide. I felt further from humanity than I ever had. "You will die in the crossing. So you must seek another answer."

Aram cleared his throat.

Everyone turned to him.

"I know of one who may have an answer," he said, staring

at a point above my right shoulder. "A friend from youth and companion through many trials. A man of honor and decency. A great and powerful magic user from a line of great and powerful magic users. And the only man alive who might *truly* understand the magic behind your imprisonment in Faerie."

I fought down my desire to strangle him to death, revive him, and then strangle him again. He'd probably taken drama class with the Gray Knight and the Princeling; it wasn't his fault the school systems in Faerie only taught Suspenseful Reveals and Dire Predictions.

"Who is this person, good-brother?" Sahir asked, probably sensing my murderous intent through our incontrovertible soul bond or something.

"Roman, of the Wild Fae," he said. The stillness that fell over the table felt foreboding.

"The Princeling promised to introduce me to Roman, if I complete the tasks he has set out for me," I said.

Aram's keen eyes found mine. "What was your bargain, child? The exact phrasing."

My forehead furrowed. In books, people always remembered prophecies and bargains.

"I don't remember," I said. "Let me check my emails."

I pulled my phone out and searched for emails to the Gray Knight.

When I found the relevant chain, I held the phone out across the table. Sahir took one look at Aram's expression and took the phone from me. He cleared his throat, sighed for effect, and read it out:

You will teach my people of humans, whenever they ask and whatever they ask, for ten years. For that period, you will also retain your job—this should be manageable for you. And if you can complete both of these tasks to my satisfaction, then all of my resources will be laid at your feet.

Aram nodded. "And he told you that his resources included Roman?"

"Yep."

"The bargain is poorly worded," Aram said, looking at Grumps. "I imagine the Princeling did not expect the human to think about it overmuch."

Grumps shrugged. "The bargain provided him with an immediate service, and"—he glanced at me—"I assume you work as many hours as Sahir?"

"More, usually," Sahir said.

"Then by keeping her in her job, he has effectively ensured she will have no time to search for an escape." Grumps took another helping of yogurt. That dude probably had a fantastic gut biome. Did the Fae have a similar anatomy to us? Did they host gut bacteria?

"If Roman is truly the Princeling's best guess—" Aram cut himself off.

But Rijska had lost patience. "If Roman is the Princeling's best guess, then the poor girl has *no reason* to wait over nine more years in this...*state*"—she gestured at me, which I took mild offense to—"when you can end her anticipation with an introduction!"

But Aram shook his head. "Would it were that easy, love,"

he said. "As you remember, Roman passed through our home some days ago. He did not share with you his destination, but I will do so now. He has taken a project in the Queen's realm, the restoration of some ruins at the edge of her sacred wood. He anticipates that he will stay in her realm for…" He counted on his fingers. "I think two human years at least."

"You mean past the Queen's soldiers on the roads?" I clarified.

He nodded. "Yes, and in the heart of a Court where a human can be destroyed on sight."

This was displeasing information.

"And you think Roman will know how I can avoid exploding myself?"

Aram shrugged. "At the least, Roman can perhaps explain some measure of his father's magic. If he grants you nothing else, he will grant you knowledge."

Sahir and I exchanged a glance. He seemed to be thinking *Is knowledge worth dying for?*

I was thinking *An entire quest? That's so much walking.*

"Roman will not grant us knowledge for nothing," Sahir said. Aram made a face like *Obviously not, you absolute child.*

"If you choose to pursue him, tell Roman that I grant you leave to call in my favor."

I glanced at Rijska, curious what she thought about this situation. She was staring intently at her plate. Fair. If Jordan had brought some strange girl to dinner and told Thea and me that he planned to escort her into enemy territory, I would likely also not want to get involved.

"Won't the Princeling be angry?"

"Your bargain has not forbidden this quest," Grumpy said, munching on a lettuce-adjacent purple leaf. She had a little plant fiber stuck in her teeth. "You may seek Roman on your own at any time."

"Do not tell us what you decide," Aram cautioned. "So that we cannot betray your trust, even under duress."

Rijska rolled her eyes. "You are quite dramatic, husband," she said. "Do not scare the human."

"Or the child," Grumps added, looking at Everly. She'd fully buried herself in her father's armpit.

Aram opened his mouth, as if to begin some philosophical diatribe about the nature of truth and fear.

Grumpy patted my hand. "We will discuss this no more. Let us eat with our son."

I looked at Sahir; his dark eyes shone.

"Miriam, my brother is the truest soul I know," Rijska said. "He will help you."

"I'm sorry," I said, still looking at him.

He shook his head. "Everly." He glanced down at her. "Are you in school?"

The little girl peeked out from under her father's arm.

And we continued with our meal.

Chapter 16

In Which I Tell Jordan the Truth

"Why did you bring me here?" I asked Sahir, when the lights of the town had faded behind us. He turned off the path toward the paddock, where our two horses stood. The starlight silvered their coats.

"I swore an oath," he said. "To keep you healthy, not just to keep you alive. And I will not break it."

I frowned at his broad back, the green of his tunic gray in the semidark. He whistled; the horses looked up and started toward us as one.

"And," he added, "sometimes, we cannot carry ourselves. At those times, it helps to have a friend."

A friend?

But he wouldn't look at me. Sparkles trotted up to my side. I saw the familiar glow along her back as the saddle appeared for me.

"It will be better if you help carry yourself, Miriam," he said. I wasn't entirely sure if he meant onto the horse, or in the context of the larger metaphor. I nodded, though, and when he came to lift me onto Sparkles, I grabbed the saddle and pulled myself partway up.

I thought I heard him chuckle into my backside and stiffened. But when I straightened in the saddle, he was already astride his horse.

"Did you understand what my good-brother and sister and mother and father said to you, Miriam?" he asked. The horses, unprompted, started toward the path.

"Kind of," I said. "But I still don't fully understand all of the Courts. How do they relate?" *Tell me about the human torture*, I thought. *Am I going to get tortured?*

"Hmm." He tapped a hand on the pommel of his own saddle. I watched his nails spark, more like polished glass than keratin. "The Princeling is, ah, like a governor."

"What?" I sputtered. "This much ceremony for a *governor*?"

"An important governor," he added, sounding almost defensive. "Like, the governor of California."

I actually laughed aloud at that.

He looked at me, startled.

"So the Queen governs faeries who want to torture humans?" I asked, because I couldn't hold it in anymore.

Sahir bit his lip, a white flash against the warm brown of his skin. "The Queen governs faeries who do not want to engage with humans but will not hesitate to kill them. Faeries do not—well, we used to torture humans. Our grandparents did."

"Until what, they all died?" I asked sarcastically.

He frowned at me. "Yes. That generation is fading. The last of them will disappear soon."

"I thought faeries were functionally immortal," I said—though I remembered Milo telling me otherwise, all those months ago, I'd never confirmed it with anyone else.

"To a gnat, you live for eons, and hunt its children and its children's children for sport." He shifted forward on his horse, looking for something up the trail.

"So I'm a gnat."

He must have heard some threat in my voice, because he answered quickly. "Perhaps a dog is more apt. A dog's great-grandson might witness the death of its master, and the lore of the master's birth could conceivably pass through four generations."

This answer wasn't much better, but I refrained from further comment on his choice of metaphor.

"But Aram is older than you? He said he remembered…"

Sahir sighed. I wondered if I'd hit a sore subject. "Rijska loves him, and he is very wise. But they both know she will have centuries without him."

We rode in silence for several minutes. Perhaps he was contemplating his brother-in-law's death and his sister's loneliness.

"So the Princeling inherited the role when his father died…" I prompted.

"No," Sahir said. "We elected him. We elect a new leader every…" He paused, thought. "I suppose every twenty-five human years."

In the distance, the lights of the Court shone out against the black of the hillside.

"Why is your elected leader called a Princeling?"

"Do you have no stupid traditions in your democracy?"

I chuckled at that, though I also felt a twinge of disappointment. In a book, there would've been a fantastic and history-rich explanation. "I guess we do," I said.

Sahir frowned at me. "I will see that we speak with Roman," he said. "It is my duty as your knight, and my honor as your friend."

"We don't need to," I said. "We can wait until I fulfill my bargain with the Princeling."

The look Sahir gave me physically hurt. "Do you think you can wait that long? It has only been three months, Miriam. Can you do this thirty-nine more times?"

I clutched at my stomach. "No," I whispered, weak and ashamed. "Probably not."

Sahir didn't push me any further.

We ascended the path to the Court's entrance and stopped the horses. I patted Sparkles on the neck while Sahir got down from his horse.

I didn't hesitate this time to slide into his arms. He caught me, hands on my ribs, and put me down gently. I gazed up into his eyes, unable to stop the thought that it would be *nice*, having Sahir around to catch me. That he followed the rules of my childhood reading: the sense of honor and justice and duty. My hands slid from his shoulders to his arms. He also had the unreasonably muscled body of most fantasy books. His fingers slid down to my waist, tightened almost convulsively. He had the unfair beautiful fringe of dark lashes that for some reason only blesses men. They shadowed his cheekbones as he stared down at me, his lush lips slightly parted.

"Thank you," I whispered, that thought whirling: *He can catch you; he can always catch you.* And the unwelcome follow-up—that I wanted to be able to catch him, too, and was currently about as useful as an easel in a hurricane.

I pulled away, and his hands fell from my hips to his sides. I turned abruptly and kissed Sparkles on her warm nose. She nickered, huffed in my face.

"Bye, Sparkles," I said.

Sahir and I walked inside together.

I focused on the floor passing beneath our feet, the sound of my breathing in my ears.

"Thank you," I said again. "For helping me go outside."

We stopped in front of my door. He took a step toward me. I leaned against my door, stared up at him. "You are welcome," he breathed.

I glanced at the dent in his upper lip. At the lush curve of his lower lip. I couldn't stop. He had a thin line, a scar, on the dimple in his chin. His throat worked as my eyes followed it down to the crest of his clavicle, half-bared by his disarranged green tunic—

Nope.

I squeezed my eyes shut. "Thank you," I managed, like a broken robot. I could hear the click of his heel as he took a half step closer, feel the warmth of his body inches from mine.

"You said that," he whispered, his breath hot on my lips. His cinnamon smell surrounded me.

I inhaled.

He pressed his forehead to mine.

"Good night, lady," he said, and was gone.

———————————— • ————————————

Safely in my room, I sat up in bed, Doctor Kitten beside me. My resident will-o'-the-wisp had taken up his preferred spot on my nightstand, curled into the nest I'd made for him from an old T-shirt. He glowed a warm, soothing bedtime yellow.

I needed help. I thought about Thea and Jordan. I wouldn't call Thea for advice; she was loving, lovely, and not very practical.

Jordan, however, was an engineer who wrote Dungeons and Dragons campaigns in his spare time. If anyone would have practical and well-reasoned advice off the bat, it was him.

"We have to call Jordan," I said. Doctor Kitten mewled in agreement.

I scrolled through my contacts for Jordan's name and clicked on it before I could think too hard. It was one a.m. He might not be awake.

But he answered on the second ring. "Mir?" He sounded groggy.

"Jordan?" I said.

"Are you okay?" He paused. "I haven't heard from you in a while."

"I'm fine," I said, staring at my empty hand. "Work is just hard."

I hadn't even checked my email when we got in. I had been offline for six hours. For all I knew, something was on fire.

"This job is terrible for you," he said. I could hear his voice change as he shifted closer to the phone. "Is it worth it?"

"Yeah, I mean…" I trailed off. Heaved a deep breath. "Jordan, I have to tell you something and I need you not to panic."

"Okay," he said, slowly. His tone had lost its sleep-rough edge. "What is it?"

"Swear not to tell anyone, not even Thea," I added. "I have to tell her myself. When I'm ready."

"Are you pregnant?" he asked. He sounded baffled. "When did you even have *time*—"

"No, shut up!" I said, suddenly so exasperated I couldn't be nervous. Which had probably been his goal. "I'm trapped in Faerie, Jordan, and I need your advice about going on a quest to find a way home."

As if he knew I needed him, Doctor Kitten uncurled himself from my side and stepped into my lap. I hunched around him, breathed heavily into the phone, and didn't speak again. For several seconds, there was silence between us. Then I heard Jordan take a few slow, deep breaths.

"Ah," Jordan said, his tone even in the way that meant he was suppressing panic. "Well, that would certainly explain why you've been completely avoiding us."

Something in my stomach unclenched.

"Yeah," I agreed.

"How'd that happen?" he asked.

I splayed out on the bed and told him the whole story.

At the end of it, Jordan hummed thoughtfully. I sat up again and leaned back against the headboard.

"I can see why you didn't tell any of us, but the point of your friends is to lighten your burdens, you moron." He sighed.

I made a vague noise. I couldn't speak yet.

"Well, what's Faerie like, then?" Jordan asked.

"It's—" I stopped. I hadn't allowed myself to think about it, really. "It's different."

"No way," he gasped. "Faerie, the pocket dimension populated entirely with magical people and famously separated from the human realm for at least a hundred years, is *different*?"

"Oh, shut up," I muttered. But that wasn't what I wanted to say to him. "It's like you'd expect," I tried again. "Everything is slightly brighter. And there's a colony of vampire nudists, I think, who skybathe on the lawn most days."

He snorted. "Of course that's what you notice."

"I'm mentioning it for *your* benefit," I snapped. "But what do I do about this quest, Jordan?"

"Are you joking?" he asked. "It seems obvious to me. You...go on the quest."

"It could be dangerous," I reminded him. "The Queen is deadly to humans."

"It sounds like staying in Faerie at your job is also deadly to humans," he said. "Or, human. You specifically."

"If I die, will you tell everyone what happened?"

Jordan made an uncomfortable noise. "Don't die, Miri. I don't want to have to explain any of this to Thea. Or worse, your mother."

I sighed. "I'll do my best."

"You should tell Thea, too," he said.

"I don't know how," I admitted.

"Just starting is usually the best way." Jordan sounded sleepy again.

"I have to go to bed," I said. "I love you."

"Love you, too, Mir."

After we hung up, I didn't go to bed. I logged onto my computer and spent three hours editing the formatting in an Excel model.

———————•———————

In my dream, a thick hairy hand reached out and pulled the ring from my finger. "This is mine," a voice said, and the world around me cracked and shook.

I shouldn't have been surprised to wake up to Lene, Gaheris, and Sahir standing over me like three not-very-wise men, Lene shaking me and Gaheris's flaming hair providing most of the light in the room.

"Good morning," I said, sitting up. "Is this an intervention?"

"You're taking off work," Sahir said. "I know where Roman is."

I pulled my covers up my chest, trying to retain the last bit of sleepy warmth.

"I know where Roman is, too, Sahir," I said, in tones of deep irritation. "He's at the edge of a sacred forest repairing some ruins."

"Miriam," Sahir started, and then stopped. "Ah," he said. He looked around the room and settled on a bare patch of wall near his left arm. "I realize that perhaps humans are not aware of geometry," he said, flicking his fingers toward the wall. A large grid appeared in the dirt.

"Geometry," I repeated, a bit dazed.

"This is a square," he said, outlining a four-by-four square with another flick of his fingers. "The area of the square is sixteen—do you see?"

He proceeded to count each of the smaller squares contained in this large square, tapping each with his finger.

I stared at him.

"And this is a rectangle," he said, outlining an eight-by-two rectangle. "It also contains sixteen squares. The area is still sixteen. But the *perimeter*"—he emphasized this word with two pulses of light around each perimeter—"is different for each of these shapes. The one has a perimeter of sixteen. The other has a perimeter of twenty. Do you see?"

Unable to form words, I nodded.

"Do you see also why it would not be convenient to walk the perimeter of the forest, looking for ruins with no further guidance?" he prompted.

We stared at each other.

"Uh. Yes," I said, because it felt easier than explaining the traumas inflicted on me by my geometry teacher.

"Good. Then get up."

"What about Doctor Kitten?" I asked, looking at the cat in question.

"We will be gone for two nights," Sahir said. "The cat will be perfectly safe."

He must not have found my expression particularly reassured. He glanced at Lene, helplessly.

"We will take Doctor Kitten," she declared.

"Will that be safe for him?"

Lene and Sahir exchanged another look.

"My sister, Nele, will stay with Doctor Kitten," she declared, with the same level of confidence as before.

"*Who?*" I scooped my cat into my arms.

"Her sister, Nele," Gaheris said. "She also has an affinity for cats."

"You have a *sister*?" I asked, staring at Lene. "Why didn't I know that?"

She blinked back. "You have not asked many questions about me."

Well, I was a bad friend.

I slid out of bed and rocked Doctor Kitten gently. He patted my cheek with his paw. "Okay, fine, but let me prepare for this. I need to request time off. I want to meet Nele before I leave her with Doctor Kitten. And I have no idea why you couldn't have waited until breakfast to tell me this."

"It is breakfast time," Gaheris said. "You were just still asleep."

Sahir stalked over to my desk and unplugged my laptop. "Here," he said, thrusting it in my general direction. "Email your boss now. Gaheris will retrieve Nele."

Gaheris turned with alacrity and exited the room.

I went for my suitcase, still on the floor by my bed, and grabbed the clothes on top—the soft green leggings and long tunic the Gray Knight had made for me all those months ago.

"Can you all let me get dressed?"

Lene, who had picked up Doctor Kitten, sat on the bed, her short legs dangling over the edge. "Please do," she said.

I stared at Sahir, who stared back. I raised an eyebrow. Sahir sighed with the gusto of a man performing his favorite activity and pushed past me, his arm jostling my shoulder, to leave the room.

"Nele is lovely," Lene said as I pulled the leggings on beneath my nightdress. "She will care for Doctor Kitten as well as I do."

"I'm sorry I didn't ask questions about you." I turned my back to Lene and attempted a complicated maneuver involving a sports bra, my left arm, and the neck of the nightdress. It ended with my shoulder jammed into my left cheek.

"Friendship can be difficult when one party is imprisoned against her will in a magical land and the other party sleeps for eighteen hours a day," Lene said, in the tone of someone stating a fairly evident fact.

"That's very wise," I said, attempting to dislodge my shoulder. Then I glanced at her, sitting primly on the bed with my cat.

"Lene, is it dangerous for you to help me find Roman?" I asked. "I'm sorry, I don't fully understand the intricacies of inter-Court politics," I added, when she glanced up.

She shrugged. "I will brave the danger as fair return for what you have given me."

I glanced down at the cat, not sure if she meant she thought I'd given her Doctor Kitten. He stared back at me, implacable. I pretended his expression meant *You're stuck with me forever* and not *This is my new mom.*

"Could they . . . kill you?" I asked, in a voice that sounded awkward to my own ears. What would I do if she said yes?

"No," she said, which was a relief. "Have you never been a political prisoner before?" she continued, which was not a relief.

"Ah . . . no," I said, shoulder still stuck to ear. "Have you?"

I extricated myself from my nightdress and straightened everything out.

She looked bewildered. "Of course. It is fairly common when we travel the roads in Faerie to be waylaid by overzealous soldiers of one Court or another."

I blinked at her. She blinked at me.

"So then what happens?" I asked, rubbing my arm to bring some feeling back into it.

She wrinkled her nose. "The soldiers bring you to their liege as tribute. Their liege offers you an opportunity to swear fealty. If you choose not to, they will negotiate with your liege against your return." She paused and frowned at me. "I do not know what would happen if the Queen encountered you," she said. "As humans are usually killed on sight at the Queen's Court, I do not know humans who have met her."

"Very cool," I said, grabbing my shirt and yanking it on.

"Cool?" she repeated. "I do not see the connection to temperature. Is this a human idiom?"

"Uh. Yes." I patted myself down to smooth any disarray. "I'm dressed," I added, still at a normal volume, and Sahir opened the door immediately. "Creep," I said, mostly for my own benefit.

"I am not a creep," Sahir said, leaning against the doorway. "I am efficient with everyone's time." He'd folded his arms across his chest, his biceps straining at the sleeves of his shirt. This felt intentional. The man had magic shirts; he could have sized them appropriately if he wanted to.

Gaheris came up behind him, leading a small woman who looked remarkably like Lene, with the same brown fur and delicate features. "Efficiency is an odd value," he said. "It never interested you before you went to the human realm."

"Hi, you must be Nele," I said to the woman with him.

"Oh, yes!" Gaheris exclaimed; he was an enthusiastic, if indifferent, student in my human classes. "Nele, I hope all is well with you. This is my Miriam."

Gaheris looked at me hopefully.

"Very close," I said, gently. "I'm your friend Miriam, not your Miriam."

"Well, you *are* my Miriam," Gaheris said, perplexed. "I do not have another."

"Hello, Doctor Kitten," Nele said, ignoring us both. She walked past me and hopped onto the bed next to her sister.

As Lene had months before, Nele started yowling at Doctor Kitten. My shoulders sagged as he yowled back. Even if I did find a way back to the mortal plane, Doctor Kitten would miss Lene—and now Nele—terribly.

I hadn't expected to coparent my cat with a faerie, but sometimes life surprises us.

"Thank you for staying with him," I said.

Nele ignored me.

"As soon as Jeff agrees to your request, we will leave," Sahir said.

I grabbed the computer off the bed, Nele and Doctor Kitten still yowling in a miserable duet, and opened it. "Does the Princeling know?" I asked, typing in my password.

"I have told him that we will go into the woods, for your health," Sahir said. "He does not know much about mortals, but he knows you have been unwell."

Feeling an insane mixture of anxiety and disinterest, I drafted an email to Jeff. The faeries settled in around me: Sahir on the other side of the bed, and Gaheris on the floor by Lene's and Nele's feet.

For a moment, I considered not sending the email. *The bargain—My job—*

But Roman was the Princeling's only bargaining chip. And unless Roman had a way to set me free, I would be trapped forever, whether or not I took two days of vacation right now.

Hi Jeff,
I was wondering if I could take a few days off to recharge. I have been feeling under the weather. I was thinking today and tomorrow might be good since the workload is lighter. I know this is short notice so let me know if this does not work. The Princeling knows I want to take off and has agreed to it. I will of course be available for calls and as issues arise. Please let me know if this works.
Miri

His response was immediate. *Yes.*

Wordlessly, I showed the exchange to Sahir. He grunted. Gaheris and Lene stood up.

"Should I take my phone?" I asked.

"The Court is the only area with cell service," Sahir said. "But do as you will."

I'd just lied to Jeff, then. I would *not* be available.

I sent a text to my mom. *Busy few days—won't be able to call.* Then I texted Thea and said, *Insane work assignment, don't expect replies for a bit,* texted Jordan *I'm going on the quest,* and locked my phone.

I kissed Doctor Kitten on the top of the head, and Nele stretched out on the bed next to him. With one backward glance to see the two of them already snuggled up like absolute traitors, I followed Sahir, Gaheris, and Lene out of the room.

I shouldn't have been surprised to find four packs leaning against the wall in the hallway, but I was briefly horrified by the way they lay out in the open as streams of faeries passed us in both directions. Everybody would see that we were leaving. Any spies on the inside could inform various bands of kidnapping soldiers that the human was about to embark on some kind of quest. Did Sahir have no sense of self-preservation?

Sahir gestured toward a pack, so I shouldered it, since there was nothing else to do at this point. Gaheris and Lene took up the other two, and together we left the mountain.

———————————— • ————————————

We walked for most of the morning.

I hadn't been exercising much.

At all. I hadn't been exercising at all. My calves burned before we'd even reached the forest at the far end of the clearing. By the time we hit the shadows of the first trees, I had an ache in my left buttock and a stitch in my side. The day was cold, but I sweated through my shirt beneath the pack. My fingertips turned blue, and I wished I had gloves.

There were constant trills of bird call, so frequent I found it jarring at first. Over time, the noise faded into a background melody entwined with the rustling of tree branches and crunch of leaves underfoot.

No one spoke. I thought about all the times I'd wished I could go on a quest, like my favorite characters. I thought about how fervently my favorite authors had derided questing, and how I'd always thought they were being buzzkills.

They were not being buzzkills. Walking all day in a state of anticipation rapidly becomes boring.

Sahir seemed uninclined to talk. Behind me, Gaheris and Lene walked side by side, their low voices blending into the sounds of the nature around us.

I tripped over a tree branch, and Sahir caught me by the arm, his fingers digging into my flesh. "Walk better," he instructed, a man born to be a teacher.

I opened my mouth to retort and got a faceful of dirt. I tried to breathe but couldn't.

There was a weight on the pack on top of me. I flailed my arms.

"Stop moving," Sahir hissed. The weight lessened, and I tilted my head to the side, gasping. His hot breath ghosted across my cheek. The curtain of his hair filled my line of sight and the sharp cinnamon smell of his shampoo filled my nostrils.

He used one hand to pull his hair away so I could see that he'd flung himself nearly on top of me and then levered himself onto all fours, crouched over my backpack.

Lene wriggled up next to me, flat on her stomach with dead leaves caught in her whiskers. "Get to cover."

"Where is cover? Cover from what?" I whispered. I went to lift my head, and Sahir's hand clamped down on the base of my skull.

"It's Kamare," Lene said, digging the claws of her left hand into the earth. The flex of her lightly furred fingers left long furrows in the ground.

"What?" There was a branch beneath my neck, jabbing into my carotid artery.

"The faerie who tried to poison you," Lene clarified.

"The lunch lady?" I asked blankly.

Sahir's sigh ruffled my hair and the leaves beneath us.

I abstained from further clarifying questions, my heart pounding against the leaves below me. Slow minutes ticked past, and my left calf started cramping.

Finally, Sahir's fingers loosened. I propped myself up on my elbows—inadvertently whacking Sahir in the stomach with my pack. He exhaled in a low and displeased huff. The warmth behind me disappeared, and I rolled over to see that he'd stood up.

When I glanced past him I saw that Gaheris's hair was extinguished; he'd huddled into the trunk of a nearby tree, eyes shut and skin shockingly well camouflaged.

"I didn't notice anything," I whispered.

Sahir rolled his eyes. "Of course you did not notice anything," he said. "There were twelve faeries. They moved with the wind and stopped when it died. They appeared to have one tracker, but from the sound of his breathing, he is experiencing a head cold."

"I believe that his head cold prevented him from smelling us," Lene chimed in.

Gaheris finally stood and came toward us, trembling on stick-thin legs.

"The Queen's soldiers distress me," he said. "They have hungry eyes."

I closed my own eyes. "Sahir," I said. "How much more walking before we find Roman?"

"About three hours," Lene said, when Sahir didn't reply. "If we walked at our usual speed. With you?" She looked me up and down. "Seven. We will camp tonight an hour from the sacred site, so that you can present yourself well to Roman in the morning."

With this encouragement, I brushed the dirt from my knees and gestured for her to lead the way.

●

By late afternoon I was crying softly, limping along several paces behind Gaheris.

The blister on my left foot was bigger, but the two on my right foot had somehow both developed between my big and second toes. This can-do attitude earned them a place of pride in my mental litany of complaints.

"Have you dreamed of our quest, Miriam?" Gaheris asked. "Guidance would be to our benefit."

I jerked to a halt. "*What?*"

Sahir glanced from me to Gaheris and back to me. "Well, it is a fair question."

Several horrible realizations clicked into place.

"Is *that* what 'Lady of the True Dreams' means? That I have prophetic dreams?"

"What did you think it meant?" Gaheris asked, looking baffled.

"I didn't think it meant *anything*."

Now Sahir looked irritated. "We have had several very involved conversations about names, Miriam. Why would the Princeling have given you a meaningless name?"

I flung my hands up so hard I almost unbalanced, the pack pulling me toward the forest floor. "Political cachet?" I guessed wildly. I regained my footing. I'd thought the Princeling had given me a title to protect me in his Court.

Lene, who had been pretending not to listen, turned around, too. "Is this a human prank?" she asked. We'd covered practical jokes, pranks, and April Fools' Day in one of our recent human classes.

My jaw dropped. "So I *do* have prophetic dreams?"

At this, Sahir emitted a sigh so vociferous it disturbed some nearby birds nesting in a tree. "Miriam, obviously you have prophetic dreams," he said, and turned his back to me definitively.

I trailed the three of them as we continued on our trek, my feet crying out and my head spinning. "Who was that obvious to?" I asked. Then I remembered the conversation between the Princeling and his knights on that Teams call months ago—about my fractured eyes and weird zygomatic bones. If my dreams were prophetic, why were they so much sexier than my waking life?

None of the faeries answered me, so I subsided into baffled silence. Hours passed as we walked.

Finally, at a signal I didn't discern, the three faeries stopped in a small clearing.

They didn't verbalize the division of labor but moved with

the ease of long familiarity. Gaheris touched my arm and jerked his head in a gesture that probably meant *Come with me* and not *Wow, the strain of these backpacks has caused me a lot of neck pain.*

While Sahir and Lene raised the tent, Gaheris and I collected wood for the campfire. This entailed me trailing him and humming in agreement whenever he picked anything up. Gaheris was uniquely suited to this task, touching each piece of wood in turn to determine if it would burn. We collected two armfuls—enough for dinner, but not enough to keep the fire going through the night.

When we got back to the campsite, a large A-frame cloth tent had been raised. I found myself wondering who I would sleep next to, a little stressed out about the idea. I was used to falling asleep in front of Sahir. And Lene was used to falling asleep in front of me. Gaheris and I were each vastly removed from the other's sleeping habits, and this made me nervous.

The air had a bite to it, cleaner and sharper than autumn in New York. Gaheris and I gathered several large stones and marked out a circle in the dirt.

"This should be enough," he said, leaning a few logs against each other in our makeshift fire pit. He left a hand on the wood, and a tongue of fire twisted down his head and neck, along his shoulder, and out over his fingertips. The wood caught, and he pulled a hand away.

"Why doesn't your hair set anything on fire?" I blurted out, finally vocalizing a question that had bugged me for months.

He looked up from where he knelt on the ground. "Because I do not want it to," he said, frowning at me. "Do you want it to?"

"No, of course not." I turned away from him, toward the discarded packs. I reached for the nearer one and opened the top to find a stack of wooden bowls. I pulled it out, and then grabbed the food containers underneath.

A loaf of bread. Some more of the purple hummus-adjacent spread. Something that looked like precooked lentils.

I put my hands in the air and stretched upward. I didn't hear Sahir come up behind me.

"That looks edible," he said, his cheek nearly pressed to mine as he peered over my shoulder. I suppressed a shiver and arched my back. The motion nestled his chin farther into the crook of my neck, where the rough stubble on his cheek rubbed against my skin.

"I like the purple stuff," I said. I could see half of his face, lit by the crackling flames.

Gaheris looked up at us. "Dinner will be ready in a moment. Where is Lene?"

"She is in a tree." Sahir pointed up.

I followed the line of his finger, letting myself lean into the flex of his biceps, and saw her reflective green eyes staring down at us.

"I hope we didn't say anything rude." I winked at Gaheris.

"We did not," he said earnestly.

Sahir hadn't moved, letting me stand in the half circle of his arm, my face nearly pressed to his shoulder.

"Is dinner ready?" Lene called to us, her voice thin in the night air.

"Yes," Gaheris said.

She stood up on the branch, heedless of the way it wobbled,

and walked back toward the trunk. I watched her sure steps until she was swallowed up by the darkness.

A few moments later, she appeared between two trees and joined us in the clearing.

Sahir stepped away from me. I tried not to have any feelings or opinions about his moving, but in his absence, I felt the cold even more acutely.

Instead, I went back to the packs and grabbed the four bowls and spoons they'd brought. We all sat around the fire, cross-legged on the ground.

Gaheris ladled each of us a bowl of stew, rich with purple potato-like chunks and silvery beads that tasted like peas. We topped it with the purple spread.

For the most part, we ate in silence. I watched Lene shift on the ground, searching for a more comfortable seat.

"Won't the Queen's soldiers see the light of our fire?" I asked.

"We would not light an unwarded fire," Gaheris replied. "Unless they stumble upon us, they will not notice even the glimmer of our wards."

"But maintaining silence will be safer," Sahir said, a quiet reproach.

To entertain myself, I came up with a list of questions for Roman, ranging from *Hi Roman, do you know a way for me to go back to New York?* to *Hi Roman, what are your top tips and tricks for magical mayhem?*

I couldn't maintain any level of fear or misery; I mostly felt hysterical. It didn't really matter, in the end, what Roman said. I couldn't *let* it matter. I knew that these faeries—my friends, I was forced to acknowledge—had only taken me on this wild-goose chase to bring me out of a depressive funk. Maybe, at most, to give me some more clarity over the molecular changes wrought by faerie food that made my escape impossible. They'd done as much as Thea and Jordan ever had—more, even, since Thea and Jordan only ever brought me candy and said mean things about exes, due to the fact that it's passé to go on quests for wise old magic-wielding mentors in New York.

And I couldn't stop the same miserable, loathsome thought that had squirreled its way into my head since the first time I touched magic. Maybe my friends were putting themselves in danger, ferrying a human through the Queen's territory, for absolutely no reason. Maybe there was a world where I lived happily in Faerie, if I could only figure out how to articulate what I wanted.

After dinner, I helped Lene scrub out the bowls with dirt while Gaheris banked the fire. Sahir had disappeared into the tent. I kept glancing toward that tent flap, longing for a windbreak. The air had gotten colder, and I was shaking.

Gaheris went into the tent first; Lene and I followed after, bringing our packs in, too.

I didn't have time to wonder where I would sleep, because she jerked her chin toward Sahir, who sat on one of the two middle bedrolls. Gaheris lay on the other middle bedroll, and Lene went to his other side.

Which put me next to Sahir.

I looked at him. His expression was implacable. I shivered again, still cold. Then I crawled onto the bedroll he'd set up for me and kicked off my shoes. I kept my socks on, slid under the thin top blanket in my clothes, and squeezed my eyes shut.

"Why don't faeries have space heaters?" I whispered.

Sahir's words were so quiet I might have imagined them. "Humans cannot endure inconvenience."

"Hypothermic death isn't inconvenient," I hissed, warmed a bit by the force of my own irritation.

His brown eyes gleamed in the darkness. "I always find your offices too warm," he said. "Perhaps faeries have warmer blood than humans."

I wrapped my arms around myself. "That is very interesting scientific theory," I said, gritting my teeth to keep them from chattering.

I'd expected some sort of magical warmth, but the blanket was apparently heated by my body and nothing else. I continued shaking and curled in on myself to conserve heat.

As my body had the same ambient temperature as a refrigerator, this did nothing.

I opened my eyes to find Sahir staring at me, his face inches from mine.

"Do you need me to warm you?" he whispered.

"You're offering to be a bed warmer?" My voice stayed light, amused. My body vibrated beneath the thin blanket he'd laid out for me.

"You're shaking." He'd propped himself up on an elbow, a dim silhouette in the tent. I glanced past him, at Lene's and Gaheris's prone forms. And then another shiver racked my body, so hard I felt my stomach muscles clench.

"Don't be ridiculous," I said through my teeth.

"I am sworn to your health, Miriam," he growled, eyes flashing. "So I ask again. Do you need me to warm you?"

I lay and looked at him for several long seconds.

"Yes, fine," I hissed, after another shiver racked me so hard my neck cracked.

He sighed and levered himself up onto his hands and knees. I started to roll to my side, but he caught my shoulder and pushed me onto my back—the same way the Gray Knight had, months before. I sucked in a gasp, afraid to show him that I'd liked it. He crawled over me, his knees outside my hips and his elbows caging my face.

I'll get claustrophobic if he stays like that, I thought, in a stellar example of *lying to oneself*. I wrinkled my nose, and he raised an eyebrow. I wiggled my knee against his calf until he lifted it, then repeated the motion on the other side.

With a sigh, he lay down against me, sliding one arm beneath my back as he did. His cinnamon smell enveloped me, so thick it was almost suffocating.

I wrapped my arms around him and held him to my chest. He sank into me completely, pressing me against the bedroll. My lips were dry, my tongue heavy and limp in my desert of a mouth, and I couldn't breathe from his weight. But he just nuzzled against my neck, apparently unaffected. His hips fit into the cradle of my legs, his lips on my collarbone as he breathed in a steady rhythm.

Minutes passed, and I waited for my heart to slow. But every shift of our bodies brought a new exquisite pain to the forefront: the curl of his hair on my cheek, the feeling of his forearm where he'd tucked it beneath me as it arched my chest up toward him, the unrelenting pressure of his hips against me.

He pushed up and propped himself on his forearms; I

followed the slide of muscle in his right biceps, my eyes half-lidded. I could feel the desire written all over my own face but couldn't hide it.

He looked down at me. "Are you any warmer?"

My shivering had stopped. I nodded. I knew my eyes were too wide, too unfocused as I stared up at him.

My lips parted. "Yes, thank you," I whispered, hoarse. We stared at each other. He didn't move any closer. I couldn't stop my frantic heartbeat, couldn't stop myself from feeling the way his body pressed into mine from my lowest rib down, the pressure delicious and suffocating.

The seconds ticked on, our faces inches apart. His thick lashes shaded his half-lidded eyes.

And then—I watched his brown eyes flick down to glance at my mouth. A question, or a temptation, or an involuntary response.

My heart stuttered, and instead of blood it pumped pain, a weltering agony inside me. I was frozen, torn between wanting his lips to brush mine and a terror that he would not like how I kissed.

He rolled himself off to the side, leaving my body cold and too light.

After a moment, he put his lips to my ear.

"Good night," he whispered, the heat of his shoulder burning mine.

I lay awake and stared at the roof of the tent until my eyes ached, unable to stop replaying that flicker in his eyes.

Chapter 17

In Which I Learn About Myself

I woke to a sudden gust of cold air, so sharp my eyes flew open.

The faeries had taken the tent down around me instead of waking me up. Lene, standing by my side, held out her hand to me. I grasped it and she pulled me up. Gaheris and Sahir both knelt nearby, vigorously rolling swaths of fabric.

This appeared to be the unappealing back end of camping, wherein one discovers that one must clean up after oneself.

Gaheris smiled at me. "Would you like to fold your bedroll?" he asked, as Sahir performed a gesture that made both of their bedrolls shrink to half their size.

"Miri, I would speak with you," Lene said, saving me from the terrible task Gaheris was attempting to assign. She grabbed my hand and pulled me away.

Lene took me a short distance into the trees.

"Roman may have knowledge from his own father," she said, her voice careful. "But he may not. And he may not be…correct." She'd unsheathed her front claws and started scratching at the tree trunk.

"What does that mean?"

She wouldn't look at me. "Faeries are not like these human *lie detectors* that Gaheris tells me about," she said. "We can only tell the truth as we believe it. But belief is not fact. If Roman misremembers information his father shared, or forgets entirely…" She trailed off.

"If he's wrong, I'll die," I translated.

Lene stared down at the splintered wood at her feet. "Would staying in Faerie be the worst fate?"

I cleared my throat, unsure how to answer. But she didn't seem to expect anything more from me—she turned and led me back the way we'd come.

Sahir and Gaheris had disassembled the entire campsite and stood waiting for us, both staring at nothing. They already had their packs on, and expressions like mountaineers on their way to a pet goldfish's funeral.

"Shall we?" I asked, aiming for cheer. Sahir frowned at me with absolutely none of the heat I remembered from the night before, and I resolved not to speak again unless spoken to.

"We must assume that the Queen will have more soldiers along this way," Sahir said. "As these ruins are sacred to her, and Roman is not her subject."

I nodded, jaw clenched.

"Are you…okay?" Gaheris asked me, clearly using the word in the hopes of cheering me up. "You look distressed."

I attempted a close-lipped smile. Gaheris flinched.

"Just follow behind me," Sahir said, with the resolve of a man expecting to be punched in the face.

He started toward the far end of the clearing. I filed behind him, with Lene and Gaheris bringing up the rear.

———————•———————

Our journey felt terribly slow: Sahir stopped us every few minutes to slip his pack off and scout forward. I never saw any sign of the Queen's soldiers, or of any other faerie.

The treescape changed abruptly into something resembling a swath of palm trees. The ground beneath our feet was drier, sandier.

I opened my mouth to ask about it, but Sahir held up an imperious hand. He hadn't even been looking at me. I closed my mouth again, recommitting to my vow of silence.

We came upon the first built structures without warning. There was no break in the trees, no change in the light.

The ruined pillars, in among the swaying almost-palms like so many more trees, rose up in two identical lines. We stood at the first of them, staring down the rows at the place where sheets of familiar blue magic were strung across like banners hung on invisible walls. I took a step forward, and Sahir caught my arm. Lene and Gaheris separated, each creeping along the outside of one of the rows of pillars, their heads on swivel. Sahir stood with his back to the ruins, staring the way we'd come.

I did my part, too: I tried not to move, breathe, or think.

I looked around for my friends, but they'd disappeared into the trees—presumably scouting for more invisible enemies. I slumped, leaning against one of the pillars. The scratchy edges of mosaic tiles pressed into my arm in the swirling colors of the undersea images the Gray Knight had shown me.

"Oi!" someone said, irate. "Get off that, you lug."

I straightened, looking around.

The Builder who I'd met at the Princeling's factory stepped between the two nearest pillars, picking his way over some of the larger stones scattering the sandy ground.

"*You're Roman?*" I hissed. "*You?*"

Sahir appeared from nowhere. He stood next to me and bowed his head, his face impassive. "Builder," he said in greeting.

"What's this, then?" Roman asked, looking me up and down. "You're that human girl the Princeling called *lady*."

He sounded like a man who had, in childhood, seen a film where an American actor from New Jersey portrayed a Cockney chimney sweep, and then made that his personality.

"What's a human doing in the Queen's Court?" Roman continued, scratching his head between his two curling horns. He shook his head, jowls vibrating, and dislodged some dandruff from his scalp.

Perhaps I shouldn't have been shocked that he'd been putting on airs for the Princeling. The accent was really throwing me for a loop, though.

"You were in the Princeling's Court a few months ago!" I exclaimed.

"I am aware," Roman said.

Sahir stuck his elbow so far into my ribs that it came out the other side of my body.

"I have come to see you, Builder," I said, adopting the title and an attitude of serenity.

Sahir took a half step in front of me, so I had to peer over his shoulder. He seemed tense.

Not for the first time, I wondered how much stress I had avoided in life simply by failing to grasp the consequences of anything happening around me.

After another bow, Sahir spoke. "Builder, I am sent by my good-brother Aram. I bring with me my lady, the Lady of the True Dreams, and two companions, who have gone to ensure our safety while we speak with you."

Roman squinted at him. "Aram," he said, wrinkling his nose. "Aram…" He frowned, thinking. "You're Rijska's brother?"

Sahir inclined his head in acknowledgment.

"Fantastic woman, that sister of yours," Roman said. I was flabbergasted and bamboozled; he spoke more like a human than anyone I'd met at the Court, barring Chad and Milo.

He waved his hand in a curling gesture; at the apex of each curl, a sheet of blue light sprang from his palm and floated above him. He flicked his index finger, and the blue lights began to spin around us in rapid rectangles. "And now we can speak freely."

I raised an eyebrow at Sahir, to ask him why he never used a ward against eavesdropping. The face he made back told me that he wasn't able to create wards against eavesdropping, but thanks for making him feel inadequate.

"Why'd you bring a human to the Queen's Court? To be killed?" Roman asked, still staring at Sahir and not at me.

"I brought her here to beg a boon of you," Sahir said.

Roman crossed his arms and sat on a stray hunk of stone. "A boon," he repeated. "That's an odd word, for the Fae."

"Aram grants me leave to call in his favor," Sahir said, changing tack.

"Feels like *I* should be allowed to call in the favor," I muttered; they both ignored me.

"What, then, do you owe him?" Roman asked, smirking. It seemed like he didn't get out much, like maybe this was his socializing for the month.

"He has been in my debt for many years," Sahir said. "It was my blessing that ensured his happiness."

"Oho." Roman glanced at me. "Interesting."

Tired and frustrated, I sat on another hunk of stone, staring at Roman. If he wanted me to move, he could just say so.

Roman said nothing. Instead, he gestured at Sahir to continue.

Sahir sat as well, his eyes still on Roman. He shrugged out of his pack, two thin lines of sweat down each side of his chest. I kept my own pack on in case someone tried to stab me from behind.

"Your father built the passageways between the worlds," Sahir said.

Roman's attitude changed slightly; he straightened on the stone and squared his shoulders. When he spoke again, he sounded more like the Builder I'd met previously. "Your blessing meant more to Aram than it does to me. For this favor, I grant you questions three," Roman replied.

"Then let me be brief."

I squeezed my eyes shut. We didn't even need three questions, did we?

No questions were asked. I opened my eyes. Sahir was staring at me.

"Miriam may have my questions," Sahir said. "As she will bear the consequences of your answers."

I inhaled. "Thank you," I said.

Roman's eyebrows had disappeared into another pocket dimension. His smirk was wider than the English Channel.

"How does faerie food prevent humans from leaving this realm?" I asked.

Roman sounded amused. "The same way as faerie gold and faerie fools," he replied.

This did not illuminate anything for me. I hoped desperately that Sahir understood more than I did. I could hardly look at either of them. I stared instead at the rapid whirling of the magic Roman had erected around us, so different from the silver-rain umbrella of the Gray Knight's ward or the green brambles of the Princeling's.

"Why will I die if I step through a portal?" I asked.

Roman looked down at his hands, twisting a hunk of stone between his fingers so it flowed and changed.

"I cannot divine why anyone will die. Am I a god, to be so wise?"

Sahir and I exchanged a glance. I had only one question left, and Roman wasn't playing nice.

"*Will* I die if I step through a portal?"

"You will die if you step through a portal, and you will die if you do not. We all die, in some way and at some time."

Roman must have looked at my face and seen his own imminent death, because he stood hastily.

He bowed his head again, more perfunctory than polite. With a lazy finger, he dissolved the spinning blue wards around us.

"Wait!" I said. "Why does everyone think it will kill me?"

Without the wards dazzling my eyes, the entire clearing felt gray.

Roman stared at me steadily. "I owe you no questions, child," he said. "What will you give me?"

I opened my mouth. Closed it. Looked down at my hands.

"I don't have anything with me except my pack and my clothes." I held up my empty palms for emphasis.

He looked at my raised hands without interest, and then looked again, squinting. He pointed at my index finger. "That ring is of faerie make," he said. "Where did you get it?"

I touched my ring, as was my habit. "It was passed down, mother to daughter," I said. "And now it's mine."

"Give me that ring, and I will give you your life."

I looked at Sahir, wondering why he'd never expressed interest in my ring. He shrugged, probably to indicate that he had never studied the finer points of jewelry making and the provenance of my ring was of no interest to him.

Roman watched me hesitate.

"Human," he said, "I require no questions. The ring is worth all my knowledge and more. I will owe you some other fair recompense, too."

Some small part of me wanted to refuse; the ring was always on my finger, and had been my mother's and my grandmother's. I shut that thought down. My mom and grandma would much rather have me than a ring.

"The deal is made, Builder," I said, twisting the ring off my finger. I held it out to him.

He leaned forward and snatched it from my hand, too fast for my eye to follow.

Which obviously didn't make me thrilled about parting with the ring.

"The magic wrought by my father and his companions wrung pockets of space from the breadth of our planet. The land of Faerie is a patchwork of earth, of mountainsides and desert spans. Imagine a sewn quilt, with magic for each seam. To enter, and to leave, my father and his companions left crevices in the quilt, places where they did not sew as tightly." He frowned at me, to check if I understood. "There are several crevices, which you call portals."

I nodded, which I would've done even if I didn't understand.

"There is a physiological difference between humans and Fae," Roman continued. "But it is largely benign."

He paused. "Well, there are many physiological differences," he amended, staring judgmentally at my non-goat-adjacent legs. "But only one relevant to this explanation. Fae are anchored in time but not in space. Humans are anchored in time and in space. Their inchoate sense of *place* is more stable than ours..." He trailed off.

"Sorry, what?" I said, before I could stop myself.

"It is the difference between..." He stopped again. "Imagine stepping through a doorway, knowing that the vacuum of space presses down on you from beyond the lintel."

I nodded.

"Now imagine stepping through a doorway *into* the vacuum

of space, and seeing in the far distance another doorway, which will bring you home if you can reach it."

"Oh," I said. I stared at my own knees. "I don't get it."

"Faerie food is a manifestation of faerie magic, and its consumption destabilizes…" He trailed off, presumably regretting his life choices. "It does not matter, child. I will not explain the biochemistry to you."

"Well, it kind of does matter," I said, but he spoke over me.

"I speak truly, and with the knowledge of my father and his father, and the magic of the moon in my blood," Roman said, staring into my face. His features had taken on a noble cast, stronger and sterner. "If you stepped through a portal, you would not die."

I couldn't breathe. I could hardly hear over the rushing in my ears.

"I wouldn't be bone shards and blood mist?"

"You would not," he agreed, sage and serene. "You would emerge whole, and could enter and exit Faerie at will."

"Is this all?" Sahir asked, coldly. "Is this your answer? There is no explanation. There is no *proof*."

Roman didn't look at Sahir. "I owe him no answers," he said, twirling my ring between his fingers. "But I will tell you this. Faerie will call to your blood."

Ominous. I shrank inward.

Luckily, I didn't have to reply, because Sahir was full of indignation.

"Why do you speak in these riddles?" he growled. "Why do you not tell us plainly?"

"I do not owe anyone my allegiance," snapped the Builder.

"Why will Faerie call to my blood?" I asked, my voice thin and weak.

"It calls to the blood of anyone who consumes Fae magic," he said with a disinterested shrug.

I wanted to let it go; he clearly wanted to be done talking. But I also didn't want to traipse through a portal without a little bit more information.

"How do you know I won't die?"

For a long moment it seemed as though he wouldn't answer. The Builder stared down at me with implacable, pitiless eyes and an expression as carved as the stone around us.

But then Roman held the ring out in the palm of his hand, as precious as water. "This is a wedding band, child," he said. "A wedding band my father made. If the women of your line wore it, then a man of your line must have gifted it." He made a strange noise, almost strangled.

Sahir whipped to his feet like a ballerina in a music box. I'd seen Draculas rise from their coffins with more knee action than that. He clenched his fists, looming over Roman. "You risk her life on *conjecture*," Sahir exclaimed, looking ready to perform a murder.

In a stroke of good fortune, the Queen's soldiers chose this moment to burst through the spaces between the jagged pillars.

Chapter 18

In Which I Am Royally Screwed

Twelve soldiers in crimson jackets surrounded us. Sahir stepped in front of me. I covered my head with my arms.

"Get *up*," someone said above us. I rolled my eyes up to the extent possible without moving but only saw a knee.

"Miri, get up," Sahir said, slightly less rudely than the attacking soldiers.

I stood, staying behind him. This only mattered for those soldiers in front of us; there were still six at our backs.

The soldiers had found Gaheris and Lene. I knew this because Gaheris and Lene stood between two soldiers, their hands in the air, their packs on the ground, and their expressions more resigned than afraid.

I stared into the snake eyes of Kamare, my would-be poisoner. She was flanked by two other faeries, each of them wearing crimson clothing.

"That's a fantastic uniform," I said, going for bravado. I leaned around Sahir to smile brightly at Kamare.

Kamare glanced in confusion at Lene, who shrugged.

Sahir shoved me back behind him.

Kamare straightened. "Look who we have caught," she said menacingly, apparently determined to have a monologue. "The human who cost me my place in the Princeling's Court."

I felt a pang of guilt, so sharp I couldn't be afraid.

"*You* cost yourself your own place in our Court, when you tried to poison someone you'd been instructed to feed," Sahir retorted.

Oh yeah.

I felt slightly less guilty.

"Details," Kamare muttered, waving a hand. "It is no matter." She paused, considering. "I should kill the human on sight," she said, "and bring the rest of you to the Queen for tribute."

I shot a look at Sahir, who had the good sense to look flustered.

Then I glanced at Lene, who shrugged, as if to say *C'est la vie.*

Even if it *was* la vie, it might not be *my* vie for very long. And I'd just discovered that I had a lot to live for. I turned to see three of the other faeries picking their way toward me over the jagged debris, swords in hand. I very much did not want to die by sword. I stared into the face of the nearest faerie, who stared back without interest or expression.

"She spared your life, Kamare," Gaheris said. "You owe her a blood debt."

The three faeries stopped—one midstep, a foot dangling in the air.

I whipped around to look at Kamare.

Kamare frowned.

"She cannot die by your hand nor by your order," Gaheris pressed.

My friend was so afraid that the fires on his head had completely extinguished, and he looked small and strange without them—but he didn't quail beneath Kamare's stare.

"He speaks truly," Sahir said. "You are bound by your honor and the gift of your breath."

The soldier to Kamare's left whispered something in her ear. She deflated visibly, like the snake-balloon in *Shrek*.

"Come along, then," Kamare said. "You will be a tribute to the Queen as well. But you may regret the choice to live that long."

No one spoke. I frowned at Roman, who frowned back at me in an expression that mingled sympathy and resignation. He'd slipped the hand with the ring into his pocket.

"And do not think I've forgotten you," Kamare said, turning her eyes on him. "I will inform the Queen of your... *liaising*."

Roman shrugged. "She is not my Queen and I am not her subject. If she wills it, I can cease construction on your sacred sites. I doubt that she wills it."

Kamare huffed. And with that witty retort, she led our merry band away.

———————————•———————————

To her credit, it took about twenty minutes for Kamare to start gloating. She kept me and Sahir close to the front; me, as the star prisoner, and Sahir because whenever she tried to separate us he bit the other faeries, and they didn't want to touch him anymore. The faerie next to me had a full dental impression on his cheek that would probably be sufficient to construct a retainer for Sahir.

At the exact moment that the silence started to become boring instead of suspenseful, Kamare spoke.

She turned her head back to look at Sahir. "You know, when my contacts in the Court told me you were bringing the human into the woods with only those two, I thought they must be wrong. I did not think you could be so stupid." Her forked tongue flicked between her lips, retreated in a pink dart.

This was clearly a dig at Gaheris and Lene. "There's no one I'd rather have with me," I snarled, but this only made her laugh.

"You are a bigger a fool than any of them," she said, "if you value loyalty over power in a companion."

"I'm really regretting saving your life right now," I muttered.

She hissed at me. "That is the only reason you still breathe," she said. "When ordinarily, I would have recourse to kill you on sight. I abide by the laws of my land and my magic, human. What laws govern you?"

"The Ten Commandments?" I said, mostly as a question.

Kamare did not condescend to a response. I amused myself by trying to remember the Ten Commandments. I definitely knew *Thou shalt not steal* and *Thou shalt not murder*. I felt fairly confident also about *Thou shalt not sleep with your neighbor's wife even if she's superhot* and *Thou shalt honor thy parents, ye ungrateful cretin, lest ye have a daughter JUST LIKE YOU*.

I continued in this vein for the remainder of the walk, hardly noticing when the ground transitioned back to the loamy black soil of the American northeast. The trees around us sprouted more branches, and I felt the occasional side-sweep of an evergreen against my cheek or shoulder.

Lene managed to slip up beside me and slid her hand into mine.

Ever since I'd gone off on the Gray Knight in my bedroom, I'd had this coiled feeling inside my stomach, like a gutful of cobras. Whenever the numbness faded, I wanted to irritate people. Or I wanted to make other people uncomfortable. To make them feel as bad as I felt, trapped and powerless.

Kamare seemed like a great target for irritation.

"So, like, what are you soldiering about?" I asked, making my voice nasal.

Kamare made a hissing noise, her back stiff. To my surprise, she answered, a practiced cadence to her voice. "We should not open our borders to humans. They will bring destruction into our home."

"Kamare, you have not seen the sun, as I have," Sahir said. "And if I lose my life to human malice or mishap, I will not regret it, having had that warmth on my skin."

The other soldiers crowded forward as Sahir spoke; I felt them at our backs. When I turned my head I saw Gaheris at the head of a knot of them, only a foot behind me.

I didn't like the thought of Sahir losing his life. "But that's not likely, right?" I asked.

Lene squeezed my hand once, then let go and stepped back to walk with Gaheris.

"Oh, it is quite probable," Gaheris chimed in. "It would only—ow!"

Since Gaheris and Lene were behind me, I could only speculate as to what had happened. But I'd probably speculate correctly.

"It's possible I tripped," Lene said, confirming my suspicions.

"Ow," Gaheris said again. And then, "Kamare, there are many Courts that will not allow humans at all. Our Princeling is an outlier. There is no need to engage in this crusade."

"She might be bored," I interjected. "Since none of you have anything to do all day."

Lene made a soft yowling noise, and I regretted my comment.

"I am not bored," Kamare snapped. "Our risk is great, Gaheris. Once a human has entered our realm, she may travel freely between the Courts, and poison anyone she meets along the way."

"Is human sweat poisonous to you?" I blurted, rubbing the scratches Lene had left on my skin.

"What?"

"Well, if a human can poison anyone she meets along the way, maybe the faerie poison is sweat." I fidgeted with my hands, with the lighter band of skin where my gold ring had rested on my index finger.

"No, human sweat is not poisonous to us," Kamare said. She batted away a branch so hard that it snapped and fell to the forest floor. "That is utterly ridiculous. The Princeling implied that you were intelligent."

"He *did* only imply it," Gaheris mused. I shot a glare over my shoulder, missing him entirely. The faerie I glared at stopped midstep and hunched their shoulders like a prey animal appearing smaller.

I looked forward again, at Kamare's back.

"So...is it human saliva?"

Sahir closed his eyes in a swift and silent prayer for release from this hell. Unfortunately for him, he'd signed himself up for a human lifetime of my company.

"No, it is not human saliva, nor any other bodily excretion," Kamare said.

"So...is it some kind of textile?"

Kamare stopped in the path and turned around. "Can someone silence the human?"

I tripped again, and this time I fell onto the dirt. I caught the worst of the fall on my palms.

As was his wont, Sahir hauled me up by the straps of my backpack. He set me on my feet, his hands on my shoulders.

"Miri, I do not think we should play twenty questions with things that kill faeries," Sahir said in my ear.

I nodded and mimed zipping my lips shut and throwing away the key.

Kamare's eyes followed my elaborate gestures. "What is the human doing now?" she snapped. "Is this some arcane magic? Is she summoning a vision?"

I mimed unzipping my lips and said, "It's a gesture humans use to indicate their silence."

"Such an odd people," Kamare said. "Imagine a culture where you speak so much that you must have a hand signal to indicate silence. Do they use the hand signal because others are talking at the same time?"

"Um." I shrugged, Sahir's hands still heavy on me. "Anyway, I won't ask any more questions. I only hoped to understand the argument. It makes sense that you don't want to let strangers into your home, but I don't see why you would need to."

Kamare turned her back to me. Sahir dropped his hands, and we all continued along the way. I thought she wouldn't answer; she took several minutes before she spoke again.

"It is a fair exchange," she said. "If we are permitted to enter your lands, so you should be permitted to enter ours."

"I don't think any humans have asked for that," I said. "And we don't have anything like that with the other—species."

But that wasn't true, was it? I thought about the Bureau for Vampire Relations, which had initiated a form of population control that prevented new vampires from turning without years of paperwork. Humans were wriggling themselves into everyone's business in any way possible.

"I hear the lie in your voice, human," Kamare said. "And I know more of your world than you might expect. Your people have always taken more than you are owed. My people are bound by magic to act equitably, and your people have no such restraints. How can we treat together, when our limitations are so different?"

"I don't know," I said. "And I'm sorry that my being here put you in this position. But I was trapped, too—you know I had no choice and didn't want to stay."

"Your death would have solved both of our problems," Kamare said, which quashed any sympathy I might have had for her.

For the next hour, we traveled in silence. I hardly noticed when the terrain changed again, until Lene elbowed me and pointed out the shapes of the trees.

Where previously, we'd been traveling under what I might have called oaks and conifers, these trees were long and slender, almost tropical. Their colors verged on jewel tones, red and orange trunks soaring skyward. The air warmed, too, and the path widened, the stones lightening and smoothing out under our feet, as they had at the sacred site. At our sides, waving blue-and-purple-fronded plants dotted the ground instead of underbrush. Here, the leaves hadn't fallen. I glanced up at a gorgeous blue sky, like threaded turquoise. Thin, wispy clouds promenaded along their stately way.

I was so busy staring up, mouth open, that I didn't see Kamare disappear.

Lene grabbed my arm, hard, and I glanced around. Kamare was gone, and the other crimson-clad Fae had come into a wide clearing with us. At our feet was a hole in the earth, dark and deeply unappealing. It was so narrow only one person could possibly enter at a time.

Lene unshouldered her pack, then helped me with mine. Sahir and Gaheris shed theirs as well, and we made an untidy pile at the side of the hole.

Sahir glanced at me. "I will enter first, and catch you at the bottom, Miriam." He pressed his hand to my cheek, so quickly it almost hurt, and then stepped backward into the hole.

I gaped as he disappeared, then glanced at Lene. Her face was expressionless.

"In," she ordered.

"You want me to *jump* into a *hole* in the *ground*? Do you know anything about human anatomy? Is the fall hundreds of feet? I could die."

Lene rolled her eyes. "It was a short fall when I jumped last. In, coward," she said, which stung.

In the spirit of compromise, I got down on my hands and knees, crawled to the edge of the hole, and slowly rolled myself over the side until I was dangling, staring up at her.

"Are you sure about this?" I asked, fighting the strain in my fingertips.

Lene reached over, stuck her fingers under mine, and yanked.

I sucked in a breath to scream but had already landed in Sahir's arms. He'd somehow caught me in a princess carry, despite my falling down feetfirst.

"That took longer than I expected," he observed, carrying me away from the opening. Lene landed where we'd just stood, unfazed, and Gaheris followed her so fast I was surprised they didn't tumble over together.

"The human required reassurance," Lene said, examining her extended claws.

"Okay, Scar," I muttered, but she ignored me. Sahir set me down.

"Miri is right," Gaheris said. "We do not know about human anatomy. I still think she might grow horns if fed enough enchanted cake."

May I live long enough for us to try, I thought.

I kept a hand on Sahir's shoulder as I looked around the dim subterranean space. We'd landed at the end of a corridor, and clearly the entrance to the Queen's Court. God only knew why they couldn't just put in a set of stairs or a ladder like normal people.

The corridor was at its narrowest about thirty feet from where we stood. *Defensive point*, I thought, like a warrior and not like a short American woman whose father described her soccer days as "an exercise in picking dandelions."

But it *was* a defensive point. The entire setup was—the narrow and inconvenient entrance with no means of egress; the corridor that would require us to walk single file. It was a far cry from the open entrance and wide hallway of the Princeling's Court.

"Let us continue our journey," Kamare said, interrupting my thoughts. I glanced around. Apparently none of her faerie guard were coming with us.

She took point once again, giving Lene her back in a show of bravado. Since Lene showed about as many violent tendencies as Doctor Kitten, who I'd once caught stealing a slice of cheese from my plate to share with our resident kitchen mouse, Kamare had really hedged her bets there.

When Kamare reached the narrowest part of the corridor, she turned sideways to get through. Lene and Gaheris followed, and then I sucked in my stomach and copied them.

The rough stone protrusions scraped me on both sides, and my left boob got caught for a second, but I made it.

On the other side, the corridor widened enough to fit five people. I glanced back to see Sahir wiggle through as well, the gray stone catching at his green tunic. The tug of stone pulled the fabric tight against his shoulders, his sculpted chest.

He stuck for a moment, his mouth a priceless O of absolute shock, and then propelled himself through the gap on the strength of mortification alone.

Unlike the Princeling's Court, the Queen's Court didn't open into a residential wing. There were no doors on either side, just long walls of rough striated gray and black stone. I looked around for the will-o'-the-wisps I'd become accustomed to, but the corridor was lit by long glowing strings pressed into the crevices in the stone and ceiling. They suffused the hallway with a comforting golden light.

Stay vigilant, I reminded myself. Anything could happen, and probably would.

Sahir strode along at my side, his face solemn. The fact that he could turn into a mass of angry vines at will *did* soothe me a bit. Though, if pressed, I wouldn't have been able to describe a single useful thing that a mass of angry vines could do in a fight.

The corridor ended in a large stone archway, which opened into the throne room.

Kamare stopped at the threshold, and I looked over her shoulder, unsure of what to expect.

Not much, was the answer.

The throne room was small, and darker than the corridor,

lit by a central fire that crackled and guttered and smoked. The Queen sat on the far side of the fire, staring into the flames with glowing, slit-pupiled eyes. Her left hand moved in impossible contortions, and shapes appeared and dissolved in the smoke above her head.

The shadows played on her dark skin, and a glowing golden diadem lay on the thin braids in her black hair. She rested her head in her right hand, elbow on the arm of a similarly golden throne.

She looked…bored.

On either side of her, two faeries stood, all four holding giant-ass spears. Like, really big. Like, two faerie-sized hands couldn't wrap around the hafts. This seemed excessive, given the number of magic users about.

"My Queen," Kamare said, sweeping a bow.

I couldn't stop looking at the faeries on either side. This must be the Queen's entourage: her equivalent of the Gray, Red, and Blue Knights, and the Crone.

Why did they need the spears?

They were, honestly, comically large.

I tried to imagine one of the faeries sweeping the spear down and impaling someone with it. I couldn't. There was no way they'd have the requisite control.

Sahir stepped on my foot.

I jumped back, glaring at him, but he was right. I needed to be looking at the Queen, not imagining her knights swinging their giant poles around like the spinning-plates act at a circus.

So I looked back at her.

She straightened and stared across the flames at the five of us. The room was so small I could feel the heat of the fire from where I stood.

"You come to relinquish your prisoners as tribute, Kamare," she said. It wasn't a question. "And you, Miriam Geld, come to beg for your life." I found myself watching her mouth for a flash of shark teeth. She tapped a finger on her full lower lip. She had ruby red nails.

"I know enough, you see," she said, her eyes glazing past me with studied disinterest. "And so long as I am ruler of this Court, any faerie may bring me petition, and I will hear them fairly."

Something passed across the leftmost guard's face when she said that.

I debated being interested and then decided I had enough of my own problems.

"The humans must not be allowed into our realm," Kamare said. "I submit these prisoners to you as fair barter for the closing of the borders to Faerie."

At this, the Queen stood.

And I panicked. *Prisoners*, Kamare had said. And *Plead for your life*, the Queen had said, as though living was an option. Was I about to be traded to a different royal faerie? Would she have different quirks than the Princeling, which I'd have to learn, and work around? Oh god, *work*. I didn't even have my work laptop with me.

My mind jerked to a halt. I was trapped in Faerie, a political prisoner to a proven poisoner, being traded to a Queen. I'd been embroiled in a battle I didn't understand and that would probably kill me, and I was worrying about my emails.

More than that—I looked right, at Sahir, Gaheris, and Lene, lined up in a row facing the Queen. I'd brought my friends into this, intentionally or otherwise. If they were harmed, it was my fault. *And I was worrying about my emails.*

"Four prisoners, three of them residents of another Court, and the fourth a human whose blood is forfeit on my soil," the Queen mused. She stared at Kamare. "Do you think the Princeling will not come looking?"

"I took them according to the laws of prisoner exchange, and they will acknowledge this themselves, if asked." Kamare looked a bit flustered.

I shot Sahir a look that said *It is insane that you live in a world where prisoners can be traded for favors from the Queen.* And he returned it with a look that said *I've been to New York; don't get too self-righteous.*

"As the humans often say, there is the letter of the law, and the spirit of the law."

What a *weird* thing for the human-killing ruler to say. The Princeling had never quoted humans to me.

The Queen took three side steps around the fire, and my heart stuttered. I'd never seen anyone move with such grace. She moved at a human speed, so my eyes could track her, and every muscle bent and stretched until at the third step, I found myself crying.

The Queen looked at me, still several feet away. She seemed unsurprised by my tears. "There is also something in the way that humans watch magic," she said musingly, and gestured at my face. Even the sweep of her arm mesmerized me.

Kamare turned to me, too, and her forked tongue flicked out between her lips—tasting the air for my tears?

"They can kill us," she said, "without intending to. They bring destruction in their wake. You know that."

The Queen shrugged. "The humans have always salted the earth," she said, her tone indifferent.

I didn't expect the rage with which Kamare responded—she screamed and flung herself at the Queen, her fingertips extended into claws. I gasped and started forward, but before I'd taken half a step, the Queen's guard were in front of her, spears leveled.

As I stared at the sharp, pointed tips, the spears didn't seem so funny to me.

"You will fall," Kamare said, but she backed up, until she was next to me in our row.

"We all fall." The Queen still seemed disinterested. "You may leave, Kamare. I am your Queen, and my strength is my people, and I will not allow harm to befall you."

Kamare slunk backward until she was out of the room. I watched her go with a strong feeling of relief.

The Queen's eyes flicked to me. "Did you intend to assist the soldier, or protect me?"

I stared at her long black eyelashes, the regal sweep of her nose. "Defend you, I think," I said.

One of the guards snickered—a tall one with wings. I wanted to differentiate them, but they all looked a lot like androgynous Elvis in various colors, and I was having trouble.

Sahir stepped forward to stand beside me. The Queen flicked her hand at him. A spark jumped from her fingertips to his chest, and he exploded into vines.

"Do not hide your form from the Queen," she said. In third person.

"Apologies, Queen," Sahir said, his familiar voice coming from the center of the vines. He was much stiller than he'd been last time the vines came out, everything drooping like chagrined shrubbery.

"Speak your plea," she said to Sahir, imperious and still so disinterested. "That I can end the mortal's life and cease to ponder this."

"You are a Queen, and a faerie, and fair," Sahir said. "If you deem her harmless, give us leave to bring her back to the Princeling."

"No human is harmless to us," she replied. If she felt that to be true, there was no hope for me.

"Then if you deem her worthy of respect," Sahir tried. "If you hear our accounting for her and believe she has earned the name Friend of the Fae."

She *tsk*ed gently, almost sad. "You know that if I let one human walk freely past my borders, more will follow."

I had the strange distant thought that I was about to dissociate through my own death.

"Then give her leave to attempt a portal crossing," Gaheris said.

Sahir groaned under his breath. The Queen looked at Gaheris.

"This is hardly a mercy," she said.

"It is a chance," Gaheris replied. "If you deem her worthy of it."

The amount of adrenaline thrumming through my veins could have exploded a pony. I felt every nerve ending, heard the thump of each heartbeat in my chest.

Obviously we'd *planned* to hurl me through a portal at some point. I just hadn't expected that point to be imminent.

The Queen and I looked at each other.

"Well," she sighed. "If nothing else, it will break the monotony."

Again a flicker of movement on the face of one of her faerie guards. Again, a decision on my own part to avoid noticing.

"I shall hear from each of you in turn," the Queen said. She stepped nimbly around her guards and glided over to Gaheris. I tracked every step she took, my head swiveling on my neck.

Gaheris inclined his head, the fires of his hair brushing her forearm as he kissed her outstretched hand. I watched the flames lick toward her elbow. I felt an inexplicable urge to separate them, to protect her.

Sahir whacked me in the thigh with a vine. I glared at him, but the pull to the Queen had been severed. I looked back toward her where she stood facing Gaheris.

"Tell me why you are here, Gaheris."

He lifted from his bow, straightened, and looked at her. I stared at his profile, his long arms and legs and face, and his thin mouth. I felt overwhelmed by a sense of something— gratitude or friendship or pride.

"Sahir has been my companion for many years, long and short," he said. "We have exchanged many bargains. I will always assist him, if I am able."

She nodded, as if she understood. The golden diadem shone in the firelight. "You have come at Sahir's behest, and with fair recompense for your risk." She started to turn away from him, toward Lene.

"In part," he said, sounding anxious; his eyes fell to the floor. The Queen froze, and readjusted to face him head on.

"When Sahir wanted to go to the human lands, I was afraid," Gaheris continued. "You know the ease with which we can die there. He went for his own reasons, which I shall not share, by your leave." He stopped and glanced at her, fear and a desire for approbation warring in his eyes.

The Queen nodded again, encouraging him to go on. I stared at her, feeling a burgeoning desire to one day be that powerful. I was well-adjusted, and knew that the feeling was just in response to a lack of control in my own life. Like any well-adjusted person, I pushed the feeling down and vowed never to examine it.

"About a year after Sahir started the job in the human world, he began to speak of a woman who had joined the company."

I jerked my head to look at Sahir so fast that my neck hurt. He'd spoken of me to his friends? We were office mates; we hadn't spent any significant time together.

Sahir was still a tangled mass of vines, so I couldn't exactly see his face.

"The other humans were cruel to him, as I understand it. They laughed when he spoke, or pretended not to understand him. They would not be alone with him if they could avoid it. These were forms of cruelty I did not know to fear, until Sahir explained them to me. But she never treated him any differently."

I flushed. Sahir had talked about me at length, apparently. He'd mentioned me often enough that Gaheris knew who I was before I ever came to Faerie. And—Sahir had been miserable at work, and in all these months I'd never asked him about it. I'd been too wrapped up in my own misery to think about his. My stomach dropped.

Sahir's arm vines had started twitching in agitation.

"I had to think about cruelty and kindness, Queen," Gaheris said. "And I found myself relieved that my companion had one kind face during the hours he toiled in the mortal realm," Gaheris continued, oblivious to my inner turmoil. "And so I was indebted to Miriam before I ever met her."

If a mass of vines could look embarrassed, Sahir did. I raised an eyebrow at him, but he didn't speak.

"This does not explain why you felt the need to trespass upon my lands," the Queen said, her jaw set. "Nor why you spoke with Roman, the Builder, of the portals between our realms."

"We trespassed to speak with Roman," Gaheris replied. "Our need was great, and his work had taken him into your Court. When we learned that he might know something of the magics trapping Miriam here, we knew we must go to him for assistance, even if we would miss her when she left," Gaheris finished. He had finally raised his head to look at the Queen again.

The Queen looked into his eyes for another minute, her expression implacable. Then she nodded, like she had come to a decision. "Our people do not prize kindness, Gaheris." It was a rebuke.

His face dropped, but to my shock, he stood tall, the fire on his head small but vital. "My Queen, I believe we do not prize kindness because we do not understand cruelty."

The Queen frowned but didn't comment. Instead, she took a step to her side, stopping in front of Lene. She moved with the same grace, but I didn't feel the same awe as before.

"And you?" The Queen's red robe had spread out around her feet in a perfect circle. *That* was cool magic.

Lene rolled her shoulders. "I love her cat, Doctor Kitten. He is soft and warm, and we sometimes watch birds together."

I glared at her. *Eleven weeks* we'd been hanging out. That was it?

She looked at me across Sahir's undulating arm-vines. "And I like her," she added hastily, seeing my expression.

Small comfort that faeries couldn't lie.

The Queen seemed to be suppressing a smile. "The mortal offered you no gifts for your companionship?"

Lene shrugged. "None that I could easily name."

"And you joined her anyway," the Queen said.

Lene nodded.

"Did her knight treat with you?"

Lene shrugged a second time. "No more so than usual," she said. "I came here without expectation of recompense."

The Queen did not reply.

Instead, she took another step, toward Sahir. "And you? Why did you tie your life to a mortal woman, the moment she set foot in our realm?"

His voice came from the center of the vines. "It is as Gaheris explained."

She snorted, which made me like her slightly more. "Sahir," she said gently, "I would like to hear from you."

Behind the Queen, her Elvis-impersonator guards stood in

exactly the same place, their spears once again raised, and their eyes blank. I kept sneaking glances at the matching slicked-back hair framing their matching stony faces.

Sahir sighed. "May I speak with you alone, my Queen?"

I felt my stomach clench—did he not want to tell her the truth in front of me? Her eyes went to me as well, like she knew why he hesitated.

"No."

A rush of relief, followed by a much bigger rush of guilt, went through me. "I don't mind," I said. "I can step out, if it's easier."

"Your mind is of no matter to me," the Queen said dismissively, flapping a hand at me to emphasize her point. This made me like her less again. My good opinion was as mutable as Play-Doh fresh from the container.

Sahir's vines stiffened, but he only said, "If I am to speak of Miriam, I would prefer to do so in the form she recognizes."

This seemed like a stupid thing to request from the Queen. I waited for one of her knights to kill him, wielding a comically large spear.

To my surprise, she nodded. He coalesced quickly into a humanoid shape, his face smooth and comfortingly familiar, and his visible hands still corded with thin twining branches. Maybe this was a compromise for her.

"My gratitude, Queen," he said.

She gestured again, a clear demand for his explanation.

"As Gaheris said, Miriam was kind to me in the human realm. And as you so wisely noted, kindness is not prized here, nor there. Perhaps it should not be. Perhaps it is a weakness.

But Miriam was a light in my long, lonely days, and a softness when the mortal realm was tough."

My eyes were inexplicably damp, probably from the cold. I stared at the side of his face, but he didn't look at me. He'd clenched his fists.

"The day that the Princeling brought Miriam into Faerie, I saw her at work in the mortal realm. It was time for the midday meal, and she and I stood together in an enclosed space. A third man could have joined us, but when he saw me, he turned away. I seethed with anger and disdain. Who were these weak mortals, to shun me? But she noticed my turmoil. She turned to comfort me. Miriam made me smile, when my heart could have hardened against humans."

Again, the Queen glanced at me, her golden eyes flickering to my face and away before I could interpret her expression.

"Miriam is sharp, and bold, and unafraid, and brilliant, but even if she were not any of these things, it would not matter. She lives and breathes, feels and thinks, and should not have been trapped anywhere. I swore fealty to her to right a wrong I saw, as I have watched her right wrongs that she sees. I beg your eye, Queen, in seeing someone worthy and honorable, though her honor is different than ours."

The Queen was quiet for a long time.

I shifted from foot to foot, suspended in terror and anticipation. I'd thought imminent death would make me more aware of my heart, of my lungs, of the flex and pull of my muscles. But I was mostly feeling fatigue in my arches.

The Queen took a step toward me, and I thought she would ask me to defend myself. But she only looked at me.

I inhaled.

Was I about to die?

Exhaled.

Would it hurt?

Inhaled.

Her somber eyes. Her golden diadem.

Exhaled.

She might have been reading my mind. If she was, she didn't find my thoughts very interesting.

"Roman said I'm part faerie," I blurted.

She blinked.

The moment stretched on.

I had an itch behind my knee. I needed to scratch it.

Inhaled.

I kept my shoulders straight. Matched her steady stare.

And it ended.

"Be that as it may," the Queen said. "I deem it irrelevant to the issue at hand."

She turned away from me to look at Sahir. "You may take her through my portal," the Queen said. "I wish you short and easy mourning, if the Builder was wrong and her guts explode upon your faces."

She waved her hand, like a woman brushing crumbs off a table. Sahir grabbed my wrist and pulled me backward. The four of us backed away in silence, heads bowed.

Even through my seething rage, I knew that was the smart thing to do.

When we'd slid backward into the tunnel, I tried to sag against a wall, but Sahir continued dragging me away. I scratched at his hand around my wrist, but it was still wooden, and he didn't notice. I, on the other hand, got splinters under a few fingernails, which *hurt*.

The shadows in the gray striations on the walls followed us, and the glowing strings of light only made the darkness more evident.

We squeezed back through the rock crevice in single file, Sahir pushing me ahead of him. I wondered if he planned to defend our backs, but no one came after us. When I looked up toward Lene, I saw that she had her claws out; they glinted in the dimness. Was she worried about Kamare lying in wait for us?

Only once we'd stopped beneath the small circular hole in the ceiling did Sahir seem to relax slightly.

Lene leapt up without a problem, catching the rim of the entrance and pulling herself skyward. Sahir held out his cradled hands for Gaheris to step into and levered the fire faerie upward with a grunt. Lene leaned down, one hand outstretched, and caught Gaheris's hand, pulling him out, too.

Sahir maneuvered me upward by grabbing my thighs and lifting me, and Gaheris pulled me up by the arms. Sahir followed last, and Gaheris hoisted him out. He was covered in a smattering of dirt and looked irritable as usual.

And absolutely nothing happened.

Chapter 19

In Which I Educate My Companions About NJ Transit

We stood in the small clearing, not looking at each other. Our packs were gone—requisitioned, probably, by Kamare and company. I imagined another night in the freezing forest, this time without a tent.

I broke the silence. "No chance we can just walk away?"

"I do not think the Queen will permit that," Lene said, staring determinedly at a tree in the middle distance. Her bottlebrush tail stuck out like she'd been electrified.

Sahir cleared his throat, scuffed his toes through the dirt. "If Roman is correct, you may well live."

"And if he's not?" I asked.

"We do not really have a choice," he said, his throat working. "I cannot defend you from all the Queen's legions. I cannot even defend you from all the Queen's magics."

I breathed deep. "Okay, then there's no point putting it off," I said.

"If you die, I will be displeased," Gaheris told me.

Sahir sighed, a sound that warmed my heart. "Miriam can leave Faerie," he said. "Probably. So we can travel through the Queen's portal, take the train in the mortal realm, and enter through the Princeling's portal. Once Miri has stepped through the portal, the Queen will consider the transgression repaid."

Confronted with my own mortality, I searched desperately for anything else to focus on. Otherwise, I would never be able to keep myself upright.

Lene made a noise like a cow attempting to sing a Christmas carol. I surged toward her, arms open. "Are you okay?"

"I've never been in the mortal realm," Lene said, falling into my outstretched arms like a 1920s starlet. I sagged under her weight.

Gaheris took it more stoically. "I have," he said. "And it will be interesting to see all of the electricity again."

I glanced at Sahir, who shrugged.

"Lene?" I asked. "Would you like to travel with Gaheris through the Queen's lands?"

Lene touched my face with soft fingers.

"Lead us," she said. "We must complete our quest with honor."

At this point, we all seemed to realize that we didn't know where the portal was. Sahir raised an eyebrow at Gaheris, who only blinked back at him.

Sensing that none of us would be useful, Sahir sighed again.

"Well, then," he said, and scanned the clearing with slow eyes. "She will keep the portal close under her gaze, I think." He walked a few steps toward one tree, then backed up again, probably trying to sense magic but appearing for all intents and purposes uproariously drunk.

I hefted Lene upright and we followed Sahir toward one end of the clearing, my arm around Lene's waist.

We approached two tall, thin trees that leaned into each other, meeting overhead in a keystone arch. Their trunks were branchless, but where they tangled overhead they sprouted dozens of tiny branches covered in silver petals and gold leaves. Sahir put his left hand on the nearer trunk, and the tree shivered, dropping silvery petals onto the sandy dirt. As each petal fell, it trailed light, until the entire archway was filled with a shimmering glow.

This portal felt showier than the Princeling's, which hadn't glowed *at all* and didn't involve denuding a tree. I tried not to judge, but to be honest, I didn't try very hard.

When I looked at Lene's face, it became evident that she wanted me to go through with her. What part of *bone shards and blood mist* had she not processed? I motioned for her to go first, but she shook her head and held her hand out to me.

"You sure?" I croaked.

Her lips tight, she nodded. I slid my hand into hers. Sahir took Gaheris's hand, and Gaheris took my other hand.

I cleared my throat. "If I die," I started, and then stopped, staring at the shivering silver petals dancing between the two trees.

"If you die, I will comfort Doctor Kitten," Lene assured me. She was going to comfort Doctor Kitten either way, so I wasn't impressed by this declaration.

I looked past Lene at Sahir. "If I die, it will not be your fault. You have served me with honor."

He stared back at me, his jaw set and still sporting a few small branches.

"I'll ask only that you tell my parents what happened," I said.

Sahir jerked his head in a single, short nod, his black hair curtaining his face.

"Then let's go," I said, closing my eyes and inhaling deeply.

I exhaled at once, remembering that when you're scuba diving if you hold your breath while you ascend you will explode.

Lungs empty and daisy-linked to the others like children, I let Sahir lead me back into the mortal realm.

———————————•———————————

My first breath of mortal air in eleven weeks was gray and smoky. I gasped and opened my eyes.

The four of us stood in a long glass corridor highly reminiscent of a New Jersey Transit train station. I looked out to the right and saw tracks. I wondered if I'd died and was now experiencing my own version of a train station denouement with some beloved and criminally negligent professor.

I looked out to the left and saw a squat and unhappy-looking city filled with smog and cursing passersby.

"Are we in the Trenton, New Jersey, train station?" I asked, too shocked to process that I hadn't died.

As with all of my traumatic experiences, I assumed the terror would hit me in approximately twelve hours, and I would become insensate with distress at that time.

"Train stations are highly convenient," Sahir said defensively, apparently displeased with my tone. "And often sited upon ley lines."

Lene's breath came in quick panting gasps.

I looked up, hoping to see the sun through the glass ceiling, but the day was cloudy and dull. I glanced around for something to calm her.

"This is ugly," Gaheris said. "Why would anyone choose to live here?"

I squeezed Lene's hand, hard. She stared at me, her slitted pupils dilated in terror. "It's okay," I said. "We can always go back." I turned her toward the portal, still shimmering behind us.

"Sahir, is that always visible?" I asked, pointing.

He frowned. "Not usually to humans," he said.

Lene's eyes had fixed on the shimmering magic veil, and her claws dug into my upper arm. I let her latch on to me, relaxing my jaw to breathe through the pain. *Treat her like any other cat*, I reminded myself. *You wouldn't dislodge a cat for your own comfort.*

This was perhaps not conventional wisdom, but I lived by certain principles.

"We cannot go back through the Queen's Court," Sahir said, "as she might consider it a second trespass and decide to kill you."

Delightful.

The corridor was fairly empty, one man in a corner wearing a tan trench coat and another man by the door holding a vape pen. I looked around, trying to determine the time. A large digital clock over the far doorway proclaimed 2:18 p.m.

"Sahir, we need to stop at my parents' on the way back to the Princeling's Court," I said. "I need to see them before I go back to Faerie."

I expected him to argue, but he only sighed. "I know," he said.

"They live in Princeton, so we can just get on the train." I took several confident steps toward the ticketing area, dragging Lene along with me.

"What is a train?" Gaheris asked. "I do not think my sister told me of them when we went to the aquarium." I wondered if his hair could feasibly look red from a distance. Then I saw that the vaping man had started to back away from us, which answered that question. Unless he'd seen Lene's furred face. Or her tail.

"A form of transportation that brings you from place to place at great speed," Sahir said.

When we reached the ticket machine, I stopped and patted my pockets like a dude trying to get out of paying for a date. "I think I don't have my wallet," I said, feeling guilty. "I can Venmo you," I added when Sahir reached for his own pocket.

Sahir slipped a credit card from his autumn-leaf wallet. "I do not know what that means," he said sagely. "Nor do I care."

He printed four tickets to Princeton Junction, and I brought us across the station hall to the turnstiles.

"Go through," I said to Lene, feeding a ticket into the machine.

She stared in horror as the mechanism guiding the glass panels whirred, separating them. "What dark art is this?" she whispered.

Gaheris, displaying a startling presence of mind, shoved her in the back so that she stumbled through.

The gate closed behind her, and she yowled at volume, startling the few other people in the station. When they looked over and saw three faeries, they all looked away again.

I felt a surge of anger at that.

Sahir fed another ticket to the machine and Gaheris sped through, gathering Lene into his arms. He squeezed her until her feet left the floor, and she quieted.

Sahir and I let ourselves into the station and shepherded Gaheris and Lene onto an escalator.

Lene's keening started again when she realized she was standing on moving stairs.

"I remember this from the aquarium," Gaheris explained, patting the rubber railing. "It is an excavator."

"Escalator," I corrected. "Lene, it's okay. There's a motor below us that moves the stairs. It's all mechanical."

"I don't know what any of that means," she said between howls. My head throbbed.

We stepped off onto the platform, Gaheris lifting Lene bodily so she didn't fall over. The train sat in the station, doors open.

I glanced at the sign above our heads. "The train leaves in six minutes," I said to Sahir, my eyes on the highly vocal

Lene. "Do we, like…" But I trailed off, well aware that if you knock someone out in real life, they can get a pretty nasty concussion.

He raised an eyebrow in a way that indicated the beginning of a headache and then took Lene's arm. "Lene, listen to me," he said. "I come to this world every week. I have survived everything we will do today."

"You've never met my mother," I muttered, but Sahir ignored me.

"I am going to lead you onto the train," Sahir said, staring into her face. "It will move, but it will not hurt us."

"You can hold on to me the entire time," I offered, already regretting it.

We moved in a pack, shuffling like turtles on a highway up the step into the train.

Gaheris took everything in calmly, his face alert and interested. Lene had her face in Sahir's chest, her feet on his like a child dancing with her father.

I led them to a set of four seats facing each other. Sahir put Lene on the inside with her back to the train wall. Gaheris sat across from her, still blandly untroubled. "This seat is unpleasantly made," he observed. "The fabric feels displeasing."

"It's called plastic," I said. "I think. It might be something else, I don't know." I watched Sahir sit next to Lene, boxing her into the wall. She relaxed slightly.

Gaheris reached across the open space between us and held her hands. I reached out, too, and put a hand on her knee.

"Sahir, what day is it?" I asked, unsure if my parents would even be there.

It wouldn't matter; I needed to try, at least.

"It's a Sunday," Sahir said.

I flushed, realizing I had requested off from Jeff on a weekend. But honestly, I'd worked every single weekend since I'd been trapped in Faerie. The time-off request was necessary.

"My family will probably be home." I tried not to think about walking into my house, or how it would feel to look at my mother. If my grandma would be awake, or napping in her bedroom and unwilling to be disturbed.

The train whistled, and I watched Lene's claws shoot into Gaheris's palms. "Ow," he said. He stayed motionless, though, and let her claw at him. He curled his fingers up to touch her wrists.

"It is just the train telling us it will start moving," Sahir said, staring out the window at the platform below us.

The train jerked to a start, and Lene mewled. I squeezed her knee. "It's all okay," I said. "It'll only be twenty minutes."

It was twenty painful minutes for all of us, which served as a compelling reminder of why I never took Doctor Kitten anywhere.

Lene alternated between trying to curl onto our laps and yowling and scratching our arms whenever the train changed velocity, turned slightly, made a noise, or existed. Whenever I wasn't in pain, I felt terrible for putting her through this. And whenever she decided to claw into my flesh, I felt terrible.

When the train slowed at the Princeton Junction stop, I leapt from my seat. I nearly tumbled down the stairs in my haste, then jerked to a halt in front of the train door. It didn't open any faster than usual.

I hopped out onto the small platform at Princeton Junction, staring around the parking lot. Sahir carried Lene out in his arms. She'd stuck her hands and feet in the air. Gaheris came last.

My body felt weird, sensitive and tingling. *Faerie will call to your blood*, Roman had said. I'd felt it almost immediately, buzzing in my stomach like I'd drunk too much soda, and pricking down the pathways of the nerves in my arms and legs.

"It's about a mile-and-a-half walk," I said. I really looked at my companions for the first time since we'd entered the mortal realm, foreign against the familiar backdrop of my home train station. All four of us wore the same green tunics and leggings, with soft brown boots.

Gaheris seemed taller and leaner than usual, impossibly skinny against the gray sky, with his bone-white skin and red flames that could pass for hair unless you looked closely. Lene, brown fur bristling, stood slightly shorter than me. Her ears twitched at every puff of wind or squeal of a passing car.

And Sahir stood at my side, shorter than Gaheris, broad-shouldered and stoic, with his proud beaked nose and soft eyes. He looked outward, alert and searching for something on the horizon.

"Let's go," I said, though it was already cold, and I knew my ears would hurt terribly by the time we'd walked to my parents' house. My feet, still blistered from the day before, hurt terribly already.

I led them down the concrete steps and onto the street.

We made good time, passing few cars. This was fortunate, because Gaheris seemed incapable of grasping his own mortality.

"Gaheris, get out of the road," I snapped, the first time a car came toward us.

"Miri, steel cannot kill us," he laughed. "Your myths are archaic and incorrect. I do not fear these vehicles."

"I think anything going fifty miles an hour could kill you," I said.

He didn't seem convinced.

We passed the reservoir, only stopping once so that Lene could chase a few geese who'd missed the migration memo.

When we turned onto my street, I couldn't steady my breathing. My house was halfway up the block, a two-story house with blue siding. It looked long and low from the front, with wings of windows on the first floor and a low sloping roof on the second.

I charged up the grassy slope of our lawn, ignoring the front path completely. I felt Sahir at my heels. We leapt up the flagstone steps to the front door, and I stopped, panting.

Sahir looked at me. I could feel the terror on my own face.

His jaw set. He knocked on the door, then grasped the brass handle, a spark of magic flying from his index finger into the lock.

He opened it. I didn't breathe.

"Mrs. Geld?" Sahir called. "I bring you your daughter."

Chapter 20
In Which a Family Reunion Occurs

I led Sahir inside, my heart still pounding in my ears.

Someone closed the front door behind us; I glanced back to see Gaheris and Lene. What I could see of Lene looked terrified, cowering against the inside of the door.

Our entryway was nearly pitch-black. The house had always been long and low and dark. As a child, I often tripped over shoes in the entryway, even with the dim, watery wall sconces on.

I took a deep breath, orienting myself. A wall of closets stretched away on our left, ending in a corner. The far wall held the pocket doors that separated us from the living space.

I kicked off my boots and gestured to the faeries to do the same.

Then I went to the pocket doors and pushed them open.

This was my grandmother's house first; we'd moved in when she got sick and I'd grown up with her. My mother insisted that the house was the height of '70s chic and had refused to redecorate for the past several decades.

The entryway opened directly into the TV. Not the TV room. The TV, which was a square box about half a foot across. On the left, a long, narrow, windowless hallway dwindled into darkness. On the right, a wide living room redolent with green couches and a wall of windows looking out onto a wide grassy lawn. Sahir pressed against my back, his right hand curling around my right arm. I shuffled us forward, so that we all stood next to the TV. The watery gray daylight barely reached under our eaves, so most of the light came from the kitchen, above and below the white saloon doors my grandma so deeply loved.

My mother burst out of the kitchen and stopped, a silhouette against the light.

My dad followed on her heels, bumping into her so they nearly tumbled forward.

We all stood still for a moment, caught up in shock as we stared at each other. I wondered if Gaheris's hair was backlighting me, making it as difficult for them to see my face as it was for me to see theirs against the light from the kitchen.

"Hello," Sahir said, using his grip on my arm to step in front of me.

I elbowed him in the ribs and pushed forward. "Mom," I said. "Dad."

We all stared at each other, their eyes the only bright points in their faces.

My dad reached out and flicked a light switch, illuminating everyone.

"Miriam Rachel Geld, *what* are you wearing?" my mom asked.

I deflated.

"How are you here?" my dad asked, pushing past my mom and reaching for me.

I threw myself into his arms, and he held me so tightly I wheezed.

"I wasn't trapped," I whispered, feeling my eyes well up. I squeezed my eyes shut until the urge to cry evaporated.

My dad let go of me.

I felt my mother's hand, tentative, on my back.

"What's going on?" my dad asked, relinquishing me to her. "I thought you would die if you left."

I squeezed my mom, my chin on her shoulder. I stared at my dad, standing behind my mom like the Queen's guard.

"There was a way out," I said, unsure how to explain what I hadn't even accepted. "Um, these are my friends," I added, gesturing behind myself with one arm while I held my mom with the other. "Lene, Gaheris, and Sahir."

"I am also friends with Doctor Kitten," Lene said, not looking at anyone. She'd noticed the books on the shelf next to her and begun perusing the titles.

"He's a good cat," my dad said.

"You are the tall warm one he speaks of." Lene's eyes flashed to my dad. "You are the one who pets him against his fur until the air is full of hair. Then you say, 'Who is a good puppy?' even though he is a cat."

My dad raised an eyebrow at me. "I didn't tell her that," I said. "Doctor Kitten did."

Sahir interrupted with a cough. "I am not only her friend," he said, and my face heated up. He clasped his right fist to his chest and bowed to my parents. "I am your daughter's sworn knight and will defend her with my life."

Sahir conveniently didn't mention to my parents that he'd just led me through a portal we weren't totally sure I'd survive with very little advance thought.

"So you have a sworn faerie knight now?" my dad asked, sounding slightly too amused for my liking.

"Can we just all sit down?" I snapped, already irritated.

My parents grouped themselves on the couch across from the TV. Gaheris sat in the armchair nearest them. Lene sat in the armchair inexplicably positioned directly under the TV, and Sahir and I took the love seat across from them.

A painful silence descended.

"Does anyone want anything to drink?" I asked, at the same moment my mom asked, "Did something happen at work?" and my dad asked, "So is this knight thing romantic?" and Lene asked, "Do you happen to have any cats here?"

I shot up. "It's not romantic, there are no cats, and nothing happened at work," I said, answering in priority order. "I'm going to go make some tea. You guys just…" I trailed off, unable to decide what the appropriate verb was for this situation. "Sit," I finished lamely.

My mom stood, too. "I'll help," she said. We went into the kitchen.

"Your knight is very hot," my mom said, loudly, the second the saloon doors swung shut behind us.

Saloon doors, for reference, take up about half of a doorway.

They start around your knees and end slightly above your head. They are not, in fact, soundproof.

"Thank you for the feedback, Mom." I grabbed the electric kettle and started filling it with water.

"I know you think he's hot, Miri. I saw you ogling him worse than you did Jacob Feldman in tenth grade. And if your eyes were claws, Miri, Jacob Feldman would *not* have flesh anymore."

I considered my options: leaving, spontaneously combusting, or suffering through the next half hour. "Wow, Mom, how long have you been sitting on that reference?" I asked.

"Not as long as you've been hiding this hunk," she said.

For a second, I tried to spontaneously combust, but clearly that wasn't one of my magic faerie powers. Instead, I shut off the water and plopped the kettle on its hot plate.

"Mom, did you know our ring was a faerie ring?" I asked, to distract her.

"I knew I was a witch," she said, sounding unfazed. "Maybe one of our ancestors was a faerie."

I debated explaining the differences between witches and faeries to my mother. I debated telling her I'd survived because we had faerie blood in the family. I resolved to do neither, and to schedule the genetic update later.

I started pulling coffee mugs out of the corner cabinet. Most of our mugs were white porcelain, chipped around the rim from decades of use.

"So is the other one half cat?" my mom asked, pretending to whisper at the exact same volume as before. She'd grabbed the tray of tea bags from the pantry across the room.

"Mom," I groaned. "Not right now."

"Fine," she said. "I'll go ask everyone what tea they want." She went back into the main area.

I gripped the counter, reminding myself that I loved her dearly, as she asked people for their tea preferences.

"What is tea?" Gaheris asked, and I pressed my forehead to an upper cabinet.

"Leaf water," Sahir said, before my mom could answer. "We would appreciate three peppermint tisanes, if you have them," he added.

My mom came back in and started putting tea bags into mugs. "He's hot *and* bossy," she reported, still at full volume. My soul slithered down to my feet.

Nobody spoke in the living room.

The kettle clicked off, and I started pouring cups of tea. My mom took two cups out into the living room. "Here we are," she said. "Miri's knight, will you go help Miri with the rest of them?"

I set the empty kettle back on its stand and stared into the darkening depths of a teacup. Sahir slid up behind me, so quiet that I only noticed his presence when his arm appeared beside mine. He bent to whisper conspiratorially in my ear, caging me in against the counter. "Does your mother speak truly? Do you think I am…*hot*?" he whispered, so softly I could barely hear him.

"I hope a bird nests in you," I muttered, and he burst out laughing.

"Here's the tea," I said, gesturing. He gathered all four cups of tea by unraveling his left hand until the vines of his fingers and palm lay flat in the approximation of a wide tray.

I didn't really want to hear what my mom would say about that, but I followed him back out.

My mom had given Gaheris the first cup of tea and taken the other.

"Nifty," my dad grunted, taking a cup of tea off Sahir's hand-tray. Lene took the second, and Sahir brought the last two to our couch. I sat down as close to the edge as I could, and then he plopped in the middle, pressing his thigh firmly against mine.

Another immeasurable silence descended. My stomach joined my soul in the bottoms of my feet. My brain remained unfortunately alert.

Before anyone could muster up the courage to speak, we heard my grandma coming down the hallway from her bedroom. She shuffled to a stop next to the TV and stared at all of us, sitting in a tableau in her living room.

"Who are you?" she asked the general populace. Grandma had lost much of her sight several years before, and much of her memory as well.

"I'm Gaheris," Gaheris said cheerfully. Grandma stared at him, clearly attempting to process that his head was on fire.

"Grandma," I said, standing and putting the teacup down on the table. "It's me, Miri. I brought some friends." I crossed the room and put my arms around her.

"Miri?" she repeated, then buried her face in my shoulder. "Oh, Miri. I missed you." She put her arms around me and pulled me in close, an enveloping familiar vetiver-scented warmth that eased the knot in my throat.

"Here, why don't you sit down, and you can have my tea?"

I offered, bringing her to the couch. When Sahir didn't move in either direction, I put her on his other side and handed her my mug.

I sat down next to Sahir and pulled my knees as far into the arm of the couch as I could.

Grandma looked over at Sahir and then reached out and touched his face. "Who are you?" she asked.

"I am Sahir," he said gallantly. "It is lovely to meet you, mother of Miriam's mother."

Had Sahir...*learned manners*?

"You're very handsome," Grandma said, rubbing his cheek with absolutely no shame. Apparently, in addition to faerie blood, tact in the face of attractive men had been passed down through my mother's side of the family.

"I appreciate the compliment. You are beautiful as well, like your daughter and granddaughter." I could hear my dad snort.

I tried once more to spontaneously combust but hadn't developed the ability in the past ten minutes.

My mom cleared her throat. "This is a lovely surprise, but how are you here?"

I cleared my throat, too. "Well..." I reviewed the events of the last forty-eight hours and tried to construct a summary that downplayed how much danger I'd faced.

"She escaped," my dad said, without clearing his throat first.

"That doesn't explain *how*," my mom said, and her jaw set. My dad and I looked at each other; she was gearing up for an *interrogation*.

He waylaid her with possibly the worst distraction he could've picked.

"Can you stay, Miri? Will the Princeling come after you?" my dad asked, his nostrils flaring. He glared at Sahir. Then his eyes flicked back to me. "Can you trust these people?"

Gaheris was sniffing his tea bag and Lene had curled up into a little ball on her armchair. I couldn't imagine finding them alarming in any way, even with the furry face and the fire-hair.

"Yes, Dad, they've been helping me." I put my hands out, placating. "These are my friends."

"You never really explained how you got trapped in Faerie. Did he trap you?" my dad asked, pointing to Sahir.

I glared at my dad, who was supposed to be defusing the situation and had instead chosen violence.

"Um, Jeff and I went to a client dinner," I started.

"Your boss Jeff?" my mom interrupted.

"Yes, my boss Jeff. We went to a client dinner—"

"Where was the client dinner?" she asked.

"In Faerie," I said, trying not to clench my jaw. "We talked about it, remember? You told me to wear heels." Her face remained blank. "At the client dinner, I ate some food that I thought was human food, but it wasn't."

"You ate food in Faerie?" my mom asked. "Haven't you seen the *Just Say No* advertisement? Miri, really," she scolded. "It's everywhere."

Next to her, my dad wore his Solemn Face. This meant that he was highly amused and unlikely to be much help.

I rubbed my eyes. "I've seen the ads, Mom. Jeff was pretty adamant that I eat the food so I didn't embarrass him."

"You ate faerie food, knowing it might alter your life forever, because your boss told you to?" my dad asked. The Solemn Face had disappeared; he looked like he was going to throttle me.

Sahir, unconcerned, leaned back and flung an arm around me. He'd flung his other arm around my grandma, who was still staring at his profile with open hunger. I couldn't even be mad at her.

I glanced at Gaheris and Lene. Gaheris was listening to the exchange with a bemused sort of interest. Lene had fallen asleep.

"When you put it that way it feels dumb," I said. "But it wasn't dumb. I didn't want to get fired."

"You ate faerie food, knowing it might alter your life forever, because you didn't want to get fired," my dad repeated. It was a statement and not a question.

"I—" I shook my head. "We have to get back to Faerie soon. I just wanted to see you and let you know what was going on. I'll be able to come home more now."

"Or we could come visit," my mom said. "Is there a beach?"

"What?" I tugged at my ear, like I'd misheard her.

"In Faerie, is there a beach?"

For a moment I felt frustrated. She wasn't going to think critically about the ethical implications of my kidnapping? We were going to play "all's well that ends well" with the most miserable three months of my life? She was going to pioneer Faerie's tourism industry with nothing but sheer force of will and an unending dedication to her daughter?

"There are beautiful beaches," Gaheris said. "The water is always calm, and the sand is soft beneath your toes."

"And is there skiing?"

I put my elbows on my knees and my head in my hands, inadvertently knocking my knee against Sahir's. He kicked my shin with his heel in retaliation. I debated murder.

"What is skiing?" Gaheris asked.

"You strap two pieces of wood to your feet and go down a snowy mountain face-first," I said dismissively to the floor. "Mom, I don't think faeries ski."

"Two pieces of wood?" Gaheris repeated. "This is quite odd. We strap one piece of wood to our feet and go down sideways."

I lifted my head to gape at him.

"Faeries snowboard?" my dad asked.

"Is this what you call it?" Gaheris shrugged. "We like to go fast."

We all absorbed this information for a moment.

"Miri, why didn't you tell us you were trying to escape?" my dad asked, shattering the silence.

"I didn't want you to worry." I stared down at my knees.

"We're your parents, and that's our job," my dad said.

"I didn't want you to try to storm Faerie and rescue me," I tried again.

My dad looked at my mom.

"What?" she snapped, indignant. "You think I would try to storm Faerie and rescue her?"

My dad and I shared a look.

Sahir squeezed my thigh with his free hand, and I jumped. "We must continue on, Miriam. We need to update the Princeling, and I do not want to expose Gaheris and Lene to more of this world than is absolutely necessary."

"Right." I looked at my parents. "We're going back to New York. Any chance you could drive us to the train?"

"I'll take you into the city," my dad said. He nudged my mom and nodded at my grandma, which meant *Can you stay with your mother?*

She nodded, unsubtly. Grandma had her hand in Sahir's hair.

I stood and the faeries followed suit. I pressed my lips to the top of my grandma's head. She looked a bit distraught that Sahir was leaving, until he knelt before her and kissed her hand, his hair falling in curtains around her knee.

My mom hugged me, then let me go.

We went as a group into the entryway.

My dad gestured to the front door, and I led the way outside toward the driveway. His car was parked in front of the garage.

"Lene, this is like the train, but smaller," Sahir said. My dad unlocked the car. I gestured for Gaheris to get in the front—he had height advantage—and slid into the back seat with Lene and Sahir. I buckled her in between us. My dad reached around Gaheris, heedless of his fiery hair, and buckled him in, too.

Sahir buckled himself.

My dad backed out of the driveway, and Lene stuck her claws into my thigh, but when he put the car in drive, she relaxed slightly. "I can see forward," she said, staring out the windshield. "It is like a horse without the wind."

"Thank you for escorting us in your chariot," Gaheris said to my dad, showing off his human class skills. "We are in your debt," he added, like a faerie.

"It was selfish," my dad said. "I wanted to spend more

time with my daughter." Our eyes met in the rearview mirror. "Are things okay otherwise, Miri? Is work getting any . . . easier?"

I looked away as we pulled onto the highway. "Jeff's just a little grumpy," I said, reluctant.

"The human man is insignificant and miserable," Lene chimed in. "His requests are extraneous and unwarranted. His attitude is abysmal. He is rude without reason, and he is not even clever about it. Doctor Kitten and I sit through all of Miri's meetings with her, and we find him unsatisfactory."

The top of my dad's cheek lifted as he smiled. "Do you and Doctor Kitten chat very often?" he asked.

"Oh, yes," she said, growing animated. "We share many opinions. In fact, we are even contemplating starting our own business, a human invention called a cat café. He is the most sensible of all."

She patted Sahir's knee. "Please do not take offense, Sahir. I like you, though you lack sense."

"Doctor Kitten is a very excellent cat," Gaheris added, perhaps incorrectly interpreting my dad's reaction to mean that everyone should heap praise on Doctor Kitten. I caught Sahir's eye and shook my head so that he wouldn't jump on the bandwagon, too.

"An excellent cat indeed," my dad said, and drove us into the city.

Chapter 21

In Which We Renovate My Room Again

My dad dropped us off in the Upper West Side at the 97th Street park entrance at Sahir's request. He got out of the car and gave me a big hug. "We'll see you soon," he promised. I stood and watched him drive away, merging wildly in front of a yellow taxi like he'd been born into New York traffic.

"Come, Miri," Sahir said, putting a gentle hand on my arm. "We will speak with the Princeling, and then you can come to the office with me tomorrow."

I glanced in the direction of my apartment, frowning. The fizzy feeling in my veins had gotten stronger all day. I understood what Roman meant about Faerie calling to me.

I'd need to break my lease, which I'd held on to both out of sheer denial and because my landlord was probably on the run from the law, in another country, and thus ignoring all of my texts, calls, and emails.

We trekked across the park, Lene cowering behind Sahir and Gaheris. The park was freezing and almost empty. I kept my hands clamped firmly over my ears for warmth.

"You look a bit mad," Lene said when she noticed. The observation seemed to make her feel better, so I let her have it.

The sky was overcast, loweringly gray. I looked up, wishing ineffectually that the sun would peek out so my friends could see what their Princeling was fighting for.

As we approached the entrance to the Princeling's Court, I felt the tug in my veins get stronger. My strides quickened, but so did the others'.

"You feel it," Sahir said, looking back at me. Some emotion sparked in his eyes when I nodded. He reached for my face—brushed a rough thumb across my cheekbone—turned away.

We crested a hill and I saw it below us—the glimmering veil, as transparent as a rising puff of steam on a winter day.

Lene charged for it and leapt through, Gaheris on her heels shouting her name.

Sahir and I followed more slowly. We stopped in front of the portal. He held his arm out for me and I took it.

Together, we strode back into Faerie.

<hr>

On the Faerie side of the Princeling's portal, we stepped out into a circle of toadstools, not visible from a distance. Sahir helped me over the mushrooms so that I didn't crush any caps or dislodge the mycelia.

"Where did they go?" I asked, looking across the lawn. There were figures scattered in pairs and trios and large wild circles, strolling or laughing or dancing.

Having seen the Queen's Court, I decided that perhaps if I had to be kidnapped by someone, the Princeling was the better option.

"I assume to your room," Sahir said. "Lene will want to see her sister."

"I want to see Doctor Kitten anyway," I said. We walked together up the path to the Court. We passed faeries and vampires still sprawled in the grass outside, lying on patchwork blankets or jackets and staring up at the clouds. The wide dirt entrance to the Court felt friendly, familiar.

We approached my room and found the door open. I had a moment of pure terror and sprinted forward to find Lene on the bed, sobbing into a disgruntled Nele's lap, while an even more disgruntled Doctor Kitten looked on.

"Hello," I said. Nele looked up.

I waited for her to speak.

She didn't.

I looked around for Gaheris and found him elbow-deep in one of the portals he'd left in the baseboards on my wall. I looked away hastily, utilizing my favorite policy, which is that if you aren't looking, nothing bad can happen.

"Thank you for watching him," I said to Nele. I went over to the bed, my hand out toward Doctor Kitten. He stood up and nuzzled my fingertips with his face.

"Hello, my little potato," I said. "I missed you."

He licked my pointer finger.

Unable to resist any longer, I scooped him up and kissed his face. He bore it without complaint. Also without delight, but you win some, you lose some.

"It appears your quest was an eventful one," Nele said, disentangling herself from her sister, whose claws were now ripping holes in my quilt.

"Indeed," Sahir said. He reached around me and scratched Doctor Kitten's head.

"Should we go to the Princeling now?" I asked.

Sahir put his face in my hair, sniffed me, and scrunched up his nose. "If you would like him to associate you forevermore with the smell of a decomposing badger, you are welcome to visit him in this state, Miriam."

I glowered at him and put Doctor Kitten back on the bed. Lene curled around him, sniffling. "Fine. Let's all shower and reconvene in thirty minutes?"

"Very bossy," Sahir said. "Perhaps even hot and bossy, as a wise woman once described me." He waggled his eyebrows in the general direction of an invisible audience. If Sahir decided to develop a sense of humor, it might be the last straw for my sanity.

I lamented introducing him to my mother.

"I don't want to shower," Lene said, her eyes red. "I don't ever want to leave this bed again, and I certainly don't ever want to go on an excavator to a train."

I looked at Sahir, expecting him to take all the faeries outside with him so that I could bathe.

"Well, if you're going to be staying here for the foreseeable future, you might as well have a bathroom with a door,"

Sahir said instead. He clapped his hands together and then did something anatomically improbable with his fingers. Tendrils of chestnut magic dripped from his palms like vines, crept across the room with stubborn intent. Where they stopped, columns of brown fibrous matter erupted from the wooden slats of my floor, twisting upward around each other like strangling ivy on a trellis. The twining pillars widened until they'd all connected, forming a textured wall that hit the ceiling. As I watched, the wall dimpled and developed an inset complete with a wooden door, which was inset itself with a small circular cat flap with pointed ears.

And suddenly, I had an en suite bathroom.

I gaped at him. "You could have done that at any time?" I growled.

Sahir wisely made his exit, grabbing Gaheris by the back of his tunic and dragging him along.

Gaheris pulled a mouse out of the portal as he went.

Nele, Lene, and Doctor Kitten tracked the mouse, dangling by its tail from Gaheris's hand. I felt relieved when he pulled the door shut with his trailing foot on the way out.

"Okay, I'm going to shower," I said, approaching my new, very, very long and narrow bathroom. After a moment's hesitation, I pushed on the handleless door. It opened soundlessly, revealing the same layout as before: the sink, toilet, and shower across the back wall, and Doctor Kitten's litter box beneath the window.

I shut the door, remembered I needed clean clothes, and reopened the door.

Along the brand-new inside wall was a brand-new wooden

dresser. I frowned at Lene, who was now sitting upright. She shrugged.

Next to her, Nele pretended not to watch us.

"Sahir is right," Lene said. "It should be a home for you." And with a complicated twisting motion, she sent all of the clothes scattered across the floor and shoved haphazardly into the suitcase flying across the room. Sparks of green-gold magic danced between them, and everywhere a spark touched, the clothes folded themselves. I realized that I'd never thought about Lene as a proficient magic wielder, and that I should probably revise that opinion.

The dresser drawers opened and I watched in awe as my clothes sorted themselves appropriately.

"Thank you," I said, a bit stunned.

"Of course," she said. With another, far more careless gesture, she sent my suitcase to rest in one of the newly created corners of the room. I rummaged for underwear and a new tunic and leggings. By the time I'd pulled them out, Lene and Nele had set up a cat obstacle course on the wall above my bed. I turned around and frowned at it. It was a series of platforms, some covered in carpet, that ran from the floor to the ceiling, and horizontally across the entire wall.

"Making it a home?" I asked.

"It's Doctor Kitten's home, too," Lene said. Doctor Kitten didn't appear interested in the new platforms. I imagined he wouldn't be interested until three a.m., at which point he would be both interested and loud.

I went back into the bathroom and shucked off my dirty clothes. I got into the shower, reveling in the waterfall's pressure and the soothing smell of the lavender soap. When I'd scrubbed myself clean, I stepped out and into the drying stream, then dressed.

"That was less than ten minutes," Lene said.

I thought about checking my work email, but the prospect of hundreds of unread emails made me hesitate. On some level, it didn't matter if I checked my email or not. If I sent Jeff a response, he would be angry about it, and if I didn't send Jeff a response, he would be angry about that.

Instead, I napped on the somehow-wider bed next to my cat and my friend and my friend's surly sister for fifteen minutes. When Sahir knocked on the door, I left Nele, Lene, and Doctor Kitten curled up together, sleeping.

I stepped outside and closed the door softly behind me.

Sahir and I had dressed in matching blue outfits, and I snickered.

He glanced down at me and smiled. "Well met."

"Should I wake Lene?" I asked, reaching for my ring out of habit. Finding my finger unadorned, I wrung my hands together instead.

He shook his head. "I let Gaheris stay behind as well. They will come if the Princeling requests it, but there is no reason to bring them now."

He held out his arm for me, and I slid my hand into the crook of his elbow. My stomach flopped with a mixture of confusion and pleasure. Together we trod the path to the Princeling's throne room.

"Hang on," I said. "It's a Sunday night. Is he going to be there?"

Sahir laughed like I'd told a good joke. Did faeries not take weekends? I realized it probably wouldn't make sense for faeries to conform to the American notion of a five-day workweek—especially because I'd never seen evidence that they conformed to "weeks" at all.

"Yes, the Princeling will be in his throne room," he said.

Sahir was in a very good mood, almost smiling as we walked.

"Must be a very boring job," I muttered, determined to be ornery. "If he's there on a Sunday night."

"I cannot speak to whether it is boring, but he is in the throne room because I requested an audience with him," Sahir said.

We stopped in front of the ornate door to the throne room, where the magical mural of the waterfall down the sheer cliff continued its unabated flow. Sahir knocked on the wall next to the door, and the door swung open. He released my arm and pushed against the small of my back so I entered first.

The Princeling sat on his throne, his entourage arrayed around him. He'd let the Crone sit in a small chair at his right hand, and the Gray Knight stood at his left.

We hadn't really spoken since our fight in my room—I was still upset with her for the cavalier way she'd suggested I just give up and work for the Princeling. And, if I was honest, for casually spurning me when I asked to slow down whatever had happened between us.

"Sahir," the Princeling drawled. I'd forgotten how green his eyes were, and how thick his thighs. "I see you have returned from your…camping trip."

"My liege," Sahir said, bowing his head. I followed suit. My hair, which I'd left undone, fell over my face. The floor had an inlaid pattern I hadn't noticed before, a subtle checkerboard of brownish stones.

"Lady of the True Dreams," the Princeling said. "Stand and face me."

I rose. Sahir stayed beside me, head bowed. I took a step toward the Princeling on his throne, my eyes on his stern face.

"You left Faerie." His expression remained unreadable, his eyes like emerald chips in his face. I reached for my phantom ring. It wasn't there. I fought the urge to twist my hands in front of me and kept them uncurled at my sides.

"I did." I straightened my back and squared my shoulders.

"And yet you are neither bone shards nor blood mist, let alone both combined."

"I am not," I confirmed, though I did discreetly pat my own thigh as I spoke—just to check.

"How was this possible?" He didn't look angry, exactly. Just baffled. I looked at the Crone, but she had a faraway look on her wrinkled face, her eyes focused somewhere outside the room.

Sahir lifted his head and stepped up next to me. "We bargained with the Builder Roman for information about his father's magics. Roman shared information that helped us understand the portals better. Miri should be able to pass freely through your portal without fear."

Sahir proceeded to explain our journey into the Queen's lands and then through the treacherous halls of the Trenton train station. Sahir's version of the story was truncated and lacking the vibrant details I would have included. He also called my grandmother "a woman of surpassing grace and dignity," which was a vibrant detail I would not have included.

My attention wandered, so I was surprised when he trailed off. The Princeling opened his mouth to speak, but Sahir cleared his throat. "If you allow it, lord, Miri can come to New York with me during the day, and return here at night."

The Princeling sat for a moment.

"This changes nothing," he said.

"Excuse me?" I said. My mind blanked.

The Princeling shook his head, like he was dislodging an errant leaf from his hair.

"It changes nothing. You will remain in my Court and continue to work remotely. It is good for my people to see you here."

"Wouldn't it be better for your people to see humans as living beings with agency?" I snapped.

The Princeling tapped his chin with his fingers. "I do not believe this will matter to my people." His fingernails glinted in the dim lights.

"That's your problem," I said. I flung my arms up, too frustrated to stand still. "You're so focused on how your people will integrate with humans, if they want to leave—but how can they integrate with humans if they don't see humans as *people*?"

He frowned at me. "Do you believe I have a *problem*, Miriam?" he asked, his voice low and dangerous.

To my surprise, the Gray Knight leaned down and whispered something in his ear.

He turned to look at her, his expression dark. She whispered something else, her silver hair brushing his shoulder.

"You may speak," he said, waving a hand at her.

"The Lady of the True Dreams is correct," the Gray Knight said.

I looked at the Red Knight, who was staring at his nails with the desperate intensity of a man who doesn't want to be consulted. Then the Blue Knight, who was picking his nose and seemed uninvested in this conversation. I frowned at the Blue Knight; he *should* be invested in this conversation, since it impacted the people he claimed to represent.

He looked up, like he felt my eyes on him. His finger dropped from his nostril, and he turned his attention to the Gray Knight.

"For an exchange to succeed, our people must be exposed to humans as they are, with their associated privileges and freedoms. Our people need to know that humans are dangerous, in addition to being kind or loving or just or whatever it is we're calling Miriam now." This felt a bit dismissive to me; I looked at the Red Knight, who jerked to attention when the Blue Knight jammed him in the ribs with an elbow. "If we do not provide full information, we are lying to our people," the Gray Knight concluded.

She'd been looking at me throughout this surprising speech; I'd felt the force of her gaze. I couldn't take it anymore—I met her eyes. She spoke to me more than to the Princeling. "If they do not see what it would truly mean to have humans live among us, including their comings and goings and the choices they make for themselves, then we have not represented the truth fairly."

The molten silver glow of her eyes caught mine, and she

gave me the faintest of smiles. My heart fluttered. As apologies went…

The Blue Knight coughed.

"Yes?" the Princeling said, sounding irritated.

"I agree with the Gray Knight," he said. "Our people are curious about humans. Many are not interested in leaving our realm and seeing the sun or moon. Even those would like to meet a human, to understand what lies beyond our borders. But they do not need to have constant access to the human. The human can leave and come back, if she chooses. More humans could come, too, and teach our people their ways."

The Princeling jerked his chin in a nod, then tilted his head toward the Red Knight.

The Red Knight shrugged. "I have no dissent," he said. "When we agreed to this experiment, we knew the terms would evolve. If the human can leave Faerie by day, and any other humans we accept would also leave Faerie by day, then there is no reason to keep her trapped here."

Sahir shifted closer to me, like the warmth of his arm against mine would provide comfort. I couldn't breathe as I stared at the Princeling.

His eyes found mine again.

It seemed the entire room held its breath.

"It would be wise to allow her freedom of movement," the Crone said, in a voice so low I might have imagined it. The words wisped through the room, echoed against the walls.

"It is decided, then," the Princeling said, his nostrils flared. "Sahir will bring you to the office tomorrow, and you will return home together after work. You are dismissed."

Sahir took me by the elbow and pulled me backward. I got the sense that this was a more formal dismissal than I was used to with the Princeling, and I shouldn't muck it up.

"Thank you," I said aloud. Sahir hooked an arm around my waist and dragged me out like Little Bo Peep with an armful of sheep before I could ask for anything else.

Chapter 22

In Which I Receive a Performance Review

I expected to leave for the office on Sparkles while Sahir rode his own horse, but he surprised me by leading me out of Faerie on foot. We stood together in the toadstool portal as it shimmered, and Sahir pulled me into the mortal realm on a sideways step.

I stumbled into him, and he caught me, steadying hands on my shoulders. "No horses?" I asked, hefting my backpack onto his fingers. He pulled away with a wince and shook his head.

"I would not inflict this city upon a horse," he said as he tapped on a nearby rock. The rock face cracked open and Sahir pulled out a small red motorbike. "And this bike is very cool," he added, sliding his backpack onto my shoulders on top of mine.

I snorted, sure I looked ridiculous.

He popped the seat and pulled two helmets out.

"Hop on," he said, closing the seat again and passing me a helmet. I jammed it onto my head, fumbling with the clasp for a moment before he took pity on me. He grabbed the straps, his fingers under my chin, and pulled them together until the helmet sat snug on my head. His fingertips lingered at my jaw. Then he put his own helmet on and straddled the bike.

I jumped on behind him, wrapping my arms around his waist.

We sped through the streets so fast I felt sure he was using magic, and when we reached our building, he tapped a wall that most definitely had a restaurant on the other side and no space for a motorbike. The wall split, revealing another space for the bike. "Convenient," I said.

When we went through the revolving doors into the lobby, I stuttered a step. It was so sterile, white and wide and empty. The security guard stared determinedly at a spot above my head, his jaw set. I waved at him. He didn't notice.

I fumbled for my key card, grateful I'd never taken my wallet out of my backpack.

Sahir and I tapped into the elevator bank and waited for an elevator to take us to our floor. When it opened, we stepped inside together.

The doors closed, and I flung myself at him with the violence of unadulterated terror, pressing my face against his shoulder. "I'm scared," I whispered.

I felt him startle before he put his arms around me. "Do not fret, Miriam. It will—" He stopped. He couldn't tell me it would be okay. He didn't believe it. "I will be nearby," he said.

The elevator stopped at our floor, and we pulled apart. He patted me once on the arm, attempting comfort and probably leaving a bruise.

The doors opened and Sahir tapped us into the secure area of the floor. We parted there, him turning right and me left.

Entering the office was surreal—nothing had changed and yet everything felt different. The grays of the carpet felt more aggressive than ever; the dull white walls bore into my soul. A pang hit as I realized how much I missed the dirt-made structure of the Court.

I came to our row of desks and found everyone already settled, preparing for our nine a.m. meeting.

"Miri?" Levi said, looking up at me as I opened my backpack and put my computer on my desk. "What are you doing here?"

I ground my teeth together. Levi should attend some remedial human classes on manners. "I found a way to leave Faerie," I said.

I waited for him to comment.

He grunted and nodded. No one else said anything, and none of them looked at me: I felt like some awful insect they couldn't face.

I sighed and put my bag down.

"I guess I can just get Jeff," Matt said. "Since we're all here, we don't need to have a morning call."

Matt stood up and knocked on Jeff's open door. I looked at Corey, who finally smiled at me but didn't say anything. I sat in my chair and swiveled until I faced my teammates.

Jeff and Matt came back, Matt pulling out Jeff's chair for

him. Jeff sat down while Matt was still moving, and Matt grunted but pulled him the rest of the way. When Jeff saw me, a range of expressions crossed his face: shock, confusion, and then annoyance.

Everyone settled and we all looked at each other.

"Miri, you haven't been here in a while," Jeff said in a flat voice.

I stared at him. "I've been trapped in Faerie."

"Oh, right," he said, and then looked at Levi, dismissing me entirely. "What do we need to discuss today?"

"We have a lot of pitches," Levi said.

"We always have a lot of pitches," Matt muttered.

"There's the vampire novelty T-shirt company," Levi said. "We could pitch them for a capital raise."

Jeff shook his head. "Too new."

"And the Faerie project, of course," Levi added. "Which should close soon."

"Not sure what Miri will do after that," Jeff sighed, like my presence was making his life harder. I gaped at him.

"I can come back here every day now, Jeff," I said. "I won't be remote anymore. So you can put me on a new project."

I reached for the space where my ring had once sat, but my finger was bare. So I twined my hands together and looked at him. His neck sagged into the starched white collar of his shirt. He was wearing a tie with his alma mater's logo on it.

"Your pitch decks haven't led to any new deals," he said, his icy eyes on my face.

"Neither have Matt's or Corey's," I said. "No one has gotten any new deals—not just me."

He brushed this off with a half shrug, his jaw set and his features hard.

"Jeff, don't you have anything to say to me?" I asked. "Or to Matt and Corey?" There was a buzzing in my ears, a sound like a swarm of venomous bees rising around me in a maelstrom of impotent rage.

"You need to work on your sales strategy, Miri," Jeff said. "Don't bring your colleagues into this."

My head exploded like a bottle of champagne. I was surprised to find it still attached to my neck when I inhaled again.

"Jeff, I have done everything you asked me to, even when it went against my better judgment, and even when it actively harmed me. I have worked hundred-hour weeks—"

"Then you need to utilize your hours better," Jeff interrupted. "Because your work output doesn't support that statement."

Levi snickered. Matt and Corey had the decency to look uncomfortable: Matt looked like he'd just walked in on his own grandma naked, and Corey also looked like he'd just walked in on Matt's grandma naked.

"Jeff, you—" I stopped, racking my brain for options:

A. Run-of-the-mill dingbat
B. Absolute turdwaffle
C. Shitstain on a shower curtain
D. Might be right; I'm sorry

No. Not *D*. Never *D* again. I hadn't faced down kidnapping, magical prejudice, a controlling asshole prince, and a hostile magical Queen just to cower in front of this man.

My rage turned potent. I stood up, so that for once I was taller than him. I stared down at the thinning dishwater hair crowning his head.

"Jeff, I've seen true power," I said, the words coming out so hard they nearly cracked my teeth. "You are powerless."

My hands shook at my sides. "You are useless." There was hot anger gathering in the corners of my eyes. I blinked it away.

His stupid pink face remained impassive. "You are pointless and irrelevant." My breath scraped its way up my trachea, hurt as I exhaled.

He crossed his arms, crinkling his suit jacket. "Are you done?"

"No, you festering bag of pustulent dicks," I growled.

Matt snickered; I shot him a glare so virulent that he folded up into his seat like a discarded marionette.

I turned my attention back to Jeff, who sat apparently unaffected, except for two hectic spots of pink on his cheeks. "Jeff, you are a needlessly cruel man. If you have any redeeming qualities, I haven't personally encountered them. I've had bacterial infections that provided me with better mentorship than you have."

"Miri, I'm giving you a warning," Jeff said, finally leaning forward. "You can't talk to me like that. I'm your manager and I can make your life hell."

We stared at each other. What—what did he think he'd been doing to date?

He didn't deserve any more of my energy, but *I* deserved to tell him what I needed to. I squared my shoulders. "Jeff, you're the most incompetent boss I've ever had the displeasure of working for. You communicate like you *want* us to be scared and confused, you make up problems to feel important, and you haven't brought in a single client because you're too busy arguing with them about their daughters. You're clearly not invested in my success, and, other than trapping me in Faerie, I don't think you've given me anything I'll remember."

I hoisted my backpack onto my shoulder.

"I quit. Effective immediately."

His mouth dropped open.

I didn't wait to see anyone's response. I left my computer on the desk, turned my back on the team, and kicked my chair away so hard it spun behind me.

I crossed our floor to Sahir's desk, where he sat with empty chairs on either side of him. I glared at his teammates, who had the gall to stare unabashedly back at me. "Sahir," I said quietly. He looked up; his eyes were so wide I could see white all around his irises, and he'd gripped his desk until the particle board had splintered.

"I did not want to interrupt," he whispered. "But I felt a lot of pain. Are you harmed?"

"I'm fine," I said, a little hoarse. "I just quit, is all."

His shoulders relaxed, and he stood up, too close to me for an office setting. "Should we leave?" he asked.

I shook my head. "I'll go home without you," I said. "I don't need to disrupt your day. But let's eat dinner with Lene and Gaheris after work."

A lock of his hair had escaped its bun—it curled against his temple, the tip sprouting a small green leaf. I put a hand to his face and brushed the leaf behind his ear. "I'll see you soon," I said, and stepped away, still staring daggers at his teammates.

With that, I left the Tartarus building for the last time. I waited for the crushing weight of regret, but it didn't come.

I meandered uptown, taking in the noises and smells of New York City on a winter morning. I let the sun warm my cheeks, the top of my head, the tip of my nose. I looked into the windows of the antiques stores and restaurants and clothing stores, staring at the uniform faces in their muted palette of human colors.

A man bumped into me on 50th Street and started shouting. "It's like the invasion of the body snatchers," he yelled. "With all the bumping and grabbing. If you think you can take my body, you're crazy, lady!"

"Why would I want your body when I have mine?" I yelled back, fighting a smile. His shouts followed me for the next few blocks.

I'd missed this city so much.

I almost went back to Faerie immediately, but when I passed 54th, I turned east instead. Thea would be working at home.

Though it had been three months, her doorman recognized me and let me in with a smile. I took the elevator up to her floor and then stood on the beige carpet outside her door for several minutes. *She wants to see you,* I reminded myself. The flutters in my stomach didn't seem so sure.

I knocked on the door.

"Hello?" she called out, sounding surprised.

Of course she was surprised; it was midmorning on a workday.

"It's me," I said, sounding hoarser than I expected.

"Me?" she repeated, her voice closer now. "Who's—" as she opened the door.

She stood in the doorway, half of her body behind the door, and her jaw dropped. "Miri?" she shrieked, flinging her arms out to hug me and instead launching herself into the still-open door. "Ow," she added.

I stepped inside and threw my arms around her. "Thea," I said, unable to do anything but take in the feel of her squeezing me.

"Oh my god, you aren't dead," she said, burying her face in my shoulder. I felt wetness seeping through the fabric of my shirt, and then her body began to shake. I held her tighter.

"Thea, Thea," I said, stroking her hair back from her forehead. "Are you okay?"

"Okay?" she repeated. "No, I'm not okay, Miri! You've been avoiding me for three months! Where have you been? Are you mad at me? Are *you* okay?"

I kicked the door shut behind me and held her by the shoulders. "Mad at you? Thea, of course I'm not mad at you." I led her to her giant blue couch and sat us both down.

She wiped at her nose with the back of one hand. "How is that *of course*, Miri? Where the hell did you go? You barely answered my calls, and when I went to your apartment you didn't even answer the door."

"Ah," I said. I dropped my hands. Waiting had not made it easier to tell her.

She stared at me. I stared at her.

"I've been stuck in Faerie," I said.

"You *what*?" she said.

"I got stuck in Faerie. I wasn't sure I'd ever be able to come back," I said, enunciating.

She gaped at me, startled out of tears. "Did you eat their food?"

"If one more person asks about my terrible life choices," I muttered, and she flung herself around me so hard we fell back into the couch cushions. I couldn't tell if she was punching my arms or squeezing any flesh she could to make sure I was really there.

"You were trapped in Faerie and didn't tell me?" She pulled away.

"I didn't tell you," I repeated. "I'm sorry."

"Oh, Miri," she said. Her eyes were rimmed red. "Don't be sorry. I'm so sorry I didn't notice something was wrong."

"What?" I grabbed her hand. "No, Thea, I'm sorry I didn't tell you."

We apologized mutually for nearly a half hour before her computer pinged and she remembered she was supposed to be working.

"I'm going to call out sick," she said. I watched from the couch while she went to her computer, scrubbing her hair until it fell in matted tangles around her shoulder. She sat down and hunched forward in her chair, and then called her boss.

Her boss answered and Thea did the most pathetic little half cough I'd ever heard in my entire life.

"Hey, Katie," she said. "I'm not feeling great." She listed to one side, as though unable to hold herself upright.

"Oh my god, please sign off and get some soup," Katie said, sounding worried.

"Okay," Thea said, clearly attempting reluctance and instead sounding gleeful. "Thanks, Katie." She hung up and turned back to me with a wide grin. "Great, my afternoon is clear."

I snorted. "But now you'll get me sick."

She ignored this absolutely hilarious joke.

Thea had her phone in hand. "I'm texting Jordan to come over," she said. "And then you can apologize to *him* for a half hour about not telling him you got stuck in Faerie."

I winced.

"No," she gasped.

"I'm so sorry," I said again.

"You *told Jordan*?"

"Just two days ago!" I said, though my voice was muffled by Thea's entire body because she'd flung herself upon me and seemed to be attempting murder by smothering. "I needed advice about going on a quest."

Good lord—had it only been two days?

"A quest?" Thea sat back, though her hands found mine, and her eyes went wide. "Okay, I think you'd better tell me from the beginning." She squeezed my fingers. It was evident from the pressure that she hadn't decided whether to berate me or welcome me home like the prodigal son.

I sighed and then bit back a smile, thinking of Sahir.

"Wait, is that a *crush smile*?" Thea shrieked. She threw her hands up. "What is *happening*, Miri?"

"Let's just wait till Jordan gets here," I said, "because I don't think I can explain all of this twice."

Thea's eyes narrowed again. "Hang on, aren't you supposed to be at work?"

I sucked in a breath.

Luckily, Jordan lived very close to Thea, and a loud *thud* on the door interrupted this line of questioning.

I got up to let him in; he'd kicked the door with his foot because he had arms full of alcohol. "Did someone order delivery?" he asked, cradling the ciders.

"Jordan, hey," I said.

"Miri, hey," he replied. "Give me a second to put the ciders on Thea's grandma's coffee table." If you're friends with someone for long enough, you know exactly which deceased relative they got all of their nice furniture from. He swept past me and deposited the ciders.

Then, arms empty, Jordan came back and yanked me into a hug. "Don't *ever* do that again," he admonished. "I was pretty sure you were going to die and then I was going to have to write the most creative and heart-wrenching eulogy ever and deliver it to a crowd of adoring mourners, including your hot cousin, which you know I'd *totally* hate doing."

"Both of you, fucking *sit*," Thea called from the couch. "I won't cause either of you bodily harm, if you tell me everything right this second."

Jordan and I went to the couch, still tangled together, and sat down. Thea came in close and wrapped her arms around my upper arm.

"Okay, so you know my boss, Jeff?" I asked.

"No, but he sounds lovely," Jordan deadpanned. Thea groaned.

"Yes, Miri, please talk faster," she said, and rested her cheek on my shoulder.

"Okay, so Jeff and I had a client dinner in Faerie in"—I thought for a second—"in August."

"And you didn't tell us?" Thea gasped.

"Let's assume that I was a bad friend throughout," I suggested. "Since it'll make the story go faster."

"You weren't a bad friend," Jordan said, with startling solemnity. "You weren't sure how to process what happened to you and didn't want to make other people who love you suffer for no reason."

I glared at him. "Jordan, stop being so well-adjusted," I said. He held up his hands in surrender, and I regaled them with my tale.

To their credit, they were a much better audience than my parents: They booed the Princeling, gasped at my recollections of being poisoned, were enraptured with my descriptions of the Faerie Court. And of course, I told them about Sahir, Gaheris, Lene, and the Gray Knight.

"So are these people your new roommates?" Thea asked, making a face.

I hesitated for a moment. "They're my new friends," I said, staring at my lap, where all of our hands were clasped. "I'd love for you to meet them."

"Did she make the face?" Jordan asked. "I couldn't tell from this angle."

"She made the face," Thea confirmed.

"What face?" I asked, my cheeks already flushing.

"The *crush face*," Jordan said, exuberant. "So which one is it?"

"Or is it more than one?" Thea asked.

I ducked my head. "I don't know what you two are talking about. I quit my job, by the way."

I'd done that intentionally. They both exploded.

"Way to bury the lede!" Thea shrieked.

"I don't think she *did*," Jordan said. "I think that's genuinely the least interesting thing that's happened to her in the past ninety days."

"I told Jeff I've had bacterial infections that provided me with better mentorship than him," I said, because that was probably my favorite part.

Thea cackled.

I glanced at the table, where the drinks we hadn't even cracked still sat.

"You could come visit me," I offered. "In Faerie. I promise I wouldn't let you eat the food."

I didn't know if they could visit me, but I planned to petition the Gray Knight as soon as I got back. She owed me *several* favors.

"Come to Faerie?" Thea sounded startled. "Really?"

"Only if you want to," I tossed out casually.

Jordan found a pillow behind his back and whacked me with it.

We all dissolved into giggles. Thea grabbed a few bottles of cider and passed them to me and Jordan. We twisted the caps off in sync.

"A toast," Thea said, twisting off her own bottle's cap. "To somehow avoiding any real consequences."

"To avoiding consequences," Jordan and I chorused. We clinked our bottles together, and together, we drank.

———————— • ————————

Hours later, I left my best friends, feeling lighter than I had in months.

When I reached Central Park, I stopped a few times to touch the grass, and once to try to climb a tree. I fell onto my butt from a few branches up. I made the rest of the trek to the shimmering portal with a mingled sense of embarrassment that I'd tried to climb a tree, and relief that no one had seen me fail.

Eventually, I came to the portal. It was exactly where we'd left it that morning, a glittering haze against the deepening blue of the sky. I stood for a moment in front of it, my eyes closed and my cheeks turned up toward the setting sun. I held my hands out, palms up, as if to catch the rays in my fingers.

I let myself enjoy the air, and the sky, and the sounds of people around me, for as long as my frozen ears could tolerate it.

When they became so cold they hurt, I sidestepped home.

———— • ————

After a lazy early evening spent napping with Doctor Kitten on my bed, I woke in time for dinner. I passed Lene's door on the way to the dining hall but didn't knock, choosing instead to let myself be swept along in a crowd of faeries. We entered as a group and formed an orderly line by the serving area. Milo must have been off, because three people I didn't recognize stood at the three stations.

I took my tray and slid it along the counter, stopping at each one. None of the servers looked surprised to see me, and none looked angry either. I smiled my thanks as the first handed me a grain bowl, the second handed me a purple salad, and the third handed me a moderately sized slice of pie.

I sat at an empty table near the doors and picked up my fork, relieved to have these moments of silence.

Sahir joined me just as I finished my salad, putting his tray opposite mine and sitting across from me. "How do you feel?" he asked, his eyes wary.

"How does she feel about what?" Lene asked, sliding into the seat next to me. She had two pieces of pie on her plate. Gaheris sat down across from her, with three pieces of pie and absolutely no vegetables.

"I think I'm happy," I said. "They weren't very nice to me, were they?"

"Happy about what?" Gaheris asked.

"I quit my job," I said, twirling my fork around my fingers.

"Congratulations," he said, smiling at me.

"They were not very nice to you," Lene affirmed darkly. "And further, this is a relief for me and Doctor Kitten. Now we do not have to listen to that odious man while we are try-ing to sleep."

I snorted. "I'm sorry about that," I said.

She shrugged, starting in on her pie. "Water passes beneath the bridge."

"Does this mean we can spend our time in more important pursuits?" Gaheris asked, staring intently at me.

"Sure," I said, feeling generous. "What are more important pursuits?"

"Perhaps we can find a way to give you wings," he said. "I did not want to say anything while you were so unhappy with work, but I am sure you would like wings."

"Is that an option?" I asked, diverted.

"I highly doubt that it is an option," Sahir said, looking a bit alarmed. "Human bone density is wrong for wings, Gaheris, which you would know if you *ever listened in science class*. And if it *is* an option, we should see a specialist about it."

"Maybe with my free time I'll take a faerie science class," I said.

Sahir glared at Gaheris. "You can join her," he said, "as you clearly need a refresher."

I giggled, relief making me heady. "Sahir, do you think I could invite my other friends to Faerie, if I don't give them any food?"

He turned his glower on me. "I am sure you can do whatever you like, Miriam, but why would you not meet them in the mortal realm, where it's safer?"

I thought about the way I'd felt when I first touched the magic barrier in my window. And I thought about how much I'd like my friends to meet Lene and Gaheris, who didn't seem up for another visit to the mortal realm in the near future. "I think my friends would like to see Faerie," I said. "It's special to us, the way our realm is special to you."

He grunted in reply and started eating his purple vegetables, because Sahir was the most responsible person in our friend group.

Another shadow fell over us.

"May I join you?"

I looked up, though I didn't need to; I would always recognize the Gray Knight's voice. I glanced at Sahir, who shrugged, as if to say *Your choice*.

"Yes," I decided.

She sat next to Sahir, and I looked at her. Her gray eyes

were hooded, but her chin tilted up defiantly. She didn't have a tray of food with her.

"Miriam, I have chosen to apologize for my role in extending your sojourn into Faerie," the Gray Knight said.

"Thank you for the apology," I said, though *extending your sojourn* was perhaps not how I would describe *feeding you faerie food without your knowledge.*

We looked at each other.

She cleared her throat. "I heard you speaking. You have left your job? You will not be closing our deal?"

I fiddled with the hem of my shirt. "I can assist you from here, if it is required," I said. "But I will no longer be at the bank. And I suppose this means I have broken my agreement with the Princeling."

She hummed thoughtfully. "I suppose," she echoed. She twirled a lock of silver hair around her finger.

"You told me once before that you thought I could work in the Court," I said to her. "Do you think a position could be created for me?"

She shrugged. "If you had a compelling argument for it."

I looked behind her, at Chad and Milo eating at another table. There were no faeries sitting with them.

"I want to be a human-faerie liaison," I said. "I feel that the Princeling has great need of a human to help him understand human . . . things."

"This is not news, lady," she said drily.

"I could educate faeries about humans, and humans about faeries," I said, testing out the idea. I pictured myself formalizing the human classes. I imagined standing with a projector and a PowerPoint, explaining electricity or zippers to a roomful of faeries.

"You could." Her face gave nothing away.

From over her shoulder, Chad waved at me. I smiled back at him.

"I would like to," I said.

She shrugged again. "We can work together on a proposal for the Princeling. I do not think he would reject the opportunity to offload the human-related portions of his work."

Another opportunity to sit next to her at a desk, to bend our heads close together over a computer screen or printed document.

"Thank you," I said. "I appreciate your offer of assistance."

"This sounds nice," Lene said. "But have you considered sitting in a tree and watching people pass below?"

"No," I said. "I haven't. Maybe I'll take a little time off and do that, too."

"If we could give you claws, it would be easier to climb a tree," Gaheris told me.

I laughed. Sahir laughed. The Gray Knight smiled reluctantly. Lene hadn't been listening.

And together we enjoyed a very pleasant dinner.

Epilogue

The email was titled: *Making an introduction...*

Between you and Miri Geld, the new human-faerie liaison for the Princeling. Miri has been a great help to us as we work to mitigate misunderstandings and build stronger connections between our human employees and faerie workers interested in joining our teams.

Miri has told me she'd be happy to chat with you about some strategies to navigate smoother integration, ensuring respect between all of your employees.

But I'll start with the best advice she's given me so far!

1. Do not commit to anything you will not deliver

2. Do not agree to anything you cannot accomplish

3. Do not offer anything you will not part with

4. Do not dissemble or lie

I'm happy to tell you more about her work—bottom line, don't look any further. I've found your consultant.

ACKNOWLEDGMENTS

This book wouldn't have been possible without the small village of friends, family members, and nemeses who carried me through:

My parents, who have been unfailingly supportive for my entire life—which is a very long time to be unfailingly supportive of anybody.

My brothers Ezra and Jake, one of whom loves the picnic basket, and the other of whom finds the picnic basket deeply distressing. They are my biggest hype-men and an unending source of comic relief in my life.

Alina, the little sister I finally have: She shares book recs with me, which is the only thing I wanted from a sister to begin with, and makes my brother super happy, which is a fun but unnecessary bonus.

My in-laws, who've cheered me on through this process, and my brother-in-law Gabe, the food inventor who filled my fridge with experiments and my phone with memes.

My cats, Felix and Adjunct Professor Moo, who took turns sitting on my lap and editing the manuscript by stepping on the space bar. And Velcro—I promised you nine lives; here's one.

Acknowledgments

Jonah, who supports and encourages me in all aspects of my life. Most importantly for this book—he pushed me to submit my manuscript.

Special thanks to Ben, Claire, Davy, Glynis, Jameyanne, Sarah, and Shermila, who read the first draft of *A Fae in Finance* and laughed at all the appropriate moments. Stewart, who gave me Richard Nixon facts; Miranda, who gave me book facts; and Asha, who let me make all my *Paradise Lost* references to her so I didn't put them in the book. Molly, queen of romance books, who gave me some great advice. Ben, who didn't give me any great advice about romance books but who is my dear friend all the same. Tali and Maia, who read an early draft and let me talk to them about it for literal years after.

Ana Maria and Evelyn, I *literally* (not figuratively) couldn't have done this without your unfailing support.

Uncle and the kids—none of you were particularly additive to my writing process but I love you very much.

My fantastic, delightful editor Stephanie Clark—you've made this book 10x better. Thank you for all of your brilliant ideas and advice. My incredibly thorough copyeditor Amy J. Schneider, a hero who did math so I wouldn't have to; my cold reader Rachel Oestreich; marketing team, Maggie Curley and Alex Lencicki; art design team, Lauren Panepinto; cover artist, Chloe Quinn; managing editor Bryn A. McDonald; and the whole Orbit team: Thanks for taking a chance on me.

And finally—my inexpressible thanks to every coworker and manager I've ever had. I learned so much from each of you. You've all been lovely, and this is fiction!

MEET THE AUTHOR

JULIET BROOKS lives with her spouse, two cats, and a lot of plants. In her free time, she plays board games with her friends while the *Pride and Prejudice* BBC miniseries plays on loop in the background. She's been informed that someday, they may move on to *The Lord of the Rings* (extended editions).

Find out more about Juliet Brooks and other Orbit authors by registering for the free monthly newsletter at orbitbooks.net.

* 9 7 8 0 3 1 6 5 8 7 6 8 6 *